HETTY FEATHER HAS BEGUN a new chapter in her life story. Escaping from Tanglefield's Travelling Circus with her friend Diamond, Hetty is determined to find them positions as music-hall artistes.

The pair quickly become the Little Stars of Mrs Ruby's show at the Cavalcade, alongside many colourful acts – including a friend from Hetty's past, Flirty Bertie. But the music hall is both thrilling and dangerous, and Hetty must fight to protect her darling Diamond, who longs for a normal childhood. Meanwhile, Hetty struggles with her feelings for Bertie – and for Jem, whom she has never forgotten.

Hetty dreams of a glittering future for herself and Diamond. The bright lights of London beckon – will Hetty become a true star?

Starring a cast of wonderful characters, both old and new, this is the fifth fabulous *Hetty Feather* story.

www.**randomhousechildrens**.co.uk

HAVE YOU READ THEM ALL?

WHERE TO START
THE DINOSAUR'S PACKED LUNCH
THE MONSTER STORY-TELLER

FOR YOUNGER READERS
BURIED ALIVE!
CLIFFHANGER
GLUBBSLYME
LIZZIE ZIPMOUTH
SLEEPOVERS
THE CAT MUMMY
THE MUM-MINDER
THE WORRY WEBSITE

FIRST CLASS FRIENDS
BAD GIRLS
BEST FRIENDS
SECRETS
VICKY ANGEL

HISTORICAL ADVENTURES
OPAL PLUMSTEAD
QUEENIE
THE LOTTIE PROJECT

ALL ABOUT JACQUELINE WILSON
JACKY DAYDREAM
MY SECRET DIARY

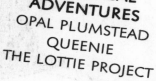

FAMILY DRAMAS
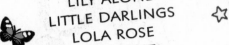
CANDYFLOSS
CLEAN BREAK
COOKIE
FOUR CHILDREN AND IT
LILY ALONE
LITTLE DARLINGS
LOLA ROSE
MIDNIGHT
THE BED AND BREAKFAST STAR
THE ILLUSTRATED MUM
THE LONGEST WHALE SONG
THE SUITCASE KID
KATY

MOST POPULAR CHARACTERS
HETTY FEATHER
SAPPHIRE BATTERSEA
EMERALD STAR
DIAMOND
LITTLE STARS
THE STORY OF TRACY BEAKER
THE DARE GAME
STARRING TRACY BEAKER

STORIES ABOUT SISTERS
DOUBLE ACT
THE BUTTERFLY CLUB
THE DIAMOND GIRLS
THE WORST THING ABOUT MY SISTER

FOR OLDER READERS
DUSTBIN BABY
GIRLS IN LOVE
GIRLS IN TEARS
GIRLS OUT LATE
GIRLS UNDER PRESSURE
KISS
LOVE LESSONS
MY SISTER JODIE

ALSO AVAILABLE
PAWS AND WHISKERS
THE JACQUELINE WILSON CHRISTMAS CRACKER
THE JACQUELINE WILSON TREASURY

☆ ABOUT THE AUTHOR ☆

Jacqueline Wilson is one of Britain's bestselling authors, with more than 35 million books sold in the UK alone. She has been honoured with many prizes for her work, including the Guardian Children's Fiction Award and the Children's Book of the Year. Jacqueline is a former Children's Laureate, a professor of children's literature, and in 2008 she was appointed a Dame for services to children's literacy.

Visit Jacqueline's fantastic website at
www.jacquelinewilson.co.uk

Jacqueline Wilson

A Hetty Feather Adventure

LITTLE STARS

ILLUSTRATED BY
NICK SHARRATT

STARDOM!
THRILLS!
HEARTBREAK!
LOVE!

DOUBLEDAY

LITTLE STARS
A DOUBLEDAY BOOK 978 0 857 53319 7
TRADE PAPERBACK 978 0 857 53320 3

Published in Great Britain by Doubleday,
an imprint of Random House Children's Publishers UK
A Penguin Random House Company

This edition published 2015

1 3 5 7 9 10 8 6 4 2

Penguin Random House is committed to a sustainable future
for our business, our readers and our planet. This book is made
from Forest Stewardship Council® certified paper.

MIX
Paper from
responsible sources
FSC® C018179

Set in New Century Schoolbook LT

RANDOM HOUSE CHILDREN'S PUBLISHERS UK
61–63 Uxbridge Road, London W5 5SA

www.**randomhousechildrens**.co.uk
www.**totallyrandombooks**.co.uk
www.**randomhouse**.co.uk

Addresses for companies within The Random House Group Limited
can be found at: www.randomhouse.co.uk/offices.htm

THE RANDOM HOUSE GROUP Limited Reg. No. 954009

A CIP catalogue record for this book is available from the British Library.

Printed and bound in Australia by Griffin Press

www.randomhouse.com.au
www.randomhouse.co.nz

To Rhian Harris, with many thanks.

Hetty Feather wouldn't exist without you.

1

I WOKE WITH A START, my head hurting, aching all over. For a moment I didn't know where I was. Indeed, I felt so fuddled I didn't even know *who* I was. Hetty Feather, Sapphire Battersea, Emerald Star? I had three names now.

Was I Hetty, curled up in my soft feather bed in the cottage or shivering in the narrow iron bed in the Foundling Hospital? Was I Sapphire, tossing and turning on the servant's truckle bed in the attic or still as a statue in my mermaid's costume at the seaside? Was I Emerald, still reeking of fish in my nightgown, or exhausted in my caravan bunk, with Elijah the elephant trumpeting in the distance?

I could hear shouting, thumping, scraping. I must be at Tanglefield's Circus. Oh Lord, was Diamond in trouble? I had to protect her. Had that evil clown Beppo beaten her cruelly because she'd tumbled during her act?

'Diamond?'

'I'm here, Hetty,' she murmured, clinging to me, strands of her long yellow hair tickling my face.

'Oh, Diamond, you're safe!' I said, holding her tight.

'Of course I'm safe. We ran away,' she said sleepily.

We ran away – yes, of course we did. I'd grabbed the clowns' penny-farthing, little Diamond balanced on my shoulders, and I pedalled and pedalled and we got away from Beppo and Mr Tanglefield. I felt my ear throbbing. Tanglefield had caught the tip of it with his whip, making it bleed. But we'd escaped! We were miles away from the circus camp. We'd fetched up in this little town, and here we were, huddled in a shop doorway near the marketplace.

I gently nudged Diamond to one side and sat up straight, stretching and yawning. I peered around anxiously, worried about the bicycle, but there it was, leaning against the wall beside us. It was still very early, but the market square was full of carts and burly men setting up their stalls with fruit and vegetables. I watched for a minute or two, fascinated by the way their great ham fists delicately arranged a row of apples, a ring of cauliflowers, a circle of salad stuffs upon the fake green grass of their stalls so that they looked like a prize garden in bloom.

One man looked up and saw me watching. He frowned and started walking purposely towards us.

I grabbed Diamond's arm, giving her a little shake. 'I think we'd better get going,' I said urgently, because I trusted very few men.

But as we stumbled to our feet and I tried to right the penny-farthing, he cried out to us. 'Don't run away, little girls! You mustn't be frightened. I don't mean you any harm. Why, I've brought up three little lasses of my own – plus a son, but the less said about him, the better. You look so cold and tired. Let me buy you each a hot drink.' He seemed genuinely concerned. It was clear by his tone that he thought me not much older than Diamond. It was a curse to me that I was so small and slight, but sometimes it had its advantages.

'That would be very kind, sir,' I said.

'And what are your names, little girls?'

'I'm Hetty and this is my sister, Ellen-Jane.' I used our real names. Emerald and Diamond would sound too fancy for this plain market man, and it seemed a wise precaution to keep quiet about our professional names.

Mr Tanglefield might try to hunt me down, and Beppo would certainly do his best to find little Diamond. She'd become the star of his Silver Tumblers acrobatic act, a real little crowd-pleaser. He'd paid her father five guineas to own her, body and soul, and he'd certainly got his money's worth.

I glanced at Diamond, hoping she wouldn't find it odd that I'd used her old name, but she was beaming. Her face was pale and tear-stained, her hair tangled and her clothes badly creased, but she still looked angelic.

'Sister!' she murmured, putting her hand in mine, clearly loving the notion.

I squeezed her hand tight.

'Aaah!' said the market man. 'Bless the little cherub! Well, I'm Sam Perkins, and that's my stall over there. Perkins, pick of the crop! Finest root vegetables and greens.' He gave a little bow.

'Good morning, Mr Perkins,' I said, bobbing him a curtsy, and giving Diamond's arm a little tug so she'd do likewise. 'We're pleased to meet you too.'

'Oh, you pets! Ain't you got lovely manners! But look, the little one's shivering. Let's warm you with that hot cup of tea.'

There was a small teashop at the side of the market, open from the crack of dawn for the market trade. We followed in Mr Perkins's wake. I gave Diamond our little suitcase while I carefully wheeled the penny-farthing. I was reluctant to leave it leaning up against the wall of the teashop.

'It'll be safe there, don't you fret,' said Mr Perkins. 'Hey, you – young Alfred!' he called to a boy at the nearest stall. 'Keep an eye on this here contraption, will you? Give us a whistle if anyone so much as walks near it.'

Alfred gave a nod and a wave. Mr Perkins was obviously well respected at the market. He led us into the warm steamy interior of the teashop. It was thick with the smell of bacon and sausage, so strong it made us reel. I felt starving hungry. I also had another pressing urge. I went and whispered to the large lady behind the counter, and she let Diamond and me through to her WC at the back of the shop. When we had relieved ourselves, we had a quick wash in the basin and I tried to comb Diamond's tangled curls with my fingers.

'There now!' said Mr Perkins when we came back. 'Bessie, three mugs of tea and three special breakfasts, if you please.'

'Certainly, Sam. Are these two your grandchildren then? Hello, dears! Have you come to see your grandpa at his work?' Bessie asked. She was all over smiles, her round face rosy red, her curly hair damp, her white apron pulled taut over her plumpness.

Mr Perkins led us to a table away from all the other market men. 'Not mine, Bessie. Two new little friends,' he said cheerfully.

'And where do they come from, then?' Bessie asked.

'Ah, it's a long story,' said Mr Perkins, sitting down beside us. He lowered his voice. 'I thought you'd maybe want to keep your circumstances to yourselves, rather than broadcast them to all and sundry.'

'That's so tactful of you, Mr Perkins,' I said gratefully.

'That doesn't mean that *I* don't want to know,' he said. 'Not just out of nosiness. I'd like to think I can help in some way. You're a pair of runaways, aren't you?'

'Yes, sir,' I said, because it was pointless denying the obvious.

'Well, I'll let you get your breakfasts first, and then I'll want to hear the whole story,' said Mr Perkins.

I bent down, unlatched the suitcase and felt for my purse. 'I can pay for the breakfasts, Mr Perkins. We're not destitute,' I said.

He roared with laughter. 'Bless you, dear, I didn't think it for a minute. I can see you're two nicely turned out little ladies. Such fine and fancy dresses clearly cost a pretty penny.'

I smiled, because I'd made both our outfits myself. I kept my purse in my hand, but Mr Perkins shook his head.

'Now, pop that purse back in your case. The breakfasts are on the house. Bessie's a dear friend of mine, and very kind-hearted. A good cook too. A good plate of Bessie-food will put some roses in those peaky little faces.'

It was wonderful food. Beppo had half starved Diamond

to keep her as light as possible for her acrobatic tumbling, and I had been feeling so tired and run down these last few months at the circus that I'd barely been able to choke down my own food. But now we both made short work of our bacon, sausage, egg, tomato and fried bread, and had enough room left for several slices of buttered toast with marmalade.

'Oh, my!' said Diamond, rubbing her full tummy. 'Bessie-food is the best food ever!'

'Did you hear that, Bess? The little lass thinks you're a rival to Mrs Beeton,' said Mr Perkins.

'Better than Mrs Beeton,' I said. I'd tried several of her recipes with Mrs Briskett when I first went into service, and it had seemed an awful lot of fiddling about for very average results. Or perhaps it was simply my culinary skills that were lacking. I wished I'd had more time with Mama so that she could have taught me. I felt a longing for her as sharp as toothache and bent my head.

'What is it, lass? Come now, whet your whistle with your tea and tell your Uncle Sam all about it,' said Mr Perkins, patting my hand in a kindly fashion.

I wished he were really my uncle. I had a moment's fantasy that he might take a shine to us and treat us like real grandchildren. We would no longer need to try to earn our own livings. I could be a little girl again, safe and cosy, still at school. Diamond would become the pet of the whole family. Mr Perkins would show her that men could be kind instead of cruel. I thought of her father selling her for a handful of silver guineas, Beppo beating her savagely if she made some slight mistake. The tears in my eyes spilled over.

'Hey, now, don't you start crying or you'll set me off. I blub like a baby, I'm warning you,' said Mr Perkins, pressing his own crumpled handkerchief on me.

I sniffed and dabbed at my eyes fiercely. I told myself I was only tearful because I was tired. I knew Diamond was looking at me anxiously.

I gave her a watery smile, managing to control myself. 'I'm sorry. I'm being silly,' I said. I wondered if I dared tell Mr Perkins the whole truth.

'Are you going to tell me what you two are doing here? Who have you run from? You've no need to be frightened now. If it's anything truly bad and you're scared someone will come after you, we'll whisk you over to Sergeant Browning at the police station. He happens to be a pal of mine, and he'll look after you and keep you safe.'

That brought me to my senses. Sergeant Browning might be Perkins's pal, but he was still a policeman. If he knew who I really was, then he might well march me straight back to the Foundling Hospital to be disciplined and then sent off into service again. And what about Diamond? Beppo had his official document saying that she belonged to him now. I couldn't risk that fate for her.

It was better to lie – and through necessity I had become very good at it.

'It's nothing like that, Mr Perkins, I promise you. Ellen-Jane and I are sad because we're grieving for our poor mother. She died of the consumption. She suffered something cruel.' Tears poured down my face again. I felt bad when I saw the concern on Mr Perkins's face, but after all, we *had* both lost our dear mothers, and still sorely missed them.

'What about your pa, dear? Can't he manage to look after you two girlies?'

'Oh, Pa's a sailor and away at sea,' I said glibly.

'So who's been looking after you two, then?' he asked.

'That's the problem. They put us into a home for destitute girls but it was quite hateful. There was a wicked matron who treated us cruelly and we had to wear hideous brown uniforms with white caps and pinafores and we were punished if we dirtied them. We weren't allowed to keep our own dolls or story books and they threatened to cut off our hair,' I said, remembering all too well the regime of the Foundling Hospital.

'Cut off your pretty hair!' echoed Mr Perkins, looking at Diamond's beautiful long blonde curls.

'And then my sister made some little childish mistake and they threatened her with a beating, so we decided to run away, didn't we, Ellen-Jane?' I said.

Diamond nodded, though she was clearly muddled by my account.

'And no wonder,' said Mr Perkins. 'But where are you running to? Do you have any plans? We can't have you two little girls walking the streets and sleeping rough. There's all sorts of dangers, especially when you're such a pretty pair.'

I knew perfectly well that I wasn't pretty, with my carroty hair and pale peaky face, but Diamond's beauty was undeniable. I guessed it would trouble him if I said we had plans to join the Cavalcade music hall. I'd been out in the world long enough to know that men might like to enjoy themselves in a music hall, but wouldn't think it a place for women to work, especially 'genteel' girls.

'We're going to the Cavalcade,' Diamond blurted out, before I could stop her.

Mr Perkins looked horrified. 'You're never! That den of iniquity! What are you *thinking* of?' he said to me, suddenly furious.

Diamond clapped her hands over her mouth. She was always terrified when men lost their tempers. She had so often borne the brunt of Beppo's fury.

'Oh, Mr Perkins, please don't get angry. Diamond is only little, she doesn't understand. She saw a poster bill and asked what it was all about, and when I told her it was ladies singing and men telling funny stories, she took a fancy to going to see for herself. But of course I'd never *dream* of taking her to such a place.'

Diamond stared at me, astonished.

'We have plans, Mr Perkins, don't you worry,' I continued hastily. 'We're going to stay with our uncle and aunt. We have written to let them know. It is all arranged. We couldn't cover the entire distance yesterday, but will be there by lunch time today if we set off shortly on our bicycle.'

'Well, that's a relief. You're a rum one, knowing how to pedal that monstrosity. And what does the little one do, run along beside you?' asked Mr Perkins.

'I balance on Hetty,' said Diamond proudly.

'You never! A little lass like you! Surely that's highly dangerous?'

Diamond looked at Mr Perkins as if he were a little soft in the head. Balancing on a penny-farthing was a trivial feat compared with hurtling off a springboard and landing on the top of a human column of three boys, the act for which she was famous.

'Ellen-Jane is brilliant at balancing, I promise you,' I assured him. Diamond nodded her head eagerly.

'You're a droll little pair,' said Mr Perkins. 'I still feel anxious about letting you wander off on your own. I'd accompany you myself, but I can't abandon my stall all day. Perhaps I'll ask Sergeant Browning if one of his young bobbies can walk along beside you.'

'Oh no, that's not at all necessary,' I said quickly. 'I dare say Uncle will come and meet us halfway. We will be fine, Mr Perkins. We're well set up now with our delicious breakfasts. We'll never forget your kindness.'

We said goodbye, thanked Bessie for our superb meals, and went outside to grapple with the penny-farthing. I couldn't mount the wretched thing properly with Mr Perkins and half the market watching me. I got my skirts caught, and then, when I clutched my suitcase, I over-balanced and very nearly landed on my head. The boys on the stalls laughed raucously, but Mr Perkins looked worried.

'My dear Hetty, I think you're too little to ride that iron monster. How old *are* you? Ten? Twelve?' he said.

I wanted to toss my head and tell him firmly that I was fifteen years old and had been entirely independent for a good year, but I didn't want to disillusion him, especially when he'd been so kind to us. And in spite of my embarrassment and irritation I was also pleased. My childishness had helped when I was Tanglefield's ringmaster. People were amused by my loud expressive voice, my swaggering air of authority, my overblown introductions, impressed that a little girl could take command.

I needed to appear a child to the manager of the Cavalcade. It was clearly my winning card. Diamond looked much younger than her age too. We could pretend she was a tot of five or six. Folk loved a performing infant. All we had to do was bounce on stage and act cute and they'd start clapping.

This thought buoyed me up – literally so, because at the third attempt I hitched myself neatly onto the saddle, so that Diamond could scramble up after me.

'Sit behind me, sharing my seat,' I whispered, because I feared her shoulder stand would look too flamboyant. We were already drawing far too much attention to ourselves.

I freed one hand to give Mr Perkins a little wave, and then started pedalling determinedly.

'Goodbye, Hetty! Goodbye, Ellen-Jane. You take care now!' Mr Perkins called, waving his handkerchief at us.

'Goodbye,' we chorused, feeling truly sad to leave him.

Diamond was muddled by my glib lies. 'Are we really going to see our uncle, Hetty?' she asked. 'I didn't even know we had one.'

'No, Diamond,' I said patiently. I suddenly wondered if I had a real uncle. Mama had never mentioned having a brother, but then she'd never mentioned her family at all. I'd met her father once, when I was up north finding *my* father, but this grandfather of mine was such a demented, angry old man I was determined never to go near him again, not even to find out if I had any other family.

It had been a pleasure getting to know my own

handsome red-haired fisherman father, though I was less enthusiastic about his new wife. Father had never mentioned a brother or sister either, come to that. I was an only child too, if I didn't count my two half-siblings.

If I ever married, I resolved to have a whole handful of children, just so they should never feel alone. I knew I could have had dear Jem as a sweetheart and married him some time in the future. He would have made a truly loving husband. And yet I had run away to the circus because I knew, deep down, that I didn't love him in quite the right way. I was too restless to stay in that little hamlet for the whole of my future life. I wanted excitement, glamour, adventure . . .

I thought I'd find all these in the circus. I suppose I did at first. But then I realized that it was a cruel, tawdry world and constantly pitching tents and travelling to the next gaff was dreary and depressing. It was such hard work too, performing twice, sometimes three times a day, and then falling asleep bone-weary. If it was hard for me, it was five times that for poor little Diamond, forced to crick her bones to make them abnormally bendy, rehearsing her act many times a day, and then performing in the ring long past a child's bedtime, always white with fear in case she didn't please that gargoyle clown.

'Hetty?' Diamond said insistently.

I realized she'd been trying to get my attention while I'd been daydreaming. 'What is it, darling?'

'Where *are* we going?'

'We're going to the Cavalcade, remember?'

'But Mr Perkins said it was a den of something-or-other. Isn't it a bad place?' asked Diamond.

'It's a music hall, that's all. I think it sounds wonderful. You and I are going to be music-hall artistes,' I said, and I turned my voice into a trumpet and tooted a fanfare.

A cluster of children hopping about in the gutter jeered at me. I gave them a little bow and consequently made the penny-farthing wobble dangerously. That made them laugh hysterically. Poor Diamond fell to the ground in the process, though thank goodness she'd been taught how to take a tumble.

'Yes, very funny, ha ha,' I said sarcastically to the gaggle of children. 'I'm so glad we amuse you. We will amuse you even more when we take our rightful place on the stage of the Cavalcade and get paid good money for our antics.'

They stared at me blankly, clearly not following.

'So can you please tell us the way to the Cavalcade?' I asked, gazing around at them all.

Their faces were still as blank as china dolls.

'What's the Cavalcade when it's at home?' the biggest boy asked.

'It's the music hall. Isn't it here? There's an advertisement for it in the market place,' I said, helping Diamond to her feet and dusting her down.

'Oh, I get you. It's in Fenstone, that music hall, miles and miles away,' he said.

My heart sank. My legs were stiff and sore from yesterday's pedalling. I didn't feel ready to tackle another marathon journey. 'How many miles?' I said wearily.

'Three. Maybe four,' he said. 'It'll take you an hour or more.'

'Oh, for heaven's sake, that's nothing!'

I'd been brought up in the countryside till I was nearly six. I used to walk over the meadows and through the woods with Jem for hour after hour, and when my worn boots got too tight, I simply tugged them off and went barefoot.

'Thank you, boy,' I said in a lordly fashion.

He sniggered and made a very rude response. I ignored him and remounted the penny-farthing (successfully, thank the Lord). Diamond scrambled up too. I let her stand on my shoulders, just to show off. I pedalled off, and this time several of the children clapped and cheered.

'Idiots,' I murmured to Diamond. 'Better sit down when we're out of sight. Phew, this pedalling is hard work!'

'Let me take a turn,' Diamond suggested, though she was so small her feet couldn't even reach the pedals.

'Maybe later,' I said tactfully. 'You're a dear little sister, do you know that?'

Diamond giggled. 'You're a dear little *big* sister,' she said.

It wasn't a very pleasant route to Fenstone: drab terraced houses and dark factories. The grey roads were littered with reeking horse manure. But I was now in such high spirits that I could have been bowling down leafy lanes, past picturesque thatched cottages, breathing in roses and honeysuckle.

Diamond was in good spirits too. She started singing hymn after hymn, her voice high and sweet. When she didn't remember the words properly, she invented her own.

'Praise my soul the King of Heaven,
To his feet – oh tingaling,
Ranting reeled restored forgiven,
Who like Hetty and Di-mond bring . . .'

'You're a funny sausage! Where did you learn all these hymns? Did you go to church when you were little? *I* had to go to chapel every single Sunday but I don't know half as many hymns as you,' I said.

'Mama used to sing them,' said Diamond. 'I sat on her lap and she sang to me. Did you sit on your mama's lap while she sang to you, Hetty?'

I shut my eyes momentarily because it was so painful. This was a mistake. I had to swerve violently to avoid the carriage in front of us, stationary because the horse was contributing to the mire on the road.

'Whoops,' I said as we wobbled past. 'No, I wasn't with my mama when I was little enough to sit on her lap. You know I was at the Foundling Hospital.'

'But your mama worked there, you said.'

'I didn't *know* she was my mama for years and years. And then, when I found out, she was sent away. And then – and then . . .'

I couldn't talk about that terrible summer when Mama slowly faded away and died.

Diamond was quiet for a minute or so too. Then she stroked my hair and said softly in my ear, 'I think your mama and mine have made friends in Heaven. They peer through the clouds at us every now and then to make sure we're being good girls.'

'Well, my poor mama must get very agitated, because I am often a *bad* girl,' I said.

My mood lightened again when we saw a signpost to Fenstone. It was a proper town, with heavy traffic. The road was so crowded that eventually I thought it safer to dismount and push the penny-farthing along the pavement. Pushing was harder than pedalling, but Diamond kept me amused by choosing which house she wanted to live in when we were grown up and rich and famous.

'Which do you like best, Hetty? The house with the

pretty blossom trees, or the house with the green shutters, or the house with that dome thing on the roof?' she asked earnestly.

'If we're going to be *really* rich and famous, couldn't we have a much bigger house? A mansion or a castle with a hundred rooms, and we can choose a different bedroom every week. How about that?' I suggested.

'No, I wouldn't like that at all, it would be far too big and scary. I'd get lost, and what would I do if I forgot which bedroom you were in?' said Diamond, taking me seriously. 'No, Hetty, please let's have one of these houses – they're so pretty and not scary at all.'

'Very well. Let's have the one with the dome. That can be our bedroom. And we'll bolt the front door so no one can ever get in, but if a very dear friend comes visiting, we'll open a window and let down our hair like Rapunzel and they can climb up to see us.'

'Oh yes, I like the dome house best of all too. But we're going to have to grow our hair right down to our feet,' said Diamond.

'That's a good idea. When we're music-hall stars we'll be known as the Hairy Sisters and our famous hair will flow out behind us as we walk, like a bride's train. Woe betide anyone who steps on it!'

'We're going to use up an awful lot of bottles of rainbow shampoo,' said Diamond. 'Hetty, what's that house right over there, past the shops? The big, big house with the

19

beautiful pale green roof? Is it a palace? Do you think it's where the Queen lives?'

'I very much doubt Queen Victoria has a palace in Fenstone,' I said. 'But let's go and see.'

It certainly looked like a palace, with its fine red brick and weathered copper roof, all towers and cupolas. The steps to the grand gilt doors were covered in deep red carpet, and through the windows we could see the glint of a grand chandelier.

'It *is* a palace!' said Diamond.

'No it's not. Read that great big word in gilt lettering, Diamond.'

'You know I'm not very good at reading.'

'Try, go on!'

'Cav . . . cav-al-cad?'

'Cavalcade! We're here, Diamond. This is the music hall!'

CAVALCADE

2

THERE WAS A BIG poster on either side of the doors advertising all the artistes. The names at the top were in large fancy writing. Lower down the list the writing grew smaller. I walked right up until my nose was nearly pecking the poster. I reached out and touched the name on the bottom line. *Little Flirty Bertie.*

Could he be *my* Bertie, the cheeky butcher's boy? I had walked out with him when I was a reluctant servant in Mr Buchanan's household. Dear funny Bertie, who had been so self-conscious about reeking of meat. Bertie, the boy who had taken me to the fair and won me the little black-and-white china dog that was in my suitcase now, carefully wrapped in my nightgown to prevent any chips.

'Them dogs always come in pairs,' Bertie had said. 'You put them on your mantelpiece either side of the clock. All married folk have them. Seems like I'll have to win you another, Hetty.'

He said it light-heartedly, but he'd blushed as red as a side of beef. And I felt my own cheeks grow hot, because he might well have been hinting that *we* become a married couple one day. I liked Bertie very much, but I couldn't take him seriously. If I'd been prepared to settle down with any man, it would have been with dear faithful Jem.

It had been so painful rejecting him. I thought he'd be happier with my friend Janet. I knew I would have led him a merry dance, but Janet would stay dear and true. She loved Jem with all her heart.

I'd loved Mama so much I still felt only half a girl without her. I loved Diamond now as if she were truly my sister. But I didn't love any man that way. So why was my heart thumping now, as I looked at Bertie's name?

Of course, it probably wasn't my Bertie at all. But he *had* told me of his ambitions to be a music-hall artiste.

He'd sung to me and taught himself a jaunty tap-dance routine. I could imagine him in a straw hat and striped blazer striding about the stage, entrancing any audience. Had he really given up his steady job at the butcher's shop to have a go?

It would have been such a big step for him to take. I was surely mistaken. Bertie was a common enough name, even bestowed on royalty. But I would be so royally proud if Bertie really had taken to the boards and was a true music-hall star, albeit at the very bottom of the bill.

I let my eyes slide upwards. Araminta, the Exotic Acrobatic Dancer. Sven the Russian Sword-swallower. Peter Perkins and his Comical Capers. Lily Lark, the Sweetest Songbird, was right at the top, with a picture of a woman singing, songbirds flying all around her head.

I wondered if one day Diamond and I would share top billing. Diamond, the Acrobatic Child Wonder! Emerald Star, Compère Extraordinaire! Oh yes, it had an authentic ring.

'Are we going in?' said Diamond, slipping her hand in mine. 'I can't wait to see if it's like a palace inside too. Will it be all gold, like in a fairy story? Will they have gold furniture and gold goblets to drink out of, and even a gold water closet?'

'I'm not sure about that, but I've heard there's going to be a real little fairy there, and she has golden hair,' I said, giving one of Diamond's locks a gentle tug.

'Don't laugh, but I really feel like a fairy!' said Diamond. 'Let's go *in*, Hetty!'

'No, no. We must prepare first before we accost the manager, whoever he is.'

'Prepare?'

'Rehearse our acts,' I said. 'Hush a moment, I need to memorize all these folk on the playbill. Oh dear, there are so many!' I opened up my suitcase and started scribbling down the names on the back of one of my memoir notebooks with an old stub of pencil.

When I had them all written down safely, I smiled at Diamond. 'There! Now, we must find some kind of temporary lodging. We need to have a proper wash as we still look very travel stained. We'd better have a nap too. You have such dark circles under your eyes, people will mistake you for a baby panda. Now come along.'

'But I'd much sooner stay at the Cavalcade. Maybe they have gold beds for all their artistes!'

'I don't think it very likely. We'll probably have to make do with ordinary iron beds just for now,' I said. 'Come on!'

I started pushing the penny-farthing while Diamond trailed behind, dragging the suitcase. She kept looking back wistfully.

I had no idea where to search for lodgings. It had been much easier when I spent the summer in Bignor. Seasides had hundreds of boarding houses, all competing for business. Fenstone seemed very different. There were row after row of private houses, then wider shopping streets, then rows of private houses again. Not one had a sign up advertising board and lodging.

I found a hotel near the railway station. It was large, and perhaps it had been impressive once, but now it had a decidedly seedy air, with peeling paint and cracked windows. The smell of stale frying fat wafted out of the open door. Surely such a place couldn't be too expensive? I'd had the presence of mind to take my purse with me when Diamond and I were running away. I had a week's meagre wages and some savings. I hoped there would be enough to last us a little while. Then we would start earning, wouldn't we?

I didn't want to leave the penny-farthing outside, not with all sorts of cheeky lads milling around the railway station. Even if they didn't steal my bicycle, they might very well try a ride on it for a lark, and then they'd be bound to wobble and crash and damage it.

I wheeled it inside the front door and marched along the hallway. Diamond tiptoed after me. The smell of stale fat was worse than ever, and we breathed shallowly.

'Hello?' I called. I tried again, with no result. I walked up to a little table, seized hold of a bell and shook it vigorously. Diamond put her hand over her mouth at the clamour. It worried me too, but I tried to look calm and confident.

An old man in undershirt, trousers and carpet slippers

came shuffling into the hallway from the nether regions of the hotel. He was clutching a mop that smelled sour. He did too.

He glared when he saw us. 'What are you two kids playing at? How dare you mess about with my bell! Go home to your mothers.'

'We can't. We haven't got any,' said Diamond, her voice shrill. She rubbed her eyes as if she were crying and then gave me a sly glance. She was clearly playing for sympathy to help our cause. It was a pity she wasn't a very convincing actress.

'Well, that's not my fault,' he said, unimpressed. 'Now scarper!'

'But we require board and lodging for a week,' I said quickly, in my most authoritative voice.

'Oh yes? And you two little guttersnipes have the fifteen shillings it will cost?' the man sneered.

Fifteen shillings! Was he truly serious?

'Perhaps we will simply take the lodgings and never mind the board,' I said. It would be easy enough to buy buns and apples and meat pies. We were both used to eating frugally.

'Oh yes? And perhaps you'd like a room without a bed for a further reduction?' he sneered.

'You don't have to be so unpleasant. I've said we will take the room. Look, I have the money here,' I said, showing him my purse.

'And who did you snatch that from, you little varmint?'

'How dare you speak to me like that! I'm a young lady,' I said, tossing my head.

I'd convinced dear Mr Perkins that I was a little girl, but now I was trying to pass myself off as a young woman. It wasn't working. It didn't help when Diamond stuck her chin in the air and declared that *she* was a young lady too.

'Scram, both of you,' the man said, and he raised his smelly mop at us.

We had to make a run for it. It was hard work manoeuvring the penny-farthing back over the brass step. He started screaming that we were scraping his polish, though it was clear that step hadn't seen a scape of polish for months.

'What a nasty man,' said Diamond when we were safely outside.

'Absolutely foul. And the hotel was ludicrously expensive,' I said.

'It smelled horrid too.'

'So we wouldn't have wanted to stay there anyway.'

But we still had to find *somewhere* to stay, and wasted the rest of the morning looking. We went to a tearoom to have a bite to eat for lunch, but it was nowhere near as pleasant as Bessie's.

Diamond pointed at slices of pink-and-yellow cake under a glass dome. 'Look! It's Madame Adeline's cake!' she cried.

We were both immediately filled with longing for dear Madame Adeline who had looked after us as best she could – until she had to retire from circus life. We ordered a slice of cake each, but it was flavourless and stale, a bitter disappointment.

'I wish we could go and see Madame Adeline,' said Diamond, chewing without swallowing. Her eyes brimmed with tears. 'I do miss her so. Hetty, couldn't we go and stay with her for just a little while and *then* become music-hall stars?'

'No, love. Madame Adeline and Mr Marvel can scarcely look after themselves. We can't impose on them. And they live much too far away. There's a limit to my pedalling. Cheer up. We'll find a place to live soon, I promise.'

We asked the tearoom lady if we could use her facilities, but she wasn't kind like Bessie.

'What do you think this is, a public convenience? I'm not having you rampaging through my private property, snatching whatever takes your eye. Do you think I was born yesterday? Be off with you!' she said, loud enough for the whole tearoom to hear.

She actually put her hand on our backs and pushed us towards the door while folk stared. Diamond was pink in the face with humiliation. I expect I was red with rage, especially as I'd actually left her an extra penny as a tip, even though her cake was stale and her tea indifferent.

'Oh, Hetty!' Diamond wailed, once we were outside. 'And I really badly need to go!'

'Don't worry,' I said, though I was worried myself. But I was nothing if not resourceful. I pushed the penny-farthing along, Diamond hop-skipping beside me, down older, quieter streets until we found a narrow alleyway. It reeked a little. Clearly other people had also used it for the purpose I had in mind. I went first and then sent Diamond, promising that I wouldn't let anyone else go down the alley while she was using it.

Then we went on our way, relieved but still down-hearted. We were in a much poorer part of Fenstone, which wasn't really a good idea. A weasel-faced old man eyed our penny-farthing and sidled up to us, asking if he could examine our marvellous bicycling machine.

'No, I'm sorry, we're in a hurry,' I said firmly. 'No! Absolutely not! Leave go or I'll call a policeman!'

He laughed unpleasantly – it was unlikely a policeman would wander down such dismal streets – and seized hold of the handlebars, elbowing Diamond sharply out of the way. That was enough. I was wearing the beautiful hard leather boots I'd worn in the circus ring. I raised my leg swiftly and kicked him extremely hard in his softest and most vulnerable place. He collapsed, groaning, and we started running back towards the town centre.

I knew we were safe when we got to wider streets. In fact, we soon found ourselves in the most stylish part of town, with rows of interesting shops. We urgently needed to find lodgings and prepare our acts for the Cavalcade, but we both became momentarily distracted. Diamond leaned her forehead against the window of a toyshop, dazzled by the dolls, gazing longingly into their blue china eyes.

'They're just like real children!' She pointed at their jointed legs, their dainty knitted stockings, their kid leather boots. 'Do you think they can *walk*?' she wondered.

'No, they're only dolls,' I told her.

'But such dolls!' said Diamond. 'I wish Maybelle had little leather boots.'

Maybelle was her own home-made doll. I had sewn features on her plain rag face and fashioned her a little outfit, but of course she wasn't anywhere near as fine as these china beauties.

'If only I could have one of these dolls,' said Diamond. But then, conscious of Maybelle stuffed into our suitcase, she said loudly, 'But I will always love Maybelle best because she is my first born.'

I suddenly remembered the rag baby my foster mother Peg had made me when I was tiny. She had done her best, but she was not a fine seamstress. The rag baby had ill-matching limbs and a lumpy face, but I remembered loving that ugly little doll as truly as any mother loved her child. It was such a shock when I arrived at the Foundling Hospital clutching my cloth baby to have her snatched from me by Matron Peters. She burned my baby, along with all my Sunday best clothes from home.

I'd grown up in the Foundling Hospital without any toys at all, and Diamond's early childhood had been equally bleak. We gazed at the toys in the window with awe, coveting each and every one, even though I at least was long past the age for such things. But I still longed to sink my hands in a tub of glass marbles, ached to fly a red-and-yellow kite with a long tail, and yearned to sit on the great rocking horse I saw stabled at the back of the shop.

'Can we go into the shop, just to look?' Diamond asked.

I hesitated. But then I heard a church clock strike three. 'No, there isn't time. And they'd probably chase us away. But I promise that when we're stars at the Cavalcade, we will come back here with my first wage packet and I'll buy you a present. I probably won't be able to afford a china doll just yet, but perhaps I could buy Maybelle a pair of boots.'

'Oh, you would absolutely love that, wouldn't you, Maybelle?' said Diamond, talking into the suitcase.

'*Yes, yes, yes!*' she said again, in a tiny Maybelle voice.

We carried on along the street, hoping that when the shops petered out there might be suitable lodgings nearby. But then I was stopped in my tracks by another shop. It was a small fashion emporium. GIBSON'S GOWNS said the sign above the door, in discreet gilt lettering.

There was a window either side of the door, with just one finely dressed mannequin in each.

I was startled to see such a sparse display. I was used to shops stuffed with a hundred and one items.

'Just look, Diamond!' I said.

Diamond looked obediently, but didn't seem impressed. 'The windows are nearly empty,' she said dismissively.

'Yes, because this is a very special, elegant shop,' I said, as if I knew all about it. 'They don't need an enormous vulgar display. They are content to let each gown speak for itself. And so it does. Eloquently!'

Diamond wrinkled her nose. 'Why are you talking so silly, Hetty?' she said.

'Well, you're just a little girl. I don't suppose you could understand,' I said.

I felt *I* understood, even if it was just by instinct. Each mannequin stood serenely in her own window, white arms outstretched as if bestowing queenly blessings on passers-by. The one on the left was dressed in a blue and violet gown with extraordinary huge sleeves. They made such a statement that the rest of the dress was restrained, almost subdued. It was breathtakingly effective.

The one on the right was a deep emerald green, almost the exact shade of the velvet gown I'd once made, and then cut up in an attempt to fashion myself a mermaid's costume. At the time I'd thought it a masterpiece, but I could now see that it had been clumsily designed and cobbled together. This green gown was silk, with an iridescent gleam as it caught the sunshine. It was styled in a perfect hourglass that would make any woman's waist look minute.

I thought how that bright green would set off my red hair, though I knew I was being ridiculous. I could tell by the sweep of the skirts that the gown would be at least nine inches too long on me, and the style and stitching told me that it would be extremely expensive, beyond my pocket even if I got star billing at the Cavalcade.

I sighed wistfully and wouldn't budge, though Diamond was pulling at my arm, starting to get bored. Then the door to Gibson's Gowns opened with a musical trill of the bell, and a very stout lady peered out at me, twitching her pince-nez up her snub nose. She was dressed in severe black satin.

I started, though I had been doing nothing wrong.

She looked at me enquiringly. 'Have you come to collect your mistress's gown?' she asked. Her voice was surprisingly girlish and high-pitched.

I flushed. 'I am not a servant, ma'am,' I said with dignity, although I had been exactly that the year before.

'Oh my dear, I do apologize. Then might I ask why you've been staring at my windows for the past ten minutes?' she asked, sounding genuinely curious.

'I was admiring your gowns. I have never seen

anything like them before. Did you invent the new styles yourself?' I asked.

'I did, though I'm influenced by the French fashion journals,' she said.

'French fashion journals,' I repeated. 'Oh, where can you buy them?'

'I send for them from Paris.'

'Paris!' I echoed, as awed as if she'd told me she'd sent for them from the moon.

'You seem very interested in fashion.' The woman's small eyes peered through the pince-nez at my dress. 'Did you make that dress yourself?'

It was my best dress, and I'd worked hard at the stitching, but now I felt ashamed of the cotton sprigging and girlish styling.

'This old thing,' I said hurriedly, blushing.

'Why, Hetty, it's your bestest dress,' said Diamond. 'And this is *my* best dress. Isn't it lovely?' She held out her blue skirts and crumpled pinafore and twirled around happily.

'It is indeed lovely,' said the stout lady, and she didn't sound as if she were mocking us. She even took two steps out onto the pavement and examined Diamond's collar and hem.

'I didn't have a proper pattern,' I said hastily. 'And it's a little tight on her now because she's grown.'

'I can grow as big as big can be now, because I'm no longer a circus girl,' said Diamond.

34

'Ellen-Jane!' I said sharply.

But the stout lady looked interested rather than shocked. 'Circus girls!' she said. She nodded at the penny-farthing propped against her windows. 'Well, I guessed you were something out of the ordinary. And you have an air about you.'

'An air,' I echoed, relishing the phrase. Oh yes, I loved the idea of having my own air. I'd spent nine long years in the Foundling Hospital, clothed exactly like all the other girls, in hideous brown dresses and white caps and aprons. All my life I'd fought so hard to be myself, whether I was Hetty Feather, Sapphire Battersea or Emerald Star.

'But we're not going to be circus girls any more,' Diamond confided. 'We're going to be music-hall stars.'

'Are you indeed!' The stout lady looked at me. 'Is that true?'

'Yes, it is,' I said. I decided to trust her. 'We are going to try for work at the Cavalcade.'

She didn't seem too shocked. 'Well, it's one of the finest music halls. Folk say it rivals any London hall. All the stars have appeared there.'

'Have you been to see them?' I asked.

'No dear, not to a show! I'm a single lady. It wouldn't be proper. But some of my best clients are Cavalcade artistes. As a matter of fact, I make all Mrs Ruby's gowns,' she said proudly.

I raised my eyebrows as if impressed, though I'd never heard of Mrs Ruby. Perhaps she was a star performer – a fine figure of a woman, like Madame Adeline in her prime.

'Does Mrs Ruby sing or perhaps dance?' I asked.

'No, no, she's the manager of the Cavalcade,' said Miss Gibson. 'I'm in the middle of making her a gown now, with the modern leg-o'-mutton sleeve, the styling very similar to the gown in the window, but my apprentice has just let me down badly. Run off with a gentleman friend, the silly little fool. He'll tire of her in a few weeks, and then where will she be? *I* know. Saddled with a baby, her life in ruins.'

I felt my face flushing fiery red, because Mama had done something similar. 'Perhaps she fell in love and couldn't help herself,' I said.

'Love!' The stout lady said it contemptuously, but there was a wistfulness about her expression. She was past middle age, but I suddenly saw her as a young girl, still much too stout, but her ringlets brown instead of grey, her face a smooth white moon, her eyes gleaming hopefully behind her tiny spectacles.

I glanced at her left hand and saw she wore no rings. Did she regret her staid spinster life, or was she perfectly content with her elegant little shop and wealthy clients?

'So you're off to the Cavalcade then, girls?' she said.

'Yes, but we badly need to find lodgings first. We've

been looking for hours for somewhere suitable,' I said.

'Hours and hours and hours,' said Diamond, sighing.

'We tried at the Station Hotel but—'

'Oh, you don't want to go there! It's a hovel now, and not at all suitable for young girls . . .' The lady had her head on one side, thinking. 'I tell you what. You can have my girl's room for tonight. It's in the attic and there's only one narrow bed, but I dare say you can double up.'

'Oh, that would be wonderful! Thank you so much, Miss . . . Gibson? What sort of charge did you have in mind?' I asked joyfully.

'How about working for your board? Can you tack? I've pinned most of the pieces for Mrs Ruby's costume. If you tack the skirts and bodice into place, I can concentrate on those tricky sleeves.'

'When would you need me to do that?' I asked.

'Well, right now. There's no point going to the Cavalcade till six thirty or seven – it will all be shut up till then,' said Miss Gibson.

I hesitated. Diamond and I needed to rehearse, didn't we? But when Miss Gibson showed us a yard behind her shop where we could safely stow the penny-farthing, I set Diamond practising her routine there.

'But what shall I do?' she asked. 'I can't perform the human column without the Silver Tumblers. I can't do the springboard without them. I can't curtsy and clap if they're not there.'

'Stop saying "I can't" all the time! Of course you can. Work out your own little solo routine. Didn't you use to perform all by yourself for pennies?'

'You mean like I did in the marketplace when I was little?' said Diamond.

'Yes, yes! If it impressed Beppo, it must have been good,' I told her.

Diamond's face darkened when I mentioned his name, but she started circling the yard obediently, turning cartwheels.

'The little pet!' said Miss Gibson. 'Now, dear, what's your name?'

'My stage name is Emerald Star. Mama's chosen name for me was Sapphire. But most folk call me Hetty,' I said.

'Then I shall call you Hetty too. Let us see your sewing skills in action.'

For the next three hours I sat stitching away at a very distinctive purple costume in Miss Gibson's back room. When I'd finished all the tacking, she set me hemming, standing over me to make sure that my stitches were tiny and even, and then leaving me alone when she was satisfied.

I stitched and stitched, my hand cramping, my neck aching. All the while I muttered under my breath. *Lily Lark, Peter Perkins, Sven, Araminta, Flirty Bertie . . .*

3

'**D**ON'T BE NERVOUS, DIAMOND.** We'll do splendidly,'
I said, taking her hand.

My own palm was damp. I'd had such confidence when
I rapped on Mr Tanglefield's wagon, bounced in and
talked myself into the job of ringmaster. But that was
just a small travelling circus, a ring of shabby wagons
and a bedraggled big top. The Cavalcade was very
different, so grand, so gold, so beautiful.

The doors were open now. We went up the marble steps and entered the theatre, clinging to each other. There was more gold inside, and red flock wallpaper, and a gleaming chandelier like a giant glass star sparkling above us. Diamond looked up at it and had to shield her eyes.

A man in dark green uniform with gold brocade was frowning at us. 'What do you two girls want, eh? The show doesn't start for another hour.'

'Please, sir, we've come to see the manager,' I said, my voice high-pitched with nerves.

'What? Blooming cheek! Now run along,' he said, giving us little dismissive waves with both hands.

'We're here about a position. We're artistes,' I said.

He burst out laughing. 'Yes, and I'm the Queen of Sheba. You're just little kids. Now push off.'

Diamond took a step backwards, but I held fast to her hand, making her stand her ground.

'Yes, we are children,' I said, my voice firmer now. 'That is the whole point. We are *child* artistes. This is Diamond, the Acrobatic Child Wonder. And I am Miss Emerald Star, Compère Extraordinaire. We have an appointment with Mrs Ruby, so we'd be grateful if you'd show us to her office.'

His look of scorn wavered when I showed that I knew the name of the manager. 'Well, you should have said. And why come in the front entrance? The

40

stage door's round the back,' he said. 'Stan will show you up.'

I thanked him grandly and pulled Diamond down the marble steps.

'Are we going now?' she whispered.

'No, of course not. We're seeing Mrs Ruby. We have to go through some special door,' I said.

We made our way down the side of the Cavalcade. It wasn't quite so grand at the back. The stucco needed a new coat of white paint, and there were ugly brown water stains down the wall where a pipe had burst.

'Maybe he was having us on,' I said angrily. 'This can't be right. There's no door back here.'

I was looking for more marble steps and twin doors with etched glass and big gilt doorknobs. I almost walked past the actual stage door. It was a shabby plywood affair, badly scuffed where it had been kicked open. There was a tiny sign above the portal. STAGE DOOR.

'My goodness,' I said. 'Oh well, in we go.'

Diamond hung back. 'I don't want to. I don't think I want to be a music-hall artiste any more.'

'Don't be silly, Diamond. We haven't come all this way for nothing. Take a deep breath.'

Diamond gulped in air.

'That's the ticket.'

I knocked on the door. I knocked again. There was still no answer, so I seized the handle and pushed hard.

The door was so stiff I could see why people had given it a kicking. I had to put my whole shoulder to it to make it budge. But it gave way at last, and Diamond and I tumbled in.

Because the sign said STAGE DOOR I'd assumed we'd step right onto the stage itself, but we were in an ordinary dark corridor. There was a little cubbyhole opposite, with an old man dozing in his chair, a pipe still clenched in his teeth.

I coughed and his eyes opened. He stared at us. 'Who are you two?' he asked suspiciously.

'Good evening, Mr Stan. We are child artistes, come to see Mrs Ruby,' I said, trying to sound confident. 'Could you tell us where to find her?'

'She knows you're coming, does she?' he asked.

'Yes, of course,' I lied blithely.

'Then along the corridor, up the stairs, two flights, go left – no, wait a minute, is it right? Well, you'll doubtless find her if you follow your nose,' he said. He set about lighting his pipe, obviously feeling he'd given us enough information.

So we set off. We found the stairs easily enough and counted the two flights, but then we were lost. We went the entire length of the second-floor corridor peering at all the doors. Some were open, showing little dressing rooms with big mirrors, and an interesting array of paints and powders all over the table tops. Some were closed, with names on the doors. I saw MISS LILY LARK and mimed fancy singing to Diamond, which made her smile nervously. I looked and looked, but I couldn't find a door with MRS RUBY on it. We paraded the corridor twice, to no avail.

I sighed, wondering if we should trail all the way back down to the unhelpful Sam. He was probably asleep, and wouldn't appreciate being woken again. I knocked on Miss Lily Lark's door to see if she could direct us, but there was no answer. I tried a door inscribed MISS EVA RUBICHEK. She sounded very foreign. I pictured her dark and exotic, maybe a contortionist with a lithe muscled body. She'd have a guttural voice, and mix up half her words.

But the voice that called out was an unmistakable London voice, loud and lively. 'Come in, then. Chop chop!'

Diamond and I looked at each other and then peeped round the door. It was a much bigger room than the other ones we'd seen. This wasn't really a dressing room at all, more like a lady's boudoir, with little gilt tables set with silver photo frames and pretty ornaments. There were pink velvet chairs and a magnificent pink chaise-longue. Miss Rubichek was lying decorously on the chaise-longue, wearing an amazing Prussian blue silk ensemble, her neatly crossed feet shod in silver kid slippers with high heels that emphasized their arches.

43

I wondered if she'd been a dancer in her youth. Her dancing days were clearly over now, but she still cut an impressive figure. Her magnificent blue bosom was a wonderful display cushion for her strings of milky pearls, and her many-ringed hands were lightly clasped on a smooth mound of stomach, but her waist was still impressively small. She was clearly wearing a very strong corset under her blue gown.

'Well, don't just stand there gawping. In you come, in you come. My, my, what are you two girlies doing here?' she asked.

'Please, ma'am, we're looking for Mrs Ruby,' I said.

'Well, look no further. Here I am!' she said, with a grand theatrical gesture that set her diamond bracelets tinkling.

'Oh! But it says Miss Eva Rubichek on the door . . .'

'Yes, well, that's me too. I once married Mr Rubichek – big mistake, that was – but even though I got rid of him soon enough, I decided to hang onto his fancy name. Better than plain Smith, the name I was born with. Most folk can't get their tongues round anything different, so they shortened it to Ruby, and though I'm a single lady now – well, most of the time – I'm given the title Mrs out of respect. Like a cook!' She cackled with laughter. 'Oh dear, I expect I've confused you.'

'Not at all, Mrs Ruby,' I said. 'I understand perfectly. Our circumstances are very similar.'

'You're never telling me a little girl like you has been married!'

'No, no! But I was called Hetty Feather as a child, and then I took the name Sapphire Battersea because that was Mama's name for me, and then, when I became an artiste, I called myself Emerald Star,' I said.

'Good heavens. Your story's even more complicated than mine! And what about you, little sweetheart?'

Diamond looked fearful and fidgeted with her pinafore.

'Cat got your tongue?' Mrs Ruby asked.

Diamond put her hand over her mouth, as if a real cat were about to steal her tongue.

'Bit simple, is she?' Mrs Ruby said to me.

'Oh no, ma'am, she's as bright as a button, and extremely talented, but she's a little over-awed,' I said quickly.

'That doesn't seem to be *your* problem, child,' said Mrs Ruby. She put her head on one side. '*Are* you a child? It's hard to tell. How old are you?'

I thought quickly. 'I'm as old as you need me to be,' I said. 'If you employ me as an artiste, I will have more novelty value as a child performer. I think I can pass for twelve, maybe even younger. But I am actually nearly sixteen, with an old head on my shoulders, so you need have no worries about chaperones – and I take full responsibility for Diamond here.'

Mrs Ruby laughed. 'Yes, you've certainly got an old head on your shoulders, Hetty-Sapphire-Emerald. So you are both child artistes? What is the nature of your double act?'

'Oh, we perform separately. We have very different skills. Diamond is the really talented one,' I said proudly. 'She is an acrobatic wonder. If you will permit us to get changed into our costumes, we will show you what we can do.'

Mrs Ruby gestured to a Japanese screen in the corner of her room. 'Pop behind there then, dears. Best be quick about it – I've only got ten minutes or so before all the real artistes start arriving.'

She didn't seem to be taking *us* seriously as artistes. There was a gleam in her dark eyes, as if we were amusing her in the wrong way. Well, we would show her!

'Chin up, Diamond,' I whispered, unsnapping the suitcase.

I wished there had been time to iron the satin bodice of Diamond's fairy costume and my own crumpled scarlet jacket. My boots could do with a good polish, and the star on Diamond's wand was drooping.

'There now! Don't we look grand?' I whispered firmly in Diamond's ear as we dressed behind the screen. 'We're going to cut a fine figure, aren't we?'

Diamond nodded, but she still looked frightened.

'What's the matter?'

'Will she beat me if I tumble?' she murmured.

'No, absolutely not!' I said.

'But Mister beat me.'

'Yes, and that was awful, and I wish I could have stopped him. But Mrs Ruby's not cruel like Beppo. If she so much as raises her hand to you, I'll kick her in her fat tummy, and when we get back to Miss Gibson's, I'll stick pins inside her new costume,' I murmured.

I was trying to make Diamond laugh, but she took me seriously. 'Will she really raise her hand to hit me?' she said.

'Oh, Diamond, for goodness' sake! No. A hundred times no. Now come on, she'll be getting impatient.' I took Diamond's hand and led her out into the room.

Mrs Ruby chuckled at the sight of Diamond in her fairy outfit and me in my scarlet ringmaster's coat and riding breeches. I swept her a bow and told Diamond to curtsy.

'Very pretty,' said Mrs Ruby. 'Very well, let's get on with it. Give me a little snippet of your performance. Three minutes each, maximum.'

'You first, Diamond,' I said, thinking she'd better get it over quickly.

She looked around the room anxiously. 'It's not a big enough space!' she hissed.

'Well, use your initiative, dearie. Only do mind my

ornaments. Adapt your act,' said Mrs Ruby.

I didn't have much idea of Diamond's new act because I'd been cooped up sewing. She didn't seem to have much idea of it, either. She did a back-flip, she walked on her hands, she cartwheeled around Mrs Ruby's chaise-longue, but each acrobatic trick was hesitant and awkward and the performance didn't flow. She pranced a little and waved her hand and smiled, showing all her teeth the way Beppo had taught her. It had looked effective in a circus ring but it seemed bizarre here.

'Right, dear, I think I've seen enough now,' Mrs Ruby said after less than two minutes. 'Now you, Little Miss Breeches. Are you going to somersault too? I hope not!'

'No, I have another speciality. But perhaps you'd like to give Diamond another try first? If she could only use the stage, I'm sure she would be able to show herself off to more effect. She was positively the little star of Tanglefield's Travelling Circus. Folk came from miles to see her,' I said.

'I dare say,' said Mrs Ruby. 'But she's had her turn now. We can't possibly use the stage. There will be men fiddling with the lighting and rushing around with props. We have a show to put on.' She consulted her gold fob watch. 'You'd better get started, pronto.'

I didn't know what to do. I was worried that Diamond had blown her chances. It was all my fault. I should have supervised her rehearsal. It was ridiculous to expect her to adapt her act herself. I sometimes forgot how little she was, and still so cowed by her life with brutal Beppo that she could scarcely decide anything for herself. I had let her down badly. I could hardly bear to look at her now, her head bent, her face hidden by her golden hair. Her hands were clenched tight. Her wand had fallen to the floor. Her skinny legs looked about to buckle.

I should scoop her up and take her out of this place – but we had to find some way of supporting ourselves. It was our best chance. If I became a star of the Cavalcade, I could earn enough to keep the two of us. I could pay the rent, buy us food, get Diamond a little treat from the toyshop. She could go to school so she could learn to read and write properly and make some friends her own age. When she came skipping home, I'd be there to make a fuss of her and give her a mug of cocoa and read to her, and then after she'd had her supper, I'd tuck her up in bed, kiss her goodnight and make my way to the Cavalcade for the performance.

So I started my spiel.

'My lords, ladies and gentlemen, plus all you good humble folk and little children like myself, welcome to the great and glorious golden Cavalcade, the cream of all music halls in this country and beyond,' I declared, striding around the room and waving my arms.

Mrs Ruby burst out laughing and poured herself a

drink from a dark red bottle. This was surely a good sign! I concentrated hard, trying to remember the list of names on the poster.

'Come and see the littlest chap on the bill – but, oh my goodness, this young man stands tall with talent. Hold onto your hats, sirs – and hold onto your sweethearts too, because although he's pocket-sized, he certainly attracts the loveliest of ladies. He's little Flirty Bertie, who'll sing his heart out and dance the two-step till your own toes start tapping.

'Then, my goodness me, marvel at the magnificent Araminta, our exotic acrobatic dancer, who will lure your eyes with her lithe body. Araminta's artistic acrobatics will set your hearts a-thumping – and they will thump again when Sven, the Russian Sword-swallower, swaggers on stage. Sven's manly charms set every girl in a dither, and the way he swallows six-foot swords is enough to make anyone swoon—' I stopped, because Mrs Ruby was choking, drops of red wine dribbling down her big white chest.

'Are you all right, Mrs Ruby? Diamond, thump Mrs Ruby on the back!' I said anxiously.

'No, no!' Mrs Ruby waved her away, and mopped herself with a white embroidered handkerchief.

When she'd recovered, I started on Peter Perkins and his Comical Capers. I wasn't quite sure what comical capers *were*, but I capered about as comically as I could, and set Mrs Ruby laughing all over again.

'Oh, child, you'll be the death of me,' she gasped, mopping her brow this time. 'No more!'

'Could I not just announce Miss Lily Lark? I have such a glorious introduction for her. It even rhymes, to make it special,' I gabbled. I threw back my head. 'And finally, top of the bill, we all know the drill – oh my, what a thrill! Put your hands together and applaud until they sting when you hear Miss Lily Lark sing. Oh, what a glorious angelic chorus. Her soaring soprano will certainly floor us.'

I had to stop again, because Mrs Ruby had fallen back on her chaise-longue, shrieking.

'Mrs Ruby?' I asked.

'Oh my Lord, you've certainly floored me!' she said. 'Help me up then. I'm stuck on my back like a stag beetle!'

'So you like my showman skills?' I asked eagerly as I hauled her upright again. It was a good job Miss Gibson was such an expert seamstress. Mrs Ruby was straining the stitches of her gown to bursting point.

'I absolutely relish them, Hetty-Sapphire-Emerald!'

Diamond perked up and clapped her hands. 'So can Hetty be your ringmaster, Mrs Ruby?' she asked.

'We don't have ringmasters in the music hall, dear. We have a master of ceremonies,' said Mrs Ruby.

'Then am I your new little mistress of ceremonies?' I said, peering at her expectantly.

'What? Don't be ridiculous, child! Of course not,' she said.

I felt as if she'd stamped all over me. 'But you liked my introductions! They made you laugh!' I protested.

'Indeed they did. You're a real little comic, and very inventive, I'll give you that. But you can't possibly believe you could run my whole show, a slip of a girl like you! The audience would eat you for breakfast.'

'I'm very used to keeping the rowdiest crowd under control,' I said indignantly.

'I dare say, in a two-bit travelling circus. How many seats are taken on a rainy Tuesday, eh? A hundred, if you're lucky. And them mostly country bumpkins, too dumb to heckle,' said Mrs Ruby.

'You needn't be so insulting. Country folk are just as bright as city slickers,' I said, feeling as if she were personally insulting my Jem.

'The Cavalcade seats a full two thousand, and the bar does a roaring trade. After the second interval it's hard even for me to keep them under control, and I've been in the business over thirty years. No, dears, it's no go for both of you, I'm afraid. But thank you very much for the entertainment. Off you go now!' said Mrs Ruby, downing the rest of her drink.

'You're making a big mistake, Mrs Ruby. You have to give us another chance. We can come back during the day. Put us on stage and you'll see for yourself. Diamond's a little tired now from our long journey, but she will twinkle like a true star tomorrow, I promise you. And if you care to sit right at the back of your magnificent theatre, you will find my voice so powerful it will carry past you, right through the wall and out into the street! If anyone in the crowd grows restless and tries to insult me, I shall quell them immediately. I am absolutely the *queen* of quell.'

'Don't set me off again, please! Look, dear, you get a gold star for persistence, I'll grant you that. But my music hall is no place for two little girls. See for yourselves . . .' She scribbled a quick note and thrust it at me. 'Present this at the box office in the main entrance. They'll give you two tickets to sit in my own personal box. You shall watch the show tonight and then you will understand.'

She heaved herself off her chaise-longue, straightened her gown, steadying herself on her feet. They were a little swollen and bulged out of her tiny silver slippers, but she walked as lightly as a girl as she crossed the room.

'Off you go, dears.' She ushered us out, and then shut the door in our faces.

We stood staring at each other in the corridor.

'So we're not going to be music-hall stars after all?' said Diamond.

'I don't think she's totally made up her mind against us,' I said. 'Maybe we should rehearse all tomorrow and then try again.'

'I did rehearse, but I couldn't seem to do it right,' said Diamond. 'Beppo would have beaten me. Hetty, maybe *you* should beat me and then I might perform better.'

'Nonsense. I'm never, ever, ever going to beat you, you silly girl,' I said. I clasped her hand. 'We mustn't give up, Diamond. I'm sure all true artistes have to fight and struggle for a while before they are given a chance to star.'

I spoke with spirit, but inside I was doubting. It was such a shock to be rejected. I had always persuaded people to take a chance on me before. They'd let me manage a market stall, yelling my head off to attract new customers, until half the girls in town were vying with each other to buy my silks and satins. I'd dressed as a mermaid and talked Mr Clarendon into letting me be part of his extraordinary Seaside Curiosities. I'd burst into Mr Tanglefield's wagon and strutted about in my makeshift costume, convincing him I could do a better job than he could. I was a showgirl to my very soul. Why couldn't Mrs Ruby see that? She was clearly a businesswoman, shrewd and sharp. Why didn't she see my potential?

I found out why when Diamond and I sat in Mrs Ruby's box watching the show. It was nothing like the circus. This wasn't a family show. Diamond was the only child in the entire theatre. There were courting couples and several rows of ladies – though they didn't quite seem like ladies, with their painted faces and raucous laughter. There were crowds of excitable young men joshing each other, and throwing sweet wrappers and orange peel at the so-called ladies. There were older men, the smell of beer wafting from them like rotten perfume. Many were the coarse, red-faced, big-bellied kind, looking for trouble. There were toffs too, all top hats and cloaks and walking canes, equally raucous.

Diamond shrank back in the box, but I leaned over the edge, eagerly observing everyone. I still thought I *might* just be able to entertain them. Surely they'd have to quieten and settle when the lights went down and the curtain went up. But they didn't. The lights went down and the curtain went up right enough, but then they all started roaring. When Mrs Ruby herself walked out on stage they made such a noise we had to put our hands over our ears.

Mrs Ruby didn't seem a jot perturbed. She sashayed across the boards, looking like a voluptuous girl with her wasp-waist figure. She waved her hands, waggling her jewelled fingers, and then threw back her head and addressed the crowd.

'Hello, all you naughty boys and girls!' she said, smiling with newly reddened lips. 'Out for a night on the tiles, eh? Well, you've come to the right place. We have beer, we have mother's ruin for the ladies – and, oh my, many a mother will doubtless be ruined before the night is out!'

'What does she mean, Hetty?' Diamond whispered while the crowd roared.

I wasn't terribly sure myself.

'Welcome to the Cavalcade, dearies!' Mrs Ruby continued. 'Sit back on my lovely plush seats – ooh, there's a treat for you! – and wiggle your toes happily because you're about to enjoy an unforgettable night. Feel free to totter backwards and forwards to the bar as often as you like, swell my profits – ooh yes, that's what I like – and appreciate all the stars of my amazing show. And here to be our master of ceremonies tonight and introduce them is my dear boy, Mr Samson Ruby himself.'

'She has her own little boy as part of the show?' Diamond whispered. 'So why wouldn't she let *us* be stars too?'

But he wasn't a little boy at all, and later I discovered that he wasn't her child, he was more like her sweetheart, though he was certainly much younger than her. He was a strapping young man, well over six foot, with broad shoulders and a very determined chin that belied his foppish appearance. His hair was long and curly, his moustache elaborately waxed. He wore a frilly white shirt, a crimson velvet smoking jacket, and trousers so tight it didn't look as if he could sit down. He held his fat cigar aloft in an affected manner.

There was a lot of whistling from the crowd. The ladies were especially shrill. He played up to them for all he was worth, striding about, pointing at several in the audience, even inviting one up on the stage and pretending to hypnotize her with his pocket watch. He spoke with Mrs Ruby's innuendo, even wiggling his eyebrows suggestively.

'That man's being silly,' said Diamond.

'Yes, he is,' I said. 'I think we've made a mistake, Diamond. I don't want to be a music-hall star any more. I'm *glad* Mrs Ruby turned us down. When this stupid Samson person has finished his spiel, I think we'll make a bolt for it.'

'Now it's time to stop all this jesting,' said Samson Ruby. 'I'd better get on with the job in hand.'

'It should be *your* job, Hetty,' said Diamond loyally.

'Let's go, Diamond. Come on,' I said, seizing her hand. We felt our way in the dark towards the door at the back of Mrs Ruby's box.

'It gives me great pleasure to introduce the first of tonight's artistes. He's a little chap with a great big heart, and the twinkliest toes that ever trod this stage. Ladies and gentleman – if there *are* any in the audience – please put your hands together to welcome little Master Flirty Bertie, our pocket-sized princeling.'

'Hetty? Aren't you coming?' Diamond hissed.

'Just wait a second,' I said.

I watched a small young man bounce out onto the stage, waving his straw hat in the air, his white spats and black patent boots moving so fast they blurred. His hair was slicked flat with pomade, his eyes were ringed with black paint, his cheeks reddened with rouge. I recognized him instantly, even in this bizarre guise. It really was my own dear Bertie!

4

HE WAS GREETED BY a roar of applause. He threw his hat in the air in acknowledgement, grinning broadly. I knew that grin so well!

I hadn't even said goodbye to him when I lost my position with Mr Buchanan. I tried to seek him out, but I'd given up easily, telling myself that he had other girls interested in him, especially the ones in the draper's shop nearby. He wouldn't miss me one jot.

Maybe that was true. But I'd missed Bertie. I realized now that I'd actually missed him terribly. It was so strange to see him strutting his stuff on stage, doing an elaborate dance while singing a funny song with a very catchy chorus:

'Bertie's my name and flirting's my game,
I've an eye for every girl. Don't give a fig!
I have a little chat, then give 'em a pat,
Yes, it's bliss,
Trouble i-i-i-s-s-s,
I'm slightly small and they're all BIG!'

A succession of very tall, glamorous girls swished up and down the stage as he sang. They were dressed in bright red costumes that showed a great deal of their shapely legs, and wore white kid boots with very high heels. I guessed they were dancers from another act, but they made a perfect foil for Bertie.

He winked and grinned and raised his hat to them, though he barely came up to their waists. He tried dancing a waltz with one, which looked very comical. It was even funnier when he attempted to kiss another – he had to jump up to reach her lips, his legs shaking with the effort.

He performed slickly, his timing perfect. He could have been on the stage all his life. It was hard to picture him in his striped butcher's apron, juggling sausages and chops.

'Is he *your* Bertie?' Diamond whispered.

'Yes, he is,' I said proudly, though I wondered if he would even remember me. He was the same Bertie, and yet so different now. He was a true music-hall star. I was a nobody. Mrs Ruby had turned me down flat, and now I could see why. My childish patter would never work for this adult audience.

I'd been so proud working as the ringmaster for Tanglefield's Travelling Circus, but now I saw I'd simply been an infant novelty in a very small affair. I certainly couldn't compare myself to Bertie. I suddenly felt I'd failed at everything I'd tried. I'd been a very poor servant, argumentative and slapdash. I'd made a passable market trader, but I'd only lasted five minutes. I'd been a reasonable attraction at Mr Clarendon's Seaside Curiosities, but there was no skill involved in lying on a patch of sand pretending to be a mermaid.

You're a child of Satan, Hetty Feather. You'll never amount to anything at all!

Had Matron Bottomly been right all along?

I bowed my head, struggling not to cry.

'Hetty?' Diamond whispered anxiously. 'Are you all right? Don't you feel very well?'

I sniffed fiercely. 'I am fine,' I said.

'Don't you care for your Bertie's act?' she asked.

'I think he's very talented.'

'I wish *I* was talented,' said Diamond. 'I'm not a child wonder any more, am I?'

'Yes, you are,' I said.

'Mrs Ruby thought I was hopeless.'

'You were just a little under-rehearsed, that's all,' I said. '*I* am the hopeless one. I can't do any acrobatics, I can't sing, I can't dance, I can't even announce any more, not for a great big rowdy crowd like this.'

'Nonsense, Hetty,' said Diamond firmly. 'You can do everything!'

She said it with such utter conviction that I was suddenly cheered. I had no business being down-hearted and self-pitying. I couldn't give up now. I had Diamond to look after. Perhaps I could still figure out *some* way to make us music-hall stars.

I watched the following artistes with great concentration. I'd been right about the tall girls. They danced in a very bold way, showing off their long legs in a line like cut-out paper dolls. I couldn't be a dancer – I was only half their size.

Peter Perkins was a comedian, wearing a tweed suit, with a bowler hat perched on the back of his head. I didn't understand half his jokes, but the audience seemed to like him and laughed in the right places. I couldn't be a comedian because I didn't know the right sort of jokes to entertain a crowd like this.

Signor Olivelli, the maestro of Italian opera, was extremely bald and extremely stout and extremely old. It looked as if he'd been a maestro a very long time ago. I expected his voice to be wavery and cracked, but it was still incredibly powerful. He gave a very energetic performance, waving his arms about, his shiny head flung back, his chin vibrating. The crowd didn't act like opera lovers, but they sang 'La-la-la' to the familiar bits. Several men did their own Signor Olivelli imitations. I hoped he was too wrapped in his performance to notice. I certainly couldn't sing operatically.

Then there was Araminta, the Exotic Acrobatic Dancer. She wore another very brief costume and didn't even have fleshings covering her legs. She waved them around a lot, doing the most extraordinary high kicks, so that her knee pressed against her powdered nose. I knew for a fact that I couldn't do that.

'Could *you* do that, Diamond?' I asked, because she was remarkably bendy.

'I'd have to be cricked really hard and it would hurt,' said Diamond. 'But I'll try if you really want me to, Hetty.'

Araminta then arched backwards and walked like a crab.

'You *can* do that, Diamond, I've seen you do it a hundred times!' I said.

Araminta climbed onto a little platform, still bent

63

over backwards. She bent even further – until her head stuck right through her legs in the most peculiar and disconcerting fashion. She revolved like a bizarre top while the audience squealed.

'I couldn't possibly do that!' said Diamond.

'And I wouldn't want you to either. She looks revolting, all tied up in a knot,' I said.

There was a ventriloquist act next – Benjamin Apple and Little Pip. Little Pip was a bizarre doll with a very pink face, red cheeks and a big square mouth. He sat on Mr Apple's lap and spoke in a strange high-pitched voice.

'Is he a real little boy?' Diamond asked.

'No, he's a painted doll,' I said.

'But he can talk! Dolls can't talk, not even Maybelle.'

'I don't think he's really talking. The Apple man is doing the talking for him.'

'Mr Apple's mouth isn't moving, though.'

'I think it is, just a very little bit, only we're not close enough to see.'

'No, I think Little Pip's a real boy, a very tiny one. I like him!' said Diamond.

I suddenly wondered if Diamond and I could possibly perform a *pretend* ventriloquist act. I could sit on a chair with Diamond on my lap, pretending to be my doll. I would do all the patter and poke Diamond in the back when I

64

needed her to respond. She certainly looked convincingly doll-like, with her big blue eyes and long fair hair.

I started tingling with excitement. Yes, this was a truly original idea! Mrs Ruby could have a little novelty act immediately after Benjamin Apple and Little Pip. It was a trick often used in the circus – real acrobats would do their act, and then the clowns Chino and Beppo would come gambolling on and imitate them, with disastrous results.

'I have an idea!' I whispered in Diamond's ear.

She looked at me anxiously. I suppose she had every right to be wary of my ideas now, but she didn't protest. She just leaned against me, her head drooping a little, and by the time the first act finished she was fast asleep.

Everyone went to the bar to take refreshments. I was hampered by Diamond, who was leaning heavily on my shoulder. I was very thirsty now and my stomach rumbled because we'd had no supper.

I thought I would simply have to put up with this state of affairs, but then the door to the box opened. A curly-haired waiter with a long white apron came in carrying a silver tray. It held a pitcher, two glasses, and a plate of little pies.

'Lemonade and oyster patties, compliments of Mrs Ruby,' he said, putting the tray down on a table at the side of the box.

'Oh my goodness!' I forgot Diamond altogether and jumped up. She tumbled sideways and then rubbed her eyes sleepily, looking bewildered. 'Look, Diamond, Mrs Ruby's sent us a little feast!'

'What is it?' Diamond sniffed the patties suspiciously. 'Are they meat? It's not horse, is it?'

She had unwittingly eaten stewed horsemeat at the circus and it had horrified her.

'No, no, they're oyster patties! I've read about them in books. They're a treat, the sort of food you have at parties,' I said.

'I don't think I like them,' said Diamond.

'Then all the more for me,' I said, taking a big bite. 'Ooh, delicious! Come on, Diamond, try a little nibble.'

We ate and drank the lemonade, which was freshly squeezed and sugared to take away the tartness.

The waiter returned after five minutes to collect the tray. 'If you should care to use the facilities, Mrs Ruby says you're very welcome to go to her private closet just down the corridor,' he murmured in my ear.

We did care to use them. They were a revelation, so grand that Diamond sat on the lavatory for a long time, pretending she was a queen on a throne. There was even a wash basin with golden taps.

'Do you think they're *real* gold?' Diamond asked.

'Goodness knows,' I said. I lathered my hands with beautiful violet soap. I dabbed a little froth on my wrists and behind my ears, as if it were perfume. Even wealthy Mr Buchanan hadn't had perfumed soap, just plain carbolic. This Mrs Ruby really lived like royalty.

Sven, the Russian Sword-swallower, started the second act. Diamond wasn't so sleepy now and we had a whispered discussion about him. She was convinced that Sven was swallowing his long steel swords right up to the hilt. It certainly looked like that, but I was sure there was some trick involved, though I couldn't work out what it was. Then Sven started juggling with fire sticks, even thrusting them into his mouth in an alarming manner. If I tried that, I'd end up with my insides skewered and my hair burned black.

Then there was a ballet with a painted woodland backdrop. The girls wore filmy white dresses with white satin ballet slippers. They went right up on their points. Diamond stood up in the box and tried to stand on the tips of *her* toes, but she toppled over onto the floor.

'How do they *do* that?' she whispered, scrambling up again.

'Goodness knows,' I said. I liked these graceful ballet girls more than the showy dancers with their bare legs, but the ballet did go on rather a long time.

There were two principal dancers, Vladimir and Véronique, who were dressed as a king and queen. They struck poses and twirled about interminably. Diamond curled up with her head on my lap and went back to sleep, and I found my own head nodding. Fortified by their interval drinks, the crowd grew restless and rowdy, but Mr Samson Ruby thumped his gavel and glared at the worst offenders.

The next act was a singer called Ivy Green. She was clearly a big favourite with the crowd, because they clapped and cheered the moment she came on stage.

Diamond woke again, and peered over the edge of the box at her. 'Isn't she pretty!' she said. 'She's just like you, Hetty!'

Ivy Green was a redhead like me, but her hair was darker, thicker and longer, tumbling down to her tiny waist. She was small like me, but very curvy, and her green and white dress was cut very low to show off her chest. She had a loud voice like me, but she used it to sing powerfully, making her clearly audible even at the back of the theatre. She sang several songs because she was so popular.

The last one was clearly everybody's favourite, because they cheered when she sang the first line. It was a long comical ditty about all the men who were in love with her: they were all sweet boys, but somehow she couldn't lose her heart to any of them. As she sang, different men pursued her on stage, going down on their knees, presenting her with bunches of flowers and blowing her kisses. I recognized Sven, now in evening dress with a swirly cloak. There was the waiter, his curly hair squashed down under a top hat, which he flourished at Ivy Green. Peter Perkins was dancing attendance too, a rose between his teeth. And there was Bertie, my Bertie, two-stepping all around Ivy Green and then coyly kissing her hand. This got a special laugh from the audience.

Diamond laughed too and then looked at me. 'It's Bertie! Don't you recognize him?' she cried.

'Yes, it's Bertie,' I said flatly. He looked as if he really, really cared for Miss Ivy Green. Who could blame him? She was so pretty, so talented, so successful. Bertie wouldn't be remotely interested in me now, not when he had the chance to charm a girl like her.

It was painful watching them. I was very glad when the Ivy Green act ended the second half. Diamond and I waited hopefully, and after five minutes the waiter reappeared in our box. He was back in his white apron, his curls a little flat now, and carried another silver tray – this time with a silver teapot, delicate rose-coloured cups and saucers, and a plate covered with pink and white sweets.

'Rose-petal tea and Turkish Delight confectionery, with the compliments of Mrs Ruby. She hopes you're enjoying the show,' he said.

'Please thank her very much and tell her we're enjoying the show immensely,' I said.

'We especially like Ivy Green!' said Diamond, and looked puzzled when I glared at her.

There was no milk or sugar on the tray, but we discovered that rose-petal tea tasted splendid just by itself. The Turkish Delight was unbelievably good too. At first I thought it would be polite to leave a few on the plate, but we tucked in greedily and they were soon gone. Then we licked our sugary fingers. Diamond actually tried to lick the plate, but I took it away from her.

The third act seemed even longer than the others. We both dozed through Mr Daniel Dart, the Demon Knife-thrower, and Ali Baba, the Mysterious Magician. The barks of Miss Sally Sunshine's performing spaniels woke us up. Diamond was more of an animal lover than me, and practically fell out of the box she was leaning forward so eagerly. She clapped and clapped each doggy trick, and was especially delighted when they were all dressed up as a family, with the littlest spaniel a baby in a bonnet and long trailing dress that tripped her up.

'She's just like Mavis!' she cried. 'Oh, Hetty, couldn't we have monkeys and form our own animal act?'

She had been very fond of Mr Marvel at Tanglefield's Travelling Circus. He had a troupe of performing monkeys. Diamond loved them all, especially the littlest one, Mavis. I wondered if we *could* start up our own animal act. But Mr Marvel had raised his monkeys from · infancy, and had spent years training them. We didn't have years. We didn't have months or even weeks. We needed to perfect a good act immediately, while we were fresh in Mrs Ruby's mind.

I tried out various mock-ventriloquist routines in my head while further acts trooped on and off stage. Then there was another ballet – just Vladimir and Véronique this time. She wore a much shorter white dress with a full skirt that emphasized her large thighs. Vladimir wore a white tunic on his broad torso, but oh my goodness, he wasn't wearing any trousers at all, not even short breeches! He wore very tight white fleshings that showed off his long muscled legs. Indeed, they showed off more than his legs! Diamond and I watched, our mouths open.

The spectators were less reticent, particularly those in the gallery. They roared with laughter, they cat-called, they shouted out incredible insults. They must have been clearly audible to Vladimir and Véronique, but they danced on as if oblivious, only listening to the orchestra in the pit. They were beautiful dancers, much better than the girls in their woodland ballet, but Vladimir's abbreviated costume made it hard to concentrate.

They were followed by a troupe of comic tumblers, wiry little men in clown costumes. They were a clever choice to put on after the ballet dancers. The crowd could laugh some more and let off steam. However, those clown costumes brought back horrible memories for Diamond and me. She climbed onto my lap and hid her face in my

71

neck. I stroked her back and whispered soothingly to her, and yet inside my head I was thinking that this could be part of our ventriloquist routine. She would look so sweet. I was certain the audience would adore her.

Then, last of all, Lily Lark appeared. She was much older than I'd imagined, and not really very pretty, with a round red face and a top-heavy figure. I was surprised that Mrs Ruby had put her top of the bill, but Samson introduced her as a music-hall legend. When she started her act, I could see why.

Her voice made Ivy Green sound like a mere warbler. Lily Lark sang real operatic songs, but with her own made-up comical take on a woman's lot in life. It was extraordinary hearing her sing little ditties about soothing a crying baby or scrubbing the doorstep to such surging dramatic music. It made you want to laugh and cry simultaneously.

When she finished her act, people threw flowers at her. She gathered them all up, fashioning them into a neat bouquet, and then selected just one rose. She peered around at the audience, smiling coquettishly, while all the men held up their hands hopefully. She took aim and threw the rose right up to a box on the opposite side, and a gentleman caught it, held it over his white waistcoated heart, and blew her a kiss.

It was the perfect way to end the evening. When we came out of the box, I looked for Mrs Ruby, wanting to thank her, and to pave the way for another chance at an audition, but the lurking waiter said she was busy and mustn't be disturbed.

'Besides, it's time you little girlies hurried home to your beds,' he said.

I was indignant at his tone, because I reckoned he was only a year or so older than me, but he was certainly right about the time. I was shocked to see that it was gone eleven. Diamond was drooping again. I was glad we had come to the Cavalcade on foot. I think she would have fallen off if we'd tried to ride the penny-farthing.

I was very tired myself, and disorientated in the sudden dark after the bright chandeliers in the theatre. I wasn't at all sure how to get back to Miss Gibson's. We had come out of a different door. I took Diamond's arm and steered her round the corner – we seemed to have come out at the back of the theatre by mistake. Yes, there was the shabby stage door.

'Come, Diamond, I think it's this way,' I said, practically holding her up.

'I'm so tired,' she murmured fretfully. 'I want to go to sleep!'

'Yes, darling, but we have to get home to our beds,' I said.

'Which home is it? I've forgotten,' she asked.

I could well understand her confusion. So much had happened, and so fast, it was hard to remember where we were and what we were doing. She was so tired now she could barely walk, so I gave her a piggyback. I set off, glad she was such a light little thing.

Then I stopped in my tracks. Someone was shouting. Someone was shouting at *me*.

'*Hetty Feather! Hetty Feather, stop!*'

5

'**H**ETTY! SOMEONE IS SHOUTING** after you!' said Diamond, craning round.

'I know. Quick! We must run,' I said instinctively.

'But they *know* you, even though we don't know anyone here.' Diamond was still peering. 'No, wait, we do know him! It's your Bertie.'

'Let's still run,' I said, grabbing her by the wrist and hauling her along.

'But he's your friend! You wanted to see him! You're being silly, Hetty!' Diamond panted.

I knew I was being silly, but I couldn't help it. I had wanted to meet Bertie – I'd *longed* to see him – but I felt different now. I was almost scared of talking to him. Perhaps it was because he seemed so grand now, a professional artiste, a star of the music hall. Or perhaps it was because he seemed overly fond of Miss Ivy Green, who was superior to me in every way. Why had I ever thought Bertie would be pleased to see me?

He was close behind us now. 'Hetty Blooming Feather! Stop running, will you! It's me, Bertie,' he called.

It was ludicrous to go on running. I slowed to a halt and turned. There he was, grinning at me in the lamplight. He wasn't in his smart striped blazer and white flannels now. He wore an old thick jersey, a shabby cord jacket and trousers patched at the knee.

'Hello, Bertie,' I said, trying to sound casual, as if we met each other every day of the week.

'I knew it was you! I saw you in Mrs Ruby's box and knew it, though it didn't make any sense. What are you *doing* here?'

'Oh, we just happened to be passing,' I said ridiculously. 'This is my friend Diamond.'

'Pleased to meet you, Miss Diamond,' said Bertie, taking her sticky hand and kissing it.

She stared up at him, thrilled to be treated like a

grown-up lady. 'We came specially to see you, Mr Bertie,' she said.

'Did you, indeed?' he said, smirking.

'No we didn't!' I said, giving her a shake.

'And what did you think of my performance, Miss Diamond? I hope you weren't too disappointed,' said Bertie.

'I thought you were very good. We both did.' Diamond pouted at me. 'We wanted to be music-hall artistes too!'

'Really?' said Bertie.

'No, it's just her little fancy,' I said, horribly disloyal. 'Come along, Diamond, it's long past your bedtime.'

'We did our acts for Mrs Ruby but she didn't think we were good enough,' said Diamond.

I felt like gluing her little lips together. She was usually so shy she would hardly say anything in company, but now she seemed intent on blurting everything to Bertie.

'So you fancy being a showgirl too, Hetty?' said Bertie. 'Well, that's marvellous. Don't worry about Mrs Ruby. She only wants experienced professionals. But I know plenty of other gaffs where they'll take a chance on lily-whites. That's what they call beginners. And I'll help you polish your act, if you like.'

I felt my face flushing as red as my hair. How dare he patronize me when he'd just been funny old Bertie the butcher's boy last year!

'We're professionals too, thank you very much. Diamond is known as the Acrobatic Child Wonder. She has been starring in Tanglefield's Travelling Circus. She's performed the famous human column with three fellow artistes night after night.'

'I know you of old, Hetty Feather,' Bertie laughed. 'You're making up stories, aren't you?'

'No, it's real. I only tumbled once. But then Beppo frightened me and we had to run away,' said Diamond.

Bertie stared, hands on hips. 'What?' He turned from Diamond to me. 'You're not telling me you're an acrobat too, Hetty? Do you wear short drawers and saucy fleshings?'

'No I do not! Take that grin off your face. But I'll have you know I was the top draw of the circus.'

'Oh, modest as always, as well as fanciful,' said Bertie, shaking his head.

I wanted to slap him. 'I was the ringmaster,' I said, as grandly as I could.

Bertie doubled up laughing. *'The ringmaster!'*

'Yes, I was. Look!' I snapped open our suitcase and showed him my scarlet tunic and cream trousers and riding boots.

'Oh my Lord!' he gasped.

'I introduced each act. Everyone said I was a magnificent spieler. The words just tripped off my tongue,' I declared.

78

'Well, I can believe that,' said Bertie. 'Oh, Hetty, it's grand to see you. There's no other girl to beat you!'

'Not even Miss Ivy Green?' I said, and then blushed again for being so obvious.

'Not even Ivy Green herself,' said Bertie, hand on heart, laughing triumphantly.

'We must get home now. Come along, Diamond. At once!' I commanded.

'I'll walk with you,' said Bertie.

'No you will not!'

'Very well. Suit yourself. But tell me where you're staying, Hetty.'

'There's no need. We are only there temporarily. I dare say we will be on our way tomorrow. Goodbye,' I said, trying to retain a shred of dignity.

'Oh, Hetty, I like it at Miss Gibson's. Can't we stay?' said Diamond.

'Miss Gibson the dressmaker? She fashioned my blazer for me! Then I'll come calling tomorrow in the hope of persuading you to stay.' Bertie gave us each a low bow and then marched off in the opposite direction.

'Bertie's so lovely!' said Diamond, far too loudly.

'Ssh! And he's not lovely at all, he's just a dreadful tease,' I said crossly.

'I thought you were sweethearts!'

'That was long ago. And we were never *exactly* sweethearts,' I said.

'Then if you don't want him any more, could he be *my* sweetheart?' asked Diamond.

'Bertie likes to be everybody's sweetheart,' I said sourly.

Perhaps we should have permitted Bertie to walk us home, because we took a wrong turning somewhere. It was very late indeed when we found our way to Gibson's Gowns at last. There were no lights at any of the windows.

'Oh dear, I think Miss Gibson must have gone to bed,' I said.

'What will we do?' asked Diamond.

'We shall have to knock loudly on the door.'

'But won't she be cross if we wake her up?'

'Probably,' I said.

I wondered if I dared try. I realized we had gone rushing off to the Cavalcade without making any arrangements with Miss Gibson. We'd stayed so late at the show. Miss Gibson would have guessed as much and probably been shocked. She'd said she wouldn't go to the Cavalcade because she was a single lady. Diamond and I were single ladies, and children too. She might be horrified. She could well have bolted the door on us for ever. Perhaps Diamond and I should march off with our suitcase and find another doorway to sleep in tonight. I'd had enough scoldings to last me a lifetime. We didn't need to return to Miss Gibson's ever.

Oh, but we *did* need to return! The penny-farthing was locked up in her back yard.

I was so tired and in such turmoil that I didn't know what to do. I leaned against the shop window, the glass cool against my forehead, and tried to figure it out.

'Hetty?' said Diamond softly, obviously thinking I was crying. Perhaps I was, just a little. I was suddenly so tired that I seemed to have used up all my courage. What if I was fooling myself about inventing a new comic ventriloquist act? And even if we did perfect such a thing, would Mrs Ruby give us a second chance? I'd been so stupid to think that two small girls would automatically get to star in a huge music hall. Yet Bertie wasn't much more than a boy. He had managed it. I was thrilled for him – and yet so deeply envious too.

'There there,' said Diamond. 'Don't you fret. *I* shall knock, and then Miss Gibson will be cross with me, not you.'

She rapped smartly on the door before I could stop her. We waited, holding our breath. Nothing happened.

'There, she must have gone to bed. She won't hear us,' I said.

But just then I saw a wavering dim light at the back of the shop, and in two seconds the front door was unlocked. Miss Gibson stood there in her cap and vast white nightgown, holding a candle aloft.

'Oh, please don't be angry with us, Miss Gibson!' Diamond said imploringly.

'Come in, girls! I'm not angry, though I must admit I've been a little worried. I dare say Mrs Ruby invited you to the show?'

'She let us use her own box,' said Diamond proudly.

'My, my! So you must have pleased her mightily. Are you really going to do your acts at the Cavalcade?'

'No, she didn't think our acts suitable,' said Diamond. 'Especially me. I wobbled all over the place and didn't do it properly. Beppo would have beaten me.'

'Who's Beppo? And how dare he beat a little mite like you? Look, girls, come into the kitchen. You're shivering. Let me make you a hot drink before you go to bed. And perhaps you might tell me a little bit about the performances? I must admit I've always been a little curious to know exactly what happens at the Cavalcade,' said Miss Gibson, relocking her front door and leading us through to the back of the shop.

She made us weak tea, and bread and milk. It was simple fare after the exotic food at the Cavalcade, but very comforting. I'd pulled myself together by this time and managed to run through most of the acts for Miss Gibson's benefit while we ate and drank.

'My, my,' she kept saying. 'Oh, my, my!'

'Tell about Bertie, Hetty,' said Diamond. 'I think he was the best of all.'

'You tell, then,' I said.

Diamond started her hymn of praise, even remembering a line or two of his special song, but soon her voice started to slur and her eyelids drooped.

'Oh dear, the poor child's falling asleep sitting up! What am I thinking of, keeping you two girls awake half the night,' said Miss Gibson. 'Let me show you your bedroom. I do hope you're not expecting anything fancy. It's very small and plain, and you'll have to double up in the bed.'

She left us her candle and shuffled off to her own room in her soft carpet slippers. I tugged most of Diamond's clothes off and then laid her down on the bed. I wandered around the room, holding the candle high. It was small and sparsely furnished, with just a bed, a washstand and a chest of drawers, but it looked spotlessly clean. I liked the rainbow-coloured patchwork quilt on the bed, obviously made from snippets of Miss Gibson's gowns.

I took off my clothes and squeezed into bed beside Diamond. I stroked the edge of the quilt against my cheek, feeling the slippery softness of the silks. I remembered the one I'd had long ago, in my foster family's country cottage. It had been plain cotton, made from scraps of worn shirts and faded frocks. I had nuzzled into it every night, fingering the stitches. I wondered if it was still there in that attic bedroom. I thought of Mother and wondered how she was faring. I knew she would be well cared for by my foster brother Gideon. He'd come back from soldiering with a wounded face and shattered nerves. I hoped he was fully recovered and happy again. And what of Jem, my dearest brother in all the world, even though we weren't related by blood? Was he happy too?

I'd been so sure I was doing the right thing when I made it plain I could never marry him, but now I suddenly wondered why. I'd hated the idea of settling down for ever in that little village, but I'd been leading a gypsy life for so long, the prospect of a proper home with the man I loved most seemed very tempting.

Had I been secretly longing for Bertie all this time, unwilling to admit it, even to myself? If so, I was incredibly foolish! Bertie had changed in many ways – and yet he was still such a flirt, it was clear I could never count on him.

What was the matter with me? I didn't want him anyway! All I wanted was to make some kind of success of myself. Mama might not be living any more, but she was here in my heart, and if I listened carefully, she would sometimes speak to me.

I lay still, cuddling Diamond, and after a long while I heard Mama's gentle whisper.

There now, dearest child. Sleep well. All will be well, will be well, will be well . . .

I felt fresh and soothed when I woke up the next morning. I wondered how I could have been so weak and tearful. I crept out of bed and quietly rummaged for the last volume of my memoir journals, taking care not to wake Diamond. She was curled up in a little ball, her long hair over her face, with just the tip of her nose peeping through the locks.

I crouched by the window for the extra light and started writing rapidly. I wasn't writing my journal, I was jotting down ideas for a comedy ventriloquist routine. I decided it would be most effective if I pretended to be a little child too. I certainly looked like one, after all. I liked the idea of us being a double act. It wouldn't be quite as frightening for Diamond standing on that stage in front of hundreds and hundreds of people. Not quite as frightening for me either, if I was honest! I remembered how the audience had heckled Vladimir and Véronique. They were such an unforgiving, rowdy crowd. If they thought that Diamond and I were very little girls, they might just be a little kinder.

We needed a name . . . Dear Madame Adeline had called me Little Star when I was a child, and it had meant the world to me. Diamond was a little star too. *Twinkle, twinkle,* little star, *How I wonder what you are. Up above the world so high, Like a* diamond *in the sky.* Little Stars was a perfect name for us.

I scribbled line after line of script, smiling to myself. After quite a while I became aware of bustling sounds down in the kitchen.

I flew down, barefoot in my nightie. I wondered if Miss Gibson had a maid, but she was there by herself, setting a scrubbed table with pretty willow-pattern plates. A kettle was whistling on the hob and eggs were boiling in a saucepan.

'Please let me help, Miss Gibson!' I said. 'You sit down like the lady you are. Shall I make us a little toast? Don't worry, I'll be very careful. I'm trained as a cook-housekeeper and know exactly what I'm doing.'

I wanted to be so obliging that she would let us stay on until we had earned enough money for bigger rooms. Of course, I'd never been a cook-housekeeper, but dear Mama had passed on some of her culinary skills and I'd been forced to skivvy all my nine long years at the Foundling Hospital.

Miss Gibson didn't seem convinced, but she let me finish laying the table. I did it neatly, the way Sarah had taught me at Mr Buchanan's, the knives and spoons just so, the napkins folded with geometric precision. I put out a little spoon for the marmalade and a small knife for the butter, which I arranged in pats on a special plate. I made the toast and aired it carefully, so it would stay crisp, and made a perfect pot of tea.

'My, Hetty, you'd certainly make an exemplary maid,' said Miss Gibson.

'And I'm going to prove an exemplary seamstress too, Miss Gibson. I do hope you'll let me do some further work on Mrs Ruby's beautiful dress today,' I said.

Miss Gibson looked at me shrewdly. 'You're doing your best to ingratiate yourself! Are you suggesting I employ you as a maid and sewing apprentice now that Mrs Ruby has put a stop to your music-hall ambitions?'

'Not at all, Miss Gibson. I will *act* as a maid and sew all day long if you wish, but I don't want any wages whatsoever. Just our bed and board, and I'm hoping this will only be temporary – because I'm sure Mrs Ruby will be delighted when I've perfected a brand-new act and decide to take us on after all,' I declared.

Miss Gibson laughed. She reached out and took my hand. 'You won't give up, will you, Hetty Feather? I like your character. You and your sister can stay as long as you wish. Is she still asleep?'

'I shall go and wake her and we'll dress in two shakes of a lamb's tail,' I said.

Miss Gibson herself was already immaculately attired in the same black satin dress with fresh white lace cuffs. She creaked a little each time she shifted. I couldn't help wondering what she looked like when her corset was removed. It must be so strange fashioning wasp-waisted gowns all day when you didn't possess a vestige of a waist yourself.

'I should breakfast in your nightgowns, dear. You

don't want to have cold egg and toast. Run up and fetch your sister.'

Diamond was still fast asleep. I shook her gently. She woke, rubbed her eyes, and then curled up again, pulling the quilt over her head.

'Diamond, come on! Breakfast's ready. We're keeping Miss Gibson waiting,' I said, pulling her arm.

'Miss Gibson?' said Diamond sleepily. 'Is she the lady in the blue dress with all the jewellery?'

'No, no, that was Mrs Ruby. Miss Gibson is our landlady now. She's the lady who makes all the gowns, remember?'

'It's hard remembering,' Diamond complained, reluctantly sitting up and swinging her legs out of bed. 'We met so many people yesterday. There were too many names. I don't want to meet anyone else today. I don't want to do anything either. I just want to stay in bed!'

'Nonsense! We have work to do,' I said briskly. 'Come on! You can wear my shawl if you're chilly. I'm warm as toast. Ah, I've *made* toast. Come and eat it, dripping with butter.'

Madame Adeline used to make us buttered toast when she'd run out of cake. Diamond loved it – and was already running across the room, wide awake now.

She behaved well, chattering politely to Miss Gibson, looking angelic in her little nightgown with her clouds of fair hair hanging down her back. When we'd all eaten, I insisted on clearing away and doing the dishes, and I swept the floor for good measure. I washed and dressed and supervised Diamond, and then sat down with her in the back sewing room, while Miss Gibson perched her large behind on a padded stool in the shop, serving the occasional customer.

I started tacking the waistband of Mrs Ruby's new purple gown, following Miss Gibson's neat line of pins.

'Can't I sew too?' asked Diamond. 'I can do big stitches like that.'

'No, these stitches have to be perfect. I need you to learn this instead.' I handed her the pages torn from my memoir book. 'This is our new act, Diamond. We're still going to be music-hall stars, I promise you.'

Diamond puzzled over the paper. She couldn't get to grips with my handwriting, so I copied it out in large print for her. As she still wasn't making much progress, I stopped stitching again and read the lines out to her over and over again. She did learn the words eventually, but she couldn't seem to say them with the right expression.

'I know you're trying very hard, Diamond, but you're not saying it quite right,' I said as tactfully as I could.

'What do you mean? I said all the words, I know I did!'

'Yes, but in such a monotone!'

'What's a monotone?'

'Speak-ing-like-this-as-if-you're-not-real.'

'But I'm not supposed to be real! You said I had to be a doll, like that Little Pip boy with the funny mouth!' said Diamond indignantly.

'Yes, but you have to have *some* expression, otherwise it sounds so dull,' I said.

'I am . . . *dull*?' said Diamond, her lip quivering.

'No! You just sound it,' I said, exasperated.

Diamond started to cry.

'Oh don't! Please don't. You make me feel so mean. Look, I think it's simply because we're not acting it out properly. Come here!' I eased Mrs Ruby's silky costume onto the table and patted my lap.

Diamond climbed up onto it, still sniffling.

'There now. You're my little dolly Diamond, my very pretty beautiful dolly, just like the one we saw in the toyshop. Remember, if we get hired by Mrs Ruby, I'm going to save up all my wages, and when I have enough, I'll buy you that special dolly,' I said, hoping that bribery might work.

'Oh yes, oh yes, oh yes!' said Diamond, childishly clapping her hands.

All the time I'd known Diamond at the circus she'd been like a sad little woman trapped in a child's body. She rarely relaxed or played games or had fun. She looked strained and wary, forever glancing around in case Beppo was watching her. But now we'd run away she seemed to have reverted to early childhood, seemingly younger and more dependent than the usual eight-year-old.

I felt a pang, realizing how distorted her entire childhood had been. I wondered if I should be pushing her so hard now. But her fairy looks and sweet little ways would be our act's biggest asset. My own looks counted for nothing – I was just a voice, so I had to use it as artfully as I could.

'Hello, everyone,' I said, in a childish lisp. 'I am Emerald and it's my birthday today. Goodness, see how many of you have come to my party! I hope cook has made lots and lots of jellies and jam tarts. Perhaps you've brought me some presents? Do you see the wonderful dolly Mama and Papa have got me? Isn't she beautiful?'

I tapped Diamond on the back as her signal to speak.

'Yes-I-am-ve-ry-beau-ti-ful,' chanted Diamond.

'No, don't do it as if you're reading – do it as if you're speaking. Just like the ventriloquist doll last night. And much louder. Really, really loud. They've got to hear you right at the back of the theatre. Positively shout it out!'

Diamond's shout was more of a squeak, and she complained it hurt her throat when I made her try harder.

And she still couldn't put any expression into her lines.

'*Act* it, Diamond!' I said.

But Diamond couldn't act. When I showed her how to move jerkily and turn her head from side to side like a little dummy, she copied me accurately enough, but she still couldn't get the right inflection to her words. I gave up coaching her in the end because we were both getting so frustrated. I decided it would have to be enough for Diamond to know the words and manage the moves. Perhaps she was right – dolls might well speak in a monotone if they came to life.

We managed to get all the way through our little piece, though it was very slow and laborious.

'Well done,' I said, falsely bright. 'Now, let's do it again.'

'Again?' said Diamond, wrinkling her forehead. 'I'm a bit tired of doing it, Hetty. It's making my head ache.'

It was making *my* head ache too, but I made us go through it several further times as I stitched. Then we had a mid-morning break while I made us all a cup of tea. Miss Gibson was in a good mood because some grand Lady Someone had come into the shop and ordered a new ball gown while Diamond and I had been gabbling away in the back.

'A real lady! Did she look very grand? Did she swish about the shop and look haughty?'

'No, she was very kind and polite,' said Miss Gibson,

'but a little exacting. She wants it just so, tight about the waist, with a firm bodice, but not too restricting because she likes to dance. And she wants it by the end of the week, which is well-nigh impossible.'

'It's not impossible if you style it, and then I tack and sew the easier bits,' I said. 'Diamond can pass the pins and brew tea and make herself useful.'

'Yes indeed,' said Miss Gibson. 'I'm starting to be very glad my last girl flounced off!'

I concentrated hard on stitching Mrs Ruby's gown for the rest of the morning, wanting to show Miss Gibson just how quick and neat I could be, though I still forced Diamond to chant through our routine with me.

'We'll act it out properly when we take a quick break for lunch,' I said.

Diamond sighed heavily. 'Are you sure we still have to be music-hall stars, Hetty? Couldn't we just be sewing girls?'

I knew this was actually a sensible suggestion. Quite by chance we now had board and lodging and I had a respectable occupation. I liked sewing too, and took pride in my work – but it still wasn't quite enough. I needed to make something of myself, to try to be truly special. I remembered vowing to myself that one day my name would be famous, recognized all over London. It meant even more to me now. Bertie had made his childish dreams come true, so why couldn't I?

Then the shop door rang again and I heard Miss Gibson talking to someone.

'Oh dear, another customer? I hoped it was lunch time now,' said Diamond.

It wasn't a customer. It was Bertie.

6

'**L**OOK WHO'S HERE, GIRLS.** A friend of yours, I do believe,' Miss Gibson said, putting her head round the door.

'A friend?' said Diamond warily.

'A certain Mr Albert Briggs?'

'Bertie!' Diamond shrieked and went rushing out to greet him as if she'd known him for ever.

I was more circumspect. I took my time carefully folding

Mrs Ruby's dress and checking for loose pins. Then I strolled slowly into the front shop, attempting nonchalance, though I couldn't stop my wretched face flushing.

'Hello, Hetty. My, you're rosy-cheeked this morning,' said Bertie.

'What are you doing here?' I said, sounding more surly than I intended.

Bertie simply laughed. 'I've come to take my three favourite ladies out to lunch,' he said. He bowed to each of us in turn. 'Might I have the pleasure of escorting you to the nearest chop house?'

Miss Gibson giggled. 'Get away with you, Bertie! You don't want to take an old maid like me out to luncheon. The very idea! Besides, I can't leave the shop.'

'Indeed I do, Miss Gibson. It won't do any harm to hang your closed sign on the door for a couple of hours. We have to go out to celebrate! I've been pining away this past year, wondering what happened to my dearest sweetheart, Hetty. She ran away without even saying goodbye – but now, quite by chance, we're reunited. Did you regret your hasty departure, Hetty, my own love, and come running after me?'

'Stop your saucy nonsense! And we were never sweethearts. I'm the only girl who *didn't* break her heart over you,' I snapped.

'Oh, I dare say you'll fall for my fatal charms soon enough,' said Bertie.

'Don't bank on it. I'm not falling for you or anyone else,' I said tersely. 'I don't ever intend to fall in love. I shall follow Miss Gibson's sensible example and stay single.'

Miss Gibson laughed uneasily. She looked wistful as she shut up her shop. The four of us walked along the pavement together.

'What about Jem?' Diamond hissed. She was trying to whisper, but she might as well have yelled under an echoing bridge.

'Oh, is the sainted Jem still on the scene?' asked Bertie, a sudden edge to his voice.

'Hetty ran away from him too,' said Diamond. 'But she sometimes looks sad when she mentions him.'

'Oh, she does, does she? And does she ever mention me, might I ask?'

'Yes!' I interrupted. 'I say, *Watch out for Flirty Bertie, Diamond. No girl is safe while he's around.*'

'You're safe as houses with me, Diamond,' said Bertie. 'Hey, come and have a piggyback down the road. Can you jump that high?'

'Huh! Go, Diamond, show him!' I said.

Diamond tucked up her skirts and took a running jump. She landed lightly on Bertie's shoulders. He shouted out in shock and staggered, so that Diamond had to hang onto his hair, which made him shout even louder.

'Keep still, silly, or she'll fall,' I said.

'Oh my!' said Miss Gibson. 'Would you believe it! She's only a little mite, yet she leaped five foot in the air!'

'I told you she was the star of the circus,' I said proudly.

'Well, wriggle down so you're safely sitting on my shoulders, little Diamond. I'll be a circus pony and take you for a ride,' said Bertie.

Diamond did as she was told, and Bertie 'neighed' and tossed his head and set off at a bizarre gallop, picking his feet up comically.

'That boy!' said Miss Gibson. 'But you have to laugh at him, don't you, Hetty?'

I *did* have to laugh. I couldn't stay distant and snappy with Bertie over lunch. He steered us towards the chop house. It was the perfect place, clean and friendly and not too expensive, and we all had a plate of lamb chops and mashed potatoes and cabbage. Even Diamond, who was often picky with her food, ate hers all up – though she did check with Bertie that it wasn't made of horse.

'Seeing as you've cleared your plate, little 'un, I think you deserve a serving of pudding,' said Bertie. 'You need to put a little meat on your bones. And you too, Hetty – you're another Skinny Minnie. Look at you!' He held my wrist, spanning his thumb and finger round it. 'There! And I'm missing the top of that finger too!'

He'd lost three of his fingers while learning the

butchering trade. I was worried Diamond might be squeamish about it, but she seemed fascinated. She held Bertie's hand and gently stroked the blunt finger ends.

'Poor Bertie. It must have hurt and hurt. I bet you cried lots when it happened,' said Diamond.

'Well, it hurt like damnation, but I didn't do anything as girly as crying,' Bertie boasted.

'You're very brave.'

I sighed at Diamond's tone. Bertie caught my eye and winked.

'I note you don't say *I'm* skin and bones,' Miss Gibson pouted in a girlish manner. 'Don't I get the offer of pudding?'

Bertie smiled sweetly at her and kissed her plump hand. 'You're not skin and bones, dear Miss Gibson. You're a very fine figure of a woman – I feel a helping of figgy pudding or jam roly-poly would enhance your natural beauty,' he said.

'Get away with you! Such nonsense,' said Miss Gibson, pink-cheeked.

She chose the figgy pudding with custard. Diamond opted for jam roly-poly. Bertie wanted a portion of each. I ordered a plate of rice pudding with strawberry compôte. I remembered how Mama had made the rice puddings at the hospital, and always contrived to give me the biggest spoonful of jam.

'Why so thoughtful, Hetty?' asked Miss Gibson.

'I dare say she's daydreaming about Jem,' said Bertie sharply.

'I was thinking of Mama,' I told him.

'Oh, how *is* your mother? Have you been able to visit her since you left old Buchanan's?' Bertie asked.

I was so choked I couldn't reply.

'Hetty's mama died, Bertie,' Diamond whispered. 'It makes her very sad sometimes.'

'Oh dear. I'm so sorry, Hetty,' Bertie said, sounding genuinely upset. 'I know just how much your mama meant to you. Tell you what, would you like a little glass of port as a pick-me-up?'

'Port?' I said. My Foundling Hospital upbringing hadn't been very educational.

'Fortified wine.'

'No thank you!' I said. But then I pondered. I'd had wine at my foster father's funeral and had quite enjoyed the experience. It had made me feel warm and happy and relaxed. I was feeling shivery and sad and anxious now, trying to plot a way of getting another audition with Mrs Ruby and worrying about Bertie. But most of all I was missing Mama so sorely I had to fight not to burst into tears.

Would a glass of port help? I remembered I'd had a little *too* much wine at the funeral wake and had felt ill afterwards. Perhaps if I just had a tiny glass . . . A sip or two . . .

'Is it possible to have just a teaspoon of port?' I asked.

'It's not medicine!' said Bertie. 'Have a proper glass. It'll only be a little glass, not a pint tankard! I'll have one too – and I'm sure you'll join us, Miss Gibson?'

'And me!' said Diamond.

'Absolutely not,' I said firmly. 'You're far too little, Diamond. I think I am too. But if you don't mind giving me a small sip from your glass, Miss Gibson, that would be fine. I'd like to taste it.'

After all that, I didn't like the taste *at all*. It was *exactly* like medicine. But Miss Gibson swallowed hers down with obvious relish, so Bertie insisted on ordering two more. He seemed totally unaffected by his drinks, but Miss Gibson grew even more girlish, tossing her old-fashioned ringlets and giggling at everything Bertie said. They had a mock argument over who was to pay the bill, having a tug of war with the slip of paper in a childish fashion. I had my purse with me and suggested we divide it into three, but Bertie overruled us all, insisting on paying.

This worried me too: even though he was a music-hall star, I wasn't sure he was earning very much. Last night his clothes had been very shabby. He was wearing what was clearly his best suit now, but it was shiny with wear, his shirt frayed at the collar. But I could see that paying the bill himself mattered enormously to him. He had always insisted on treating me when we walked out together, doing extra jobs to earn enough.

Miss Gibson was a little unsteady on her feet as we walked back to the shop, but Bertie tactfully tucked his hand through her arm and steered her along.

'I seem to be unaccountably sleepy,' Miss Gibson said when we were home. 'I rather think I need a little nap. Hetty, could you possibly mind the shop for me and call me if I have a customer?'

'Of course, Miss Gibson,' I said.

I helped her upstairs. She flopped down on her bed and fell into a deep sleep almost immediately. I was sure she was uncomfortable in her corsets, but I had no way of wrestling them off her. I had to content myself with gently removing her tight little shoes and covering her with a shawl.

When I went downstairs, Bertie was still there, joshing around with Diamond.

'Well, thank you for a splendid luncheon,' I said. 'Now, I have work to do.'

'And what's that, Hetty?' asked Bertie, sitting on the counter top and swinging his legs.

'Get off that!' I said, slapping at his calves. 'I have to serve in the shop.'

'But you haven't any customers.'

'And I must stitch Mrs Ruby's dress.'

'Well, stitch away then, and I'll keep you girls company,' said Bertie.

'Haven't you got anything better to do?' I said.

'That's the joy of working at the Cavalcade. I'm free until seven or so every day,' said Bertie. He jumped right over the counter, stuck a lace doily on his head and whipped a tape measure round his neck. 'How can I help you, madam? A silk or satin gown? And a large pair of matching drawers with lace frill? Certainly!'

Diamond shrieked with laughter.

'That's not funny, Bertie,' I said, though my own lips were twitching. 'We shall all get into terrible trouble if a real customer comes into the shop. Stop being such a guy and leave us in peace.'

'No, don't go, Bertie!' said Diamond, rushing to him. 'Please stay!'

'Diamond, we have particular work to do,' I said meaningfully.

Back at the circus, Diamond had done anything I told her. She'd followed me around like a little shadow and never argued. But now she seemed more independent.

'No! I don't want to,' she said. 'I don't like being that stupid doll – you'll only be vexed with me, Hetty, because I can't say the words properly. I want to play with Bertie!'

'Quite right,' said Bertie. He looked at me, his head on one side. 'You play doll games with Diamond?'

'No! I mean, yes. To keep her amused,' I said, because I didn't want to tell Bertie we were going to have another attempt at impressing Mrs Ruby. 'Yes, we play doll games. Now please go, Bertie. You're getting Diamond over-excited. She's still only little.'

'No I'm not,' said Diamond, stung. 'We're not playing doll games for *me*. It's our new music-hall act.'

'Is it, indeed!' said Bertie. 'Tell me more.'

'You *are* little, but you've got a very big mouth, Diamond,' I snapped.

'So you've not given up? You're working on a new act?' said Bertie. 'That's just like you, Hetty. You're never a girl to give up. Let me see this act, then, girls!'

'Absolutely not,' I said.

'Why not?'

'Because I'd feel silly. You'd make me feel self-conscious,' I said.

'You can't perform in front of one friend, yet you feel you'll be fine in front of two thousand strangers?'

I was silenced.

'Come on, Hetty.'

'You'll laugh at us,' I said in a small voice.

'Well, is your act meant to be funny?'

'Yes.'

'Then I'll laugh my head off,' Bertie said. 'But if there are tragic bits, I'll blub like a baby. I'm your ideal audience, girls. Come on, let's get the show started!' He sat on the counter again and started clapping hopefully.

I felt ridiculously nervous, but I didn't want to appear a coward in front of Bertie.

'Come on, Diamond, let's show him,' I said, fluffing out her hair. 'You'll have to imagine Diamond got up like a little fairy doll, Bertie. Imagine me as a little girl too, in a pastel frock and pinafore, my hair in plaits.'

'Oh, what a picture!' he said.

I placed a chair in the middle of the floor, then took Diamond's hand. We went to the side of the shop.

'Up you get,' I whispered to Diamond.

She jumped up into my arms, resting on my hip.

'Keep your arms and legs stiff, as if you really are a china doll. Stare straight ahead and do your circus smile,' I whispered. 'Right, we're going on stage now.'

I started the birthday routine and introduced Diamond, my new dolly. I felt sick with embarrassment at having to lisp coy nonsense in front of Bertie, but he gave us nods of encouragement. I'd cut Diamond's 'I am very beautiful,' speech because it gave her such trouble. I'd worked out a better way of introducing her.

I sat down on the chair, Diamond on my knee. I kept one hand on her back, as if I were working her like a puppet.

'There now, Diamond Dolly. Oh my, you're so pretty. Such lovely long hair. And bright blue eyes!'

On cue Diamond blinked her eyes and looked from left to right.

'Oh goodness!' I said, pretending to be alarmed. 'You look almost real!'

I tapped Diamond on the back. She turned her head slowly to look at me.

'I-am-real,' she said.

I gave a little scream. Diamond screamed too. We turned our heads away from each other. Then looked back – and let out two screams again.

'Why are you screaming?' I said.

'I'm-cop-y-ing-you-be-cause-you're-my-mum-my,' Diamond chanted without expression. But I could see it didn't matter. Somehow it made our act even funnier. Bertie was sitting back, kicking his heels on the counter, looking delighted.

I felt a thrill of pure joy. It was like being back in the circus ring, playing around with my announcements while the audience cheered. It was *better* because I was part of the act this time.

We carried on with our routine. I felt like hugging Diamond – she'd truly memorized everything and didn't forget her words once, not even the complicated argy-bargy of sharing our pocket money. We had a penny and a halfpenny and couldn't manage to share it equally. I said I wanted to buy a dolly from the toyshop who didn't argue with me. Diamond said she wanted to buy a girl from the human shop who didn't argue with *her*.

We tried to go off in different directions – but Diamond stood stiffly, unable to move without me, her mouth opening and closing silently. So then we kissed and made up and I picked Diamond up and skipped off with her.

Bertie was looking expectantly at us. Then he frowned. 'Is that it?'

'Yes. What do you think?' I asked eagerly.

'It's not long enough.' Bertie consulted his pocket watch. 'Three minutes tops. You're over in a flash. It won't work.'

'Well, all right, we'll make it longer,' I said impatiently. 'But you think the general gist works? You seemed to be enjoying it.'

'Yes, it was very sweet as a little party piece. I'm not sure it would work as a music-hall act, though.'

'And why not?'

'Because it's not spectacular enough.'

'I didn't see *you* jumping through flaming hoops or catapulting out of a cannon,' I said crossly. 'You just sang and danced.'

'No need to get shirty, Hetty. I'm just trying to help,' said Bertie.

'Aren't we good enough, Bertie?' asked Diamond.

'You're absolutely wonderful, little Twinkle,' said Bertie. 'You make a brilliant dolly, sweetheart.' He looked at me. 'But you need to do something else with her. Look at the way the kid can jump – right up onto my shoulders! You should capitalize on her skills. She's the little star.'

It was as if he'd thrown a bucket of icy water all over me. It was hard admitting it, but *I* wanted to be the star.

Or if I didn't have any special talents, *I* wanted to be the director of our act. I resented Bertie's suggestions bitterly, even though I knew he was right.

I mumbled some excuse about needing the privy, and ran out of the door into the yard.

'It's not fair!' I wailed, walking round and round in a temper. I kicked a bucket, I bashed my hand against the fence, I took hold of the handlebars of the penny-farthing and shook it. Then I stared at it and suddenly leaped onto the machine. I rode it around the yard, working things out in my head.

I saw where I'd gone wrong. When the clowns had capered into the ring and performed comically badly, they hadn't ended their act there. They had suddenly taken the whole audience by surprise by attempting a really difficult trick and performing it splendidly. *That's* what Diamond and I would do.

I rewrote lines in my head, changing the pocket-money dispute, working out tricks. I'd have to be patient. We'd need to rehearse for days. But we could do it. I was sure of it now.

7

DIAMOND AND I LABOURED along the road to the Cavalcade. I rode the penny-farthing, while Diamond struggled along the pavement behind me, clutching Mrs Ruby's finished gown, carefully folded up in a huge muslin bag. We were both in costume. Diamond was wearing her fairy outfit and looked adorable. I looked more comical. I'd had to work on my outfit at lightning speed, begging odd lengths of material from Miss Gibson and stitching them together in a crazy patchwork. I'd only had time to cut out the white broderie-anglaise pinafore and tack it together, leaving the hem unsewn, but I hoped a few dangling threads wouldn't spoil the general impression.

I'd applied rouge to our cheeks and tied ribbons in our hair. I left Diamond's loose and flowing, and fashioned my own into two plaits. It made me feel very much a foundling again. My skin even started itching as I remembered that harsh brown institution frock. How Matron Stinking Bottomly would gasp if she could see me now, breezing along on my penny-farthing, about to enter that den of iniquity, a music hall. She'd always declared I was a child of Satan and would go straight to hell. I hoped she wasn't right!

'Are you sure she'll like us this time?' Diamond asked.

'I'm absolutely certain,' I said. I was fibbing of course. In fact, I was starting to think that Mrs Ruby would laugh us straight out of her theatre – but we still had to give it a go.

I prayed inside my head, asking Mama for courage.

You've got more courage in your little finger than most folks have in their entire bodies, my own child.

I shoved open the stage door, feeling comforted. Stan was there, as cheerless as ever.

'Please can we store the penny-farthing with you for a few minutes?' I asked. 'I daren't leave it outside.'

'Well, you can't leave it here, either. What do you think this is, a special storage shed for your infernal contraption? Don't be ridiculous,' Stan grumbled.

'I'm simply doing what Mrs Ruby herself suggested,' I lied. 'Of course, if you want to dispute it with her, then that's another matter.'

Stan looked at me suspiciously. 'What do you take me for?' he said, but he let us leave it there all the same.

We went up to the second floor and along the corridor. My heart was beating fast now, but I managed to give Diamond a determined grin. 'Chin up, lovely,' I said. 'We're going to knock her socks off.'

Diamond spluttered as we both imagined Mrs Ruby in her splendid gown, with childish socks on her fat feet. Then I took a deep breath and knocked on Mrs Ruby's door.

'Right, let's be having you,' she called imperiously.

I pushed her door open and we sidled in.

'Oh my Lord, not you two kiddies again!' said Mrs Ruby. She looked at our outfits and our rouged cheeks. 'Come on now, I treated you to a night at the Cavalcade. Enough is enough. Off you go. Vamoose!'

Diamond looked up at me anxiously. I thought quickly. 'Yes, we're so grateful to you for letting us sit in your special box. We had such a lovely evening. But today we're here to give you your beautiful gown, Mrs Ruby,' I said. I seized it and whipped it out of the muslin bag so that I could brandish the purple costume like a flag. 'Isn't it a picture? Miss Gibson has done wonders. She sends her regards, by the way.'

'Oh my, yes, it does look effective. Just what the old girl needs to perk herself up. *Lovely* colour, perfect for limelight,' she said. She circled the waist with her hands. 'Nice boning too, to keep everything under control!'

'And you can rely on those stitches, Mrs Ruby, because I sewed them myself. You could use this gown in a tug of war and it still wouldn't bust at the seams, I promise you,' I declared.

'You're a caution, you are,' she told me. 'What was your name? I think there were several!'

'Hetty Feather, though I'm known as Emerald Star professionally. And this is Diamond, former Acrobatic Child Wonder.'

'Yes, yes. From the circus. So what's your connection with Miss Gibson, dear? Are you her niece perhaps – or her little apprentice?'

'I'm more a friend who's helping her out on a temporary basis,' I said smoothly.

'Well, you're a very good little friend – and these are weeny fairy stitches even though they're so strong,' said Mrs Ruby, examining the seams carefully. 'Here, dear, this is for your trouble.' She felt in her large velvet bag and brought out a florin.

Diamond's mouth went into a little O of excitement. I felt mean dashing her hopes of a wild spending spree, but this was our chance.

'It's so kind of you, Mrs Ruby, but I wonder – could you grant us a mere ten minutes of your time instead of the shilling?' I said. 'We have a brand-new act and—'

'No! Absolutely not. Look, dears, you're very sweet, and I truly believe you were the stars of your little circus, but music hall is different. It's adult, not little girly entertainment.'

'We appreciate that. We have adapted everything accordingly. Please let us show you, Mrs Ruby. You don't want to miss this chance. We have enormous potential, I promise you,' I declared.

'You've got enormous cheek, young lady, but I can't help admiring your persistence. Very well. Get started, and be quick about it,' she said, sitting back on her chaise-longue.

'I'm afraid we can only show you the introductory part up here in your dressing room. If you are to truly appreciate the whole of our novelty act, then we all need to repair to the stage,' I said.

'What? Nonsense! I'm not playing silly beggars trailing all the way down to the stage. Do your act here or not at all,' she said briskly.

'But there's not room – and it's very clever,' said Diamond, surprising me. 'Please let us show you properly,

Mrs Ruby. Hetty has been making us practise for eight hours each day in preparation!'

'My answer's still no,' she said.

I clenched my fists. 'You're a businesswoman, Mrs Ruby. I'm sure you like the idea of a bargain. You're pleased with your new dress. It was very expensive, though worth every penny, of course. Well, I will purchase a length of beautiful material according to your choice, consult with you on style, and stitch it for you for nothing. There! Just think, a gown worth two sovereigns! And all you have to do is come downstairs with us and watch our act.'

'And what if I don't like it, Miss Hetty Feather?'

'Then I shall still honour my solemn promise and still make you a free gown,' I said. 'I am a woman of my word.'

Mrs Ruby burst out laughing, though I wasn't aware I'd said anything amusing. 'Oh, child, you'll be the death of me. Very well, it's a bargain. But I shall hold you to that solemn promise.'

'Thank you so very much! Right, Diamond, please go down to the stage with Mrs Ruby while I go and fetch our surprise from the stage door.' I charged off before Mrs Ruby could object further.

I hurtled down the stairs and found my way back to Stan. 'Mrs Ruby insists I take my penny-farthing on stage,' I said. 'Please will you show me the way? And we'd better be quick about it. Mrs Ruby can be very impatient!'

'Tell me about it,' he muttered.

He shuffled off down the corridor again, while I pushed the penny-farthing behind him. We went up and down stairs, which was a huge problem, but I heaved and hauled my machine as best I could. I banged the walls once or twice, and Stan nagged me about spoiling the paintwork, though it was already pretty scuffed, even peeling in places. The Cavalcade might look in splendid shape from the front, but behind the scenes it was very run down.

We reached the stage at last.

'I'll tuck it away in the corner,' I said, propping the penny-farthing against a chair.

'That's not a corner, that's the wings. Don't you know nothing about the theatre? And you can't leave it there – it'll trip up all the artistes.'

'*I* am an artiste – and it is only there as a temporary measure,' I assured him.

Diamond was already on stage, looking lonely and frightened. Mrs Ruby had seated herself in the front row of the stalls. She was consulting her pocket watch – not a good sign.

I grabbed another chair, set it on the stage, then whisked Diamond into these newly named wings.

'Hop up into my arms, little Diamond Dolly,' I said. 'Don't look so scared. It's going to be fine this time. She will love our new act, just you wait and see.'

I tried to sound convincing, which was quite a challenge. I was suddenly so faint with nerves that the stage itself seemed to be rolling up and down like the waves at the seaside. But somehow I managed to stride out, smiling bravely, carrying Diamond. She stuck her arms and legs out stiffly, bless her, just as I'd taught her.

I sat down on the chair with Diamond on my lap and started chatting about my birthday and my new present. We carried on our routine, not daring to look down at Mrs Ruby. When we reached the part where we both looked away and then at each other and screamed, we heard a sudden burst of laughter. I felt a little thrill. But the best was yet to come!

We started our discussion about pocket money, only this time we were wondering how to share a penny and a farthing.

'Yes, how *do* you share a penny-farthing?' I asked the empty auditorium.

'I don't know, how *do* you share a penny-farthing?' Mrs Ruby called, actually joining in.

'Like this!' I said. 'But first I'd better wind up my special dolly. She's been a bit slow so far.'

I pretended there was a key in Diamond's back and made a great play of winding her up, giving a loud creaking noise. Then I ran off the stage while Diamond started running around, no longer slow and stiff, then turning cartwheels. I hitched myself upright on the penny-farthing and then pedalled onto the stage.

Mrs Ruby laughed again, then gasped when Diamond somersaulted towards me, leaped up into the air, and landed on my shoulders. We'd tried this trick a hundred times over, poor Diamond frequently taking a tumble. I did too, unable to stop the penny-farthing wobbling and crashing to the floor. We were all over bruises under our clothes, but I was determined to get our act right, and after Beppo's cruel training Diamond had learned to be brave. The constant practice had paid off. Diamond was as sure-footed as a little gazelle, and I knew exactly how far and fast I should pedal to catch her safely.

It was easy to pedal round and round steadily while Diamond struck poses. I didn't have to do anything fancy. I felt rather like Madame Adeline's horse, Pirate, who galloped in circles while she pirouetted on his back. Then we worked up to the big finale. Diamond hunched over so that her hands were on my shoulders. I heard her suck in her breath and tense her arms. Then she did a perfect handstand while I kept pedalling.

'Wave goodbye to all the lovely people, Diamond dolly!' I cried.

Diamond's right hand dug into my shoulder as she shifted her weight and managed to free her left hand to wave. I took my own left hand off the handlebars, steering as steadily as I could, and waved too. Then we pedalled off into the wings.

Mrs Ruby clapped. I steadied Diamond, helped her clamber down, and jumped off the penny-farthing myself. We ran back on stage hand in hand and curtsied.

'Well done, girlies!' said Mrs Ruby. She stood up and clapped more.

'Oh, Diamond, she likes us!' I said, hugging her.

Mrs Ruby edged her way along the row of seats and hurried up the steps onto the stage, still clapping.

'Diamond, you were superb. A true little star,' she said, patting her on the head.

I smiled proudly and squeezed Diamond's hand.

'So who devised this new act?' asked Mrs Ruby.

'Hetty did,' said Diamond. 'She made it all up and got me to learn it, and we practised all the tricks on the penny-farthing again and again. She said we had to be absolutely perfect if we got another chance to perform for you.'

'She's a shrewd little sweetheart, then.' Mrs Ruby nodded at me. 'I reckon you're a little star too. You're a young woman after my own heart. You watched my show and worked out exactly what would work. And it's paid off. You start on Monday. Pop into my room before the performance and we'll sign a contract. Ten shillings a week for your double act. Does that suit you?'

'It suits us splendidly!' I said. 'Thank you so much!'

'Thank *you*, dear. I look forward to my new dress.'

'I shall look at Miss Gibson's latest patterns from

Paris and bring you a selection to choose from,' I said. 'It will be the dress of your dreams!'

Mrs Ruby laughed again and waved us away.

Once we were off the stage I picked Diamond up and whirled her round. 'We've done it, Diamond! We've actually done it. We really are going to be music-hall artistes!'

'We're Little Stars! Madame Adeline would love that,' said Diamond. 'Oh, will you write and tell her, Hetty? Maybe she and Mr Marvel will come to see us perform!'

'And all the little monkeys too? How they will clap their tiny paws!' I said.

I capered about like a monkey myself I was so happy. I only calmed down when we got near grumpy old Stan.

We rode the penny-farthing home. Miss Gibson was busy with a customer and could only nod at us, but the moment she'd finished her fitting she rushed into the back room and exclaimed joyfully when we told her the good news.

I was a little worried that she'd be cross with me for promising Mrs Ruby a new dress, especially as I was nowhere near as skilled as she was, but she didn't mind at all.

'Don't you worry, dear. I'll give you a hand with it,' she said generously. 'And now that you're going to be a Cavalcade girl, perhaps you can put in a good word for me with the other artistes? Especially Lily Lark? How I'd love to dress her!'

'I'll work on it, Miss Gibson, just you wait and see,' I promised. 'And I'll still act as your apprentice during the day. That's what's so wonderful about this job – it's only evening work and yet it's quite well paid.'

'Can I get a new china dolly now?' Diamond asked eagerly.

'Very soon, I promise.'

'And you're the woman who keeps her promises, remember!' she said. 'Oh, I can't wait to tell Bertie. He'll be so pleased for us.'

I enjoyed telling him too. His whole face lit up and he danced a funny little jig. 'There, girls! You lengthened the act, gave it some novelty, just as I suggested! And I was right, wasn't I?' he said.

'Oh yes, it was all down to you, Bertie. I dare say you wrote the script and trained Diamond too,' I said sarcastically, but he seemed so genuinely delighted for us that I couldn't carp for long.

'We'll go out on Sunday to celebrate,' he said.

'All of us?' asked Diamond.

'Of course,' said Bertie, but when she'd run off to fashion a dress for her doll Maybelle out of Miss Gibson's scraps, he shook his head and sighed. 'I was really hoping Miss Gibson would look after little Diamond so that you and I could walk out together, Hetty,' he murmured.

I smiled and shrugged, not sure how to react. My

heart was beating very fast again. I couldn't understand why I felt so stupidly shy with Bertie now. We'd been such easy friends before. He'd kissed me on the cheek once, and that had seemed perfectly normal and natural, but now the very thought made me blush.

Still, I was determined not to go all moony-eyed over Bertie. I had to focus on our act. We had to keep it polished and up to standard. So I worked us very hard indeed every morning, trying to devise new acrobatic tricks for Diamond, while making sure that the routine went like clockwork. Diamond didn't complain, but she had violet shadows under her eyes and equally vivid bruises on her arms and legs from inadvertent tumbles. I felt dreadful, almost as cruel as Beppo, but I was even harder on myself. I let Diamond have the afternoons off. She played dressing up with discarded material, did a little 'stitching' for Maybelle, and lay on her tummy kicking her legs while I told her a story as I worked.

I'd started on the dress for Mrs Ruby. She'd chosen an amazing flame-orange satin with a gold slub thread. I privately thought it a little garish even for the stage, but I told her that it was a wonderful choice: she'd shine like the sun itself – which seemed to please her. Miss Gibson helped me with the cutting out – my hands shook as I scissored the material because it had been very expensive. Miss Gibson had had to loan me some money until I received my first Cavalcade wage. She made sure I didn't pin any material inside out or back to front, and checked all my tacking on the complex pieces. Then I started on the sewing. I made each stitch minute because I knew Mrs Ruby was a terrible stickler. I pulled every seam when it was finished to check it for strength.

It would take days and days to complete: there were big bunchy sleeves that had to be gathered to fit into the bodice, and the skirt was another nightmare, hanging smooth at the front but bunched at the back. I needed to concentrate hard, but I managed to tell Diamond stories at the same time.

I was word perfect on *Thumbelina*. Mama had given me the story when I was at the Foundling Hospital, and I had read it every night for years. I remembered other fairy stories read aloud to us by dear Nurse Winnie and recited them to Diamond, and then made up elaborate variations of my own. I amused myself with fairy-tale alternatives, talking of beautiful princesses who were secretly evil and cruel, slapping their baby sisters and kicking their kittens. I invented hideous witches who were sweet as honey and soft as butter, handsome princes who ran in fear when attacked by dragons, gentle giants who cradled children in their massive hands, and scrawny servant girls who sailed the seven seas and became queens of all the pirates.

Diamond enjoyed all my stories, but the one she liked best was utterly prosaic. It was about two little girls called Hatty and Twinkle. Hatty had red hair and Twinkle had fair hair. They were dear sisters and lived with their mama and papa in a small house in the country. Hatty and Twinkle played all day, and then Papa read them stories and Mama tucked them up in bed, and they cuddled up close and went to sleep. That was it. The simplest story in the whole world, but Diamond wanted to hear it again and again, and protested if I ever tried to make Hatty and Twinkle go for a walk into the woods or ride on a farmer's donkeys or visit the seaside. She wanted Hatty and Twinkle to stay safe inside their house. She certainly didn't want them to run away and become music-hall artistes.

I worried about her, knowing that I was forcing her to perform when she didn't really want to, but she seemed happy enough. She was always ecstatic when Bertie popped into the dress shop. He sat cross-legged like a mini tailor, telling us all sorts of stories about the other artistes. He seemed a little too keen to convince me that Ivy Green was a perfect sweetheart.

'*Your* sweetheart, I gather,' I said crisply.

'Not at all! She's just a dear friend. You're my sweetheart now, Miss Hetty Feather,' said Bertie.

'No I'm not,' I insisted.

'*I* am your sweetheart, aren't I, Bertie?' said Diamond, tossing her long hair and fluttering her eyelashes at him like a miniature coquette.

'Oh, how lucky I am! *Two* sweethearts, one for each arm,' he said.

I told him to run away if he had nothing better to do than talk nonsense, but I was grateful when he stayed and played card games with Diamond. He started off making her a card house, but then showed her a few simple games. She was surprisingly quick to learn, and chortled happily whenever she managed to trump him.

I knew he was deliberately playing poorly and felt very fond of him. I didn't flinch away when he kissed me goodbye. Diamond was even more enthusiastic. She flung her arms round Bertie's neck and kissed him back heartily on both cheeks.

8

BERTIE SUGGESTED WE GO for a picnic on Sunday. He'd found a delightful spot which he knew we'd love. Miss Gibson had lived in town all her life and probably knew every likely picnic venue for miles around, but she clapped her hands and told Bertie he was a marvel. Diamond echoed this.

'You must let us provide the picnic, Bertie, as you treated us to lunch at the chop house,' I said.

'I want to provide the meat,' said Bertie. 'If there's one thing I know about, it's blooming meat.'

'You don't have meat at a picnic, do you?' I said.

'You do at *my* picnics,' he told me. 'But I hope Miss Gibson might provide some cake and lemonade. And I know what I want from you, Hetty.'

'What's that?' I asked warily.

'One of your magnificent apple pies!'

I was startled. When I was a maid at Mr Buchanan's, I had indeed made Bertie an apple pie, but I was astonished that he'd remembered.

'Can you cook *pies*, Hetty?' asked Diamond.

At the circus we had lived on stews, mostly scrag end or boiler fowl, and occasionally on dreaded horsemeat. There had been no pantries, no tables, no bowls and rolling pins, no ovens, so of course I couldn't possibly make pies.

'She bakes a superb pie. That old Mrs Briskett taught her well,' said Bertie.

'No, it was Mama who taught me to cook. Mama was the best cook ever,' I said. 'At the Foundling Hospital she even made our porridge taste good.'

'Were you a foundling child?' Miss Gibson asked, looking astonished.

I felt myself blush. It had just slipped out. What would Miss Gibson think of me now? So many folk looked down on foundlings and considered them little sinners. But she smiled at me and patted my hand with her own plump one, her fingertips calloused with constant sewing.

'You should feel very proud of yourself, dear, to have come so far. And it's fitting that you are now employed at the Cavalcade. *Peg's Periodical* gives little biographies of music-hall stars, and many of them come from humble beginnings,' she said.

'Yes, I've heard that the magnificent Flirty Bertie himself was once a workhouse baby,' said Bertie. He curled his hands into tiny fists, and went *'Waa-waa-waa!'* like a tiny baby, which made us all laugh.

'Oh, I'm *so* looking forward to Sunday!' said Diamond when we went to bed. 'Aren't you, Hetty?'

'Oh, I suppose so,' I murmured casually. I was actually looking forward to it enormously.

Miss Gibson went to the early church service on Sunday morning. She didn't seem to mind when we opted to stay behind. I rather wished she'd taken Diamond with her. She was very keen to lend a hand with the pie-making and was forever getting in the way, spilling flour over herself and rolling the pastry too thin when I let her have a go with the rolling pin. In the end I suggested we *both* make a pie at different ends of the scrubbed wooden table, and that was easier.

'We'll cut Bertie a big slice of each and he'll have to choose which one he likes the best,' said Diamond, putting an extra big knob of butter and two spoonfuls of sugar into her pastry mix.

'Hey, don't do that! You'll spoil it!' I said.

'But I want mine to be extra tasty,' she protested.

She worked long and hard at her strange pastry, and by the time she was ready to assemble her pie, it was grey with working.

'Oh dear, it doesn't look very nice, does it?' she said. 'I think I'd better put extra apples in to make it especially delicious.'

She tipped in so many slices of apple, she could barely cram the pastry lid on top.

'Now for the fun part,' I said. 'We decorate our pies.'

I showed Diamond how to make a pattern all round the edge with the fork, and pricked the top in a neat circle to let the steam out. Diamond jabbed happily, and then grew particularly excited when I divided up my leftover pastry and said we could now make a pretty shape to sit in the centre of our pies.

Mrs Briskett had often made a pretty pastry rose – but Mama had once fashioned something very special. I copied her now, cutting out the shape and scoring it carefully with the tines of a fork.

'What is it? Oh, I know! It's a feather!' said Diamond. 'Right, *I* shall make a diamond to show it's *my* pie.'

She tried hard, but could only manage to make

the pastry look like a blob, so she poked out the centre and made it into a letter D instead. Then we put the pies in the oven and started the mammoth task of clearing up Miss Gibson's kitchen. Diamond kept wanting to open the door of the oven to see how the pies were progressing, but I managed to make her leave well alone. The kitchen was soon full of the most delicious sweet smell.

'They're ready, I know they're ready now!' cried Diamond.

'No, not yet. We want them to get beautifully golden brown. Patience!' I said. 'Shall we go out in the yard and practise our penny-farthing tricks for ten minutes?'

'Shall we *not*!' said Diamond. 'Oh, I'm so hungry because of the lovely pie smell.'

She ate a fingerful of butter dabbed in sugar, all the apple peelings, and even a piece of raw pastry, though I said it would give her worms.

'You're such a bossy big sister,' said Diamond, laughing at me.

She seemed to have started believing that we really were sisters. Well, I was certainly closer to her than my own foster sisters, all of them grown up now, and Rose and big Eliza were certainly very bossy indeed. But of course I had a younger foster sister too, *little* Eliza, still languishing in the Foundling Hospital. I felt a sudden pang. I'd been so thrilled when she first arrived at the hospital and made her my special pet straight away, but when she started babbling about Jem and how *she* would marry him one day, I was so wounded I found it hard to have anything to do with her.

I should have tried to keep in touch with her when I left the hospital. I resolved to find her again when she turned fourteen and could leave as well. She would probably be devastated when Jem didn't come to marry her after all. He would be married to my friend Janet by then. Perhaps he was even married to her already!

I was so deep in thought that I might have let the pies burn to a cinder, but luckily Diamond begged to take a peep into the oven at just the right moment. Both pies were golden and smelled splendid. Diamond's was oozing syrup, which had burned a little.

'Oh dear, mine's leaking!' she wailed. 'And the juicy bits have gone dark brown!'

'It's leaking *because* it's extra juicy. The juice outside will taste of caramel – it'll be extra delicious,' I assured her.

'Do you think Bertie will really like it, then?' she asked.

'He'll love it. I expect he'll want to eat it all up himself,' I said.

'Well, he can't!' said Diamond. 'I shall make sure you have a big slice, Hetty, because you're really my favourite.

And Miss Gibson had better have a slice too because she's being so kind to us.'

Miss Gibson admired both our pies when she got home. 'I must set to myself now, girls,' she said.

She took off her going-to-church jacket, rolled up her black satin sleeves, covered herself in a large white apron, and got started. She made two big jugfuls of fresh lemonade, pouring them into old ginger beer bottles, and put them in the pantry to cool. Then she brought out more flour and sugar and butter.

'What sort of cake shall I make? A nice Victoria sponge? A Swiss roll? An angel cake? What's your favourite cake, girls?' she asked.

Diamond and I exchanged glances.

'They all sound lovely cakes, but there's one kind in particular that we both like,' I said. 'I don't know the name, but it's checked pink and yellow.'

'Yes, and wrapped all around with marzipan!' said Diamond. 'Oh, we love that cake, don't we, Hetty!'

'Battenberg,' said Miss Gibson. 'Yes, I love it too. And it's a good little cake to take on a picnic because it won't squash easily or lose half its cream. Right, Battenberg it is.'

Diamond and I sat at the kitchen table watching her make Madame Adeline's special cake. I knew Madame Adeline bought hers from a bakery, so I worried that Miss Gibson's home-made version wouldn't be quite the same, but when at last it was cooked and assembled, it looked and smelled perfect.

It made us both miss Madame Adeline so much that when we went up to our room to tidy ourselves and get ready, we had a little hug.

'I do wish we could see Madame Adeline and Mr Marvel,' Diamond sighed.

'I shall write to them tonight and tell them we are going to be music-hall artistes. They will be so pleased and proud,' I said.

'But I wish they were here,' Diamond wailed, nearly in tears. 'I especially miss Madame Adeline.'

'Well, shut your eyes and I'll see if I can conjure her up,' I told her. 'Go on, hide your head in the pillow – and absolutely no peeking.'

Diamond did as she was told. I hitched my dress right up to my thighs, kicked off my boots and stockings, and loosened my hair. I seized a floor mop, straddled it, then struck an attitude, arms out, toes pointed.

'I am Madame Adeline, and I am about to perform my amazing acrobatic routine on my beautiful horse!' I cried in Madame Adeline's accent. 'Wake up and watch me, my little twinkling Diamond.'

Diamond sat up and laughed delightedly.

'Here I go!' I shouted, and 'galloped' round and round the little room, jumping over my discarded boots. I patted the mop head and cried *'Hup hup hup!'*, making the mop rear up in the air as if it were standing on its back legs.

Diamond clapped and cheered, and I took a bow and made the mop bow too, and then accept a pretend sugar lump from Diamond's proffered hand.

'There now,' I said in my own voice. 'Show's over for today – but Madame Adeline will come back tonight if you're very good. Let's get your hands and face washed, you're all sticky sugar. Good Lord, you've even got it in your hair. Watch out – people will mistake you for a stick of spun sugar and gollop you up before you know it.'

It was easy enough to jolly her back into a good mood, and she was very keen to scrub herself clean and brush her hair and put on her newly washed and ironed pinafore because she wanted to impress Bertie. I rather wanted to do likewise. I wished I had more clothes. My dress was looking so tired and limp.

My only other outfit was my red riding jacket and breeches, and they were of no use to me now. I might as well throw them away. I couldn't wear my wonderful glossy riding boots with frocks, but I was determined to keep them for ever, even if I never wore them again. Madame Adeline had given them to me and so they were doubly precious. I wished I still had the green dress I'd made out of curtains and gold braid. I had loved that dress so much – and Bertie had admired it too. But I'd had to cut it up to turn it into the mermaid's costume. Thank goodness I need never wear *that* again!

I put my grey sprigged dress on again and sighed at myself in the looking glass. 'It looks so plain,' I said. '*I* look so plain.'

I felt worse when I saw Miss Gibson. She still wore her usual black satin, but with a different black jacket, cut like a blazer with very dashing red stripes.

'Oh, Miss Gibson, you look a picture,' I said. 'I love the jacket!'

'You don't think it's too bold a look, do you?' she asked anxiously. 'I've had it years, but scarcely had the courage to wear it. Still, I do think a picnic is the perfect occasion for a blazer.'

'Absolutely. I wish *I* had one.'

'Then perhaps you'd like to borrow one of mine,' Miss Gibson offered generously.

I hesitated. I didn't like to point out that all her jackets would be vastly too big for me.

'I've got a sample somewhere,' she said. 'I made it for a schoolgirl daughter of one of my clients, but for some reason it didn't suit. Aha!' She brought out a dashing green blazer with a silver-grey stripe. 'Try it on, Hetty.'

It looked wonderful. The green contrasted with my red hair, and the silvery stripe toned with the grey of my dress. It made all the difference in the world!

'Thank you so much, Miss Gibson!' I said.

'You look lovely, Hetty,' said Diamond. She sounded a little wistful.

'Oh dear, I don't think I've got any jackets small enough for you,' said Miss Gibson. 'But I know what will look very pretty in your hair.' She rummaged in one of the long drawers in her cabinet and came out with a handful of satin ribbons. 'Which would you like, Diamond? You choose.'

Diamond looked at them all solemnly. She hesitated over a tartan ribbon, stroked a pink one with rosebud embroidery, but then picked out a shining sky-blue satin one. 'They're all beautiful, but I think I will choose the blue one. It will go with my dress perfectly,' she said, like a little fashion-conscious lady.

'It will go with your eyes too,' I said, tying it for her.

'My pa once gave me a blue ribbon,' she said un-expectedly. 'That was when I was his pet. But then he stopped liking me.'

'Well, I'll always, always, always like you, Diamond,' I said quickly.

'And I will too,' said Miss Gibson.

'Will Bertie always like me?' Diamond asked.

'Of course he will, silly,' I said.

Bertie certainly made a huge fuss of Diamond, picking her up and cradling her as if she really were a little doll. 'How's my little sweetheart, then? All ready to come on a picnic with Bertie? My, don't you look a picture. Good enough to eat. We'll be hard pressed to choose at the picnic – a slice of pie or a slice of scrumptious Diamond!'

'I've made you a special pie, Bertie. A really juicy one,' she said.

'Aren't I the lucky one! And I'll provide a juicy plate of meat fit for a little princess,' he said. There was a big canvas bag over his shoulder, with the handle of a black frying pan sticking out.

'You're going to *cook*?' I exclaimed.

'That's the general idea. Unless you'd like your meat raw. I must say, you two ladies are a sight for sore eyes too. You look splendid in those stripes, Miss Gibson. And you look quite the ticket too, Miss Hetty. That's a very saucy jacket.'

'And you're a very saucy boy, Mr Bertie,' I said. He'd made an effort with his own appearance, wearing his stage straw boater and blazer and white flannels. His newly-washed hair was as fluffy as a dandelion clock, and his fingernails were clipped and clean. He used to wear far too much pomade to disguise the stink of meat, but now he just smelled pleasantly of soap. I was touched that he'd made such an effort.

I was worried too. Here we were, the four of us, all dressed up like dogs' dinners, with elaborate bags and boxes of food, setting off expectantly, as if we were about to step onto a magic carpet and picnic in an Arabian palace garden, with fountains flowing and servants proffering silver trays of exotic delicacies. We were probably going to some dismal municipal park where we'd squat uncomfortably and spill our picnic all down our finery.

'Where exactly are we going, Bertie?' I asked.

'Aha! This is a special mystery trip. Have faith, little feathery one. I'm taking us somewhere special,' said Bertie.

'This way, ladies,' he instructed when we got to the end of the road.

There were shops and then houses as far as the eye could see. I peered hard, but couldn't see a patch of green anywhere. I looked doubtfully at Miss Gibson's tight little boots. They'd have to work very hard to support the rest of her.

'I don't think we can walk terribly far,' I murmured.

'We're not walking all the way,' Bertie told me. 'I've laid on my own select charabanc to transport us.'

For a moment I thought he'd actually hired his own carriage, but then I spotted the bus stop a few yards away.

Bertie looked at his pocket watch. 'It should be here any minute,' he said cheerily.

He must have consulted the omnibus timetables, because within seconds we saw the vehicle at the end of the street. Bertie had a pocketful of change and paid for all of us. We sat upstairs, the wind blowing in our hair as the omnibus gathered pace. I had to tie Diamond's blue ribbon extra tightly, and Bertie had to cram his boater down on his head to stop it sailing away.

'Oh, this is such fun! I've never been on an omnibus before!' said Diamond, her cheeks pink.

'You're so sweet, Diamond,' I said – though I'd only been on a bus a handful of times myself and found it equally exciting to bowl along looking into people's top windows and peering down into their gardens.

Then the houses gradually petered out and we were in the countryside. At first I thought we might be going back to the little market town where I'd first seen the Cavalcade poster, but I didn't recognize the route. We must be going in the opposite direction. Soon there were woods on either side of us, and high hills far away.

'I came this way on a Sunday school picnic long ago when I was a little girl,' said Miss Gibson. Her cheeks were pink too, her ringlets escaping their rigid curl. 'Bertie, might you be taking us to Ledbury Hill?'

'There, you've spoiled my little surprise, Miss G!'

'But it's the most tremendous surprise! I've wanted to go back there all these years, and yet somehow never had the gumption to do so. Oh, I do hope it hasn't changed.'

When we got off the omnibus and started walking into the woods, Miss Gibson declared it hadn't changed at all. There were sandy paths to make walking easier, and gorse and heather coloured the heath in dazzling yellow and pinky purple. We started climbing steadily, Bertie gallantly offering Miss Gibson a hand. We were all gasping by the time we got to the top, but it was worth it. We could see for miles across a great green sweep of countryside to the hazy blue hills on the horizon.

There was a convenient wooden bench where Miss Gibson could sit and catch her breath, while Bertie, Diamond and I searched for suitable twigs and branches to make a decent fire. Bertie had brought Bryant and May matches with him, but even so had difficulty in getting the twigs to catch.

'Let me have a go,' I said, rolling up my sleeves.

I laid the twigs in a different pattern, and used the paper wrapping my apple pie, crumpling it into little balls which I wedged in carefully. I lit a match, and within seconds the fire had taken hold.

'My goodness, you clever little witch!' exclaimed Bertie.

I was simply practised. At the circus I'd made similar fires every day. Then it was Bertie's turn to show off his expertise. He took out his frying pan, melted a large dollop of lard, and set four large steaks a-sizzling.

'Prime cuts,' he said triumphantly. 'Hetty, will you butter the loaf in my bag? We'll have steak sandwiches.'

Diamond was peering at the pan doubtfully. 'It's not horsemeat, is it?' she asked.

'Horsemeat! These are the finest Angus fillet steaks, child, ordered specially from the best butcher in Fenstone,' said Bertie, pretending to be indignant.

'I'm sorry, I didn't mean to vex you,' she said anxiously.

'You couldn't possibly vex me, Twinkle,' said Bertie.

The steaks were wonderful, ultra-succulent and so tender they scarcely needed biting. Diamond declared that she liked Angus fillet better than any other food in the world. We washed them down with draughts of lemonade. Then it was pie time!

I'd brought a knife so I could cut everyone a neat slice from both pies, and Miss Gibson had provided a jar of cream to go with them. Bertie rolled his eyes and kissed his fingers when he ate my slice, but was tactful enough to mime even more excessively when he ate Diamond's shrivelled pastry and overcooked apple.

'I'm so sorry, Hetty. You make a splendid apple pie, but young Diamond here has utterly surpassed you. What an utterly frabjous pie!'

We finished the last of the lemonade with Miss Gibson's Battenberg cake. Neither Diamond nor I wanted to acknowledge it, but it was even better than Madame Adeline's, so light and fresh, with extra jam between the squares of colour, and the marzipan especially almondy.

'My, what a feast,' said Bertie, patting his stomach.

The food and the warmth of the little fire made Miss Gibson so sleepy she lay down on the mossy bank and was gently snoring in seconds.

'Fancy going to sleep in the daytime!' Diamond giggled.

She started gathering little sticks and stones and leaves to make a tiny house for a mouse, but ten minutes later she'd curled up too, eyes closed, thumb in her mouth.

Bertie smiled at me. 'Are you going to sleep too, Hetty?'

I shook my head.

'Shall we go for a little walk and leave these two slumber-ladies?'

'If you like,' I said, though my heart had started thumping hard under my borrowed blazer.

He took hold of my hand to help me up, and then kept hold of it as we started off. We walked down the other side of the hill, heading into the woods, where it was darker and cooler.

'Not too cold, are you?' Bertie said softly. 'That's quite a skimpy little blazer, for all it's so fetching. Come here.'

He put his arm round me, looking sideways at me to see if I objected. I didn't know what to do. I felt I should flounce away and put him in his place. But his arm felt so warm and strong around me. Then he drew me closer, still looking into my eyes.

'Oh, Hetty,' he whispered, and then he kissed me.

We stopped being Hetty and Bertie. We felt like a

fairytale couple in an enchanted wood, and this was the kiss that would bind us together for ever.

Yet when we came out into the sunlight again, I chatted determinedly to Miss Gibson about the latest fashions while Bertie played tag with Diamond, as if nothing momentous had happened at all.

9

OH, THE NERVES ON Monday night, before our first performance! I parked the penny-farthing in the wings, and then we went to sign our contracts with Mrs Ruby. She wished us luck, and then sent us off to our dressing room. I'd hoped we'd have our own special room like Lily Lark, but we had to squeeze into the girls' dressing room.

It was a very shabby room on the first floor, with

flyblown mirrors, racks of clothes, a jumble of make-up on the rickety tables, and a box of resin on the floor. At first it seemed like a big room, because we were extremely early, but once all the showgirls had crowded in, we were crammed elbow to elbow.

There weren't any curtains to change behind. We were astonished when the girls stripped off in front of each other, right down to their drawers. In fact, they removed their everyday drawers altogether, wiggling into short red satin ones with a frill.

'Don't stare so, Diamond!' I whispered, but I couldn't help looking too.

I watched as they all smeared blue on their eyelids, pink on their cheeks and carmine on their lips. The showgirls were all so tall, so loud, so confident, calling out to each other and telling silly jokes. They ignored Diamond and me altogether. Some of them didn't look that much older than me when they first came into the room, and several were naturally flat-chested. They stuffed rolled-up stockings down their bodices, fashioning reasonably authentic bosoms. I wondered if this was a trick I should try.

They looked amazing when they were all in their scarlet costumes. I couldn't help feeling a little scared of them. One of them saw me staring and gave me a wink.

'Are you two kids dancers as well?' she asked, casually adjusting the frill on her drawers.

'No, we're a novelty act,' I told her.

'Is it your first time on stage? You look very nervous,' she said.

'Oh no, Diamond and I are seasoned performers,' I said, trying to sound confident. 'She used to be an acrobatic child wonder at Tanglefield's Travelling Circus.'

The moment I said the word circus she shook her head. 'The circus!' she said pityingly, and went to join her friends.

'Hetty, I think *I'm* a bit nervous,' Diamond whispered.

I saw that she was trembling and put my arm round her. 'Don't worry. I'm nervous too, but I didn't want that dancing girl to scoff at us,' I said.

I was looking around for Ivy Green, but she was clearly enough of a star to have her own dressing room.

'Beginning acts!' someone called, knocking on the door.

The showgirls groaned and then started to leave the dressing room, arms round each other, joshing and joking.

'You'll be a beginning act too,' said the last girl, peering over her shoulder at us. 'Come on, follow us.'

So Diamond and I went down the maze of corridors and narrow steps till we arrived back in the wings. There were several artistes already waiting there – Peter Perkins the comic, Signor Olivelli the Italian opera singer, and Araminta the contortionist. She was wearing an even briefer costume than the dancing girls, exposing a startling amount of muscled flesh, but Peter Perkins and Signor Olivelli didn't give her a second glance.

She was looking indignant, flouncing about with her hands on her hips. 'Who put that ridiculous machine in the wings? I nearly tripped over it in the dark. If I so much as pull a muscle I'll be out of the show for weeks! It's ludicrous to use the wings as a rubbish dump,' she declared.

'Well, let's get rid of it,' said Signor Olivelli, who spoke with a London accent, for all his Italian singing. He seized hold of the penny-farthing's handlebars as if he intended to tip it over.

'Stop it! Leave that alone! It's a very valuable penny-farthing and it's part of our act!' I said, rushing over and grabbing it from him.

'Don't talk to me like that, kid! Who the hell are you anyway? I've never seen you in the show,' he said, not letting go of the penny-farthing. 'And why are you dragging this heap of old iron around?' He gave the front wheel a contemptuous kick with his black patent boot.

'Don't you dare do that! You'll buckle the wheel. I'll kick *you* if you don't watch out!' I said.

'You cheeky little devil!' Signor Olivelli raised his hand as if to cuff me, but someone seized his wrist and spun him round, jerking the penny-farthing free at the same time.

'You leave her alone!' said Bertie. He only came up to the man's shoulder, but he was very strong and half Olivelli's age. It was clear who would win in a tussle.

Olivelli came out with a mouthful of abuse.

'Hey, hey – language, gentlemen!' Mrs Ruby herself swept up in her new purple gown. She had a string of large blue gems about her white throat – maybe cut glass, maybe real amethysts. 'What's all the argy-bargy?'

'These silly little kids are cluttering up the wings with this bally great bicycle, and when I tried to move it, the redhead kicked out at me!' said Olivelli.

'I didn't kick him, I just threatened him,' I said indignantly.

'And he tried to punch her head in – I saw him!' added Bertie.

'I very nearly tripped,' Araminta declared. 'I'm telling you, if I so much as pull a muscle, I can't work for—'

'Weeks – yes, dear, so you keep telling us,' said Mrs Ruby. 'Now, my darlings, I suggest you all calm down and wait quietly for the show to begin, or *none* of you will work for weeks. Hetty, child – or Sapphire or Emerald, whoever you want to be – I suggest you pop your penny-farthing right back in the furthest corner, out of every-one's way. There's a good girl. Now, let's all smile and behave like one big happy family. Let me see those pearly-whites, dears.'

They all bared their teeth in a smile, even Olivelli, though it was clearly a strain.

'Now, where's that boy of mine? Propping up the bar, I dare say. Someone go and fetch him, as I make it one minute to opening time. Dear, oh dear, who'd be in charge of a music-hall theatre?' said Mrs Ruby. 'Any of you wish to take over? You'd be more than welcome. I'm getting old and tired. I'd be glad of a rest.' She smiled smugly, because she was looking marvellously youthful in her cleverly boned purple frock, and she seemed electric with energy. Her little eyes were darting everywhere, checking on all her artistes, looking for her 'son' and seeing that I'd wheeled the penny-farthing further back in the wings.

Then she heard the orchestra strike a particularly arresting chord. She stood even straighter, thrusting out her magnificent chest, and sailed onto the stage, owning every inch of it. All the chattering artistes in the wings lowered their voices to whispers.

Bertie tiptoed over to Diamond and me. 'Are you all right, Hetty? That bogus Eyetie warbler didn't hurt you, did he?' he murmured.

'You stopped him! Thank you so much.'

'Well, I'll not have anyone bullying my girl. Girls,' he corrected himself, patting Diamond on the shoulder. 'How are you feeling, Twinkle?'

'I feel sick!' she said. 'Just the way I used to at the circus. Maybe *worse*.'

'It's just stage fright, dear. We all feel it,' said Bertie. 'See, I'm shivery and sick too.' He started trembling violently and then mimed vomiting.

Diamond giggled and then clapped her hand over her mouth.

We waited silently while Mrs Ruby warmed up the audience. Someone right up in the gallery had the cheek to heckle her, calling out something vulgar about her bosom.

Mrs Ruby put her head on one side, one hand behind her ear. 'Sorry, dear? Didn't quite catch that. You've got a little mouse squeak. Show yourself, my sweetheart. Ooh, I see you. Yes, a little mouse all right, hiding there amongst your big mates. Why don't you whip down those stairs and come and join me on stage, where we can have a proper conversation and you can admire my abundant figure in close proximity. How about that for an invitation? Little mousy want to come and meet Mrs Pussycat?'

This drew huge laughter and applause, and the stupid youth slunk down in his seat, not inclined to take up her invitation.

'Boys!' said Mrs Ruby, shaking her head. 'And what about *my* boy? Where's he got to? He's due up on stage with me and yet *I* can't see him. No use going through all the usual spiel about my boy Samson if he's not going to come bounding onto the stage on cue. Shall I send out a search party for the naughty lad?'

There was a sudden jostling in the wings, and Samson Ruby pushed his way through, though he paused to give one of the showgirls a big kiss on her cheek. Then he spotted me. 'Hello! Who's this funny little sprat? Ooh, and an even weenier one,' he said, patting Diamond on the head. 'Whose kiddies are you?'

'We're not anybody's kiddies,' I said fiercely. 'We're artistes.'

He laughed in my face, breathing whisky fumes all over me.

'Where are you, little Samson?' Mrs Ruby repeated on stage, an edge to her voice.

'Here, big Mama,' he said, rushing forward to kiss her hand.

I hated him, but he was very clever at bantering with her *and* dealing with the audience, because now half a dozen were cat-calling. As ringmaster at Tanglefield's, I'd had to deal with a few drunks. It was like walking a tightrope. If they were merry, everything *could* go swimmingly and they'd laugh along with you in a cheery manner, but they could suddenly snap and turn nasty for no reason, and then they were a nightmare to control. Diamond wasn't the only one who was trembling.

When Mrs Ruby came off stage, she breathed out heavily. 'Be bold, dears. They're a rowdy lot tonight. Squash 'em flat from the start.' She turned to Diamond and me. 'And keep your peckers up, little girlies. Don't show you're scared, whatever you do. You both look so sweet, I doubt that even the meanest drunk will pick on you. I'm going to my special box now. I'll be watching over you.'

'And I'll be watching over you too,' said Bertie as Samson Ruby started introducing him. He squeezed my hand, and I was surprised to discover that it was nearly as cold and clammy as mine.

'Good luck, Bertie. I think your act's brilliant,' I said.

'I do too,' said Diamond earnestly.

'There, what a lucky chap I am, having two sweethearts wishing me well!' Bertie sprang on stage with a natty little skip, waving his boater in the air.

I was glad that Samson Ruby always sat at a special table in front of the stage, ready to announce all the artistes. I didn't fancy the idea of being squashed up in the wings with him. I hated the way he'd looked at me. The girl he'd kissed was wiping her cheek, grimacing, while her friends were shaking their heads sympathetically.

I watched Bertie, marvelling at his courage as he sang and danced and cracked funny jokes as if he didn't have a care in the world.

'Bless his little cotton socks,' said one of the showgirls.

'He's a cute one, our Bertie,' said another.

I was glad he was a favourite of theirs. I didn't want

Ivy Green flirting with him, but the showgirls were talking about him as if he were a cute puppy, not a man to be reckoned with. They all trooped on stage for him to serenade them, while the audience laughed.

'That's it, Bertie, lad. Make them laugh. Then they'll keep laughing for me,' said Peter Perkins, the comic.

He didn't look comical now, he looked deadly serious, and he had to keep mopping his brow with a yellow spotted handkerchief. He shook his head when he saw me staring. 'It's all right for you two. Like Mrs Ruby said, they'll not turn on little girls. They might chew you up a little bit, but then they'll spit you out. But a big sweaty chappie like me – oooh, they'll swallow me whole if I'm not careful. Dear God, why did I ever take to the boards? I should have listened to my old dad,' he said. 'I'd have done an honest day's work down the market and now I'd be safe at home with my feet up.'

'Oh my goodness!' I said. 'I think we might have met your father. Is he Sam Perkins, with his own fruit and veg stall? He was so kind to Diamond and me. He took us for a slap-up breakfast and looked after us beautifully.' I didn't add that Mr Perkins had called the Cavalcade a den of iniquity.

'That's my dad all right,' said Peter Perkins. 'Does everyone a good turn and always has a kind word – well, except for me. I fair broke his heart when I wouldn't join him in the family business, and it was the last straw when I joined the Cavalcade. He's strait-laced, my dad – wouldn't ever set foot in a music hall. He'll barely talk to me now.'

'Oh dear, I'm so sorry. But sometimes you just have to follow your dream,' I said.

'Sometimes your dream turns into a nightmare,' he murmured gloomily.

Bertie came bouncing across the stage, all sunny smiles and cheery waves until he joined us in the wings. Then he pulled a face and mopped his brow. 'Lordy, Lordy, that was uphill work,' he said.

'You were very good, Bertie,' said Diamond. 'I think I'll be very bad.'

'Nonsense. You'll knock their socks off,' said Bertie. 'All crowds love little girls.'

There were cheers and whistles as the showgirls went back on stage to do their own routine.

'They like big girls too,' I said. My mouth was so dry I had to wet my lips to talk properly. How on earth was I going to project my voice to the back of the huge hall? Why had I tried so desperately hard to get a place here? What was really so glamorous about the music hall? Diamond and I didn't *have* to do this. We could stay at Miss Gibson's and I could sew pretty gowns and we could lead a quiet, tranquil life.

'You'll be fine, Hetty, I promise you,' Bertie whispered.

'I just feel so nervous!' I admitted. 'I never felt like

this at the circus. I almost wish I was back there . . .
No, I don't! The clown, Beppo, was so cruel to Diamond.'

She had crept to the edge of the wings, distracted by
the dancers. She unconsciously clapped her hands and
pointed her toes, imitating them.

'You're really fond of that kid, aren't you?' Bertie said.
'You're like a little mother to her. You'll be marvellous
when you have your own kids, Hetty.'

'I'm not having any kids! Or any husband either,' I
said firmly.

'Not even the sainted Jem?'

'I expect he's married someone else by now.'

'Oh, Hetty! Did he jilt you, then?'

'No he didn't. I left him,' I said shortly.

'There! You couldn't get me out of your head, could
you?' Bertie was joking, but there was a hopeful edge to
his voice.

'I didn't give you a second thought,' I said, not entirely
truthfully. It sounded harsher than I'd meant. 'Sorry,
Bertie, I didn't mean to hurt your feelings.'

'Don't worry, you haven't. I was just trying to distract
you – stop you feeling so nervous,' he said lightly.

'Well, that's very kind of you,' I said. 'Though it's not
working!'

The dancers' routine seemed to be over in a flash.
Peter Perkins bit his thumb for luck and then went on
stage, walking like a soldier – left, right, left, right – then

saluting so smartly he poked himself in the eye. It was a silly routine that had worked before, but tonight it barely raised a titter.

'Oh, poor man,' I said.

'He's a trooper, old Pete. He'll get them on his side,' said Bertie.

But poor Peter Perkins couldn't make any of his jokes work – and they started booing him.

'I can't bear it,' I said, putting my hands over my ears.

'He won't let it upset him too much. Sometimes they're simply not in the mood for jokes. They just want to be a comic turn themselves,' Bertie told me.

'And some comics are no bally good anyway,' Signor Olivelli muttered.

Peter Perkins came off looking chalk white, to hardly any applause. The other artistes turned away tactfully, though Bertie patted him on the back. Peter hurried off, shaking his head in despair.

Signor Olivelli didn't have a much better reception, but he took no notice of the restless audience, simply singing louder and louder, his eyes closed as if he were singing to himself. The crowd liked Araminta, loudly applauding her very brief costume.

Mr Apple the ventriloquist joined us in the wings only a couple of minutes before he was due on. He stared at Diamond and me. 'Who are you two?'

'We're artistes. I'm Emerald Star and this is Diamond,'

I said. 'How do you do?' I held out my hand, but he didn't take it.

'I don't hold with kids littering up the place,' he muttered.

'I'm not a kid. I'm nearly sixteen. This is my costume,' I said.

'And you've got a little boy yourself,' said Diamond.

Mr Apple glared at her.

'She means Little Pip. She was very taken with him when we saw the show,' I explained.

He sighed impatiently. But when he unzipped his bag and took out Little Pip, he handled him carefully, stroking the dummy's wild hair into place and adjusting his tie. He slipped his hand up inside Little Pip's coat and then pulled a funny face at him. Little Pip turned his head and pulled a funny face back.

I raised my eyebrows at Bertie.

He rolled his own eyes and tapped the side of his forehead. 'Barmy,' he mouthed.

I tried to concentrate on Benjamin Apple's act, to see if I could get further inspiration for our own performance, but it was hard to concentrate. We were on next!

Diamond started squirming. 'I think I need to go to the WC, Hetty!'

'Well, you can't. Not till after we've been on stage. It'll all be over in ten minutes, Diamond,' I whispered.

'Will they shout at us?'

'They might.'

'Then can we run away?'

'No, we're going to carry on, no matter what. Mrs Ruby will be watching. We can't give up. We're going to give an immaculate performance and show everyone,' I said. I took hold of Diamond's hand. 'We can do it!'

Benjamin Apple came off stage, still bowing. Little Pip was bowing too, his head bobbing up and down to show he was pleased.

'Sticky night, boss,' said Little Pip.

'But they liked us,' said Benjamin Apple. Then he took Little Pip off his arm and stuffed him back in his bag.

'*Liked us*,' Little Pip murmured in a muffled voice.

Diamond backed away from them, and I shivered because it was so creepy.

'Did you enjoy Benjamin Apple and Little Pip, ladies and gents – and naughty boys up in the gallery?' Samson Ruby bellowed. 'A real comic turn, weren't they? Well, you're in for a very special treat, because there are two little girls who are going to do their best to entertain you in exactly the same way. Oh, this is going to tickle your fancy! Please put your hands together to welcome our new Little Stars to the stage, Emerald and Diamond!'

I picked Diamond up and made for the stage.

'Wait a minute. What does he mean, exactly the same way? You're not another bally ventriloquist act, are you?' Mr Apple hissed, standing in front of us.

'Get out of their way!' said Bertie furiously, and he pulled him to one side.

I rushed on stage, five beats too late, as the audience started to murmur. I decided to exploit the situation. Instead of launching straight into the act, I stopped, acted totally startled, peered out into the audience, and then made my mouth a round O of astonishment.

'Hello! Are you *all* guests at my party? I'm sorry I wasn't here to greet you. I was upstairs, in the littlest room, doing what little girls have to do.'

The audience rocked with laughter. Diamond clutched me, surprised because I'd launched into a brand-new script. I patted her reassuringly, hoping she wouldn't panic.

'I am Emerald and it's my birthday today. Mama said I could have lots of people to my party, but I didn't realize she meant *this* many! There are lots and lots and *lots* of you. This is my best birthday present – my new dolly, Diamond. Isn't she pretty? Just like a real little girl. I wish she was!'

The audience laughed knowingly, realizing what was coming. I hoped some still weren't sure, wondering if Diamond really was a doll.

It was easy after that. We'd won them over. When Diamond spoke at last, in her expressionless chant, they all exclaimed delightedly. I lost all sense of time and place. We were simply Emerald and Diamond in the bright limelight, and I was tingling all over, because our act was working.

I'd seen how Lily Lark involved the audience, chatting to one gentleman in particular, and then to one lady. I copied this, only I called the man Papa and the lady Mamma. I stressed the double *m*. I didn't want to call some stranger the precious name Mama. It worked a treat, bringing them into the act while everyone waited to hear how they'd respond. Then a lad in the gallery called something. I didn't even properly hear what it was, but I quickly told the audience, 'Oh, that's my big brother Fred. Take no notice of him! He's forever plaguing me.' It won me another laugh.

I didn't dare milk the situation for too long. I knew Mrs Ruby was strict about timings so the show didn't drag on, and all the artistes had their fair turn. I started the pocket-money routine, emphasizing the words *penny* and *farthing*, and then fetched the machine and rode it onto the stage. Diamond was dancing around, holding her skirts out and looking pretty as a picture, but her eye was on me. With split-second timing she ran forward, leaping up as I pedalled to the right spot, where she could land perfectly on my shoulders!

The audience clapped hard, clearly taken aback. I heard Diamond give a little gasp of pleasure. Well, they were in for a bigger surprise. I wheeled us about, while Diamond held her arms out, gripping me hard with her knees, and then we worked up to her handstand at the end of the act. She did it beautifully, and then managed to free one hand to wave as I pedalled off.

There was such applause! We'd had ovations at the circus, but we'd never experienced anything like this great roar of noise. We listened in the wings, trembling with excitement. Then we heard Samson Ruby shouting, 'Wasn't that spectacular, ladies and gents? I'm sure you'd like our Little Stars to run on and take a bow!'

We didn't need to be told twice. We left the penny-farthing and ran on stage, hand in hand. I didn't have to tell Diamond what to do. She curtsied like a little fairy, and I did too, while the clapping and cheers made us reel. Then we skipped off, waving. Diamond did one perfect forward flip just as she reached the curtain, a bit of showmanship that made me laugh.

Benjamin Apple wasn't laughing. He was still in the wings, looking furious. 'How dare you come here and make a mockery of my act! You don't have any ventriloquist skills whatsoever. You're just poking fun at my performance. Yours is a complete parody!' he spat.

'That's the entire point, Mr Apple,' I said. 'It *is* a parody – and a homage to your great performance. It's a traditional thing to do in the circus. Clowns come after all the biggest talent and try to copy their skills. It makes you look even more talented, don't you see?'

'Do you think I'm a fool? You can sweet-talk me all

you like, but I know an evil little upstart when I see one. How dare you come skipping in here with your simpers and silliness and make a fool of me!' he spluttered.

'You're making a fool of *yourself*, Apple,' said Bertie. 'The girls were brilliant in their own right, and you know it. Well done, Hetty, well done, little Twinkle. You really are stars!'

'Stars! They're slum children off the street with a few slick tricks, that's all they are,' said Benjamin Apple.

'You say that again and you'll get my fist connecting with your big mouth,' said Bertie.

'If anyone says any more, they'll get my kid boot up their backside!' said Mrs Ruby, who had come scurrying down from her box. 'Shut up, the lot of you! Bertie, simmer down – less of the threats. Apple, you've done your turn, so clear off to your digs with your little chap and get over your peevishness by tomorrow or you'll find yourself out on your ear. Right! Little girls, come with me, and take that penny-farthing with you or we'll all be going farce over fit, if you get my rhyming slang.'

We followed her.

'I'm sorry about the noise just now, Mrs Ruby,' I said, struggling with the penny-farthing. 'But it wasn't really our fault.'

'Oh yes it was!' she replied.

'But – but . . .' I spluttered. I'd had too many years in the Foundling Hospital to know you never ever told tales, but this seemed monstrously unfair.

'Cat got your tongue?' said Mrs Ruby. 'You had plenty to say on stage!'

'Did we go on too long?'

'Yes, you did! You were nearly ten minutes over, a cardinal sin where I'm concerned. And then there was the extra minute when you milked the applause.'

'But we were called back!'

'Of course you were. I gave my Samson a nod to do just that. I know success when I see it. And that's why all the other artistes were so over-excited one way or another. Old Benjamin grew as green and sour as a cooking apple! You've pipped his little performance.'

'We didn't mean to!'

'Didn't you? Well, for your information, little Miss Innocent, you two ran away with the whole show. I knew you'd look sweet on stage, and the penny-farthing acrobatics are a clever idea, but I didn't realize how you two would come alive. And tonight's audience is as sticky as treacle, I'm telling you. Poor Peter Perkins died a death and the others didn't do much better.'

'Bertie did,' Diamond piped up.

'Yes, little Bertie worked his charms, as always. He's clearly very smitten with you, Emerald Star. He seems to have a penchant for little green girls, our Bertie.'

I quivered at that. *Ivy Green!*

'You two are a big success. I'm very pleased with you. I might well put you on in the second act. It's a bit saggy at the moment, with that interminable ballet. I've got some adjustments to make. But you need a better spot – and it looks like it had better be far removed from Benjamin Apple or he'll get so het up he'll bake himself. Now, off you go – and well done!'

'Can't we watch the rest of the show, Mrs Ruby?' I asked.

'No, you girls need to go home and get your beauty sleep. Look at this little one.' Mrs Ruby put her hand under Diamond's chin and tilted her head.

I saw the dark shadows under her eyes and didn't argue any further.

'See you tomorrow, girls. Pedal carefully. You're a valuable asset!' said Mrs Ruby.

'What's a valuable asset?' Diamond asked sleepily, clutching me as we wobbled back to Miss Gibson's.

'Us!' I said. 'We really are Little Stars, Diamond. We're the stars of the whole show!'

10

WE WERE STILL NERVOUS the next night – more so, in fact, because we'd been such a hit on our opening night. Perhaps we'd simply had beginner's luck, and we'd never be as good ever again. But we were, we were! The applause was still deafening and Samson Ruby called us back to take our bow.

We were circus girls and used to performing day after day, night after night, but by the Saturday we were both exhausted. Diamond was looking permanently pale and peaky, with shadows under her eyes. Now that we'd been promoted to the second act, we were at the theatre until ten, and Diamond often wasn't asleep until eleven at night, which was certainly much too late for a small girl.

I made her take a nap after lunch on Saturday. She slept all afternoon while I stitched away, fashioning Mrs Ruby's free frock. (Miss Gibson was an angel and helped me with all the extra-tricky parts.)

Diamond still seemed exhausted when I woke her. I brought her a bowl of bread and milk, with sugar sprinkled on top. We couldn't eat a proper meal before a performance in case we were sick, and Diamond had to have a near-empty stomach to manage all her acrobatics.

She could only manage a few spoonfuls, even when I tried to feed her. 'I'm not hungry, Hetty. I'm just so sleepy,' she said, rubbing her eyes. 'Can I go back to bed now?'

'No, darling, we've got to wash and brush you and get you all gussied up in your costume for the performance,' I said.

'I'm a bit tired of performing,' she sighed. 'We've done it so much. Couldn't we stay at home today?'

'You know we can't. It's Saturday, the Cavalcade's big night. Mrs Ruby says there isn't a seat to be had. We must go, whether we want to or not. We have to show we're true professionals.' I gently pulled her out of bed.

She stood before me in her skimpy nightgown, shivering. 'I wish I didn't have to be a true professional,' she said. 'I want to be a real little girl.'

'You are real, silly! Well, you have to pretend to be a doll, but that's just play-acting. You do *know* that, don't you?' I said worriedly.

Diamond nodded wearily. 'Of course. It's all right, Hetty. I'll come. I'll do the show.'

'Everyone thinks we're wonderful. Well, everyone except Mr Apple and his weird little dummy. *I am Little Pip and I copy everything my papa does.*' I mimicked his strange squeaky voice, hoping Diamond would laugh.

She smiled politely but still looked very wan.

'Diamond, I know you're very tired now, but you do *like* performing, don't you?' I asked.

Diamond looked uncertain.

'You like doing our penny-farthing routine better than doing the human column with the Silver Tumblers?' I persisted.

'Oh yes! Much better,' said Diamond. 'And no Mister beating me!'

I didn't enquire further as I washed her face and helped her dress and brushed the tangles out of her hair. I told myself that Diamond was simply in a contrary mood because she was over-tired. Of course she liked performing. She'd been out on the streets turning cartwheels for pennies when she was scarcely more than a baby. She didn't have a cruel master now. I knew she loved receiving applause at the end of our performance. She skipped, she smiled, she waved her hands.

I wouldn't admit even to myself that there was now something mechanical about Diamond's behaviour on stage, as if she really *were* a doll moving by clockwork trickery. Deep down, she really would prefer an ordinary little girl's life.

But then where would that leave me? I'd devised our act, but I knew that Diamond was the real star – she could perform amazing acrobatics, she could pass for a five- or six-year-old, and she was incredibly pretty, like a little fairy. I was a plain skinny redhead with no extraordinary skills whatsoever, just the gift of the gab. I couldn't be a music-hall artiste without Diamond.

I worried all the way to the Cavalcade. Diamond slumped behind me on the penny-farthing, dozing again. But when we got to the theatre, she perked up at last, and chatted happily to Bertie. I told him that she was feeling a little off-colour, so he was especially charming and gentle, pretending that she was little Cinderella and he was the handsome prince. He even danced with her at a pretend ball, though there was scarcely any room to move in the wings.

The waiting ballet dancers thought this charming, and showed Diamond how to point her feet and stand on tiptoe, but Sven the Sword-Swallower objected.

'I have to concentrate and prepare my throat,' he said. 'Keep the wee girls away from me, Bertie.'

He was no more foreign than Signor Olivelli. He was actually Sam McTavish from Glasgow. He used to work the Scottish halls as Bagpipe Mac, but those tartan acts were two a penny, so he'd come down south and tried something different. He shared Bertie's digs and was a nice enough fellow, often giving Diamond and me very sweet sugary lumps called 'tablet', but he was always edgy before a performance. I could understand. If his sword went awry, he could easily slice a strip off his throat or perforate his stomach.

I pulled Diamond away from Bertie and made her stand still beside me.

'Oh, poor Bertie. You've lost your Cinderella. Shall I have a little dance with you instead?' said Ivy Green.

She was the other disadvantage of being in the second act. We had to wait beside her in the wings. She pretended to make a fuss of Diamond, treating her as if she really were five, talking in such a silly voice. She scarcely said a word to me. She whispered incessantly to Bertie, snuggling up close to him, holding onto his arm. He made no attempt to shake her off.

I told myself that I was the girl he'd kissed in the woods. I was the girl he called his sweetheart. I was the girl who saw him every day, not just at the theatre. We never went anywhere without Diamond, but as she skipped along between us, we often exchanged meaningful looks over her head – and whenever she was distracted we blew each other kisses.

Bertie regularly kept us company at Miss Gibson's. He played cards with Diamond and watched me sew. Miss Gibson usually invited him to stay to tea. We sat on faded velvet sofas in the old-fashioned parlour, crammed with ornaments and vases and little tables on tottery legs. It was as if we were posing for a painting: young mother and father nodding at each other, small daughter playing with her rag doll, grandmama presiding over the teapot.

Bertie seemed devoted to me, so why did I feel a sharp pain in my chest whenever Ivy Green fluttered her eye-lashes at him?

Bertie knew, which made it worse. 'You mustn't get so worked up, Hetty,' he said. 'Ivy's just a friend.'

'I'm not the slightest bit worked up,' I said furiously. 'And you've a habit of making "friends" of your work-mates. What about those two girls you were forever flirting with in that draper's shop?'

'Oh my Lord, we were all silly children then,' said Bertie loftily, though it was only last year. 'Ivy's a fellow artiste and I'm part of her act. That's why we're friendly. She wants to be your friend too. I don't see why you're always so standoffish with her.'

I had spent my childhood surrounded by girls. Ivy

didn't fool me. She might smile and tell me in a little breathless voice that she thought our act *utterly terrific*, but I knew she wished we'd pack our bags and clear off.

Standing in the wings with her now was torture. She watched Diamond yawn and rub her eyes. 'Oh dear, little Diamond looks tired out! And she's so pale – or is that just this weird half-light? She looks like a little ghost to me!' she said, all mock sympathy.

'She's absolutely fine, aren't you, Diamond,' I hissed, although I was so concerned myself.

'Yes, I'm absolutely fine,' Diamond repeated obediently, with another yawn.

'Oh, the poor little pet. You've certainly got her trained, Emerald. She's like a little parrot,' said Ivy. 'It's a hard life for such a tiny girl. Do you have to do everything Emerald says, Diamond?'

Diamond didn't reply – she simply looked worried.

'Of course she doesn't,' said Bertie. 'You're a little princess, aren't you, Diamond, and you do exactly as you wish. In fact, you give the orders. How can I please you, your royal highness?'

Diamond giggled, happy again. 'You can please me by giving me a kiss, Master Bertie,' she said.

'Delighted, ma'am,' said Bertie, and he clicked his heels together, picked up her hand and planted a kiss upon it.

'You see,' I said, nodding to Ivy. 'Diamond's having the time of her life.'

'Well, Bertie certainly knows how to cheer her up. But if she were *my* sister I'd want her fast asleep, tucked up in bed at this hour,' said Ivy, and she shook her head and tutted infuriatingly.

It was as if she'd jinxed us. Diamond was indeed fine when we started our performance. She played the dolly routine perfectly, never muddling her responses, and managing the synchronized neck turning and eye rolling expertly. She did her little routine while I rushed to fetch the penny-farthing. She watched carefully as I pedalled around the stage, squinting slightly. I realized for the first time what a huge effort it was for her to spring right up in the air and land with such precision.

She was so keyed up, she started running a beat too early. I tried to slow my pedalling, but I didn't adjust quickly enough. Diamond sprang up – and just missed. She thumped against my back instead, sending us both sprawling.

There was a gasp from the audience.

'Are you all right?' I whispered.

'I – I think so,' Diamond said, stunned.

'Then let's make them think it's part of the act,' I said.

I sat up, rubbing myself. 'Ouch!' I said. I nodded slightly at Diamond.

'Ouch!' she said in her dolly voice, copying me.

'I don't think I wound you up enough!' I said. 'Let's try again.'

I stood up and helped Diamond to her feet. 'Poor floppy dolly, I haven't broken you, have I? Move your arms like this.'

I waved my arms, and Diamond copied. 'Now your legs,' I said, doing a little walk in a circle.

Diamond did the same, her gait doll-stiff.

'Good dolly! Right, stand still.' I made a big play of winding her up further, making loud clicking noises. 'There, that should do it. Let's try again for all the lovely guests at my party,' I said, pulling the penny-farthing upright.

Thank goodness the wheels hadn't buckled! I climbed on again and pedalled round and round. Diamond watched carefully while the whole audience held its breath, willing her to manage it this time. Then she took off at exactly the right moment and landed perfectly, like a little feather, on my shoulders.

The crowd went wild, clapping and cheering. Diamond managed the headstand too, and there was such applause at the end of our act that Samson Ruby had to call us back twice to take our bows.

'My, that was a dicky moment!' said Mrs Ruby, bobbing down from her box. 'But you worked it like a true professional, Miss Emerald Star. I wouldn't try that one too often, but you certainly got away with it tonight! Well done. Here's your week's wages.' She handed over a brown envelope. 'I normally give them out at the end of the show, but there's no need for you two to hang around. Take the little girly home and have a good rest tomorrow. Thank God for Sundays!'

I tucked the envelope down my neck and put my arm round Diamond. 'There now, let's go home. We'll just say a quick goodbye to Bertie. I wonder if we'll all go on another picnic tomorrow?' I said. Diamond would like that. She'd forget all about the Cavalcade for a day and relax and be a little girl again.

But Ivy Green was hanging on Bertie's arm, whispering in his ear. His head was bent, intent on listening. It didn't even look as if he'd been watching us on stage! He was certainly unaware of us now. And he was smiling. Smiling at Ivy Green!

'Come on, Diamond,' I said quickly.

'But we haven't said goodbye to Bertie!' She tried waving at him, but he didn't see her.

'Bertie's busy,' I said shortly. 'Come *on*.'

Diamond came with me, but she was so silent on the way home that I thought she'd fallen asleep again. Miss Gibson made us cocoa and hot buttered toast, two special treats, but Diamond only sipped her drink and chewed on a crust.

'She's still tired, poor lamb,' said Miss Gibson. 'Up the little wooden stairs to Bedfordshire for you, little Diamond.'

I undressed her and examined her carefully by the

light of the candle, worried she might have hurt herself when we took a tumble. She had a couple of red marks on her legs that might well be bruises by the morning, but nothing serious at all. I tucked her up in bed, then checked the money in the envelope. Ten whole shillings, just as Mrs Ruby had promised.

I pulled off my clothes and jumped into bed beside Diamond. 'We're rich girls now,' I said. 'Night-night, darling.' I blew the candle out.

We curled up together. Diamond usually went sound asleep straight away, but tonight she lay hot and tense. When I reached for her hand, I discovered it was clenched into a little fist.

'Hey, what's the matter, Diamond?' I whispered.

'Nothing,' said Diamond, but then she started crying.

'Oh dear, come on, tell me,' I said, putting my arms round her.

'I did it all wrong, Hetty. And we fell in front of everyone,' she sobbed.

'Yes, but it didn't matter in the slightest because the audience still loved us. Didn't you hear them when you did the trick all over again? They thought you were wonderful.'

'Yes, but you must never ever fall. Mister beat me if I fell.'

'Yes, but that was just Mister hateful Beppo. We're never, ever going to see him again.'

'I know,' said Diamond, but she didn't sound certain. She snuffled into her doll, Maybelle, rubbing her against her cheek.

'You'll be getting a new doll soon,' I said. 'In fact, we *could* go and buy her on Monday, though it would use up all our money.'

'I'd like a new doll, but I don't want to hurt Maybelle's feelings,' Diamond whispered, as if Maybelle herself might hear. Then she said, still very softly, 'I think Bertie is cross with me because I fell.'

'No he isn't! Not at all. He thinks you did wonderfully,' I said.

'But he didn't say so.'

'I know. He was too busy listening to that Green girl. No wonder she's called herself Ivy. Did you see the way she was clinging to him! She was practically winding herself all over him,' I said crossly.

'Does he like her more than us?'

'I don't know. Maybe. Maybe not. It's just his way. He'll flirt with anyone. Goodness, he even flirts with Miss Gibson!'

'I wish people didn't chop and change so much,' said Diamond.

'I know. I do too,' I said, though I was very aware that *I* chopped and changed, never quite settling, never quite satisfied. 'Now, let's go to sleep, Diamond. It's Sunday tomorrow. No performance.'

'But maybe no Bertie,' Diamond muttered mournfully.

'Oh goodness, who needs Bertie?' I said.

But I lay awake a long time, tormented by images of Bertie and Ivy Green entwined. Diamond slept fitfully, and was awake again before dawn. I woke to find her crouching by the mirror, peering at herself by the light of the candle.

'Careful! Watch your hair! Goodness, I wish you wouldn't light that candle by yourself,' I said, leaping out of bed. 'What are you doing?'

'I'm seeing if I really look like a ghost,' said Diamond.

'Take no notice of that stupid Ivy – she was talking nonsense. You're just a bit pale, that's all,' I said. 'We just need to put the roses back in your cheeks.'

Sea air!

The words suddenly came into my head. Was it Mama? Was it me? It didn't matter. It was a truly excellent idea!

11

'**I'M TAKING YOU TO** the seaside, Diamond,' I said. 'If we get up now, quiet as little mice so as not to wake Miss Gibson, we might well catch the milk train. We'll ask the man in the ticket office about the connections. I want to take you to the best seaside ever!'

'Are we running away again?' she asked.

'No, this is going to be a special day trip. It will make us feel so much better. Have you ever seen the sea? It's so wonderful – so big. We'll run on the sand and paddle and maybe ride a donkey. And then I will take you to the most special place ever! Just you wait and see.'

We got dressed and I cut us slices of bread and jam and filled a bottle with water to drink on the train. I put our wages in my purse. I also pocketed a tape measure and some scraps from bolts of material on Miss Gibson's shelves.

'What are they for?' asked Diamond.

'You'll see! Now, I'd better write Miss Gibson a note to explain where we've gone,' I said.

'Shouldn't we invite her to come to the seaside too?'

'No, she's still asleep. And she'll want to go to church. This is a special outing just for you and me,' I said, hurriedly scribbling a few sentences.

'And Bertie?'

'Oh, bother Bertie. We don't need him. We'll go and have a lovely time, just us. Come on!'

Diamond started hurrying. There was something about her automatic obedience that worried me. *Does she have to do everything you say?* I hated Ivy Green!

'You don't have to come to the seaside if you don't want to,' I said, when Diamond rushed back from the outside privy.

She stopped short, looking worried. 'Don't you want to any more, Hetty?'

'Yes.'

'Then I do too.'

'Yes, but you don't *have* to do everything I do. You can argue or shout back or tell me I'm stupid. If you want.'

Diamond blinked at me. 'Is that what you want me to do?'

'Oh, I give up! Come on then. Seaside, here we come!'

It was a much longer journey than I remembered, but Diamond enjoyed the train ride itself, standing at the door, hanging onto the window strap and peering out at the countryside.

'We're going so fast!' she kept shouting, above the noise of the train.

'Fast-to-the-sea! Fast-to-the-sea!' I sang, to the rhythm of the clacking wheels. After a few minutes all the folk crammed into our third-class carriage started singing it too.

We'd eaten our jam sandwich and drunk our water within half an hour, but everybody else had great picnic hampers, and generously shared them round. Diamond and I feasted on chicken legs and pork pies and mutton pasties and custard tarts. We wouldn't need any lunch when we got to the seaside – maybe just a hokey-pokey ice cream or two!

We drew in to the last station on the line.

'Bignor-on-Sea! Bignor-on-Sea! Your journey ends here, ladies and gentlemen. Please vacate the train!' the porters shouted.

'Bignor?' said Diamond. 'Oh, Hetty! This is where you lived once, isn't it? And your mama.'

'Yes, my lovely mama lived here too . . .' I swallowed.

I live in your heart now, my Hetty.

'Will you be sad now?' Diamond asked softly.

'No, I'm going to be very happy showing you the seaside,' I said.

I took Diamond's hand and we walked out of the crowded station, down the street, round the corner – and there was the sea spread out before us, blue-grey and glistening, the crest of the waves whipped white in the breeze.

'Oooooh!' Diamond gasped.

'Look to the left. Look to the right. Sea, all sea,' I said.

'Isn't it wonderful! And all the yellow carpet.'

'That's sand, lovely soft sand.'

'People are walking on it.'

'We'll walk on it too. Take your shoes and socks off. I will too.'

We sat on the steps baring our feet, and then jumped down from the promenade onto the beach.

'Oh, it feels funny!' said Diamond, curling her toes and waddling weirdly.

'Let's run.'

We raced backwards and forwards. The wind seized my hair and unravelled half my careful topknot, so I let it all free. It flew about my head like a red flag. Then we went right down to the damp dark sand at the very edge of the sea. Diamond went rushing forward, and then squealed because she hadn't expected the sea to be so very cold.

'It'll get warmer in a minute. We'll paddle together,' I said.

We waded in the shallows, watching bolder swimmers emerging from the bathing machines and taking an all-over dip.

'Don't they look funny in their combinations!' cried Diamond.

'You could do with some yourself. Look at your dress – it's soaking!'

'Oh dear,' said Diamond, flapping it worriedly.

'It's all right, it'll dry in the sun. Look at those donkeys! Would you like a ride on a donkey, Diamond?'

The rides were only for children, but I was small enough to pass as a child myself. I waited to ride the donkey I'd always chosen, the little grey one called Polly with a cross on her back. She gave me a little whinnying greeting, almost as if she remembered me. Diamond picked one called Rosie, and whispered to her lovingly all the way up the beach and back.

Then we went to the hokey-pokey cart and chose two vanilla ice creams with strawberry sauce.

'This is the best food ever!' said Diamond, licking extravagantly.

She got ice cream all down the front of her dress, but I didn't tell her in case she started worrying. She looked so happy now. The dark circles under her eyes were fading and her cheeks were pink again.

'I like Bignor better than anywhere else in the world,' she declared. 'Can't we come and live here, Hetty?'

'Maybe one day,' I said. 'Shall I show you the house I'd like to live in? It's very pretty.'

I didn't need to consult the big map of the town on the promenade. I'd never forget the way. We walked along the rose-pink pavement, down Victoria Avenue, all the way to Saltdean Lane. There were all the pretty villas painted cream and apricot and lilac, with bright window boxes and tubs of flowers.

'Oh yes, I love these little houses!' said Diamond. 'Which one shall we choose? Could we maybe have the very pale purple one?'

'We *could* – but wait till you see number eighteen,' I told her.

It was painted cream with a blue door, and there were the pink hydrangeas on either side, looking so fresh and pretty.

'Oh yes, this one's lovely! I wonder what it's like inside,' said Diamond.

'It's crammed full of knick-knacks and it's all rather old-fashioned and dark and stuffy because the owner is a mean old lady who doesn't care for anyone but herself

– but when we move in, we can make it beautiful. We shall just own a few beautiful things and have modern cotton curtains in designs by Mr William Morris because we'll be very artistic ladies,' I declared. 'We'll change every room except one – the little attic room right at the top of the house.'

'Why won't we change that one?'

'Because that's where Mama slept,' I said quietly.

'Oh, Hetty.' Diamond put her hand in mine.

'She's sleeping all the time now. Shall I show you where?'

Diamond nodded doubtfully. 'Is it a graveyard?' she asked.

'Yes, it is. I need to go there, just to say hello to Mama, but you don't have to come if the idea frightens you. I can leave you sitting on the seafront with another ice cream and then come back and collect you.'

I thought she'd jump at this, but she shook her head. 'I'll come with you,' she said.

The graveyard was cool and quiet after the sunny hurly-burly of the seafront. Great yew trees towered on either side of the lych gate, showing that we were entering the land of the dead. Stone angels balanced on grave-stones, their wings outspread.

Diamond shivered when she saw them. 'Has your mama got an angel?' she asked.

'No, I couldn't afford one. But she has a proper headstone,' I said proudly.

I'd had to work for many weeks at Mr Clarendon's Seaside Curiosities before I saved enough money. It was a simple white stone, but I asked if the stonecutter could possibly carve a small violet at either top corner, and he'd done just that. The carving said: EVIE EDENSHAW (IDA BATTERSEA), BELOVED MOTHER OF HETTY FEATHER. Then the date of her birth and death, and finally two more words: SORELY MISSED.

Oh, *so* sorely missed! I knelt down in front of the stone and tried to imagine Mama beneath me, lying in her white nightgown.

'I love you so, Mama,' I whispered. I closed my eyes, but tears trickled down my cheeks.

Diamond dabbed at them very carefully with the sleeve of her dress and then put her arm round me.

I hadn't thought to bring any flowers and I didn't feel I could trail Diamond all the way back to the town to buy any. I searched the path nearby for little white pebbles instead, Diamond helping me. When we had enough, I spelled out a few words in front of Mama's gravestone: I LOVE YOU MAMA.

Diamond read them out slowly. 'That's lovely, Hetty.'

'Perhaps one day we'll go and find *your* mama and we can spell out a message for her too,' I said, standing up and stretching. 'Do you know where she is buried?'

'It was at the church near home. She loved going to church, my ma. But I don't want to go back to find her, in case Pa sees me,' said Diamond. 'I don't want to see my brothers either because they always plagued me. I'd quite like to see Mary-Martha because she was a kind big sister, but I love you much more, Hetty. I don't think I want any family but you.'

'I shall always be a sister to you, I promise,' I told her.

'This is your very special place, isn't it, Hetty,' she said.

'Yes, it is.'

'So do we have to go back home now?' she asked.

'No, not yet. We're going visiting. I have a friend here in Bignor.'

'Really! Is she in one of those pretty houses?'

'No, she lives in a very strange place. At least, I hope she will still be there. Let's find out.'

We left the quiet graveyard. I stopped at the lych gate and turned to wave at Mama. Diamond waved too. Then we made our way back to the seafront and walked along the promenade to the red-and-white striped tent right at the end.

'No!' said Diamond, stopping still. 'I don't want to go there! There will be clowns!'

'It's not a circus, I promise, Diamond. Look, see the notice. Spell it out.'

Diamond tried, but she had problems with words of more than one syllable.

'It says *Mr Clarendon's Seaside Curiosities*,' I said.

'Now, you mustn't be frightened. There are some extra-ordinary people inside and they look very strange, but they are all perfectly fine. I worked there myself for a while.'

'But you don't look strange, Hetty.'

'I dressed up as Emerald the Amazing Pocket-Sized Mermaid. I cut up my best green dress to make a mermaid tail. I had to lie on a little mound of sand and comb my hair.'

'Did folk think you were a *real* mermaid?'

'Probably not. They just used to like to stare at me.'

'And all you had to do was comb your hair? You didn't have to say any lines or do any tricks? I should like to be a mermaid!' said Diamond.

'Prepare to be truly amazed!' wafted along the promenade.

'Who's saying that? And why does it sound so funny?' asked Diamond, looking around.

'It's Mr Clarendon and he's speaking through a loudhailer – that's why it sounds so tinny.'

'I can't see him!'

'That man all in red, to match his tent.'

'Oh my goodness. He's even got a red bowler hat! He sounds funny and he looks funny,' said Diamond.

'If you think Mr Clarendon looks strange, wait till you see all the living curiosities,' I said. 'But promise you won't say anything to hurt anyone's feelings.'

We approached the tent. Mr Clarendon spotted me, stopped yelling into his loudhailer, and did a theatrical double take. 'Oh my, it's Miss Emerald Mermaid herself!'

'I've two legs and no tail at all,' I said.

'I'd know that red hair anywhere! It's good to see you, girl. And who have we here? Oh, what a picture. I can just see it now – little Snowdrop, our Living Fairy!'

'I used to have wings and a fairy wand,' said Diamond obligingly.

'There you are then! How about a little tableau – two beautiful mythical creatures for the price of one? *That* would pull the crowds. I'd pay you royally, of course.'

'I'm sorry, Mr Clarendon, we're in another line of business now. We're music-hall artistes,' I said proudly. 'We're here to see Freda. She is still part of the show, isn't she?'

'She is indeed. My top draw – though you rivalled her while you were here. Sure you don't want to change your mind? I've heard the music hall can be very gruelling, whereas here you could be a little lady of leisure reclining on your sand.'

'I'm afraid you can't tempt me, Mr Clarendon.' I stepped into the tent, pulling Diamond with me.

'That will be sixpence each, please,' he said.

'What?' I said, astonished. 'You're going to charge us?'

'You're here to see my Curiosities, aren't you? Well,

one of them. Look, I'll let you in for sixpence the pair – that's children's rate.'

I sighed and handed him sixpence, then took Diamond inside, past the first little seaside section of shells and stuffed fish, through to the living exhibits. I led her past Henry, the Man with One Hundred Tattoos and Pirate Pete, Scourge of the Seven Seas. They both nodded at me. Diamond held my hand tight.

We hurried to the next partition and, oh joy, there was my dear friend Fantastic Freda, the Female Giant. She was standing on her upturned bucket to make her look even taller, wearing the special dress I'd made for her.

'Oh, Freda, dear Freda!' I cried.

'Emerald!' She stepped down from her bucket, bent down and picked me up in her great hands.

'Don't drop her!' Diamond said.

Freda cradled me gently in her burly arms. 'I've missed you so, my dear friend,' she said.

'She's *my* dear friend now,' Diamond insisted.

'Yes, this is Diamond, Freda.'

'Hello, my dear. My, aren't you little and pretty! And so is my *new* dear friend. Please let me introduce you,' said Freda.

She set me down very carefully and led us to the next partition. She had to bend down to get through. We followed her – and there was a minute little person sitting cross-legged on a rug. At first I thought she was a tiny child, even though she was dressed in a fashionable gown and her hair was in a bun. But when I looked at her face closely, I saw that she was actually a grown woman, though of course she had scarcely grown at all. Even Diamond towered above her.

'Meet Lucy Locket, the Littlest Woman in the World,' Freda announced proudly. 'Lucy, this is Emerald, who used to be the Amazing Pocket-Sized Mermaid here, and was always so kind to me. She made me my beautiful dress!'

'Pleased to meet you,' said Lucy Locket, holding out her tiny hand. Her voice was as little as her person, and very pleasant.

I shook her hand warmly. 'This is my friend Diamond,' I said.

'*Dear* friend,' Diamond corrected, but she shook hands politely.

'Freda's told me so many stories about you, Emerald. When we can't get to sleep at night, I always ask for another tale about you. You were very kind to my Freda,' said Lucy Locket.

I was so happy that Freda had found such a good friend now. I'd always been worried that she would be lonely after I left Clarendon's.

'And her dress is exquisite! I had to have my costume specially made for me and it cost a fortune, but Freda said her gown was a gift,' said Lucy.

'Yes indeed – and I'm here to measure Freda for *another* gown,' I said. 'I promised to make it a long time ago.'

'You're going to measure me? Why, do you think I've grown!' said Freda, joking easily about her size.

I wondered how I was going to get Freda's correct upper measurements, but Lucy kept a stepladder in the corner of her booth so she could reach things, and this came in very handy. It seemed rude to ignore Lucy, so I offered *her* a new gown too, and took her weeny little measurements as well. I showed them the samples of material. They both liked the same print – white with red cherries.

'But we can't really have the same,' said Lucy wistfully. 'You have the cherry print, Freda.'

'No no, my dear, it will suit you much better. It will look enchanting. You must have it,' said Freda.

'Why don't you both have the cherries? They will be wonderful for work – red and white to match the awning of the tent. And then, when you are strolling down the promenade together, you will be a walking advertisement for the Curiosities. Mr Clarendon will be thrilled,' I said.

I was fully aware that the dresses were going to be a challenge, and I was only halfway through Mrs Ruby's promised gown, but I felt that Freda and Lucy deserved special new outfits. They were exceptionally grateful.

Diamond and I waited until Mr Clarendon closed the

tent at five, so his artistes could have an hour's break before the evening session. Freda and Lucy Locket insisted on taking us both to a delightful fish restaurant on the seafront. We all had cod and fried potatoes. Lucy cut her fish in half and gave it to Freda, and donated most of her fried potatoes too. We all toasted each other in ginger beer and declared firm and lasting friendship.

Then Diamond and I had to scurry back to the station to catch our train. Diamond slept for most of the journey, practically walking in her sleep when we had to change trains. But when at last I tucked her up in our own bed at Miss Gibson's, she murmured sleepily, 'Promise you'll make *me* a new dress, Hetty!'

12

I **LET DIAMOND SLEEP** late again the next morning and went downstairs for breakfast by myself.

'Good morning, Hetty,' said Miss Gibson, a little coolly. 'Do you have another day trip planned for today?'

'It's work today, Miss Gibson. Sewing all day, and the Cavalcade tonight,' I said. 'You didn't mind too much that we went to the seaside yesterday? I did leave you the note explaining I was going to introduce Diamond to a dear friend.'

'Yes, I know you did, dear. I didn't mind at all,' she said, though she sounded reproachful. 'Of course, I worried a little.'

I felt guilty, though I couldn't see why it was such a crime to take Diamond out for the day. And why should she worry? I might act like a baby in the music hall, but I was a grown girl now, fully capable of caring for one small child. I shuddered at the thought of the Foundling Hospital, but at least life had been simple there. You knew what the rules were, and if you broke them you were severely punished. You didn't have to fuss about hurting people's feelings.

'I'm sorry, Miss Gibson,' I said all the same, because I liked her and didn't want to upset her.

'Oh, it's not me you should apologize to, dear. It's your Bertie,' she said.

'He's not "my" Bertie,' I told her.

'He's your sweetheart, isn't he?'

'He's everybody's sweetheart.'

'Well, he's been a very good friend to all of us, hasn't he? Remember what a lovely time the four of us had the Sunday before last? And he was all prepared to take us out again. He came round yesterday lunch time with all kinds of plans. When he heard you two had gone off on this sudden adventure, he seemed very surprised and upset – especially when I showed him your letter,' said Miss Gibson.

'Oh, for goodness' sake! Bertie didn't *say* he was coming round on Sunday. We can't sit around all day hoping he'll put in an appearance,' I said crossly.

'You're a strange girl, Hetty,' said Miss Gibson. 'I thought you *liked* Bertie. You want to hang onto him or someone else will come along and snap him up.'

'See if I care,' I said childishly.

I *did* care, and we both knew it. I spent the day hoping that Bertie would come round, even if it was just to pick a fight with me, but he stayed away. So I stitched diligently until I'd finished Mrs Ruby's orange and gold gown. I ironed it very carefully, praying that it wouldn't shrivel or scorch, and aired it in the back yard. It still seemed a little plain for a flamboyant lady like Mrs Ruby. I'd have to add a little extra decoration – something that would sparkle in the limelight.

'You've done a lovely job on that, Hetty,' said Miss Gibson. 'We'll keep that design just for Mrs Ruby as she's my best customer and very particular about wearing a bespoke outfit, but I dare say we can adapt it a little and sell a ready-made version in the shop. You'll work on it with me, won't you, dear?'

'Yes, of course, Miss Gibson,' I said. I wondered how I was going to manage an enormous gown for Freda, a fiddly tiny gown for Lucy Locket, *and* a new dress for Diamond. I remembered dear Nurse Winterson reading us *The Tailor of Gloucester* when we were little girls, darning all afternoon at the Foundling Hospital. How I wished there were obliging little mice in the Gibson wainscot, ready to scuttle out at night and sew my dresses for me.

I tried to teach Diamond to sew, but her fingers were clumsy and her stitches uneven. She had come bouncing downstairs at ten, refreshed at last. I was so pleased to see that she still had rosy cheeks and a light suntan from her day in the fresh air. At first she seemed cheery, but became increasingly restless as the day progressed. I kept trying to set her little tasks or invent games, but she wouldn't settle.

'I wish Bertie would come visiting,' she said every ten minutes.

Miss Gibson looked meaningfully at me and raised her eyebrows, though she didn't say anything.

I made Diamond practise our act out in the yard.

'*Again?*' she said, but she went through it all obediently, and managed the leap onto my shoulders perfectly.

We set off for the Cavalcade at half past seven. As we rode along on the penny-farthing, some lads called out, 'Hey, there's the Little Stars! Good luck, girls!'

'They know who we are!' said Diamond.

Two women pointed at us too, and one said, 'There's those clever little kiddies from the Cavalcade!'

'We're famous, Diamond!' I said.

Diamond wanted to go straight to the wings when we got there, to see Bertie perform.

'You've seen him do his act lots of times. And you'll see him in the second act too, with Ivy Green. We're much better off staying in the dressing room. We'll only get in the way. And I'd sooner keep clear of Mr Apple just now,' I said.

Diamond pouted but did as she was told. We waited with the ballet dancers. They all made rather a fuss of Diamond and showed her how to do the five basic foot positions, and then a few simple twirls. They laughed with delight when she picked them up almost immediately.

'Hey, hey, less noise in here, girls,' said Mrs Ruby, putting her head round the door. 'Ah, the Little Stars. I see you're learning another party piece, Diamond. Very pretty. Mind you manage your little penny-farthing trick tonight, dear. You both carried it off splendidly, but I don't want you to make a habit of it, understand?'

'Perfectly, Mrs Ruby. And we'll *be* perfect, I promise,' I said.

All the same I had a little knot of anxiety in my stomach. When the bell went for the start of the second act, I suddenly wanted to grab Diamond and bolt from the Cavalcade altogether. I thought of that little cream villa with the pink hydrangeas in Bignor. I could set myself up as a gown-maker and build up a business just like Miss Gibson's. *Miss Feather's Fancy Fashions.* We would see our friends Freda and Lucy every day, walk on the promenade in the evening, and I would have a quiet word with Mama as often as I wanted.

I'd left the penny-farthing at the stage door with grumpy Stan. We could jump on it and pedal off at top speed. But we didn't, of course. I wheeled it into the wings while Diamond squeezed through the queue of waiting artistes to find Bertie.

Samson Ruby was at the back of the wings too, kissing one of the dancing girls. He didn't seem at all abashed when I came upon them. He sent her on her way with a proprietary slap on the backside. It didn't hurt her and she just laughed. I was the one who winced.

Samson saw and laughed at me. 'There! That's what you get if you're a naughty girl,' he said.

'Well, I'm exceptionally good so you'll never have cause to lay a finger on me,' I said, parking my penny-farthing.

'Oh, you're a sharp little miss and no mistake. I bet you've got a temper too, with that bright red mane.' Samson reached out to touch it, but I quickly tossed my hair out of his way.

'Hoity toity!' he said. 'Success gone to your head? Getting above yourself, are you?' He said it calmly, but there was an edge to his voice that bothered me. He might be a lecherous drunk, but he was also a Ruby, and second in command of the Cavalcade. If he took against us, we were done for.

'Not me,' I said. 'I'm just a little girl who's got lucky.' I spoke in my stage voice, trying to make myself seem even younger.

'Just a lickle baby, eh? So what are you doing, cavorting in front of all the crowds with that little sister of yours? Where's your ma, then? Doesn't she want to keep an eye on you?'

'She can't. She's dead,' I said, and my voice wobbled.

'Oh.' His face softened. 'Sorry to hear it.' He patted me on the shoulder. 'Run along then.'

I ran, double quick. I rubbed at my shoulder, hating the feel of his fingers, though the pat had been meant kindly. I resolved to keep right out of his way in future. I found Diamond hanging onto Bertie's hand, while he was whisper-singing his Flirty Bertie ditty to her. He glanced at me and then carried on singing, not missing a beat.

Ivy Green wasn't in the wings yet, which was a relief.

I stood there, shifting from one foot to the other, while he totally ignored me. I stuck my head in the air to show I didn't care – though of course I did.

When Bertie finished at last, he swept Diamond a deep bow and then kissed her hand, which made her giggle.

'Oh, Bertie, you're so funny,' she said.

'So, did Jem sing you a special song and kiss your hand?' asked Bertie.

'Jem?' said Diamond, puzzled.

'You know, the special dear friend of Hetty's who you saw yesterday.' There was an edge to Bertie's voice.

Oh my Lord, he'd seen the note I'd written to Miss Gibson and jumped to entirely the wrong conclusion!

I sighed and shook my head. 'You've got it all wrong, Bertie,' I said.

'Oh, hello, Hetty. I didn't see you standing there,' he said casually. 'You had a good time on Sunday, I take it?'

'A very good time,' I said. 'Diamond, tell Bertie all about my dear friend.'

'No thank you. I've heard quite enough about him already,' said Bertie.

'It's not a *him*,' said Diamond, giggling again. 'Hetty's friend is a lovely, very, very big lady called Freda, and she stands on a bucket and silly people come and stare at her. She's a giant. And *she* has a friend called Lucy Locket who's very, very tiny – in fact, she only comes up to Freda's kneecaps, and she's a fairy. But they get along very well, and Hetty is going to make them each a new dress and she's making me one too. I don't know which colour material to choose. What's your favourite colour, Bertie?'

Bertie was staring at her as if she'd started to talk in Jabberwocky language. 'Come again, Diamond?' he said.

'What's your favourite colour?' she repeated.

'For a dress? Puce, with blue and yellow stripes.'

'Oh, Bertie! That would look *horrid*!' Diamond squealed.

'Less noise, little 'un,' said Sven. 'I need to concentrate on my breathing exercises.'

Bertie was looking at me at last. 'Have you told her to tell me this stupid fairy tale? What sort of a fool do you take me for?'

'A prize one. It isn't a fairy tale. I took Diamond to the seaside, where I lived after I left Mr Buchanan's. For a while I worked as a mermaid in a show tent of Seaside Curiosities – a sad freak show. Freda really is a kind of giant, but a sweet lovely girl. I'd promised her a dress a while ago, so I went to take her measurements.'

'Which are *huge*!' said Diamond. 'I think Hetty will have to use a whole bolt of material.'

'So why on earth didn't you tell me where you were going on Saturday night?' said Bertie.

'You were too busy cosying up to Ivy Green,' I told him.

'What? I don't cosy up to anyone,' said Bertie. He lowered his voice even more. 'Only you,' he said quietly.

'I saw you, Bertie – whisper-whisper-whispering with her.'

'She was simply suggesting we add more comedy to her routine. She was wanting me to chase her around the stage, and it worked a treat.'

'I'll bet it did,' I said tartly.

'Oh, Hetty. We're a pair of idiots, assuming all sorts of nonsense. I was so sure you'd taken little Twinkle to meet your Jem,' said Bertie.

'I've told you and told you, he's not "my" Jem.'

'So, am I *your* Bertie?'

I hesitated.

He took hold of my nose and gave it a little pinch. 'Say yes, or I'll twist it right off!'

'Idiot! Stop it – you'll make it all red. All right, yes. Yes, do you hear me?'

'I hear you,' said Bertie, and he bent his head and quickly kissed the very tip of my nose. 'There, all better!'

And it *was* all better too, even when Ivy Green came sauntering into the wings looking sweeter than ever, a white rose in her hair and a black velvet band circling her even whiter throat. Bertie smiled pleasantly and admired her flower, but stayed by my side. When Samson Ruby announced our act, he squeezed my hand and then Diamond's to wish us luck.

'Go and twinkle, both of you,' he said.

This time it all worked perfectly. We did the dolly routine, we chattered about pennies and farthings, I fetched the vehicle, I pedalled on stage, Diamond watched and ran and landed right on my shoulders, did her handstand, we both waved, and then came off stage to rousing cheers.

'Well, you two little girls certainly are little stars!' Lily Lark was standing in the wings, still in her silk wrapper, an embroidered turban round her hair. She was smoking a black cigarette in a long holder, a picture of languid sophistication. The other artistes were standing back respectfully to give her more space.

She was so awe inspiring that I wondered if I should drop her a curtsy. Diamond did just that, holding out her skirts prettily, and Lily Lark laughed.

'Look at you – pretty as a picture! And very talented too. That's quite a trick, leaping up onto your sister's shoulders like that. Though I hear you came a cropper on Saturday?'

Diamond hung her head.

'But *you* saved the day – turned it into part of your act.' Lily Lark was looking at me. 'Did you grow up in the theatre, duckie? You certainly seem born to perform.'

I smiled at her. She'd never, ever guess I was a foundling. No chance of performing in that strict hospital! Well, there was the Christmas living tableau in the chapel, but the matrons had never picked me to take part. They *had* chosen Gideon, my foster brother. I remembered him as the Angel Gabriel, suspended in the air in his white silk robe, his face shining with joy. Then I thought of Gideon's face now, horribly cratered by a bullet, and a twist of love and pity made me wince.

'I was a circus girl. We both were,' I told Lily Lark.

'I was little Diamond, the Acrobatic Child Wonder,' added Diamond.

'And I was the child ringmaster,' I said.

'What a pair!' said Lily Lark. 'Do you miss the circus now?'

We both shook our heads vehemently.

'So you're set on stardom in the music halls, is that right?' she said. 'Thinking you'll soon take my place at the top of the bill?'

'We're only little stars, Miss Lark, not a great star like you,' I said quickly.

'You're a smooth talker – a very clever little girl. Mrs Ruby's chosen well. You're all that she says. Well, carry on the good work, girls. We'll all have to look to our laurels, for all you're acting so modest. There's a steely glint in those big blue eyes!' She laughed again and sashayed back to her dressing room, leaving an exotic aroma of Turkish cigarettes and sandalwood perfume in her wake.

'Oh, my! Fancy Lily Lark coming to have a gander at you!' said Bertie. 'You've certainly stirred things up, you two. I've never known her to put in an appearance like that before.'

'Oh, she came specially to see me when *I* first started at the Cavalcade,' said Ivy Green. 'She liked my act. She said I was a chip off the old block – meaning *her*. I took it as a great compliment.'

'She could have meant you're just copying her,' said one of the ballet girls who'd been teaching Diamond steps.

'Yes, Diamond's performance is unique. I've never seen anything like it and I've been round all the halls,' said another. 'And she's still so little too.'

I said nothing, but I smiled smugly to myself. 'Come on then, Littlest Star, we'd better get you home,' I said. 'Bye, everyone.'

Ivy Green didn't deign to respond – though Bertie blew me a kiss.

'I do like all those ballet ladies,' said Diamond as we cycled home.

'So, you like performing now?' I asked eagerly.

Diamond was silent. I couldn't turn round to look at her without wobbling.

'Didn't you hear the applause? They absolutely love us, Diamond. Especially you. You're the talented one,' I said.

'I couldn't do any of it without you, Hetty,' she said.

'But it makes you feel good, doesn't it, when it all goes well and they clap and clap?' I persisted.

'I like it – yes, I do,' said Diamond, still sounding

doubtful. 'I really liked learning ballet with those ladies in the dressing room. I'd love one of their lovely sticking-out dresses. Oh, Hetty, could you make me one of those?'

'All right, I will. Perhaps you'd like to learn ballet dancing? I mean, properly. We could maybe pay for you to have lessons. Would you like that?'

'I don't really like doing things properly. I like doing things just for fun,' said Diamond.

I sighed. 'Perhaps it's because you're still so young,' I said.

I tried to think back to when I was Diamond's age. Had I felt the same way? There'd certainly been precious little fun at the hospital. After the carefree time I'd spent with my foster family, it had all seemed so bleak. I remembered those wonderful games up in the squirrel tree with Jem. But even then I'd longed for something more, something colourful and magical, a fairy-tale world where I could somehow shine.

Tanglefield's Travelling Circus made such an impression on me when it came to our village. I still remembered every single act from the first time I watched, when I was only five. Madame Adeline was still in her prime and had her six rosin-backed horses. Something still stirred in my blood when I thought of the circus, even though I'd seen the sad and sordid side, the cruel beatings Beppo had inflicted on little

Diamond, the callous sacking of dear Madame Adeline herself.

I was so caught up in the past, I couldn't sleep that night. Diamond nodded off almost immediately, but I tossed and turned. I heard Miss Gibson making her way upstairs and bustling about her bedroom, but then there was silence.

I took my shawl, seized my suitcase, relit the candle and tiptoed down to the kitchen. It was cold and I was glad of the shawl that Lizzie had given me. The suitcase had been Sarah's. Both were dear friends from the past. I opened the suitcase and touched each precious object reverently: Mama's letters and mine back to her, *The Tale of Thumbelina*, her little violet vase, Bertie's black-and-white china dog, my silver sixpence from Jem. Then there were four precious fat notebooks: my three volumes of memoirs, and Diamond's story, which I'd copied out when the circus was at its winter quarters.

So much had happened since. I needed to start a new notebook now! I flipped through the pages of the second volume and found the first time I met Bertie. It was strange comparing that awkward young butcher's boy to Bertie now, so cocky and confident. I wondered if it was all an act and whether he was still anxious and worried about his appearance. It made me feel even fonder of him.

Then I searched for Jem. There were long passages

in every volume, right from when I was a baby. I found it surprisingly upsetting reading about our last Christmas together. I could hardly bear to turn the pages where I left Jem and ran away to join Tanglefield's as their ringmaster. And I hadn't even written to him since.

I tore out a blank page from the back of the notebook, unscrewed my pot of ink and dipped my pen. I wrote *Care of Miss Gibson* and then my new address.

Dearest Jem,

I am so sorry I haven't written sooner. I am sure you will have been wondering what has happened to me. Or perhaps not. Maybe you never think of bad little Hetty nowadays. I wouldn't blame you.

I ran away to the circus, as I am sure you realized. I hope you didn't tell poor Mother. She always disapproved of the circus so. And with good reason. I was happy for a while, but it's no place for a young girl. I was the ringmaster there. You should have seen my costume! I don't think you would have approved. I loved being the centre of attention (that won't surprise you), but it was a hard life in many ways, and some of the circus folk were very cruel. However, dear Madame Adeline (remember her? The beautiful lady in pink spangles who stood on the back of a horse?) was like another mother to me.

I also grew very close to a little girl acrobat called Diamond and did my best to look after her. I still take care of her now.

But we are not at the circus any more. As you can see from the address above, we live in Fenstone, with a kind, respectable spinster lady who has a gown shop. I make gowns too. I have become quite skilled with my needle. But this is not my profession. I am a music-hall artiste.

Please don't disapprove! The music hall is very popular in most towns, and the Cavalcade, where I work, is exceptionally admired and considered on a par with the big London establishments. We have Lily Lark topping our bill, and I'm sure folk are humming her songs even in the countryside. There are many lovely ladies who are artistes, all perfectly respectable.

I blushed a little as I wrote this, thinking of the dancing girl kissing slimy Samson in the wings. It might be better not to go into too much detail to Jem.

I have worked hard developing an act with Diamond. She is exceptionally skilled at acrobatics – and you will find this surprising, but I can ride a penny-farthing! Our act is a comedy too, a little burlesque, and it goes down very well. I hope you won't think I'm boasting, but we are practically the stars of the show. Miss Lark herself said so!

Do come and see us if ever you are passing this way. And bring Gideon too, if you think he is up to it. I know he is sadly changed, but as a boy he was very fond of performing. Or perhaps you might care to bring Janet? She was such a dear friend to me. I know she is a dear friend to you too. Perhaps you are even a married couple by now!

I thought of crossing out this sentence. It was only a joke, but it sounded a little false and heavy-handed. I had a sudden image of Jem in a light grey suit, Janet in a long white dress, hand in hand stepping out of the church, with all the villagers clapping and cheering, and the bells ringing to celebrate their wedding. It was a sweet image, my two special friends joined in matrimony – so why did it make the tears start in my eyes?

I blinked fiercely, ashamed of myself.

Please don't ever forget that I am still your very loving Hetty

I wrote the last sentence quickly, and then found blotting paper and an envelope in the kitchen drawer.

I was tired by now, but I felt I should catch up with my correspondence. I'd been in the habit of writing regularly to Madame Adeline now that she was living with little Mr Marvel and his troupe of monkeys. Perhaps one of the Tanglefield folk had written to tell her that Diamond and I had run away? She would be dreadfully worried.

Dear Madame Adeline,

I am so sorry that I haven't written for a little while. A lot has been happening – but do not worry, Diamond and I are safe and well!

We are no longer at Tanglefield's. Beppo lost his temper with poor Diamond when she fell during a performance and threatened her with such a beating that I had to spirit her away. We left that night – though they chased us. It was all very dramatic and exciting, as you can imagine. Do you remember that penny-farthing the clowns used as part of their act? Well, I appropriated it and we used it for our escape!

We might not be circus girls any more, but we are still performers! I coached Diamond and we've developed a novelty double act: now we are music-hall artistes, promoted to the second act already. Who knows, we might be top of the bill one day! We are at the Cavalcade, a truly splendid establishment, all gold and red plush inside, with a capacity of two thousand!

If you and Mr Marvel ever consider taking a trip to this part of the country (I appreciate the monkeys might prove a problem), then please come and see us. I do so hope you would be proud of us.

We think of you very fondly every day. Diamond is asleep now, but if she were awake she would be clamouring to send her love to you. I am sending mine too. You have always been like another mother to me.

Your loving Hetty

13

I **HAD TO CATCH UP** with my dressmaking as well as
my letter-writing. The next day I worked very hard
decorating Mrs Ruby's orange gown. I sewed tiny red
glass beads all round the neckline and cuffs and hem.

'It's splendid, Hetty, especially all those little mock rubies.
She'll love all the little touches,' said Miss Gibson, holding
the dress up and shaking the skirts this way and that.

'You did the really hard bits for me,' I said.

'The gathering, yes. But I'd never have thought of the beads, or the little embroidered yellow roses down the seams at the waist, and that tiny rose inside, on the lining silk. It's a gown fit for a queen,' she said.

'Queen Victoria?' I said. 'I'd need five times the material!'

'Hush, you bad girl!' exclaimed Miss Gibson. 'Show some respect!'

'Anyway, Mrs Ruby is certainly Queen of the Cavalcade,' I said. 'Let's hope she's as keen on her gown as you are, Miss Gibson.'

Mrs Ruby was delighted. 'Thank you, dear. I like a girl who keeps a promise,' she said, pulling the gown from its tissue wrapping. '*Two* new gowns to choose from! Aren't I the lucky one?' Then she examined the dress more closely. 'Oh, my!' she said. And again, 'Oh, my!'

'I hope you like it, Mrs Ruby,' I said demurely.

'I love it! The detail! And even rubies, you clever little minx. I shall have them added to every gown in future.'

Then I'd end up with bleeding fingers – though I kept smiling valiantly.

Mrs Ruby showed off her gown to Lily Lark, who cornered me in the wings the next day. 'I'd like you to make *me* a dress, little Miss Starry Talent,' she said.

I took a deep breath.

'I know you made Mrs Ruby's as a favour. I'll pay, of course. I don't just want a copy in a different colour. I'd

213

like my own design – perhaps not so corseted. I rather favour aesthetic dress. You know what I mean,' she said.

I nodded, though I had no idea. Still, I was sure Miss Gibson would know, and thank goodness I was right.

'She'll want it loose and flowing, in Liberty silk,' she said. 'I've got a lovely apple green – I think she'll like that.'

'With a yoke, then I could embroider lilies on it! White lilies, with little gold stamens, on the green silk.'

'Wonderful!' said Miss Gibson. 'Shall I make the dress and you do the embroidery, and then we'll share the profits?'

We made a perfect dressmaking team, and Diamond proved nifty at cutting out patterns, though she still couldn't stitch very well. When Bertie came visiting during the day, he sometimes assumed a tailor's pose, sitting cross-legged on the floor, and sewed the odd button into place. He was surprisingly nimble with his fingers.

'You're very good at sewing, Bertie,' said Miss Gibson admiringly.

'I've had to be. I haven't got a little woman at home to sew buttons on my shirts or turn up my trouser hems.' He winked at me meaningfully. '*Yet.*'

I started on Freda's gown too, which was a mammoth task. I was tempted to keep it plain because it was taking such a long time, but I knew Freda would love little girly details, so I sewed cherry blossoms round the neck and cuffs, and added a white ruffled petticoat underneath. I took the dress to the Cavalcade with me and sat in the dressing room stitching.

The ballet girls marvelled at the embroidery, but burst out laughing when they held the dress up against themselves. 'It's lovely, Emerald, but it's much too long! This is a dress for a giant!'

'Mmm,' I said quietly, and took it back and continued sewing.

When the girls were changing and in a boisterous mood, I sometimes sat in the corridor instead, Diamond beside me, playing games with my cotton reels.

Mr Apple stalked past on his way home, sniffing contemptuously. 'I suppose she thinks she's everyone's darling now,' he muttered. 'She's not just content with stealing the show – she's making everyone dresses now. Well, I hope she pricks her nasty scrabbly little fingers!'

There was a muffled response from inside his suitcase, which made Diamond start nervously.

'That was Little Pip talking!' she said when they'd gone. 'He *is* real, Hetty!'

'No, Mr Apple is just a very strange man,' I told her.

'I don't like him,' said Diamond.

'Neither do I,' I said, though I'd started to feel almost sorry for him. How would *I* feel if a pair of young children came along and performed a much more elaborate comedy bicycling act and became Mrs Ruby's pets?

At long last I finished Freda's gown and got started on Lucy Locket's. I made hers more formal, a truly grown-up little costume, with an embroidered locket stitched in the centre of her white lace collar as a witty touch.

The next time Mr Apple came down the corridor, I deliberately held up the miniature gown, pretending to show it to Diamond.

'See how *tiny* this is,' I said loudly. 'Specially made for a very, very little person.'

'Stupid girl, stitch-stitch-stitching away. I hope she pricks herself,' said Mr Apple.

But halfway down the corridor there was a muffled comment from inside the suitcase: 'I'd like a costume like that!' said Little Pip.

'You'd look a right banana in a lady's costume,' said Mr Apple, shaking his suitcase irritably.

'Maybe that girl could make a little boy's costume,' Little Pip persisted. 'I could do with a new outfit, Uncle Benjamin. Mine's getting very threadbare.'

'Well, we're not asking her. You be quiet now, do you hear me?'

Diamond was staring at me round-eyed. 'Little Pip really is talking!' she whispered. 'He *is is is* real! He says he wants you to make him an outfit, but Mr Apple says he mustn't ask.'

'Little Pip's a dummy, Diamond, I promise you. Mr

Apple just pretends he's talking, the way you make Maybelle talk,' I said. 'Shall I offer to make Little Pip an outfit, even though Benjamin Apple's so horrid to us?'

'Well, Little Pip's not horrid,' said Diamond. 'I like him, even though he looks a bit scary, especially when his mouth opens and shuts.'

'Let's see then,' I said, running after Benjamin Apple. I caught up with him in a few paces, because he had an old man's shuffle. 'Excuse me, Mr Apple. Could I have a word?'

'Is she talking to us?' he asked his suitcase.

'Of course she is!' Little Pip piped up.

'I was wondering if you'd like me to make a new costume for Little Pip,' I said.

'No thank you, missy. Little Pip already has a very smart suit.'

'No I don't!' came the voice from the suitcase. 'It's threadbare – you said so yourself. Folk will see my little arms and legs and all my workings soon!'

'I wonder what sort of outfit Little Pip would fancy?' I said. 'Another smart suit? A quilted smoking jacket? Oh, I know – a little blazer and flannels and a jaunty boater!'

'Yes! Oh yes, please!' Little Pip seemed to be dancing a jig inside the suitcase.

'It's not necessary, not at all. But I suppose I can't really disappoint the little lad,' said Mr Apple.

'I'll need to take a few measurements,' I said. 'Would that be possible?'

Benjamin Apple looked doubtful. 'I'm not sure. I don't want him exposed.'

'I'll be very quick and discreet. And he won't need to take his own clothes off.'

Even so, he insisted we go into a dark corner, and when he took Little Pip out of the suitcase and laid him gently on the floor, he spread his coat out to shield him from view. I measured his prone body as quickly as I could. His head was back, his mouth sagging, the rest of him totally limp. He looked horribly like a dead person. It was a relief to hear him talking again when he was back in the suitcase.

'My, that was a bit of an ordeal! That girl didn't half tickle me! Do you really think she'll make me a blazer and a boater? I'll look such a toff!'

'Don't count your chickens. Maybe she won't keep her word. You know what these flighty young things are like,' said Mr Apple.

'I'll keep my word,' I promised – and I did.

The blazer and the flannels were easy enough, but the boater was a struggle.

Bertie found me plaiting little strands of straw and tutted at me. 'You're crazy, Hetty, fiddling around making stuff for that mean old geezer. He's never even said a civil word to you.'

'Yes, but Little Pip's starting to be very friendly,' I said.

'You really *are* crazy,' said Bertie, but fondly. 'Look, *I'm* ever so friendly. How about making *me* a new blazer?'

'I will. Eventually. I'll put you on my list,' I said.

'Who's next on your list?' Diamond asked hopefully.

'You are!'

Benjamin Apple barely thanked me when I gave him the finished outfit – not even when I put the boater on Little Pip and we could see it was a perfect fit. He just started fussing about money, telling me that he had to pay me.

'I'm not going to feel obliged to anybody. So you take this money and be done with it, missy. I dare say I've been over-generous,' he said, pressing coins into my hand.

His payment was actually on the meagre side – it didn't even cover the cost of the materials – but I wasn't going to quibble. And Little Pip more than made up for Benjamin Apple's lack of enthusiasm.

'Oh joy! I absolutely love my natty little outfit! Don't I look dashing, Uncle Benjamin? All the girls will be after me! Help me tip my new boater to Miss Emerald Star. I am soooo grateful!' he burbled.

'I'm so glad you like it, Little Pip,' I said.

He continued talking to me whenever Benjamin Apple brought him near. Mr Apple himself even deigned to nod at me every now and then.

It was so much more comfortable backstage now. Even Mr Olivelli became friendly and taught Diamond to warble in Italian. She was everyone's favourite. The showgirls and the ballet dancers dressed her up and brushed her hair and sat her on their laps, often treating her to sweets or little cakes.

There was only one person at the Cavalcade I did my best to avoid – Samson Ruby. He lurked in the wings during the intervals. Sometimes he sweet-talked one of the girls, but he often made a beeline for me.

'Here's our little Emerald Star,' he said, and made horrible kissing noises at me.

'Cut it out, Samson, she's just a kid,' said Thelma, the brassiest of the showgirls.

'She might get herself up in that little girly outfit, but she's no kid, that one,' he said. 'She's a little saucebox.'

'Why bother with a little girl when you've got a real woman right in front of your nose?' Thelma reached out and boldly drew Samson into an embrace.

I wrinkled my nose at her behaviour, misunder-standing, though I was glad to be able to slip away.

The next day Thelma came up to me in the dressing room. 'Hey, you, Emerald,' she said. She towered above me, her low-cut dress and yellow glacé kid boots almost as outrageous as her stage costume. She was still wearing her stage make-up, her cheeks rouged, her lips carmine. 'I want a word, kid.'

I couldn't help being scared of girls like Thelma. I'd seen her pick a fight with another girl who'd borrowed her hairbrush. I'd been in numerous scraps at the hospital – wrestling and slapping and hair-pulling – but this was *fist* fighting.

'What do you want to talk about, Thelma?' I asked, trying to keep my voice steady.

Diamond came to my side. She pressed Maybelle onto my lap, as if for comfort.

'Samson Ruby,' said Thelma, her arms akimbo.

'I don't like him, Thelma, honestly. I don't want anything to do with him. He's all yours!' I said hastily.

She stared at me and then laughed. 'Do you think *I* want him? I can't stand the smarmy beggar. Oh, he's handsome enough, but he's broken too many of the girls' hearts – *and* got them into trouble.'

'But you were kissing him yesterday!'

'To distract him from you, you fool,' said Thelma.

'Goodness!' I *felt* a fool, and an ungrateful one at that. 'Oh, thank you, Thelma!'

'I'll watch out for you, and so will most of the other girls. But we can't be around all the time, especially now you're in the second act. So watch out. Keep as far away from him as possible or he'll eat you for breakfast,' she said. 'Got it, kid?'

'I've got it,' I said.

She smiled, and I saw that underneath all her make-up she was only a few years older than me, and a sweet kind girl for all her rough ways.

'I wish I had lovely shiny yellow boots like Thelma's,' Diamond said, after she'd gone home. 'Will you buy me a pair one day, Hetty?'

'No, I will not!'

'That's not fair. Madame Adeline bought *you* boots!'

'Yes, riding boots. Thelma's boots are *quite* different.'

'And I like her black stockings with holes in. Can I have pretty stockings like that?'

'No, they're fishnets and totally unsuitable for a little girl,' I said, sounding as prim as a matron. I started worrying again. I knew that the music hall wasn't really the right environment for an impressionable child. It couldn't be good for Diamond to be amongst such girls all the time. They were kind-hearted and made a big fuss of her, but most folk wouldn't consider them respectable. Still, most folk would sneer at a foundling and a circus child who'd been sold by her own father.

'Thelma and all the girls who dance here are very kind girls and I like them a lot, but they're not considered "good" girls, Diamond,' I said carefully.

'*I* think they're good,' she said stoutly.

'Well, perhaps you're right,' I said. 'But I'm certain of one thing. Samson Ruby isn't a good man at all – he's very, very bad. We must both keep away from him.'

'Why?' Diamond asked.

'Because he might try to kiss us.'

'Bertie kisses us. He's not bad – he's very, very good.'

'Yes, he is,' I said.

'And he looks after us. When Mr Apple was horrid, Bertie stood up for us. So we don't need to worry about Samson Ruby. Bertie will fight him if tries to do anything bad,' said Diamond.

I thought about it. Bertie was brave and hot-headed. He *would* fight. But Samson Ruby was tall and well-muscled. Bertie was strong and a street scrapper, but I didn't see how he'd ever beat Samson. I didn't want him to get hurt. And if by some miracle *he* managed to hurt Samson, what would happen then? Mrs Ruby adored Samson. One of the artistes thought he was her nephew. Most sniggered, and implied he might be a closer companion, though he was half her age. Whatever his relationship to Mrs Ruby, she would be furious if anyone hurt him. And if you fell out with Mrs Ruby, you wouldn't last long at the Cavalcade.

'We mustn't tell Bertie,' I said firmly. 'We don't want him to get into a fight or he'll be in trouble. We'll just keep away from Samson Ruby, that's simple enough.'

I still felt a little anxious, but I told myself I was worrying unnecessarily. It was a relief to go on stage and concentrate on our act. The audience were rowdy, and one quartet of drunken toffs in the front stalls were especially annoying, calling out silly things so that folk in the stalls missed half our jokes. I tried to ignore them,

223

but it was impossible. I remembered how Mrs Ruby had confronted a heckler.

'Wait a second, Diamond dolly,' I said in my little-girl stage voice. I gently pushed her off my lap. She stared at me in surprise. 'Sit there like a good dolly. Don't move. Well, you can't, can you?' It got me an uncertain laugh. I stood up and skipped to the front of the stage, peering across the lights. 'You see, there's four fine dummies down there and it seems they all want to play with me too.'

This time the laugh was huge. I smiled. 'Do you want to come and sit on my lap, fine sirs? You're very good at saying silly things, so you'll make all the fine folk laugh.'

The audience cheered and, thank goodness, the toffs subsided. I returned to Diamond and everyone clapped hard. We had not one, not two, but *three* curtain calls that night.

14

THE NEXT MORNING I had two letters, one from Madame Adeline and one from Jem. They were both unsettling.

I opened Madame Adeline's first, pulling Diamond close so she could try to spell it out for herself. I'd been trying to encourage her, but she had grown too used to my reading everything aloud for her.

'Dear Hetty and Diamond . . .' She frowned at the next

paragraph. 'Madame Adeline's writing is too swirly to read properly,' she said. 'And where are my pictures?'

In all our previous letters, Madame Adeline had written the news, while Mr Marvel had drawn comical sketches of his family of monkeys. The littlest, Mavis, featured most prominently because she was Diamond's favourite and they'd always had a special bond. Mr Marvel showed Mavis getting up to all kinds of naughty tricks: sometimes she'd be hunched at the corner of their table, tail curled like a handle, so that she resembled a monkey teapot. In the next picture she'd be grabbing a sandwich, and then holding a whole Victoria sponge, nibbling all round the edge. He'd draw Mavis in their bed with Mr Marvel's old-fashioned nightcap on her head, so that all you could see were her paws and tail. The funniest picture was of Mavis wearing Madame Adeline's red wig, looking like an ugly little girl with Rapunzel hair. Diamond would laugh and laugh at these pictures and keep them carefully folded beneath Maybelle's belongings.

I peered inside the envelope again, but Diamond was right – there were no monkey pictures. And no mention of Mr Marvel. Madame Adeline's letter was unusually short.

Dear Hetty and Diamond,
Oh, girls, what a relief to know you are safe and sound! My last letter to Tanglefield's was returned

*with NO LONGER HERE! scrawled across it. As
you can imagine, I was very worried. I think you
were very wise to leave. I never trusted Beppo – he
was far too harsh with my little Diamond. I am
very excited that you are music-hall artistes now.
My clever girls! Please give me details of your act.
I hope the other artistes there are kind to you. I
wonder if they give you cake like your loving*

Madame Adeline

'It's too short! She always adds that Mr Marvel sends
his love too – and sends a message from Mavis. Madame
Adeline hasn't written it properly this time,' said
Diamond.

'I expect she's busy. Or tired. And my letters to her
are never very long,' I said guiltily. 'I'll write her a really
long letter next time – and you could write too, Diamond.
It will be good practice for you.'

'Writing makes my hand ache,' she whined.

'You should have been brought up in the Foundling
Hospital. We had to write the same sentence for hours,
and if we made any spelling mistakes or ink blots we had
our knuckles rapped,' I said.

It had been such a cruelly strict regime – and yet by
Diamond's age I had a clear flowing hand and could read
my way through any volume. I could sew and darn, and

parrot all kinds of general knowledge, learned by heart.

'Maybe I should enrol you in a local school now that we're settled here,' I said to Diamond.

She looked appalled. 'I don't care for school at all,' she said firmly.

'How do you know? You've never actually attended one.'

'I'm sure I wouldn't like it. Besides, I don't want to be anywhere else. I want to be with you, Hetty. And Miss Gibson. I like to join in your talking, and do my own sewing,' she said.

'I don't think Miss Gibson and I are the attraction. You only perk up when a certain Mr Bertie comes calling,' I said, pulling her hair.

'Well, I love Bertie,' said Diamond merrily, 'and so do you, Hetty.'

'Nonsense,' I said, and bent my head so that my hair swung forward, hiding my burning cheeks.

I opened the second letter. This was longer and much more informative.

Dear Hetty,

It was a great relief to all of us to receive your letter. We have been very anxious about you. It was rather a shock to hear that you are now working in a music hall. I must admit I have never been in one, but I know they are very dubious places, entirely unsuitable for young girls. What sort of act do you do? And what kind of costume do you wear? I hope it is a proper dress. I was alarmed when I saw you at the circus in those riding breeches! Dearest Hetty, it's not your fault you've had such a strange, hard life, mostly without a mother's care, but you really shouldn't flaunt yourself so. It's not right, and people will get the wrong impression.

'Oh, for heaven's sake!' I snorted, crumpling the letter in my fist. 'He sounds as old and fuddy-duddy as Mr Buchanan! What a prig! How dare he wag his finger at me in such a manner. Who does he think he is? He's never been to a music hall, so what does he know? And how can he say I *flaunt* myself? Talk about insulting!'

I ranted on for several minutes while Diamond blinked at me.

'Why are you so cross, Hetty?'

'Because Jem is being so horrid and stuffy and lecturing. He's scarcely been out of that village all his life. He knows nothing about town life and the way most people live. To think I always looked up to him and thought him so wonderfully wise!' I said furiously.

I wasn't just angry, I was unhappy too. I'd wanted Jem to be impressed that I was now a music-hall artiste, one of the true stars of the show. How had he changed so much? He had been thrilled when I rode with Madame

Adeline the day he took me to the circus all those years ago. Was he truly shocked now – or was he just jealous that I had been so daring and adventurous. I was actually a little bit famous now. There had been a tiny piece about the Little Stars in the local news journal. Well, it was mostly an interview with Lily Lark, but there was a little insert about *us*.

Miss Lark is performing nightly at the Cavalcade, along with many other stars of the music hall, including the Little Stars, two cute wee girls with a sweet novelty act.

It was irritating to be labelled a 'cute wee girl' (Bertie insisted on calling me this frequently to tease me), but flattering to be given a special mention. I bought another copy of the journal, so that Diamond could cut out the article for her biscuit box and I could stow mine in the suitcase with my other treasures.

I was so annoyed with Jem that I stuffed the letter in my pocket and didn't read the rest until that afternoon, when I was having a cup of tea with Miss Gibson, taking a break from embroidering lilies.

I read your letter out loud to Mother and Gideon, and they were so delighted to have news of you. Mother actually managed to say the word Hetty, and then shook her head fondly, as if remembering what a naughty scrap you used to be. Gideon is generally very quiet, but he became truly talkative, and chatted away about our games when we were all children. He added that you'd been a truly wonderful sister to him at the Foundling Hospital, caring for him whenever you had the opportunity.

I was very touched by this passage, and held the letter to my chest, as if I were hugging poor ailing Mother and dear Gideon. But then I read on.

Of course I didn't read out the passage about the music hall, as I knew Mother and Gideon would be as concerned as I am. I told them you were employed as a seamstress, and they both thought this a delightful occupation. Gideon remembered how you sewed black satin roses on Mother's bonnet on the sad occasion of Father's funeral.

Perhaps Mother might have been a little concerned, if she were capable of understanding the concept of a music hall in her sadly fuddled mind. She'd certainly been shocked when I'd been to the circus as a child, and had called Madame Adeline a hussy because she wore pink spangles and showed her legs when she rode her horses. But Gideon would be extremely interested. He might well think the music hall glamorous. I so wanted a brother to be proud of me. I especially wanted that brother to be Jem.

'Oh, Jem!' I said aloud in exasperation.

'Jem?' said Miss Gibson.

'This is the boy I grew up with in the country. Well, he is a man now – and seems to have become very stuffy. He's telling me off for being a music-hall artiste. The nerve!'

'I can understand his concern, dear,' said Miss Gibson, sipping daintily. 'It's not really respectable, especially for ladies.'

'How can you say that, when we're making a gown for Lily Lark right this moment, and Mrs Ruby is your most valued customer?' I demanded.

'That's business, dear,' she said placidly. 'Now tell me more about this Jem. What does he look like?'

'Oh, he's . . .' I struggled to find the right words. He was *Jem*. It was a struggle to remember him as a man. I always thought of the boy Jem first, his hair tousled, his cheeks rosy, his long limbs lithe and tanned. My foster brother Jem, the boy who taught me everything, who played with me, who cuddled me close whenever I needed comfort. It was an effort translating all these dear images into the man Jem had become.

'Is he handsome?' asked Miss Gibson.

'Yes, I suppose so,' I replied. I hadn't really thought

about it, but yes, Jem would certainly be considered handsome. Janet wasn't the only girl who thought him wonderful. Half the girls in the village had set their caps at him. 'He's got dark hair, rather curly, and he can never be bothered to go to the barber's so it's a little long and wild,' I said. 'He's got brown eyes, very warm brown eyes, perhaps his best feature. And he's grown tall, so that he towers over me. He's broad in the shoulder, and strong, because he works on the farm.'

'Oh, my,' said Miss Gibson. 'And what sort of nature does he have?'

'He's very smug and quick to judge,' I said. But then I thought about it. 'However, he's kind, extremely loyal, very gentle and caring. And although he's not exactly a gentleman, he certainly acts like one.'

'Dear goodness!' Miss Gibson shook her head. 'Poor Bertie.'

'What did you say?' I said, puzzled for a moment. Then I conjured up Bertie in my mind, making him stand beside my imaginary Jem. Bertie barely came up to his shoulders. His hair stuck up wildly. His blue eyes twinkled and he always had a cheeky grin, but no one would ever call him handsome. He wasn't gentlemanly either, and teased and tormented when he felt like it. He was also a flirt, and I still wasn't entirely sure he could be trusted.

'Well, your Jem sounds perfect in every way,' said Miss Gibson.

'He's not at all! He's become very priggish. And he's not *my* Jem. He's very likely betrothed to someone else by now.'

'Would you mind if he were?' asked Miss Gibson.

'Of course not. I would be delighted. I actually could have had Jem as a sweetheart myself, but I decided against it. He's more like a brother to me, I assure you,' I said.

Then I read the rest of his letter.

I am so delighted you wrote to us, Hetty dear. I did not know how to get hold of you to tell you my news. Janet and I are going to be married next Saturday – the 27th! We have been betrothed for the last six months and are so happy together. The whole family is delighted for us. I have had a wage rise, and can just about afford to rent my own small cottage on the estate. It is very run down and primitive, but Janet is brave and says it's beautifully picturesque. I will do my best to repair the thatch and whitewash it when we're given the tenancy, and Janet has already begun making curtains and rugs and will do her best to turn two humble rooms into a little palace.

Our wedding will be a very simple affair in the local church, with a party at Janet's parents' house. Keep your fingers crossed for us that it is sunny on the 27th because Janet wants to have dancing on the lawn. I am sure she will regret this, because I become a lumbering ox on any dance-floor, but hopefully she will make allowances for her new bridegroom!

The family will all be guests, of course – and as you are very much part of the family too, it is our dearest wish that you should come and wish us well. I now realize this probably won't be possible, as you will be performing in this Cavalcade – but please think of us at noon on Saturday, and raise a glass to Janet and
Your ever-loving brother,
Jem

There seemed to be something wrong with my eyes. I had the greatest difficulty finishing the letter. The words kept blurring. Perhaps I'd done too much sewing recently. I started to rub my eyes and my knuckles grew strangely wet.

'Why, Hetty, you're in floods of tears! Whatever's the matter? Is it bad news from Jem?' Miss Gibson came rushing over and gave me her own lace handkerchief.

'I'm sorry! No, everything's perfectly all right. I don't know why I'm crying. Yes I do! I'm happy for Jem. He's going to marry one of my dearest friends, the girl I wanted him to marry all along. Yes, I'm very, very happy for them both,' I said, scrubbing at my eyes.

Miss Gibson was no fool. She patted my shoulder and went into the kitchen to make another pot of tea. I peered after her. Diamond was at the sink, playing boats with the soap dish and three corks – a baby's game that amused her for hours. Maybelle was propped on the draining board paddling her rag feet in the water.

Miss Gibson murmured something to her and Diamond looked round at me, concerned. I couldn't bear their attention – I needed to get away by myself to try to work out what I was feeling. I thought of the penny-farthing, but that would mean drawing attention to myself. Instead I ran out of the shop, down the road, as far as I could. I wanted to go to the woods where Bertie had taken us, but that meant a bus ride, and I didn't have any money. I ran right through the town and eventually took refuge in the little municipal park.

It was not much bigger than a large garden, with a path, some grass, several flowerbeds planted with regimental precision, and a small pond without a single duck. A mother was helping her little boy float a toy wooden yacht across this uninspiring calm sea. Perhaps I should bring Diamond here? She would enjoy floating her 'boats' on the pond. But maybe I shouldn't pander to her new childishness. I didn't know how best to look after her. She needed to play now to make up for the hardships of her past, but I didn't want her stuck in little girlhood for ever.

I sat down on a bench, trying to concentrate on Diamond. But one word kept tolling like a bell in my head. *Jem! Jem! Jem!*

When I left the house, I had thrust the letter into my pocket – I couldn't bear the thought of Miss Gibson or Diamond reading it! I took it out again now, smoothing the creases, and read it through again. I lingered over the first three paragraphs, trying to recapture my feelings of wild irritation. But somehow Jem's words failed to have the same effect second time round. He expressed himself a little stiffly, but that was because he was trying to write elegantly, showing me that he might be a farm labourer but he could turn a fancy phrase as well as anyone. His tone was teacherly, but his concern was genuine.

I couldn't really blame him for being worried about the music hall. Many folk shared his prejudice. Some of the acts were more than a little risqué, and many of the costumes were alarmingly brief. I thought of the shapely legs of the showgirls and the ballet dancers, of the practically bare body of Araminta the contortionist. I knew from the raucous response of the audience that most weren't there to appreciate their dancing or acrobatic skills. Jem simply wanted to protect me from unpleasant cries and comments.

I made myself re-read the last two paragraphs. I started crying all over again, and had to duck my head so the nearby mother wouldn't see. *Why* was I reacting in such an emotional manner? I'd *wanted* Jem to marry Janet. I hadn't wanted him as my own sweetheart. I'd thought of him as my brother. So why now, when Jem signed himself for the first time as *Your ever-loving brother* did that word seem to stab me in the stomach?

I didn't understand. I bent my head even lower, until it was on my knees. I put my hands over my ears, trying to block out the chatter of the small child, the murmur of the mother, the scrunch of the gravel path as someone else walked by. I wanted to crawl into a deep, dark, silent world to try to make sense of things.

'Why, Mama?' I whispered.

Oh, Hetty! You know why. You want Jem – and yet you don't want Jem.

'So do I want Bertie?'

It's the same answer. You want Bertie – and yet you don't want Bertie.

'Why am I like this? Why can't I make up my mind?'

You've always been a contrary child!

'Well, I know one thing. I want *you*, Mama. Why did you have to go and die when I was so young?'

You were old enough to cope, dearie. Just about. You had to grow up very quickly. You should take a leaf out of Diamond's book and try being a child again. Perhaps that's the trouble. You're too young for any sweetheart, Jem or Bertie.

'Which one do *you* like best, Mama?'

I can't tell you that! You must make up your own mind.

This wasn't much help, but I felt a little more peaceful. I sat up awkwardly, conscious that the mother and child were staring at me. I wondered if I'd been talking aloud. I hurried away, hoping they didn't think I was some poor soul whose mind was wandering. Perhaps I *was*?

Miss Gibson seemed very relieved when I got home.

'You gave us quite a fright, rushing off like that, Hetty. Poor Diamond wanted to run after you. She cried when I wouldn't let her. You must try to act more responsibly, dear,' she said reproachfully.

'I'm so sorry,' I said. 'I won't do it again, Miss Gibson. Thank you for looking after Diamond for me.'

I was even sorrier for Diamond, who didn't make a fuss or start crying again. She just clung to me, her hands hot and tight about my waist.

'It's all right, sweetheart. I just needed a little walk by myself, that's all,' I said.

'I thought you were running away from me,' she whispered.

'As if I'd ever do that!' I said, smoothing her hair and kissing the top of her head.

'You promise you won't ever?'

'I promise. I tell you what, we'll go for a little walk *together* now, to make up for your fright. And we might just find you something very, very special,' I said.

I fetched my purse, and we set off hand in hand. I took her to the toyshop.

'You can choose a friend for Maybelle,' I said.

'Really? Oh, then please may I have the doll in the window?' she asked.

'Why don't we look inside too? I think we'd better inspect each and every doll, just to make sure we find the right one.'

The toyshop was a revelation. There were shelves and cabinets everywhere, crammed with the most wondrous toys. There were tiny replicas: a blue miniature steam engine with magenta and cream carriages, perfect in every detail; a black horse with a red leather saddle pulling a pitch-pine cart; a metal cooking stove with a full set of small pots and pans on the hob; an elaborate printing press with little letters; sets of small bricks, plain wood or red and yellow cubes, with alphabet squares for babies.

There was livestock: brown fur bears with gaping red felt mouths; soft pink or blue rabbits with long limbs and floppy ears; a dappled rocking horse with a real mane and long bushy tail; and, most splendid of all, a Noah's ark sheltering all kinds of wooden animals – hand-sized elephants and giraffes, down to two tiny mice smaller than my fingernail.

Then there were the dolls: large lady dolls in silks with feathers in their straw hats; a gentleman doll with a top hat and tails and a tiny spotted bow tie; baby dolls lying on their backs, their long white christening robes draping the shelf; little girl dolls, blonde, brunette and even a redhead, in cream dresses with white knitted socks and weeny kid boots; there were even very small dolls peeping out of the windows of an elaborate red-brick doll's house with gables and balconies and a turret.

'Oh my goodness, how will you ever choose, Diamond?' I said.

She wandered from one to another, whispering under her breath, clearly talking to the dolls. I was worried the shop man might become impatient, but he nodded at her and mouthed at me, 'She's like a little doll herself!'

I was also dazed by the toys. It seemed extraordinary that rich children had such choice! When I was a very little girl, I'd had my rag baby, an even less sophisticated dolly than Diamond's Maybelle, though I'd loved her dearly. We'd had no toys at all at the Foundling Hospital, and scarcely any leisure time to play anyway. If our Little Stars act proved popular and we earned even more money, I wondered whether I'd like any of these beauties for myself.

I didn't want a doll, but I liked the grinning bear. I'd have loved to take him up into my tree house with Jem. I liked the horse and cart too. I'd have had wonderful games taking it back and forth to an imaginary market. And how about the splendid Noah's ark? I knew the Bible story well. I could make Noah scurry around perfecting the ark and then help him line up all the animals in pairs so they could troop inside out of the rain. Was the ark waterproof? I imagined sailing it on the pond in the park, while the elephants trumpeted and the lions roared and Noah and his family prayed.

I could act it all out for Diamond – but I knew that this time had long gone. I couldn't immerse myself in play now. I'd left it too late.

'So, Diamond, which doll is it going to be?' I asked.

'I can really, really have one? It isn't just pretend?'

'Really.' I shook my fat purse. 'See, I have the money with me.'

'Well, they're all so beautiful. It would be lovely to have a lady doll dressed in such finery, just like Mrs Ruby or Miss Lark – and I rather fancy this gentleman doll because he's got a dear round face just like Bertie's. The baby dolls are all very pretty, though they couldn't talk to me, could they, not when they're so young. The little girl dolls are all delightful, but I can't choose between them and I don't want to hurt their feelings. The little tiny dolls are maybe *too* little and tiny and might get lost, though I'd love to carry them around in my pocket,' said Diamond, talking very fast and hopping up and down. 'So the doll I'd really, really love is the one in the window, because she waved to me as soon as she saw me and she so hopes I'm going to be her mother.'

'The sweet pet!' said the shopkeeper.

I felt Diamond might be acting for effect, but I couldn't criticize her for behaving like a baby because I asked her to do just that every night on stage. I bought her the doll, the one in the window with long blonde curls and big blue eyes, looking just like a little Diamond.

The shopkeeper insisted on wrapping her up carefully in soft linen and then storing her in a silk-lined box, before covering it with brown paper and string. It was a large, unwieldy parcel, but Diamond insisted on carrying it all the way back to Miss Gibson's, though she was very pink in the face by the time she got there. Then she insisted on holding a 'birthing' scene on the cutting-out table.

Miss Gibson looked slightly alarmed by this suggestion, but Diamond had no idea of the mechanics of real childbirth (I was actually a little hazy myself). She laid the box on the table and then shut her eyes, crossed her fingers and said fervently, 'Oh, I *wish* I had a child! I *wish wish wish* I had my very own daughter!'

Then she went *'Ping!'* and lifted her finger. 'Hark!' she said theatrically. 'I think my wish is granted!'

She snipped the string, tore off the brown paper, lifted the lid of the box, carefully unwrapped the linen and then took the new doll in her arms.

'There! Isn't she beautiful! And she's mine, she's really mine!' she said, rocking the doll in her arms.

'What are you going to call her, dearie?' said Miss Gibson, beaming at her.

'I think I will call her . . . Hetty.'

'Perhaps that might get confusing,' I said, though I was very touched.

'Then she will be Adeline,' said Diamond. 'It doesn't matter calling her that, because I never get to see Madame Adeline now, though I wish I did. It's a lovely name, isn't it? And my Adeline's the loveliest doll in the whole world!'

She suddenly caught sight of Maybelle lying abandoned on her back on the floor. 'Well, *equally* the loveliest doll in the world,' she said, snatching up Maybelle too and hugging her hard. 'Oh dear, her legs are still very wet from paddling in the sink.'

'Perhaps I'd better peg her out on the washing line,' I said. 'Don't worry, she'll like swinging there – it will be a treat for her.'

So we dried out soggy Maybelle while Diamond played with Adeline with a clear conscience. She didn't want to stop playing and get into her Cavalcade clothes that evening. I could only get her to go if we took Adeline with us. She wanted to go on stage with her and make her part of our act, but I felt it would be too cumbersome.

'I can make up lots of stuff for Adeline to say. It would be so sweet!' Diamond insisted.

'We've had enough sweet talk,' I said firmly. 'People

aren't paying good money to see you playing with your new dolly. They want a proper act.'

'I'm sick of our boring old act,' said Diamond. 'I'm not doing it! You can't make me.'

I was taken aback. Diamond always did as she was told. I tried to persuade and cajole, but she was adamant. She'd become so over-excited that she was tired out now and refused to see reason. I got her to the theatre, still clutching Adeline, and she enjoyed showing her new doll to all the girls – but then she slumped down on the floor with her and wouldn't get up.

'No, we're sleepy now,' she said, and shut her eyes.

'Oh, for goodness' sake, Diamond!' I didn't know what to do. I wasn't going to threaten her with a beating, like hateful Beppo, but she seemed immune to any kind of gentle persuasion.

I tried being artful. 'Adeline, can you ask your mama to be a good kind lady and get herself ready to go on stage, please?'

Diamond opened her eyes and laid Adeline flat on her back so that her eyelids closed with a click. 'She's asleep,' she said. 'Ssh, Hetty, you're disturbing us!'

The ballet girls all giggled, which encouraged Diamond to play up even more. But then they started drifting off to warm up and dip their feet in the resin box so they wouldn't slip. We were due on stage before them!

'Diamond!' I said urgently, shaking her. 'We're going

to miss our spot and then Mrs Ruby will be furious with us.'

'I don't care,' she muttered.

There was a knock at the dressing-room door. 'That'll be her now!' I said.

But it was Bertie, looking concerned. 'Are you girls all right? You're cutting it a bit fine, aren't you? Samson's just about to announce you!'

'Diamond's playing up,' I said, nodding at her.

'Leave her to me,' he said.

He squatted beside Diamond. 'Hello, little princess. It's your old Bertie here,' he murmured.

Diamond opened her eyes, but Bertie wasn't looking at her. He had taken Adeline's china hand. He bent and kissed it.

'My, you're looking prettier than ever today, Twinkle. But we'd better feed you up a bit. You look very *little*.'

Diamond burst out laughing. 'No, Bertie, you're talking to my new dolly, Adeline. *I'm* Diamond.'

'What? No, you can't be Diamond. Look at the time!' Bertie consulted the pocket watch he was so proud of. 'She's doing her act in less than a minute. Diamond is brushing her lovely hair' – he raked his fingers carefully through the doll's hair – 'and making sure her dress is hanging just so' – he puffed out Adeline's dress and petticoats – 'and running to the wings as fast as her little legs will carry her!' He eased the doll out of Diamond's arms and bobbed her madly in the air as if she really were running.

'No, it's me, it's me, *I'm* Diamond!' she said, and she scrambled to her feet, shook her hair, twitched her dress and started running. I ran too. We made it to the stage just as Samson finished his spiel and the audience started clapping.

I was still worried about her performance, wondering if she would dry during her speeches or miss her leap onto my shoulders again, but she did it all perfectly, looking as fresh as a daisy. But the moment we came off stage she drooped again. She wouldn't even go back to the dressing room. She just seized Adeline and curled up in a corner. She was asleep almost instantly, not faking it this time. She started snuffling with little infant snores.

Ivy Green and all the ballet girls were waiting in the wings now and they all chuckled.

'Doesn't she look sweetly pretty?' said Ivy in an irritating voice.

'Maybe, but she's obviously tired out,' I said. 'How am I ever going to get her home? I can't carry her and the wretched doll when I've got the penny-farthing.'

'Wait until after I've been on with Ivy. I'll carry Diamond home for you,' said Bertie.

Ivy pouted. 'Oh, Bertie, that's so kind of you, but I rather wanted you to see *me* home tonight. That lad might be in the audience again tonight – the one who's so sweet on me. He was waiting for me at the stage door and got quite difficult when I wouldn't go out to supper with him. He was very insistent.'

'The one who wanted to treat you to oysters and champagne? I thought *you* were quite sweet on *him*. You certainly went on about him enough, love,' said Bertie. 'Tell you what, doesn't old Ben Apply-Dapply live in digs down your road? I'll tell him to hang on and escort you home. Then you'll have two gentlemen protecting you, him and Little Pip.'

'Oh, very droll,' Ivy snapped. 'No, thanks very much. Maybe I *will* go out for supper with my gentleman admirer.' She nodded at Bertie as if that would make him care and change his mind – but it didn't.

So I waited while Ivy sang her little ditty and Bertie and all the other show lads danced about her, miming their adoration. Perhaps this wasn't too hard a task. She looked especially beautiful tonight, her long bright hair glossy in the limelight, her figure particularly shapely in a new pink dress, her legs remarkably lithe in their white silk stockings. I couldn't help feeling triumphant that Bertie had offered to help me with Diamond rather than escort Ivy home.

But when we set off back to Miss Gibson's, Bertie carrying Diamond and her doll, me pushing the penny-farthing, I started worrying, peering over my shoulder.

'What's up, Hetty?' Bertie was panting a little, because Diamond seemed to weigh a ton when she was fast asleep, for all that she was so slight.

'Do you think this man *might* pursue Ivy?' I said. 'I don't like her, but I wouldn't want her to get into difficulties because you're looking after us.'

'Oh, Ivy's tough as old boots for all she acts so coy,' he said. 'She's been out with half a dozen of her gentlemen admirers and could eat them all for breakfast. She was just being awkward because she didn't want me to go home with you two girls. *Three* girls, if we're counting this wretched doll. Who gave it to her?'

'I did. I felt she deserved a treat – but she got too excited and then wouldn't be sensible. Bertie, do you think I'm bad making her perform all the time? I'm sure it's an awful strain on her.'

'She seems to be having a whale of a time, silly. She loves all the fuss people make of her. *You* like performing, don't you? Didn't you once tell me that you rode a horse in the circus when you were only about five and that you absolutely loved it?'

'Yes, I did. But Diamond has always been really worried about performing. Beppo was forever threatening her with a beating,' I said anxiously.

'You're hardly threatening her, are you, you funny girl? You look after that little kid extraordinarily well.'

'She's like a little sister to me.'

'You're more like a mother to her, if you ask me. And to borrow Ivy's sentimental phrase, I think *that's* sweetly pretty. You'll be a lovely real mother one day, Hetty,' said Bertie.

'Do you really mean that?' I felt very near tears. Perhaps I was tired out too. Or perhaps it was just such a special thing for him to say. My own dear mama meant the world to me, but I had always thought I'd be a failure as a mother myself. The matrons at the hospital had always scoffed at the idea of any of us girls marrying, let alone bearing children. We were foundlings, only fit to be servants.

'Of course I mean it,' said Bertie. 'You never take me seriously, Hetty.'

'Because you're always joking around and teasing so,' I said. 'But you're a truly good sort, Bertie. It's very kind of you to carry Diamond all the way home. You must be exhausted.'

'Not at all. I'm bright and bouncy and the night is still young, Hetty Feather. Tell you what. You tuck little Twinkle up in her bed and then how about you and me stepping out? How about champagne and oysters? What do you say?'

I hesitated. Then I smiled.

'I say *Yes, please!*'

15

MISS GIBSON LOOKED A little wistful when I asked
her if she'd mind keeping an eye on Diamond
while I went out with Bertie.

'Well, of course, dear. Though it is a little late. Where
exactly are you taking her, Bertie?'

'Not quite sure yet, Miss Gibson. We're just going to
have a bite to eat.'

'But I can make you a special little supper here. What

do you fancy? I've got some very nice cheese and my own home-made pickle – or if you'd prefer something hot, then I could make you bacon and eggs,' she said, all eagerness, already reaching for her apron.

'Oh, you're such a lovely lady, Miss Gibson dear, but Hetty and I feel in need of a breath of air tonight. I'm sure you understand,' said Bertie, giving her a kiss on her plump cheek.

'Oh, I do, I do,' she said, shaking her head a little.

I rushed upstairs to change. I'd never get served champagne in my Cavalcade outfit. I had resolved never to drink alcohol again, but I wanted to try champagne! Diamond was already fast asleep, curled up in bed, with Adeline on one side of her and Maybelle on the other.

I changed into my grey dress, wishing it wasn't so plain. I seemed to be always making outfits for other people, but still had nothing decent to wear myself. I put on the striped blazer I'd worn at the picnic to make my outfit more interesting, and tied up my hair.

When I ran down the stairs, Miss Gibson didn't say a word about my borrowing the blazer again. 'Have a lovely time, dears. Don't worry about Diamond. Or me!'

'Oh dear,' I said to Bertie as we walked down the road. 'I feel a bit mean leaving her with Diamond. I do feel sorry for her sometimes.'

'Perhaps you're deciding against the life of a lonely spinster after all?' he replied.

'I don't think I want Miss Gibson's life – but one's life doesn't have to be lonely if you stay single,' I said, tossing my head. 'I'd rather like Lily Lark's life. Top of the bill, much admired, with gentleman admirers hanging around the stage door – though she doesn't seem to give a fig for any of them. *She* doesn't stay in cheap digs. The girls told me she's taken a mansion flat near the park for the whole season.'

'She leads a good enough life, I grant you, but I feel a bit sorry for the old bird. She's had her time in all the big London gaffs. She's on the slippery slope now. The Cavalcade's good, but it's only the provinces. Give old Lil another five years and she'll be history,' said Bertie.

'Well, I can't see Ivy Green taking her place at the Cavalcade,' I snapped.

'Me neither,' said Bertie wisely. 'It'll be you and Diamond, of course, Hetty. You're a big draw already.'

'And you can be second on the bill, Bertie – how about that?'

'No thanks. I think I'll be top of the bill at the Alhambra or the Criterion,' he said with a grin.

'No one can ever get the better of you,' I said.

'I think we're evenly matched. That's why I'm sweet on you, Hetty. You're not like all the other girls.'

'Not at all like other girls. Not pretty, not shapely, not tall, not a lady,' I said.

'Same as I'm not handsome, not a fine figure, and

definitely not a gentleman,' said Bertie. 'But we're both sharp and cunning because we've had to make our own way in life. We know how to fend for ourselves. We make out we're tough as old boots, but inside we're soft as butter and just want a little bit of loving.'

'I think you've probably had more than enough loving in your life,' I said tartly.

'And I don't think you've had enough, Hetty,' said Bertie, taking my hand.

'So where are we going, Mr Flirty Bertie? I hope you've got a suitable establishment in mind.' I adopted Miss Gibson's girly murmur. 'Respectable, I hope!'

'Ultra-respectable – in its way,' said Bertie. 'I'm taking you to Maudie's.'

'Ah, Maudie's,' I said in a nonchalant manner.

'You haven't a clue what Maudie's is, have you?' said Bertie, chuckling. 'Don't worry – it's a drinking club, but I've never seen anybody behave badly there. It's all quite swish, and you can get a bite to eat.'

'So is this one of your regular haunts, then?'

'Every night I down the old bottle of champers and generally make merry,' said Bertie. 'Nah! I've only been there once before, when Peter Perkins had a windfall on the gee-gees and took a whole bunch of us out to celebrate. Even the Rubys came. And I liked it so much, I thought if ever I got a specially lovely lady friend – one like that little Hetty Feather I courted way back when I was a lowly butcher's boy – then I'd take her there to impress her.'

'You don't have to take me anywhere swish to impress me, Bertie,' I said. 'We're both quite good at picturing, I seem to remember.'

'Yes, you were a little sport that day when I was out of cash and couldn't treat you to anything. One of our best times together, wasn't it? I've never known a girl so good at pretending.'

'Well, you got the hang of it too,' I said.

'I like to think I'm the only boy you've pictured with,' said Bertie.

I hesitated for a second, remembering all those long-ago days in the squirrel tree. 'Yes, of course.'

'No I'm *not*,' said Bertie. 'So you and Jem used to picture too?'

'You will go on about Jem. I might have had all sorts of sweethearts, you're not to know,' I said.

'Yes, but I do know you, Hetty, through and through. So it's no use lying to me, especially about Jem.'

'I didn't lie,' I lied. 'Well, only a bit. When we were little children, Jem and I used to play simple games. We had a special tree in the woods and we used to climb up and pretend we were squirrels.'

'How sweetly pretty,' said Bertie sarcastically.

'Don't you dare parrot Ivy Green to me!'

We glared at each other – but then Bertie pulled me

close. 'Don't let's spoil our special evening, Hetty,' he said.

'All right. I'll hang onto my temper. And actually there's no need for you to get all het up about Jem any more.'

'I don't get het up!'

'Just listen to you! Jem's betrothed. He's actually getting married this very Saturday,' I said.

'He's never!'

'I *told* you he had a sweetheart.'

'You were always his sweetheart.'

'When I was a tiny girl, before I went to the hospital. He made a fuss of me, the way you make a fuss of Diamond,' I said.

'And – and you don't mind that he's getting married now?'

'Of course not!' I said, my third lie in three minutes. It wasn't totally a lie. Part of me, maybe nearly all of me, was very happy for Jem and Janet. It was what I'd wanted, what I'd hoped for. But there was still a squirmy little piece of jealousy inside me, as if the five-year-old Hetty were screaming, *He's my Jem and no one else can have him but me!*

I thought of little Eliza in the Foundling Hospital and wondered if she'd been told. She would mind dreadfully. She'd set her heart on marrying Jem herself. It seemed ironic that one sweet, gentle boy had already broken the hearts of two little girls.

'You've got that dreamy look on your face, Hetty,' Bertie said accusingly.

'Maybe I'm dreaming of you.'

'I wish you were. I wish we'd just met now. I've given myself a polish, even smartened up my accent. I'm a plain lad, and I'm shorter than average, but somehow I know how to please the ladies. I reckon I'd have a fair chance with you, Hetty. But whenever you look at me now, you can't help remembering that awful butcher's boy with the pencil behind his ear and the stained apron and the stink of meat. No wonder your nose wrinkles whenever I come near you.'

'No it doesn't! Whenever I look at you I think that you're my dear friend. I don't care if you're delivering meat or tap-dancing on stage, you're still the same Bertie,' I said, and I kissed him full on the lips even though we were standing right under a gaslight.

'My Hetty,' Bertie whispered, kissing me back.

There was a piercing whistle from a passing lad.

Bertie made a rude gesture at him and laughed. 'Come on, we'd better stop this canoodling. If Miss Gibson could see us, she'd be very shocked. Maudie's is just down the street.'

It didn't look like anything from outside, a tall narrow building, rather shabby, with an uninviting black-painted door. There was no sign up, nothing to show it was a club.

'Are you sure you've got the right place, Bertie?' I asked.

'Certain,' he said.

He rapped smartly on the door and someone opened it a chink. We caught a glimpse of a tall broad man with a boxer's broken nose. He didn't look welcoming.

'Yes?' he grunted.

'We're two customers for Maudie's,' said Bertie.

'Have you got membership?'

'Not as yet, but I'll gladly join.'

'But will we gladly invite you in? No, we will not,' said the doorman. 'Go on, off you hop, small fry.'

This was so insulting! I couldn't bear to see Bertie humiliated. He looked ready to start a fight he couldn't possibly win.

'Excuse me, Mr Doorman, I don't think you realize who we are,' I said imperiously. 'We're personal friends of Mrs Ruby from the Cavalcade. She recommended your establishment herself. But if this is your attitude, then I'm not at all sure we *want* to come in.'

'Mrs Ruby?' he said, changing his tone. Then he opened the door properly, so that light shone on our faces. 'Oh, you're artistes! You're that child with the penny-farthing. You're very comical.'

'But as you can see, I'm not really a child,' I said, standing as tall as possible.

'Indeed not. Come in, come in,' said the doorman, all affability now.

Bertie sniffed at him as he stalked past, his hand

round my waist protectively. 'My goodness, Hetty, you're famous already,' he said.

'We both are. He said, "You're artistes."'

'But he remembered your act, not mine,' said Bertie.

'Oh pish-pash, what does it matter?' I said, though I knew it did.

Bertie led me down a dark corridor into a large room of little tables, with pink gaslights at every one, so the whole room had a rosy glow. I looked around at the glittering mirrors, the marble bar, the waiters in black with long crisp white aprons, the artistic folk lounging at the gilt tables, drinking and eating and smoking.

'Oh my goodness, I love it here!' I said.

One of the waiters showed us to a little table in the corner. Bertie objected, wanting the table in the very centre of the room, though it had a reserved sign on it.

'No, no, I'd much prefer this table, then we can peer at everyone,' I said quickly, wanting to avoid another argument.

We did have a tiny squabble over the champagne. Bertie wanted to order a bottle, but I wanted just one glass. I remembered drinking too much at my foster father's funeral and it hadn't ended well. But after I'd got my way Bertie relaxed a little. Perhaps he'd seen just how much a whole bottle of champagne cost. He did insist on ordering oysters. I didn't like gulping them down raw at all. They were revoltingly slimy – but I pretended to enjoy them to please Bertie.

'Shall we have something else now?' Bertie suggested. 'I think my tum needs something a little more substantial.'

We had devils-on-horseback – lovely little prunes stuffed with mango chutney and wrapped in bacon. Then we had a wonderful apricot pudding so delicious I wanted to lick round my bowl. It was topped with a crystallized apricot.

When Bertie saw me eating mine with such relish, he gave me his too. 'This is better than picturing, ain't it, girl?' he said.

'I'll say,' I agreed.

I sipped at my champagne, looking around at all the ladies to see what kind of gowns they were wearing. Some were dressed in very skimpy garments, showing a great deal of chest, and putting far too much faith in a flimsy shred of lace. Less bold ladies were making do with slightly tired evening gowns, a little stained under the arms and needing a good going over with a steaming iron. There were a few dashing women wearing what I now knew was the latest fashion. I assessed their sleeves, their necklines, the cut of their skirts, to see if I could pick up any tips for Miss Gibson.

There was one woman who particularly drew my attention. She had red hair just like mine, and she seemed to glory in it, for it was piled up on her head and adorned with a green necklace like a little coronet. She was wearing a loose purple silk dress with another green bead necklace and there was a faint jangle from her silver bracelets every time she moved her arms. She wore as much make-up as the showgirls, but somehow she still looked like a lady. She was chatting politely to a small, stout, ugly man in immaculate evening dress, his shirt brilliant white, his suit a fancy cut of cloth and his gold and pink brocade waistcoat very splendid.

Bertie was looking at them too. 'See that couple – that's you and me in twenty years' time!' he said.

'I'll never look so amazing,' I said. 'And you'll never look so ugly, Bertie!'

'Don't you think I'm ugly then?'

'I think you've got a very pleasant face,' I said.

'Only pleasant!'

'Look, I'm not going to lavish compliments on you to make you even more big-headed. You'd better ask Diamond. She thinks you're the most handsome man on earth,' I said.

'Dear little Twinkle.'

'You're very good with her, Bertie. She absolutely adores you.'

'Well, she's a sweet kid. Sometimes it seems like we're a little family now, you, me and Diamond.'

'And Miss Gibson as Grandma?'

'Perhaps not!' said Bertie.

'It's sad we've never known our real grandmothers. But perhaps it's just as well. I met my grandfather when

I went up north to stay with my father, and he tried to attack me.'

'What about your father? Surely he took a shine to you?'

'Yes, I think he did. I liked him ever so. But I didn't care for his new wife at all. I have a stepsister and -brother, but to be truthful I didn't really care for them either. It's strange – as you're growing up in a terrible institution, you long to find your blood relatives, and yet it's often a disappointment when you meet them. Apart from my dear mama, of course. Oh, Bertie, I miss her so. If only she were here now. If I tell you something, will you swear not to tease me?'

'I swear, Hetty,' said Bertie, holding my hand under the table.

'I sometimes hear her talking to me.'

'What, like Sarah's mother at those séance sessions?' asked Bertie.

'No, no – it was plain they were charlatans, though I suppose they gave poor Sarah a lot of joy even so. No, Mama speaks in my heart. Not always, just when I need her advice most. You're not laughing, are you, Bertie?'

'I'd never laugh at anything that truly matters to you, Hetty. So, have you talked to your mama about me? I hope she thinks I'm a nice cheery chap, just the ticket for her special girl.'

'You *are* laughing! And I haven't discussed you with Mama.'

'That's a disappointment! I'd hoped I might be on your mind more than somewhat.'

'Well, you are.'

Bertie still had hold of my hand. He put his face very close to mine. 'And what do you really think of me, Hetty? You know I'm truly keen on you. You're my best girl. I might have a bit of a reputation, and I don't deny I've had a few sweethearts before you, but I'll be true to you and never, ever stray,' he whispered earnestly.

'Oh, Bertie.' I held his hand tight, staring at his dear pink face, seeing he really was serious. My heart thumped hard underneath the garish stripes of my blazer.

'Do you love me, just a little bit?' he asked.

'I – I think I do.'

'Only *think*?'

I struggled to find the right response. *Did* I truly love Bertie? I certainly loved his company most of the time. I liked joshing with him, I liked holding his hand, I liked kissing him. Was that love? I knew I loved Mama. I knew I loved Diamond. I knew I loved Madame Adeline. I knew I loved Jem – like a brother?

'My, my, look who we have here! Talk about love's young dream!' It was Mrs Ruby herself, all got up in the special dress I'd stitched for her. Her eyes were sparkling, and all the red glass beads at her neckline sparkled in the gaslight too.

Bertie looked furious at being interrupted at such an

inopportune moment, but he stood up politely and nodded to her. He sat down again when he saw Samson behind her.

'It's the Little Star herself, all dressed up in a tiny sporting blazer!' said Samson, laughing at me. 'Don't she look a little cracker!' He patted my shoulder clumsily.

'Crackers can be fiery,' I said, jerking out of his reach.

'May I order you a drink, Mrs Ruby?' said Bertie, glaring at Samson.

'Thank you, dearie, but we're joining some friends.' Mrs Ruby was frowning at Samson too. 'Come along, Strongman,' she said sharply.

Samson pulled a silly face, pretending to be frightened of her. He had clearly already been drinking at the Cavalcade bar. Mrs Ruby turned on her heel and he shambled after her. They went to join the couple we'd been staring at, the red-haired stunner and the ugly stout man.

'I can't stand that oaf,' Bertie said furiously.

'What did she call him – *strongman*?'

'Well, he was. That was his act – Samson the Strongman. There's a picture of him in the corridor near Mrs Ruby's suite of rooms. He looks a total fool in a leopardskin, showing his great hairy legs. God knows why the old girl took such a shine to him,' said Bertie.

They were sitting very close together. I saw that Mrs Ruby was holding Samson's hand, out of affection – or perhaps restraining him. He craned round, looking over at me.

'Shall we go now?' I said. 'I can't stand Samson either.'

'Right you are.' Bertie waved at the waiter and dived into his pockets for money.

'Will you let me pay my half, as we're such friends?' I said.

'Never!' said Bertie, paying in full and leaving a generous tip.

He walked me back to Miss Gibson's. We went the long way round, with the darkest alleyways. In between kisses I told Bertie I really did love him.

'More than Jem?' he persisted.

'More than Jem,' I said.

'And you really don't wish it was you marrying him on Saturday?'

'I really, really don't. Though I'd like to be there for the wedding. It would be good to see all the family again – and Janet is a special friend. I think she will look a lovely bride. I wish I could go. In fact, I don't see why I shouldn't.'

'Are you crazy? It's a Saturday. You can't miss a performance.'

'Maybe I won't have to. There's an early milk train. Diamond and I caught it when we went to Bignor. Then I could change at Waterloo and get a connecting train out into the country. I'd have to find a cart to take me the last few miles, but I reckon I could still make it by twelve,' I said, calculating the hours on my fingers. 'And then, so long as I left in plenty of time, I could toast the bride and have a slice of wedding cake – and be back for the middle act. Just.'

'It sounds as if you'd be cutting it very fine.'

'Well . . . I'll leave Diamond with Miss Gibson for the day, otherwise she'd be too tired to perform. If someone could possibly walk her to the theatre, wheeling the penny-farthing, then I could change into my performing clothes somewhere on the journey and then dash straight from the railway station to the Cavalcade,' I said.

'Someone?' asked Bertie.

'Oh, Bertie, would you?' I said, in a wheedling tone.

'I – I think I will.'

'Only *think*?'

Then we kissed again, and I decided I really, really did love him.

I lay awake half the night, sometimes making feverish plans for getting to the wedding, sometimes thinking of Bertie. I told Diamond about it the next morning, and at first she plagued me to come to the wedding too.

'But you won't know any of the people, darling,' I said.

'I'm sure I do know them. You've told me all about them, especially Jem. And I'd really love to see a wedding where the bride wears a long dress.'

'I'm not sure what Janet will wear. She likes very simple clothes,' I said.

Diamond wrinkled her nose at such a thought. 'You'll make yourself a pretty new dress, won't you, Hetty?' she asked.

'I don't think there's time,' I said.

'Well, could you make one for me?' she begged. She went on clamouring to come to the wedding until I told her that if she were a good girl and stayed at home, then Bertie would come and escort her to the theatre. That pleased her immensely. Miss Gibson said she was willing to look after Diamond for me. She even let me off my daily sewing duties so that I could make Janet and Jem a wedding present. I sewed a pair of fine white cotton pillowcases, embroidering Janet's name in pink, with little sprays of pink rosebuds in each corner, and Jem's name in green, with strands of ivy twirling decoratively here and there. I added a small strand of ivy around each spray of rosebuds on Janet's pillowcase and added four little rosebuds to the ivy on Jem's.

'You've made a beautiful job of those pillows, Hetty dear,' said Miss Gibson.

She'd been busy herself, putting the final touches to an elegant primrose yellow silk dress edged with pearly grey lace, very fresh and stylish.

'It's a lovely dress and it's really quite little,' said Diamond, peering at it. 'Do you think it might fit me, Miss Gibson?'

'I think it will be rather too big for you, dear. But I'm hoping it will fit Hetty perfectly,' said Miss Gibson.

'Fit *me*?'

'You need to wear something special for a wedding.'

'Oh, Miss Gibson, you're so kind! It's a simply beautiful dress,' I said, giving her a hug.

'Careful, careful, you'll crease the silk!' she said, but she seemed delighted with my response.

So I was all set to go to the wedding on Saturday.

On Friday night Bertie walked us home from the theatre again.

'I can't really come out with you to Maudie's again, Bertie,' I said, after Diamond had run indoors. 'I have to go to bed now myself because I need to be up so very early.'

'I know, I know – but I'd like to give you this. It won't take a minute.' He put his hand in his pocket and brought out a small rounded box.

My heart started thudding again. Bertie pressed the box into my hand. 'Open it,' he whispered.

'But – but Bertie—'

'Please.'

I opened the box. There was a ring inside, a gold band with a word etched carefully on it. Not my name – a strange foreign word.

'*Mizpah*?' I read.

'It's Hebrew. It means – the Lord keep us safe when we are absent, one from another,' said Bertie.

'It's lovely.' I swallowed. 'It's not an engagement ring, is it, Bertie? I really do love you, but I think I'm too young to get engaged.'

'It's not exactly an engagement ring. I want to give you a massive diamond when the time comes – or perhaps it should be a sapphire or an emerald? But I haven't got the cash just yet. This is an *I love you* ring, Hetty.'

'Then I will be very happy to wear it,' I said as Bertie slipped it on my finger.

16

I WAS WORRIED **I** wouldn't wake up in time, but I hardly slept. I crept out of bed at four, washed and dressed myself, packed my suitcase with the pillowcases and my Cavalcade costume and a book to keep me busy, all without waking Diamond. She murmured a little when I kissed her goodbye, but snuggled up with Adeline and Maybelle, still fast asleep.

I was too excited and anxious to eat any breakfast. I

ended up running all the way to the railway station, worried I might miss the milk train – and arrived there a good ten minutes early. I stood shivering on the platform, twisting my Mizpah ring round and round my finger.

The Lord keep us safe when we are absent, one from another. I liked the sentiment. Mama and I had whispered similar words when I was stuck in the Foundling Hospital and she was working as a maid in Bignor.

I felt it about Madame Adeline too. *Was* she safe? Why was her letter so much shorter than usual? Was she feeling very weary now? And why was there no mention of Mr Marvel? I so wanted them to be living happily together, with all the monkeys as a furry family. Now that I was getting used to travelling, perhaps I could take Diamond to visit one Sunday?

I wanted Jem to be safe too. When I ran away to Tanglefield's, I'd felt too guilty to write to him. Perhaps if I'd kept in touch, he wouldn't be marrying Janet now?

What was I thinking? I *wanted* Jem to marry her, didn't I? I'd practically engineered it. I knew she'd make Jem a fine, true, loving wife. She'd cherish him far better than I could. She'd cook him good meals and tackle the washing every Monday and keep a tidy house for him and chat to him companionably by the fireside, taking all his concerns to heart. She'd be a marvellous mother too. I saw her with a baby in her arms, a little girl leaning against her knee, and a fine strong boy with tousled brown hair and his father's bright eyes smiling at her side.

As I was jolted about on the train to Waterloo, I thought about their life together. I didn't really want to be in Janet's place. I didn't want to make meals for anyone, even though Mama had done her best to interest me in cooking. I certainly didn't want to do any housework. At the hospital I'd done enough scrubbing to last me a lifetime. I'd like chatting to Jem, but I'd want to discuss *my* concerns too. It would never be enough for me to stay at home and raise my children.

I'd loved being a ringmaster, striding about in breeches and boots, even though circus life could be cruel. And I loved my life as a music-hall artiste even more. I still tingled with excitement, right down to the soles of my feet, whenever I heard that roar of applause at the end of our act. I knew it was mostly for little Diamond, who looked so fetching and was truly talented – but I was part of the act too, though it barely needed any skill to ride a penny-farthing around a stage.

I'd made up the words though. I could invent fresh ones whenever necessary. I'd always loved words, talking incessantly as a small child, and inventing all kinds of pretend games. I'd thirsted after stories, loving the fairy tales Nurse Winterson read while we darned at the hospital. I also adored the lurid accounts of murder in

Cook's *Police Gazette*. I'd read Father's copy of *David Copperfield* so many times that the pages opened at my favourite passages.

This was the book I'd chosen for my journey back to the village. I'd read it for the first time on my way back from Monksby. I read it now, all the way to Waterloo. I went on reading on the train to Gillford, but now I was getting too excited to concentrate on David's story.

I looked out of the window, counting the stations, trying to see familiar landmarks. I'd travelled the opposite way along that same rail track when Gideon and I were only five, on our way to the Foundling Hospital. We'd had no idea then that our happy carefree childhood was already over.

At long last the train drew in to Gillford station. I jumped out onto the platform clutching my suitcase. I was worried about reaching Havenford now. I didn't want to walk the six miles and arrive hot and damp and dusty, too late to see Jem and Janet say their wedding vows. I didn't want to hitch a ride on a cart either. I had grim memories of a wizened old man who demanded kisses for the favour. I hoped Gillford might have a hansom cab, though I wasn't sure I could afford the fare.

I was deliberating these options when I saw a plain woman in a surprisingly fancy gown struggling to control two little boys who were trying to run in different directions.

'Big Eliza!' I cried.

She looked up, frowning, clearly not recognizing me. *Again!*

'It's me, Hetty! We last met at Father's funeral – don't you remember?'

'Oh yes. Of course,' she said. She smoothed down her over-ruffled skirt, breathing in sharply. 'Why did you call me "big"?'

'Because Mother fostered another Eliza, remember, so she was Little Eliza and you became Big Eliza. Little Eliza isn't so little now. I expect she's taller than me, but then nearly everybody is. Still, it works to my advantage sometimes, being so small, because I'm now a music-hall artiste, and I pretend to be a child for my act. I don't want to sound as if I'm boasting, but we're a big hit. I do the act with a real little girl, my dearest friend, Diamond.'

Eliza wasn't even listening. 'Hold Wilfred,' she said, thrusting one little boy at me. 'Ernest, don't! You'll get pecked!' She scurried off to retrieve the other child, who was poking his finger into a pigeon carrier.

A thin, weedy, bespectacled man in a creased Sunday suit came hurrying up and seized hold of little Wilfred. 'Let the little boy go!' he demanded.

'Leave him be! He's nothing to do with you. He's my nephew, more or less!' I said, yanking Wilfred back. He started crying, not appreciating the tug of war.

274

'Hetty, let go of poor little Wilfred!' Eliza came running up, holding Ernest by the scruff of his neck.

'You told me to hold him!' I said indignantly. 'I'm protecting him. This man was trying to drag him away!'

'He is my husband, Frank,' said Eliza coldly. 'Frank, this is Hetty Feather, one of Mother's little foster children. She came to Father's funeral. Do you remember I told you all about her?'

'I do indeed.' Frank held out his hand. 'How do you do, Hetty. So you're the girl who ran off to a circus?'

'Yes, I did, but now I am a music-hall artiste,' I said proudly.

He raised his eyebrows so that his spectacles waggled on his thin nose. He didn't seem very impressed.

'I'm not a showgirl,' I said quickly. 'I have a proper novelty act with my young acrobat friend. We're called the Little Stars. We've been promoted to the second act already.'

'Very nice,' said Frank, though his tone implied the exact opposite. 'And might I ask what you're doing here, at Gillford station?'

'Why, I'm going to Jem's wedding, of course.'

'And so are we,' said Eliza.

'I have transport waiting outside the station,' said Frank. 'Perhaps you'd care to join us, Hetty?'

Frank's transport turned out to be a man with a cart

– but thank goodness, he was a respectable tradesman who was happy to be paid in cash rather than kisses. Frank sat up front with him, while Eliza and I squashed into the cart with the twins. Eliza was fuss-fuss-fussing about her gown, especially when Wilfred and Ernest clambered over her.

'Boys! For goodness' sake, mind your muddy boots. This gown cost a fortune!' She gave me a little nod. 'It's cut from a French pattern, you know. The very latest fashion. Still, your dress is very pretty too, Hetty, though the cut's a little skimped.'

I smiled at her pityingly. Stupid woman! That style was at least ten years out of date. *I* was dressed in the latest fashion, and she was too ignorant to realize it. She was the one who was boasting now, chattering on about her house, with its three bedrooms and its indoor water closet and her little servant girl.

'She came from the Foundling Hospital, Hetty, just like you,' she said.

My smile stiffened.

'She's a dear little thing, quick to learn as long as I'm firm with her.'

I ached for this poor foundling girl, stuck with bossy Eliza.

'She's fallen on her feet with us,' Eliza went on. 'Frank is very kind to her too, and is helping her with her general knowledge. Frank is a schoolmaster, Hetty.

We live in the school house, and it's very splendid.'

'Are you a teacher too, Eliza?' I asked, remembering how she used to play school with us little ones.

'Of course not! I'm a married woman with twin boys,' she said. 'I don't work!'

'But wouldn't you like to?' I asked curiously. 'You could teach while your foundling girl looked after the twins. I can't imagine just staying at home and not working. Doesn't it get a little boring?'

'You talk such nonsense, Hetty. Of course, you were brought up to be a working girl, so I suppose any genteel way of life seems strange to you,' she said smugly.

I was getting so sick of my foster sister I contemplated jumping out of the cart and walking the rest of the way to the village. Instead I simply ignored her as we trundled round Carter's Bray towards Havenford. I had my first glimpse of the village, hazy in the sunlight. It was going to be a beautiful day for the wedding. I looked for Pennyman's Field, where Tanglefield's Travelling Circus had camped. I peered closely at the woods, wondering if my squirrel house was still there. We passed the first few cottages – and then I saw *our* cottage, small and square, still a little crumbling, but with new thatch on the roof and the garden full of roses.

Jem would be too busy with his farm work to keep the garden tidy and Mother was long past it. So was it Gideon who tended it?

A tall man in a dark suit and an uncomfortably starched white collar came out of the front door, shading his eyes from the sun, looking at the cartful of visitors. He lowered his hand, and I saw the black patch over one eye and the livid scars on his cheek.

'Gideon!' I didn't wait for the carter to hand me down. I seized my case, held up my skirts, and jumped. 'Oh, Gideon, Gideon!'

'Hetty!' he said, and he clasped me tight and gave me a wonderful warm hug.

'How *are* you, Gid? Do you still like it here with Mother? You're not lonely?' I asked.

He held me at arm's length, smiling into my face. I stopped noticing his wounds, and just saw the dear brother I'd shared a basket with when we were babies, the brother I'd played with at the cottage, the brother I'd tried to protect at the hospital.

'I love it here. It's home!' he said simply. 'Oh, Hetty, I'm so glad you could come for Jem's wedding. It wouldn't be the same without you.'

I could hear Eliza sniffing behind me, because her family weren't getting the same welcome.

'Mother?' she called, going into the cottage. She turned to Gideon. 'I had better help get Mother dressed for the church.'

'Beth and Rosie are helping her,' he told her. 'Do come in, all of you. I have refreshments waiting!'

On the large wooden table stood two big enamel jugs, one containing fresh milk, the other lemonade. There were several plates of dark malt bread thickly spread with butter. Various small children were eating slices, licking the butter off appreciatively.

'I made the lemonade myself – and the malt bread,' said Gideon proudly. 'Of course, it's not a patch on Mrs Maple's baking. You should see what she's prepared for the wedding breakfast! But I thought folk would like a bite beforehand too, seeing as you've all travelled so far.'

I poured myself a glass of lemonade and bolted down a slice of bread, starving hungry because I'd had no breakfast.

'Oh, your malt bread is absolutely delicious, Gid! And the lemonade is perfect – not too sweet, not too tart. What a lovely idea of yours,' I said enthusiastically, though I could see Eliza raising her eyebrows and exclaiming at the chipped crockery and thick slices, the crusts left on country style.

Another foster sister in another flouncy dress started boasting about the dainty food she had, talking like some lady of the manor. This was Nora, who for all her fancy airs and graces was merely a lady's maid. She spoke in an affected voice, and when she was persuaded to try a morsel of malt loaf, she ate it with her little finger sticking out in a ridiculous fashion.

I tried chatting to her, but she practically ignored me, though she did look a little enviously at my primrose dress, knowing more about high fashion than Eliza. I went back to the table for another piece of malt bread, elbowing the children out of my way. (I had learned to elbow very effectively at the hospital!)

I heard Nora hiss to Eliza, 'Why is *she* invited to Jem's wedding? She was only one of the foundling babies, wasn't she?'

'I know, but she stayed on after Father's funeral and wheedled her way into everyone's hearts,' Eliza replied.

'Like *him*,' said Nora.

They both sniffed.

'Mother dotes on him now.'

'He's totally taken over.'

'She thinks more of him than her own kin. Goodness knows why! I mean, look at him. And he's always seemed a bit simple to me.'

They were sneering at Gideon! How dare they talk about my brother like that! He had devoted his life to Mother. I didn't give a fig what they thought of me, but their unkind words about Gideon burned my ears like a branding iron.

I had to run upstairs to see Mother to stop myself punching both my sisters in their smug silly faces. Bess was combing her hair into a neat bun, while Rosie held up a looking glass so Mother could see and approve. Bess looked the same as ever, but Rosie had grown enormous. It took me a second or two to realize that she was heavily with child. Mother had her back to me, but she must have glimpsed me in the looking glass.

'Het-ty!' she said. She slurred the word a little, but it was still clear.

'No, Mother, she lives too far away now. I don't think Hetty will be able to come to the wedding,' said Rosie, rubbing her back.

'Yes I can!' I said.

'Oh Lordy, you startled me! My goodness, Hetty, you're quite the young lady now,' said Rosie.

'There, Mother, you were right,' said Bess, amused. 'You knew who Hetty was, didn't you?'

'Of course Mother knows me!' I said, rushing forward and giving Mother a big hug.

'Careful with her! You'll make her topple!' said Bess, though Mother's large behind seemed firmly anchored.

She was looking so much better! Her mouth was still twisted sideways, but her eyes were bright, and she even managed to lift her arms to return my hug.

'Het-ty, Het-ty, Het-ty,' she said. She took hold of a lock of my hair, which was already tumbling down. 'Bright red. My bright girl!'

'No, Mother, Hetty's not one of your own girls. She was one of the foundlings.' Rosie patted her huge stomach.

'Imagine giving up your own baby. I don't know how they can do it.'

I felt as if she kicked me in my own stomach. 'They don't have any choice!' I snapped. I patted Mother's hand. 'You look lovely, Mother. This must be a very big day for you.'

'Jem,' said Mother.

'Yes, our dear Jem's getting married.'

Rosie and Bess bristled at my pronoun.

'Where *is* Jem anyway?' I asked.

'He's downstairs,' said Bess.

'No he's not!'

'Well, I saw him ten minutes ago, all got up in his wedding gear,' said Rosie. 'He was fiddling around with Mother's chair because one of the wheels has started wobbling.'

I ducked down the stairs again, noticing that someone had put a rail on either side of the stairwell to make it easier for Mother to be helped up and down. I found her chair in the corner of the living room, all the wheels intact – but no Jem.

'Where's Jem, Gid?' I asked as he poured lemonade for the children.

'I think he went outside to smoke his pipe,' he replied.

'He'll be a bit on edge,' said Frank. 'And no wonder! It's a big day in a man's life. A turning point. Maybe he's having second thoughts!'

'Nonsense!' said Eliza.

'Just a joke, dear, just a little joke,' he said quickly.

I went outside, taking my suitcase with me. I didn't want any of those unruly children peering inside. I looked up and down the lane. There was no sign of Jem. I walked round to the back of the cottage. No Jem again, but I found a new pig rootling in its pen. I scratched its back, remembering the pigs of my little girlhood. I had loved them all and wept bitterly every time one had to be slaughtered, though it didn't prevent me from enjoying the bacon and ham.

So where on earth had Jem got to? I went back to the front and walked along the dusty lane into the main village as far as the church. There were flowers in the porch, white roses and honeysuckle, their scent almost overpowering. I glanced inside, peering in the sudden gloom. A couple of families were sitting in the pews much too early, determined to get good seats for the wedding, but no Jem.

Had he gone to Janet's house? Wasn't it supposed to be bad luck for the groom to see his bride before she arrived at the church? All the same, I walked along to the Maples' house. There were trestle tables in the garden spread with white linen, with bowls of white roses in the middle, and place settings for the wedding breakfast. I knocked at the door and Mr Maple answered, still in his shirt sleeves, moving stiffly as if worried the sharp creases in his new trousers would concertina.

'Hello, Mr Maple! Remember me? I'm Hetty. I once stayed with you,' I said.

'How could anyone forget you, Hetty,' he said, smiling at me. 'I expect you've come to wish Janet luck. She's upstairs with her mother.'

I couldn't very well say I'd just popped by to see if Jem were there. I ran upstairs, marvelling at the quiet elegance of the house. I wondered if Janet would mind moving to a tumbledown cottage. She'd probably be happy living in a pigsty so long as it was with Jem. I remembered reading her diary and seeing just how passionately she loved him.

I heard girls' voices and knocked shyly on the bedroom door.

'Come in!' called Mrs Maple.

I peered round the door. There was Janet standing in the middle of the room, surrounded by girls in pale yellow dresses, and her mother in a deep daffodil gown. Janet looked incredible. I'd always thought her rather plain, though I loved her gentle face and rounded figure and long fair plait – but now she looked serenely beautiful in her long white lace gown. She had white rosebuds woven into her hair and wore a simple pearl necklace.

'Hetty!' she cried, and held out her arms.

I embraced her carefully, worried about treading on her gown or disarranging her hair, but she gave me a big hug.

'Oh, Hetty, I'm so very glad you could come! And look,

you're dressed in yellow too, just like my bridesmaids. You'll have to join in as we walk down the aisle!' she cried. She introduced me to each of them – two vaguely familiar girls from the village and two little girls she'd taught in school.

'You look a picture, Janet,' I said, almost in awe of her.

'So do you, Hetty. Your dress is beautiful. I wonder if you made it yourself? You became so nimble with a needle.'

'My dressmaking friend made it for me,' I said.

'Ah yes, Jem said you had joined up with another lady in a gown shop. It sounds like a wonderful opportunity.'

So Jem hadn't even told Janet about my music-hall success!

'Jem must be so happy to see you here for our big day.' There was no edge to Janet's voice at all. She was such a sweet lovely girl.

'Well, I'm truly happy for both of you,' I said. I hesitated. 'I haven't seen Jem yet, actually.'

'He's probably been shining his new shoes again and has got polish all over his shirt!' said Janet. 'You know what he's like.'

'Why don't you run and help him, Hetty?' said Mrs Maple, gently pinning up my stray lock of hair and tucking two spare white rosebuds on either side.

'All right, I will,' I said. 'Thank you for tidying me up, Mrs Maple. Well, I'll see you in church.'

I ran back up the lane, my case banging against my legs. I put my head in the cottage once more. Nobody had seen Jem.

'Perhaps he's gone for a little walk to calm himself,' said Gideon, sounding worried.

'Perhaps he has,' I said.

I suddenly knew where. I darted out towards the woods. When I turned off the path, I picked up my skirts and ran. I knew the way as if it were signposted. I would never forget as long as I lived. I hurried straight to the tall, many-branched tree, the squirrel house of my childhood – and there was Jem. He was leaning against the trunk, dressed in a dark suit, a tight white collar rubbing against his brown neck.

'Oh, Jem!'

'My Hetty!'

We ran into each other's arms.

'What are you *doing* here, Jem?'

'I'm waiting for you. And you look so fresh and lovely in your primrose dress! Oh, the relief! I thought you'd be all dolled up in silks and satins, with red lips and cheeks.'

'The idea! I'm an artiste, not a lady of the night! You truly are ridiculous, Jem,' I said, ducking away from him.

He caught hold of my hand, and felt the ring on my finger. 'What's this?' He peered at it closely. 'It's not a wedding ring, is it?'

'Don't be silly. I'm far too young to be married,' I said.

'But some lad gave it to you?'

'No, of course not. I saw it in a jeweller's and took a fancy to it,' I lied smoothly. It was simpler that way, wasn't it? I didn't want to hurt his feelings – perhaps that was it . . . I felt uncomfortable all the same.

'Now come along, people are starting to worry,' I said briskly. 'You're due at the church in fifteen minutes.'

'I was waiting for you in the lane until I couldn't bear the suspense any longer. I was walking up and down, up and down, and then my feet just started walking all by themselves, into the woods, to our tree,' he said.

'Eliza's tree too,' I said, still smarting from that revelation even now.

'Stop it. It's *our* tree, Hetty. Our place. Our time together.'

'Well, when you and Janet have children, you can take them to the tree and play the squirrel-house game with them.'

'I don't want children with Janet. God help me, I don't want to marry her,' he said miserably.

'What? Jem, don't be silly, of course you want to marry her. You love her!'

'I do love her. She's the dearest girl and would make the best wife in the world.'

'Then stop this nonsense and get to the church and marry her!'

'But I don't love her the way I love you.'

'You love me as a brother – "Your loving brother, Jem".'

'Yes, I know I wrote that. I tried to think it. I tried so hard after you ran away to that wretched circus, Hetty. It broke my heart. I've never felt so lonely in my life. But Janet was there – such a dear girl, such a comfort. I tried to convince myself that we'd be happy together.'

'You *will* be happy, Jem! You're just anxious and worried now, because it's such a big day. I'm sure everyone has their doubts before they marry. But you and Janet are made for each other. All the family think so. All the village!'

'I don't care what they all think. I only know what *I* think. I want *you*, Hetty. And you want me too, I know you do, or you wouldn't have come all this way. You knew where to find me. I was waiting here, and I kept thinking, *If Hetty comes to me, then it's a sign that we're soulmates and should be together.* And you did come, you *did*!'

'Jem, stop it! You're going to be late for your wedding. Come with me now,' I said, pulling at his arm.

'No, you come with me! Look, you've even got your case with you. I don't need anything. You're the girl who's good at running away. Well, run away with me. We'll go anywhere you like. I'm strong, I'm handy, I'll find a job on any farm.'

'I work in a town, Jem,' I reminded him gently.

'Then I'll come too. I can work in a factory.'

'Oh, Jem! You're country born and bred. You'd hate it anywhere else.'

'I wouldn't mind, not if I was with you,' he said. 'And you want to be with me. I can see it in your eyes.'

I shook my head – but part of me was wicked enough to glory in his words. I had yearned for Jem for so many years. He had literally meant the world to me. I had left him, I had hoped he would marry Janet – but it was still wonderful to know that he loved me best.

'I love you, Hetty,' he said, and he pulled me close again and kissed me.

It felt so strange. He kissed so fiercely, with none of Bertie's finesse – but there was something so direct and true and passionate about it that this time I didn't turn my head and push him away. I kissed him back, my hand reaching up to his neck, my fingers clutching his brown curls.

'There, Hetty!' Jem said triumphantly when at last we drew apart for breath. 'You love me too, I know you do. So come away with me. Now!'

I pictured us running through the woods, joining the path, walking all the way to Gillford, Jem carrying my case. We'd get on the first train and go wherever we fancied. We'd start a whole new life and it would be everything I'd ever dreamed of when I was a tiny girl in a white nightdress pretending to marry Jem.

Then, far away, we heard the church bells chiming for

a wedding. Jem's wedding to Janet. I thought of Janet, so serene in her long white gown, as pure as the little white pearls around her neck.

'Janet will be arriving at the church any minute. Jem, we have to go back. This is madness. I saw Janet when she was getting ready. We can't do this to her. You'll break her heart for ever. And I'll break your heart someday, because I'm too wild and restless to settle anywhere for long. I'll run away again, you know I will. Are you listening?'

He broke away from me, his hands over his face. 'I'm not listening.'

'You must! This is your home, your farm, your village. All these people are like kin to you. They all know you and respect you, and you take pride in being honest and decent and trustworthy. They'll hate you if you abandon Janet. And you'll hate yourself too, I know you will,' I told him.

'You know too much.' Jem's voice was thick, and when I pulled his hands away from his face, I saw that he had tears in his eyes.

'There now,' I said, fishing out my handkerchief. I wiped his face tenderly. 'Come on, Mr Bridegroom. Come to the church and see your Janet.'

I took his hand, and he stumbled along beside me until we were out of the woods. I looked at him carefully, smoothing his hair, adjusting his jacket, using my handkerchief to rub the dust off his boots.

'There! You look splendid, Jem. You're going to be a wonderful husband to Janet, I know you are. You're going to forget all about me,' I said.

'I shall never, ever forget you, Hetty,' said Jem.

17

THE WEDDING WAS LIKE a dream – or perhaps a nightmare. I sat squashed into a pew with Eliza and her husband and squirming children, watching Jem and Janet stand before the vicar. When he asked if anyone objected to the wedding, my throat prickled with the effort of swallowing my words. *Yes, I object! Jem belongs to me, to me, to me!*

I didn't say a thing. I sat still and silent while Jem

and Janet made their vows and were declared man and wife. Jem carefully lifted Janet's veil and kissed her on the lips. Was he thinking of *our* kiss such a short time ago? My own lips were dry and yearning.

Then suddenly it was all over. Jem and Janet walked down the aisle together arm in arm, Janet smiling radiantly, Jem keeping step with her, the bridesmaids parading afterwards in their yellow silks. Jem didn't even glance at me.

Outside the church everyone threw dried rose petals. They whirled around like pink snow. Then there was the procession back to the Maples' house for the wedding breakfast. Mrs Maple must have been up baking half the night. There were enormous savoury flans, egg and bacon, ham and mustard, cheese and tomato, all edged with curls of baby lettuce, so that they resembled gigantic sunflowers. There were sausage rolls too, and pork pies, and bacon patties – clearly more than one pig had been sacrificed. There were fruit pies too: apple, raspberry, cherry and rhubarb, all with jugs of cream and custard. There were jellies shivering gently whenever anyone brushed the table, strawberry red and lemon yellow, and two types of blancmange from a special mould, so that a pink and a chocolate castle graced the table. And there were cakes: fairy cakes, Victoria sponge, madeira cake, jam and cream rolls, a large charlotte russe – and, of course, the wedding cake. It had three dazzling tiers, with white icing rosebuds crisp enough to crack your teeth.

There was another table where the wedding gifts were displayed, mostly helpfully practical for a young couple setting up home: a flat iron, a watering can, a set of pots and pans and a rolling pin, a patchwork quilt. There was a pile of bed linen too, rather coarse and unadorned. I laid my pillowcases beside it. I hoped they would guess who had made them – but if not, I had embroidered *Hetty* in tiny chain stitch across the smallest ivy leaf. For a moment I couldn't help thinking of the brown head and the fair head laying on their pillows, and shook my head vigorously to make the image dissolve.

'Don't you like the presents, Hetty?' asked Gideon, standing beside me.

'Yes, yes, of course I do,' I said hurriedly.

'Do you like the quilt?'

'I think it's very fine.' The soft worn hexagons were made from scraps of shirts and pinafores and summer dresses, arranged into pleasing patterns of pink and blue and white.

'I made it!' said Gideon proudly.

'Good heavens, Gid, truly? I didn't even know you could sew! And you have to manage with only one eye too. You've made the quilt beautifully.'

'Do you really think so? I got one of the girls to teach me. I love sewing – though they laugh at me in the village when they see me at my fancy work, sitting beside Mother on the garden bench. They call me a great big lass,' Gideon said calmly.

'Tell me who says that and I'll give them a piece of my mind!' I said.

'Oh dear, Hetty! You've always looked after me,' said Gideon. 'They don't bother me. They're only teasing. And it's true – I love sewing, so I suppose I am like a girl.'

'Men sew too,' I said. 'In Monksby where my real father lives, all the big burly fishermen spend their days mending nets, whistling as they sew. And what about tailors? Who do you think made that fine suit of yours?' I picked up the patchwork. 'You're really good at sewing, Gideon. Your stitches are very tiny and even. Perhaps *you* could train to be a tailor?'

'I don't want to sew dull dark material. I like quilting with light soft stuffs,' he said.

'Then next time I come home I shall bring you a big bag of silk and satin scraps, that's a promise,' I said. 'I know Jem and Janet will love your quilt.'

'They'll love your pillowcases more.' Gideon's finger traced the embroidery. 'Will you show me how to do this stitch, Hetty?'

At the wedding breakfast I sat next to Gideon and talked sewing, while Mother nodded at us both happily.

'I have a notion Mother is fonder of us than of her real flesh-and-blood children,' I whispered.

'Apart from Jem,' said Gideon.

'Will you miss him when he goes to live in his new cottage with Janet?'

'I shall miss him, but I still have Mother for company, and Jem and Janet say we must come and dine with them every Sunday.'

'Perhaps one day you will want to marry too,' I said.

'I don't think so!' he replied. 'What about you, Hetty?'

'Oh, I don't know. I can't make up my mind. Maybe foundling children are so starved of love they don't know how to want to marry,' I said, wondering if this were really true.

I wasn't worrying for Gideon. He seemed truly happy living his peaceful village life. I was worrying for me.

I was tempted to have some of the cowslip wine being generously poured for everyone, but I remembered how terrible I'd felt after I drank too much at my foster father's funeral. Besides, I had to make the long journey back to Fenstone and then perform my act. I sipped lemonade instead – and held this childish glass in my hand to drink the health of Janet and Jem at the end of the feast.

'Make a speech, make a speech!' folk clamoured. 'Come on, Jem, say something, lad.'

Jem shook his head, going scarlet. 'You know I'm not one for making speeches,' he mumbled.

'You do it, Hetty!' Gideon cried. 'You said such lovely things at Father's funeral.'

My foster family frowned, but many of the villagers clapped and cheered in encouragement.

So I stood up, my fists clenched. A hundred thoughts tumbled through my head. I had no idea how to organize any of them. I took a deep breath and opened my mouth.

'We're gathered together today, family and friends, to celebrate the wedding of dear Jem and his Janet. We were children together. I worshipped my big foster brother and followed him everywhere, plaguing the life out of him. But he was always so kind and patient with me. He even indulged me in our own mock wedding. I ran around in a tattered white nightgown with daisies in my hair, a little five-year-old bride. But today Jem has his real true beautiful bride, my dear friend Janet, who will make him wonderfully happy. This is like a wedding in a fairy tale, and we're all sure that the two of you will live happily ever after. Please raise your glasses and drink a toast to Jem and Janet!'

We all drank to them – and for the first time Jem looked me straight in the eye. I knew he was saying goodbye. He was an honourable man. He would never speak words of love to me again.

I left almost straight away. There was no point staying and I daren't risk missing my train. I didn't say a proper goodbye to anyone. I just picked up my suitcase and slipped away.

I didn't know how I was going to get all the way back

to Gillford, but I trusted to luck – and a farm lad fetching his mother from market gave me a lift in his cart all the way to the station. I caught the train in plenty of time, and had a whole carriage to myself. It was just as well, because I did a lot of crying.

By the time I got to Waterloo I knew I must be very red-eyed, but I'd managed to compose myself. I went to the station indicator board to find the platform for the next train to Fenstone – and saw the gold arrow pointing to one terrible word: *Cancelled!* I kept blinking and rubbing my eyes, hoping that when I looked again, the word would vanish. It stayed there, clear and ominous.

I searched for a porter. 'Please can you tell me, why is the Fenstone train cancelled?' I asked desperately.

'Some trouble on the line, miss. The one before was cancelled too,' he said, setting down his load of cases and having a stretch.

'So when is the next train?'

He shrugged. 'Couple of hours. *If* it's running.'

'But – but I *have* to get to Fenstone as soon as possible. Don't any of the other trains go near there?'

'Not unless they've put in another line overnight – which ain't very likely, is it, miss?' He guffawed and seemed to expect me to join in.

I was nearly crying again. 'Please, can't you help me? There must be some other way of getting to Fenstone.'

'Well, I dare say you could hire a hansom – *if* you was a millionaire.'

'How much do you reckon it would be?'

He chewed his teeth. 'At least a tenner. No, fifteen. Maybe more. And I doubt they'd take you all that way as they wouldn't get a fare back. You could try asking, though.'

There was no point. I had two shillings in my purse. I wished I hadn't been so extravagant with my wages, but it had been so wonderful to treat Diamond and take trips. I stared at the useless train ticket in my hand.

'Can I get my money back on this?' I asked. Maybe I could take a cab part of the way, and then walk, or even hitch a lift . . . I *had* to be back in time for the second act. I knew what would happen if I didn't turn up. Mrs Ruby was ruthless. If you didn't show up on time, it was instant dismissal – no arguing or excuses. Artistes performed with hangovers and head colds. I'd seen Peter Perkins throw up in a bucket at the side of the stage. One of the showgirls had danced an energetic routine when she was white as a sheet and bleeding badly, but she'd still managed to kick up her legs and smile.

'Not sure about that, missy. If the cancellations are due to unforeseen circumstances, then I don't see how the company can be held responsible,' said the porter.

'Well, what *are* these unforeseen circumstances, for pity's sake?'

299

'Most likely some poor wretch threw him- or herself on the line to end their misery. So they're all right now, but they're causing endless misery to the poor lads who have to clear up the mess, to their loved ones, and to you too, missy, and all your fellow travellers. Think on if you ever feel like ending it all in the same fashion. It's a rotten selfish act, if you ask me.'

I didn't feel *quite* like jumping in front of a train – but pretty near. I couldn't believe how unfair it all was. I'd tried so hard to work out the train times. It had all been entirely possible, and yet now here I was at Waterloo, completely stuck.

The next hour and a half were the longest of my life. I prowled round and round the station, conspicuous in my primrose dress. Several young men followed me for a while, calling me duckling and going *quack-quack-quack*, but I managed to send them packing with a few withering comments. It helped to vent a little of my anger – though I was mostly angry at myself.

Going to Jem's wedding had been a terrible mistake. I had unsettled him, made him admit things that would torment him now. I had nearly wrecked the entire wedding and ruined Janet's life, when she had always been so kind to me. I had irritated all my foster sisters, who seemed to hate me.

At least Mother and Gideon still cared for me. Perhaps poor Gideon, leading his quiet little life, was the cleverest of us all. What use was it pursuing fame and fortune and falling in and out of love? It looked as if my music-hall career was over before it had begun. And I was no nearer understanding my true feelings about Jem or Bertie.

I twisted the Mizpah ring round and round on my finger. *The Lord keep us safe* . . . I was still absent from nearly all my loved ones, no nearer finding a true home. And Mama was absent for ever.

I tried to talk to her now, but the station hubbub was loud and I couldn't hear her dear voice inside me. I wished there were some way I could get in touch with Bertie so he could help me think of some plausible excuse for Mrs Ruby. I wondered about sending a telegram, but I didn't know his exact address, only that it was shared digs in one of the roads behind the theatre.

I tried sending a thought message by sheer will-power. It had worked for Jem and me. He had been waiting by our squirrel tree, willing me to come and find him – and I'd done just that. So were we truly soulmates? Had I lost all chance of happiness now that he was married to my friend?

I gave myself a shake. No, we'd simply met up at our childhood meeting place. And I didn't need any man to make me happy. I had spent so many happy times with Mama, with Diamond, with Madame Adeline; happy times writing my memoirs, sewing all my creations, performing in the circus ring and the music hall.

Though my chances of remaining a music-hall star receded as the great clock suspended from the station ceiling ticked slowly onwards. Then there was a click from the notice board above my head. A new train was announced – on the line that went through Fenstone! I opened my eyes wide, but there was no yellow arrow with its terse message.

I searched the station for the porter and seized hold of him. 'Does this mean the train is actually running? Oh, please say it does!'

He sucked his teeth again. 'Well, miss, I wouldn't like to say.'

'It doesn't say cancelled, does it?'

'Not as yet. But then the train before was due to run, wasn't it? We'll just have to wait and see.' He said it slowly, shaking his head.

I wanted to shake *him*, but I just had to stand there, staring up at the board, willing the arrow not to appear. I kept doing feverish calculations in my head. If I changed in the facilities on the train and then ran full tilt from Fenstone station, there was a chance I might *just* make it in time, before the end of the second act. Diamond and I would have to go on after the ballet, but I didn't think that would matter *too* much. The audience started to grow restless during their long performance, and some left as soon as the second act was over – which didn't please the programme-toppers, especially Lily Lark.

Maybe this could be our chance to close the second act permanently? This might actually prove a blessing in disguise, so long as Mrs Ruby didn't get too angry.

I waited and waited, not daring to look away from the board for a single second in case the arrow appeared. I *willed* that wretched board to stay arrow-free – and at last a platform number was indicated. I ran to the right one and saw a train steaming into the station.

I breathed in the sooty air as if it were the purest oxygen, rejoicing that the train was actually there, in front of my eyes. As soon as it stopped I leaped aboard, terrified that it might leave without me. When other people got into my carriage, I asked them if they were sure this train was really going to Fenstone in case I'd boarded the wrong train in my panic.

All seemed well, and right on time the train hooted, puffing out yet more steam, and we were off. I breathed a huge sigh of relief. I tried to read *David Copperfield* but I still couldn't concentrate. The words waved up and down, as if David and Little Em'ly had been sucked out to sea and were in danger of drowning like half Em'ly's relations.

I put the book back in the suitcase, fingered each of my precious possessions for luck, and then snapped it shut, laying it on my lap and drumming my fingers on it in time to the thrum of the train.

Let me be in time, let me be in time, let me be in time,

I chanted feverishly to the rhythm inside my head.

But when, by my reckoning, we were only a few miles outside Fenstone, the train slowed and then drew to a complete halt.

'Oh no!' I said.

I wrestled with the leather window sash and peered out into the dusk. I saw other heads leaning out too, up and down the line. I called to them, asking if they knew why we'd stopped, but they shook their heads.

'Calm down, dearie, I'm sure we'll get started again soon,' said a middle-aged woman, placidly continuing her knitting, her needles going *clicketty-clack, clicketty-clack*.

'I've heard there's trouble on the line,' said a man in a striped city suit.

'Someone did away with themselves. Dreadful, isn't it?' said another woman.

The knitting woman tutted in agreement.

I felt as if I were going to go mad locked up in the carriage with them. We waited five minutes. Then another five. Once the train jolted, as if we were about to start, but then it subsided again. We were fifteen minutes late now.

I had no chance of making my proper performance time. I just had to hope that Mrs Ruby would let us end the second act. But time ticked on, and after another quarter of an hour I was in despair. A railway guard came through the train: he explained that they were still clearing the track and we might be here for quite a while.

'Do you know exactly how far away we are from Fenstone? I think I'd better start walking,' I said, and I tried to open the carriage door.

'Stop that! Are you mad? You'll tumble down and kill yourself!' said the guard, seizing me by the arm and yanking me back. 'No passenger is allowed to leave the train! It's strictly against the rules.'

'I'm sure I could jump down quite safely,' I argued, though actually it did look a long way down.

'If you try that again, I shall have you arrested.' The guard forced me to sit down beside the man in the city suit. 'Keep an eye on this young person, sir, and keep her trapped if necessary. We're not having another death on this line!'

So I was well and truly stuck. I wasn't even allowed to go and change into my stage outfit. I sat there shaking with frustration – and then, ten minutes later, the train suddenly jerked into action again.

'There, dearie, off we go now!' said the knitting woman.

'See – you'd only have gone half a mile at most if you'd leaped off the train, and you'd probably have broken your legs into the bargain,' said the city gent.

I ignored them, wondering what I could say to Mrs Ruby. I invented ludicrous excuses for my absence: street

305

accidents, kidnappings, dramatic seizures. As if she'd believe a word! The second act would have ended by now, and they'd be having the long drinks interval. Poor little Diamond would have suffered the worst of Mrs Ruby's rage, though I knew Bertie would have done his best to protect her.

I felt sick at the thought that I'd let Diamond down. I'd trained her so hard, I'd lost sight of the fact that she was still only a small girl. I'd been almost as fierce with her as Beppo – all to make us music-hall stars. Now that we'd actually made it at the Cavalcade I'd totally wrecked our chances. I'd been a fool to risk such a long journey all in one day, a pointless journey that had stirred up all the wrong emotions in Jem and threatened what should have been the happiest day of his life.

I didn't want to go to the theatre now. I wanted to slink back to Miss Gibson's, pull the bedcovers over my head in our little attic room, and hide from everyone. But I had to go and rescue Diamond and face the Ruby wrath.

When we reached Fenstone station at last, the city gent released me and the knitting lady gave me a little pat and said sweetly, 'Here we are! There was no need to get in such a panic, was there?'

I could barely smile at her. I hurried to the Cavalcade, my suitcase banging against my calves, and went in through the stage door.

Stan raised his eyebrows at me. 'Looks like you're in

big trouble,' he said. 'That contraption of yours was waiting in the wings, but I doubt it was able to ride itself all over the stage. Mrs Ruby wants a word with you.'

'I dare say she does,' I said grimly, and set off up to her room. I heard raised voices inside, and then the sound of a child crying. Diamond! I ran the last few paces and rushed into the room without even knocking.

Mrs Ruby was standing with her arms akimbo, looking furious. Samson was there too, downing a very large glass of red wine. Bertie had his arm round Diamond, trying to comfort her. The moment she saw me she ran over and seized me by the waist, sobbing.

'How dare you shout at her! She's only a little girl. It's not her fault we missed our spot. It's mine. Shout at me all you want, but leave her alone, you pair of bullies!' I yelled furiously, hugging Diamond hard.

Mrs Ruby looked taken aback. Perhaps no one had ever dared shout back at her before.

Samson roared with laughter. 'There's a fiery spirit!' he said. 'A temper to match her red hair. Go on, little 'un, give the old lady another mouthful.'

'Can it, Hetty,' said Bertie. 'Listen, I did my best to explain to Mrs Ruby that you were called away because your mother's very ill, but somehow she wouldn't believe me. Tell her!'

He was trying to help me out, offering me an excuse that was far more plausible than any of my own made-up nonsense. But his hasty words suddenly brought back those terrible days in Bignor when my lovely little mama was dying in the consumption ward. That time was so searingly sad, so sacred, that I couldn't use it as a paltry excuse.

'Thanks, Bertie. I know you're trying to save me, but I won't lie, not about Mama,' I said, holding my head high. I looked straight at Mrs Ruby. 'I went to my brother's wedding. It's a long journey, way out in the country. Even so, I left plenty of time to get back, but the train was cancelled. That's God's honest truth.'

'You should never have risked it, not on a Saturday. We've got a sell-out audience, and half of them were here to see you two, the kiddies everyone's talking about. There was uproar when you didn't show up. I'm not having the show disrupted like that! They're in an ugly mood now, and it will be the devil's own job to calm them down. All my major third-act stars are very angry. It puts everyone in a bad light. I'm not having this. I'm getting shot of you two. Go on, out of here. You're no longer part of the show,' Mrs Ruby declared.

'But that's so unfair, Mrs Ruby. Hetty couldn't help it—' Bertie began.

'And you can shut your mouth or you're out too,' she said curtly.

'Hey, hey, maybe you're being a bit hasty,' said Samson, pouring her a glass of wine. 'You saw for yourself – the little girls are a big draw. Why not pop them on at the beginning of the third act – which was due to start ten minutes ago, so we'd better get cracking. It'll surprise the crowd and settle them down.'

'Put them on as third-acters? *Reward* her for a no-show?' exclaimed Mrs Ruby. 'Never! They'd all start taking liberties then.'

'They wouldn't dare. But these girls are good – you know that. I'm not saying put them on as third-acters permanent, like. Just for tonight, as a crowd-pleaser.'

Mrs Ruby's eyes had narrowed suspiciously. 'How come you're sticking up for the kid, Samson?' she said sharply. 'What's it to you if I get rid of her?'

'She means nothing to me. Like you said, she's just a kid. But we're in this show to make money, aren't we? You're meant to be the shrewd businesswoman, aren't you – *Auntie?*'

She flushed when he said the word. She drained her glass, thinking. Then she dabbed her lips with an embroidered handkerchief and faced me. 'All right. You're on in one minute. Get your skinny little rump downstairs, and take the cry-baby with you. I'll decide what to do with you after the show. Go on then, jump to it!'

We jumped.

'Stop crying, Diamond! Wipe your eyes, quick,' I said as we hurtled down the stairs. There was no time for modesty. I stripped off my primrose dress and shrugged on my stage costume in full view of everyone. Samson was lurking around instead of going to his table to quieten everyone down.

'Push off – give the girl some privacy,' said Bertie angrily, trying to shield me. 'Go and announce them!'

'You button your lip, little goblin,' said Samson, aiming a blow at him, but luckily he was too tipsy. He lurched off, though he turned round several times, leering at me.

There were resentful mutterings in the wings as we seized the penny-farthing and Samson announced the beginning of the third act.

'Welcome back, ladies and gentlemen – and others! I hope you've had a chance to imbibe sufficient liquid refreshment, my dears. And now you're in for an unexpected treat. It's been brought to our attention that some of you are a tad disgruntled because two special starry little ladies have failed to put in an appearance tonight . . .'

There was a loud response from the audience.

'Aha, I thought so! But do not despair, ladies and gentlemen. Perk up, all you others! The management understands your feelings. We love those little ladies too. That's why we've decided, on this very special sell-out Saturday at the Cavalcade, to move our miniature misses to the start of the third act! And here they are, so give a big hand to our *Little Stars*!'

As we went on stage, I couldn't help marvelling at

Samson's ability to give us a fine introduction, even though he was clearly drunk. His voice was perhaps a little huskier than usual, but it wasn't slurred, and he was completely articulate. I knew from my own experience that it was hard work getting the words to roll out so fluently.

I was conscious of Samson peering at us intently throughout the act. I thought he was simply keeping an eye on us, making sure we wouldn't let him down after he'd persuaded Mrs Ruby to give us a second chance.

Somehow, though I was bone weary and heartsick, and poor little Diamond still had tear-stained cheeks and looked exhausted, we gave what was probably our very best performance. It seemed daisy-fresh, though we'd said the same lines so many times, and when Diamond made her flying leap up onto my shoulders, she did it with such finesse that there was a great gasp from the audience, and then a frenetic burst of applause.

When we left the stage on the penny-farthing, they clapped even harder. Samson clapped too, actually standing up at his table. I still couldn't bear him, but I was so grateful to have this chance that I smiled and blew him a kiss.

18

BERTIE WALKED US HOME, telling me all about the
shenanigans of the evening, the panic when I failed
to arrive, and Mrs Ruby's increasing rage.

'Well, I never thought I'd say this, but good old Samson
for saving us,' I said, doing a little dance down the road
because I was so happy.

'You watch out, Hetty. I can't bear the way that
man looks at you. Keep away from him, do you hear

me?' Bertie took hold of my arm and gave me a little shake.

I just giggled, feeling light-headed with tiredness. Of course I didn't want to encourage Samson in any way – but he seemed to have taken a shine to me. He was considered a fine figure of a man. He wore foppish velvet jackets and big silk neck ties, but he was so tall and broad-shouldered, with such a pronounced cleft chin, that he didn't look remotely effeminate. The showgirls thought him handsome because of his thick wavy hair, his shrewd dark eyes, his high colouring. It was astonishing that such a man could be interested in a small slight girl like me, sickly pale, with flaming red hair.

'You don't *like* him, do you?' Bertie demanded.

'Of course I don't like him. I absolutely hate him. He gives me the shivers,' I said, truthfully enough. 'But thank goodness he spoke up for us.'

'I spoke up for you too. I practically tore my tongue in two, making excuses,' said Bertie. 'Were you really simply held up by the train? Are you sure you didn't stay too late celebrating at this wedding of yours? Were you having one last dance with the newly-wed?'

'You do talk such nonsense, Bertie,' I said, laughing at him.

He waited outside the door while I took Diamond in to Miss Gibson, thanking her fervently – and then slipped out again. Bertie drew me away from the porch, where the gaslight was bright. We stood together in the dark alleyway beside the shop.

He put his arm round me. 'You're a one, you are, Hetty Feather, whizzing about the country all by yourself, so devil-may-care. Doesn't anything ever frighten you?' he asked.

'Oh my goodness, Bertie, I was *desperate* when the first train was cancelled, and then the second one stopped in the middle of nowhere and wouldn't start again. I was all for jumping out and walking. This man had to hold me down. I still haven't stopped shaking!'

'There now. You're safe with old Bertie – and you two absolutely stunned the audience. I bet Mrs Ruby makes you permanent third-acters. Then there'll be some mutterings! Mine will be the loudest! How dare you jump higher up the bill from me when you've only been in the business five minutes!'

'You are joking, aren't you?' I said uncertainly.

'Course I am. I *want* you to do well, silly,' said Bertie. 'I'm proud of you, Hetty Feather. So how did the wedding go, then? Was it strange seeing your Jem wed this other girl?'

I was glad he couldn't see my face properly. 'It was a lovely wedding,' I said smoothly. 'I'm so pleased for Jem and Janet. They make a lovely couple. They'll be very happy together.'

'And you didn't have any second thoughts? You didn't wish you could be his bride?' Bertie persisted.

'Of course not,' I said.

'Did you tell him you had your own sweetheart now? Did you show him your ring?'

'Of course I did,' I fibbed.

'So you told him all about me?'

'Yes, I did.'

'What did you say?'

I paused. 'I told everyone that I had a very demanding, jealous sweetheart who flirts with any girl that takes his fancy but has a fit if I so much as smile at another man,' I said.

'Oh, ha ha. You don't know how devastating that smile of yours can be. Don't you go dimpling at that oaf Samson or he'll get the wrong idea entirely.'

'As if I would!' I said. 'But it's good that he's on our side.'

'I wouldn't count on it,' said Bertie. 'And for pity's sake, suck up to Mrs Ruby. She could still get rid of you, you know, and I couldn't bear that.'

Mrs Ruby didn't get rid of Diamond and me, although she told us that we were on a 'last warning'. If we were so much as a second late for any further performances, we'd be sacked on the spot. We couldn't keep our place in the third act either.

'I'm not having my other artistes upset by two little upstarts,' she said severely. 'You have to earn your place at the top of the bill. Let's all bide our time and see how you progress.'

For once there was no point arguing. I knew how ruthless Mrs Ruby could be. Apparently, at the end of Saturday's show, she had summoned Vladimir and Véronique and every single girl in the corps de ballet, and told them they were all sacked.

There had been an enormous outcry. Vladimir had made violent threats. Some of the artistes said he'd actually drawn a pistol, but I don't know whether this was to shoot Mrs Ruby or himself. Véronique had gone as white as her tutu and walked off in that curious manner, feet turned out like a graceful goose. Then she had suddenly collapsed on the carpet, fainting dead away. All the ballet girls had cried, so there was a chorus of sobbing, the girls clutching each other and wailing.

I was horrified on their behalf, but I *wished* I could have seen such an extraordinary spectacle.

'All the lads think Mrs Ruby's gone off her head,' said Bertie. 'First she tried to sack you and Diamond, and everyone knows what a big draw you are. And then she gets rid of the whole ballet caboodle!'

'But *they're* not a big draw,' I said unkindly. 'The girls are lovely, but their ballet does seem to go on and on. Véronique's a brilliant dancer, but Vladimir is much too old now. And he definitely shouldn't wear those skin-tight fleshings!'

'It needs a fine figure of a man to carry them off properly.' Bertie struck a ridiculous pose, his arms out, his leg raised, toe pointed. 'How would I look?'

'Extremely silly,' I said, pushing him so that he lost his balance and very nearly fell over.

He chased me then, and Diamond joined in, the three of us running round and round the kitchen table, while Miss Gibson threatened to beat us all about the head with her wooden spoon. But when we were all sitting down drinking cocoa, Bertie continued, 'Seriously, Mrs Ruby's losing her mind. Whether the dancers were a draw or not, they were a vital part of the evening. The ballet took up a good fifty minutes, and old Vladimir's dance with Véronique was at least ten. What's Mrs Ruby going to do on Monday with a whole hour to fill? The audience will start demanding their money back if they're short-changed by a whole hour.'

'Maybe *we'll* have to dance!' said Diamond. 'Oh yes, I love dancing! Bertie, will you dance with me? You won't mind, will you, Hetty?'

'I won't mind so long as he doesn't wear fleshings,' I said.

Diamond spent the rest of Sunday trying to organize her dancing act. Bertie joined in good-naturedly at first, but then became unnerved.

'You must take our act seriously, Bertie,' said Diamond when he pranced about. 'Do it properly!'

'We're not *really* going to be dancing, Twinkle,' he told her.

'Oh, we are, we are,' she insisted. 'Hetty, do you think you could make me a little ballet dress by tomorrow evening? And where can we get some of those soft ballet slippers? Bertie needs some – all he's got are those shiny black shoes and they go *clatter-clatter-clatter* and dis-tract me!'

'They're meant to clatter. They've got metal plates hammered onto the soles for my tap routine. That's the only kind of dancing I can do, Diamond. Why don't we work out a little tap-dance together? I can show you how to do the steps. I know you're a quick learner.'

'I don't want to do tap – it's too noisy and jumpy-about. I want to be *elegant*,' she said, drifting around with an ethereal expression on her face.

I'm afraid we all laughed at her and she got very cross and sat under the table with Adeline and Maybelle, all three of them sulking.

But it turned out that no one had to do any dancing or extend their usual act on Monday night. Mrs Ruby already had a new act to cover both dancing spots.

'We are lucky enough to be joined by Mr Gerald Parkinson and his theatrical company, starring the internationally famous actress Miss Marina Royal,' Mrs Ruby announced to the assembled company. 'They are joining our show for the next three months, before their autumn engagement in London.'

We all stared, many muttering that the old girl must have worked a miracle to find a substitute act so quickly. But Bertie and I knew better. Mr Gerald Parkinson was a withered little old man, with fancy clothes, a thick gold watch chain and a very large cigar held between two fingers. Miss Marina Royal was clearly middle-aged, but still very striking, with abundant bright red hair and a loose green silk gown that emphasized her full figure, set off by a very long rope of amber beads.

'They're the couple we saw in the nightclub,' I hissed to Bertie.

'So Mrs Ruby was fixing the deal with them then,' he said. 'I didn't recognize them, but they're big stars. Well, I've heard they were, twenty or thirty years ago. He was one of the biggest actor-managers, and she was really famous, playing all the great parts, with many devoted followers. There were all sorts of posh nobs in love with her – Lord So-and-so, the Earl of What-not – and she played the field with half a dozen. They were all desperate to marry her, but she's stayed fancy free all these years, saying she's married to her art.'

'My goodness, how splendid,' I said without thinking.

Bertie looked hurt. 'Well, I dare say she's regretting it

now, when she's too old to get any more suitors, past playing all the great parts and performing in provincial music halls to keep the wolf from the door,' he snapped.

I decided to end the discussion, but I brooded about it as I waited in the wings. Why did everyone assume that marriage was a girl's true destiny? Spinsters were mocked and pitied. Even women with professions – Miss Gibson, dear Madame Adeline – were considered lesser mortals because they weren't married. (*Was* Madame Adeline married to Mr Marvel now? No, surely she would have invited Diamond and me to their wedding. I thought about her recent letter. I'd written back immediately but had had no reply).

Dear Mama hadn't been married, though she had certainly longed to be my father's wife. The matrons at the hospital weren't married either, but then, who on earth would ever want to wed Matron Pigface or Matron Stinking Bottomly? Miss Sarah Smith wasn't married either – though she seemed too engrossed in her story writing and charity work to feel the lack of a husband.

I felt a pang when I thought of story writing. I had longed to be a writer, and had jotted down my daily life in the notebooks I grandly called my memoirs. If only writing were my profession, my art! I loved appearing on the stage at the Cavalcade, but it wasn't really *dignified* pretending to be a little girl and riding a penny-farthing. I could make people laugh. Was that all I really wanted?

'Diamond, what do you really, really want to do with your life?' I whispered.

'I want to be with you!' she said.

'Yes, and I want to be with you too. But what do you want to *do*? Have you got used to performing now? You're very good at it. Is this what you want to do when you're grown up? Or do you just want to get married?'

'I don't really want to be grown up.'

'Are you sure? Don't you want to marry Bertie?' I teased.

Diamond gave me a world-weary look. 'Yes, but that's just pretend,' she said. 'Bertie wants to marry you, not me. And if I stay small, I can be a little girl, your little girl, as well as your sister. And Madame Adeline and Mr Marvel can be our grandmama and grandpapa, and Miss Gibson can be our auntie. We'll be a real family.'

'Oh, Diamond! But you could go on performing even if we were one big happy family. You like it now, don't you? How could you *not* like it, when everyone thinks you're so sweet and wonderful?' I said.

'I do *quite* like it, but it gives me a knot in my tummy every night,' said Diamond, rubbing it. 'I like having fun with you and Bertie much more. And playing with Adeline and Maybelle. And making cakes with Miss Gibson.'

'Well, you like being a Little Star with me more than being the Acrobatic Child Wonder?' I persisted anxiously.

Diamond gave me a poke in my own stomach. 'You're being silly now, Hetty. Of course I do!'

Then it was time for our performance. For all Diamond's reservations she did her doll act perfectly, moving her arms and legs mechanically, swivelling her head and staying expressionless as she opened and shut her mouth, uncannily like Little Pip. She leaped and landed with perfect grace, did a rock-steady handstand, and we waved our hands in unison as we pedalled off.

Mr Parkinson, Miss Royal and a little bunch of actors were gathered in the wings now, waiting to go on. One of the ladies was very large, and rather plain, though she wore a great deal of greasepaint. She scratched her head in a rather unladylike way and her hair slipped sideways. I realized that she was wearing a wig like Madame Adeline! She saw me staring and pulled a funny face.

'Whoopsie!' she said, in a very deep voice. 'Well done, you two. You're a hard act to follow. Two fresh-faced little sweethearts outshine a tired troupe of old thespians any day of the week!'

Mr Parkinson frowned and put his finger to his lips, listening intently to Samson's introduction.

The large woman made a big O with her painted lips and waggled her eyebrows at me. Or was it *his* eyebrows? Yes, he was a man dressed up as a lady!

'My goodness, let's stay in the wings and watch them,'

I whispered to Diamond. 'I think they're going to be interesting!'

They were amazing. They performed the most astonishing play. It was all about a murder, with Mr Parkinson solving the mystery and saving Marina Royal from a similar fate – but it wasn't a tragedy at all, it was wondrously comic.

'It's called a farce,' said Bertie knowledgeably.

Diamond was worried when so many things went wrong: the actors tripped or dropped things or hid behind doors and were discovered. 'Will they get into trouble?' she asked anxiously.

'No, no, it's meant to go wrong,' said Bertie. 'That's why it's so funny.'

The audience were in stitches, and half the Cavalcade artistes crowded into the wings, hands over their mouths, rocking with laughter too.

'Bit of a change from all that dreary dancing!' said Bertie. 'Isn't Marina Royal comical when she wants to be! I love her funny way of walking. She's still a fine figure of a woman, isn't she?'

'Well, personally I think she's a little past it, poor old dear,' said Ivy Green, sniffing. 'Bit of a come-down, isn't it? I thought she used to be a serious actress?'

'I think she's doing splendidly now,' I said fiercely. 'Bertie's right – she still looks marvellous.'

'Yes, well . . .' said Ivy, looking at me and not finishing

her sentence. She clearly meant that a plain little thing like me *would* think Marina Royal marvellous.

'She can still act all of us off the stage,' I said sharply.

Bertie looked amused. He always liked it when the two of us got into a spat. He especially liked acting as a referee, trying to calm us down.

I wasn't in the mood for that. 'Come on, Diamond, let's go home,' I said.

'But we always wait till after Bertie's act, then he can walk us home,' said Diamond.

'Yes, but I think we're both tired and need to go home *now*,' I said firmly.

However, when I'd dragged her away, I stowed the penny-farthing down with grumpy old Stan, and we slipped back into the Cavalcade. As it was a Monday, we weren't sold out, so it was easy to find two seats in the back stalls. I watched the rest of Mr Parkinson's comical farce, which continued at a glorious pace until the grand finale. The applause was tremendous.

'Mrs Ruby knows what she's doing! They're so much better than the ballet,' I said to Diamond. But she had already curled up on her plush seat and was fast asleep.

I didn't wake her up. I waited during the long interval, going over the play in my head, marvelling at their comic timing. They made it all look so easy, but I realized how much practice it took to get everything so spot-on perfect.

I was tired myself, and knew I should take Diamond

home to bed and go to sleep myself, but I was keen to see what the actors would do in their third-act spot.

It was worth the wait. I was expecting another comedy, but this seemed to be a romance between two actors, Miss Royal and Mr Parkinson – Romeo and Juliet. I'd never seen or read the Shakespeare play, but I had a vague idea that it was about two young lovers. The audience knew this too, and when they saw a makeshift balcony being rolled on stage with Marina Royal standing on it and Mr Parkinson pacing below, there was a guffaw of laughter: it seemed ridiculous, two elderly people acting such parts.

Perhaps that was the point . . . Were they going to ham it up and make it deliberately foolish? I wondered. But when Miss Royal gazed out into the auditorium in seeming frustration and said, '*O Romeo, Romeo, wherefore art thou Romeo?*' I knew she was playing the scene with all due seriousness.

Suddenly she *became* Juliet, everything about her young and lissom and eager. When Mr Parkinson answered, he seemed to become an ardent passionate youth. There were still a few titters from the rowdier elements, but these soon subsided. Marina Royal and Gerald Parkinson had managed to overcome an entire semi-drunken Cavalcade audience by the simple power of their acting.

I sat bolt upright, tingling all over as their words

reached me. I believed in them, I believed in their sudden overwhelming love, I hoped that somehow they could live happily ever after, even though I sensed there would be a tragic ending. The words themselves made complex patterns in my head. They were archaic, difficult to understand at first, and yet so beautiful that it was worth the effort. Marina Royal and Gerald Parkinson seemed aware of this, and spoke slowly and dramatically, emphasizing everything with gestures, but at the same time they managed to seem utterly natural, two young people longing for each other.

I thought of my time in the wood with Jem, my dalliance with Bertie. My own romances seemed so small and stunted compared with Romeo and Juliet's grand passion. Perhaps it was simply Shakespeare's words that worked the magic. I tried to imagine straightforward Jem with his country burr proclaiming such passionate poetry, Bertie with his Cockney twang and constant teasing speaking with such ardour. It was impossible.

I wanted the scene to go on for ever, but it was only minutes before the couple parted. There was a little silence after Juliet had disappeared from her balcony and Romeo had run off stage – and then everyone clapped furiously.

I stood up and clapped too, so enthusiastically that Diamond jerked awake, startled. 'What's happened, Hetty? What is it?' she muttered.

'Oh, Diamond, I should have woken you. Never mind, we'll watch tomorrow – and tomorrow and tomorrow! They're so wonderful, especially Miss Royal! Oh, if only I could act like her!' I burbled, completely overcome.

'I'm sure you could, Hetty,' said Diamond, loyal as ever. 'In fact, I'm sure you could do it better!'

She'd thoroughly woken up now, so we stayed right till the end of the show to watch Lily Lark, who was as saucy as ever, and sang her heart out – but suddenly her act seemed almost tawdry, compared with the style and passion of the two actors. Perhaps I didn't want to top the music-hall bills any more. I wanted to be a real actress!

At the end of the show Diamond and I went out with the crowd, but I lingered outside the stage door, wanting to see Marina Royal again. There was a crowd already gathering there. Most of them recognized Diamond and me, and several asked us to write our names on their programmes.

It was the first time this had happened, and I must admit I found it thrilling. I wrote *Emerald Star* with a fancy flourish, and added a five-pointed star to set off my signature. Diamond had a little more difficulty: her *d*s were a little wobbly, with a tendency to slope in different directions, but she managed reasonably well, though she stuck out her tongue as she struggled to control her pen. She added *Star* to her name, and copied me with her own little star at the end.

The crowd thought she was the sweetest child ever, but they forgot all about us when the stage door opened. There was Marina Royal, looking tired but splendid, with a sable fur wrapped round her gown. Mr Parkinson stood at her side protectively. They were immediately surrounded, everyone babbling, *Oh, Miss Royal, you were splendid tonight; Please sign my programme for me!; I've been following your career for the last twenty years, you're the best actress of your generation; Dear Miss Royal, please accept this little posy as a token of my appreciation* . . .

I found such adulation a little sickening, and I suspect Miss Royal did too, but she smiled and signed and said a few words to each person, while Mr Parkinson waited patiently at her side.

'Are you going to speak to her, Hetty?' Diamond asked.

'I don't know,' I said. I *wanted* to, but for the first time in my life I couldn't think of anything to say. I wanted to distinguish myself from all these other sycophantic people, to say something that would really interest her, but nothing came to me. Perhaps it would be better to go straight home. I would probably embarrass myself if I tried to speak to her.

The stage door opened again. The crowd surged forward once more, hoping for Lily Lark, but this time it was Samson in his crimson cloak, an ivory cane in one hand. I ducked my head, but I wasn't quick enough.

'The little star herself!' he said.

I grabbed Diamond's hand and started pulling her away.

'No, wait – don't go!' said Samson, pushing his way through the crush. He caught hold of us, one burly hand on Diamond, one grasping my shoulder. 'There now, little girlies. My, you're a skinny one,' he said to me. 'Skin and bones! You could do with a good meal inside you. Now there's an idea! Let's go and have supper right now.'

'I'm so sorry, Mr Samson, but we have to go home straight away. It's very late, past our bedtime,' I said, as childishly as I could.

'Yes, I suppose it is,' said Samson, letting Diamond go to consult his pocket watch. 'So why did you stay to the very end tonight?'

'To see Miss Marina Royal,' I said.

'Oh yes, our illustrious new artiste. The old girl's still got it, hasn't she? But I like spotting talent when it's new and fresh and just needs developing a little.' Samson held me even tighter. I knew I'd have bruises on my shoulder the next day.

'Please, sir, your hand's digging into me uncomfortably,' I said.

'I'm just protecting you from the hurly-burly of the crowd, dear. So how do you two little ones get home, might I enquire? You don't ride all the way home on that contraption of yours?'

'Not tonight, sir. We'll walk. It's not far. Come along, Diamond!' I said urgently.

'Walk! I can't let you two chickies walk off into the night, not when there are so many big bad wolves around,' said Samson. He bared his teeth in his own very wolfish grin.

'We'll be fine, sir,' I insisted.

'Nonsense. I'll call you a hansom cab. I'll pay the fare, of course. In fact, I'll accompany you all the way home, just to put my mind at rest.' Samson leaned forward, his face close to mine, his breath hot and sour with wine fumes. 'Got to keep an eye on my little girl.'

I squirmed as far away from him as I could, searching frantically for some further excuse. But then I heard eager cries as the stage door opened again. I peered round. It was Lily Lark, arm in arm with Mrs Ruby.

'Mrs Ruby!' I called loudly. 'It was a fantastic show tonight! Miss Lark, you were in fine voice!'

They both turned towards me. Samson immediately let us go.

'Quick!' I hissed to Diamond, and we ducked away as he was forced to wave to Mrs Ruby.

We ran hard, hand in hand.

'Is he following?' Diamond panted.

'He won't follow, not with Mrs Ruby's beady eye on him,' I gasped. 'Hurry, though. Let's get round the corner before we slow down, just to be on the safe side.'

We leaned against the wall, trying to get our breath.

'I don't like Samson,' said Diamond.

'Neither do I,' I said. I'd been such a fool to blow a kiss to him at the end of the performance.

'He acts all funny. Especially with you.'

'Well, we're going to keep right away from him in future. I was very silly to keep us out so late. I should never, ever have gone round to the stage door. In future we'll always wait for Bertie, and he'll walk us home. How about that?'

'Yes, then we'll be absolutely safe,' said Diamond happily.

I very much hoped she was right.

19

ERTIE WAS VERY HAPPY to walk home with us every night. He seemed far more relaxed, perhaps because he knew that Jem was married now. I was happy too. I liked his company, I laughed at his jokes, I loved our snatched time together after Diamond went to bed. Sometimes in private I took my Mizpah ring off my right hand and tried it on my wedding-ring finger.

I wondered what it would be like to be married to Bertie

– not now, of course. I still felt far too young. But perhaps in a few years? We might both have progressed further up the bill by then. Lily Lark was getting older, and Marina Royal too, though she was only here on a temporary basis. Perhaps it was time someone much younger topped the bill. I was utterly determined it wasn't going to be Ivy Green! She was a one-trick pony, singing her tiresome songs. She wasn't an original novelty act like the Little Stars.

Even so, I tried to think of a new and even better act for Diamond and me. Bertie shared his treasured *Stage* periodicals with me and I read about all the famous music-hall acts in London. One woman had caused a sensation by dressing entirely as a man – dress shirt, fitted suit, spats and top hat. I rather fancied this idea. I'd loved wearing my riding breeches in the circus. I could enlist Miss Gibson's help and work up my own miniature man's suit, plus one in an even smaller size for Diamond. Of course, we'd have to cut off our hair to really look the part, but it would be liberating to be free of my long tangled mane that was such a bore to brush and style.

We could act as if we were a couple of little men out for a stroll at night. We could pretend to smoke cigars and swig a bottle of wine – there were all sorts of comical possibilities. I'd have to say most of the words, but that might be funny too, if Diamond just echoed me. I could sweet-talk the general handyman to make us a lamppost prop so that we could dance around it. Then maybe someone could play a few notes on a penny whistle off stage – Bertie, perhaps? We'd think it was a nightingale and go looking for it. Diamond could jump up on my shoulders and peer upwards, then propel herself right up on top of the lamppost? I'd have to make sure the post was very firm and steady, with a flat top so she could land safely, of course.

I outlined my plan to Diamond. She looked appalled and shook her head determinedly.

'But it wouldn't be hard, Diamond. I'm sure you could land on the lamppost easily, you're so clever. It needn't be a real-sized lamppost. In fact, we don't need a lamppost at all, we can think of another way to show off your acrobatic ability.'

It turned out this wasn't the problem.

'I'm not being a little man. And I'm not, not, not cutting off my hair!' said Diamond.

As she protested so rarely, I felt I couldn't press her on this, especially when Miss Gibson seemed utterly horrified too.

'Sometimes I don't know what gets into your head, Hetty! How could you possibly cut off your hair – and Diamond's too! It's your crowning glory. How could you ever look a little lady with short hair!'

That was the trouble. I wasn't a real lady at all. I wasn't sure who was. Perhaps Marina Royal?

I was thrilled when she sought me out in the dressing room.

'Are you the little girl who's so good at stitching?' she asked.

'I – I think so,' I said foolishly. I felt so in awe of her. She was so stately, so imperious, with such a thrilling deep voice. The rich tones of her abundant hair made my own look childish and carroty. Her skin was white and clear without greasepaint, her eyes green and intense. She even smelled extraordinary, wearing a rich lily perfume with musky undertones that made my noise twitch.

'I wonder if you could help me with my Juliet costume? The white muslin sleeves are all worn through. I've done my best to darn them, but they badly need replacing.'

She showed me. She might be a wonderful actress but she was clearly pretty hopeless when it came to darning. A six-year-old foundling could have made a better job of those elbows.

'If you give me the dress tonight, after your performance, I'll take it home and work on it tomorrow. I'll bring it back ready for the evening show,' I offered.

'Are you sure? It's very kind of you,' she said. 'I like your act, by the way. Very original.'

'Thank you, ma'am.'

'And your little sister's a real stunner with all that lovely long fair hair.'

Perhaps Diamond had been right to resist the idea of cutting it off!

*

335

'I'm going to have to stay behind this evening till after Miss Royal and Mr Parkinson have done their Romeo and Juliet scene,' I told her.

'But then Samson might start chasing after you again,' said Diamond.

'I'll rush up to Marina Royal's dressing room and take her Juliet dress, and then I can be out of the Cavalcade while Samson's still at his table, announcing Lily Lark,' I said. 'You can go home with Bertie, same as usual.'

'No, I'll wait,' said Diamond.

Bertie waited too. We watched the show from the back seats. I loved the comic murder mystery, impressed all over again by the immaculate timing and hilarious joshing, but it was still a lot of frothy nonsense compared to the Shakespeare in act three. I had planned to go backstage to Marina Royal's dressing room while they were performing, but I couldn't drag myself away. I shivered all over at the words, whispering Juliet's speeches myself. I'd found an old volume of *Romeo and Juliet* on a penny stall and learned the balcony scene by heart, because it meant so much to me.

Diamond dug me in the ribs with her elbow. 'Um, you're talking, and you always tell me off if I dare say anything during someone's performance,' she whispered.

Bertie whispered in my other ear, making some silly comment about old Mr Parkinson being so old and arthritic that he'd never be able to climb on top of a brick, let alone a balcony.

I took no notice of them. I just stared at the stage, enthralled. I made a dash for it while everyone applauded. I ran all the way out of the theatre, round the corner, in at the stage door, past grumpy Stan, up the stairs and along the corridor. I knocked timidly at the door with Miss Royal's name on.

'Enter!' she called, in that thrilling voice.

I went in timidly. She was sitting in front of the mirror in a silk wrapper, her hair up in a turban while she creamed her face to remove her greasepaint. She still somehow managed to look magnificent.

'You were wonderful tonight, Miss Royal,' I said. 'So heartfelt! And the way you let out a sigh after asking *Wherefore art thou Romeo!* It was so moving.'

She stared at me in the mirror, one eyebrow raised. 'Thank you, dear,' she said. Then she turned round and looked at me properly. 'It didn't seem too ridiculous, a woman of my years playing Juliet?'

'You became Juliet! I don't know how you did it,' I said.

'It's called acting, child – but it's becoming more of a struggle! I should really let our ingénue, Stella, play Juliet instead. The girl's young and pretty, but her acting's wooden as a chair leg.'

'No one could ever take over from you,' I said.

'I think you'd better come round to my dressing room

every evening to give my confidence a boost!' she said, smiling at me. 'There's the dress, hanging over the screen. Do you really think you can fix it so quickly?'

'Of course I can,' I said, taking hold of the dress.

It was a shabby little gown when she wasn't wearing it, the blue velvet faded and worn and the white muslin in tatters. It would be a challenge to fix it up – but I'd have sewn her an entire trousseau overnight if she'd demanded it.

I wanted to stay chatting with her in her dressing room, but I knew it would be foolish to risk encountering Samson again. I ran off, promising Miss Royal that I wouldn't let her down, and joined up with Diamond and Bertie, who were sitting on the steps of the Cavalcade.

'Come on, Hetty! I can hear Lily Lark singing. Samson will be out any minute,' said Diamond, jumping up.

'Has he been pestering you again?' asked Bertie.

'No, no – we just don't like him, that's all,' I said quickly. I didn't want Bertie to tackle him – it was clear who would win any tussle.

Bertie himself knew this, and he cursed Samson all the way back to Miss Gibson's, going on and on about him. Even Diamond couldn't coax him out of his mood. When Bertie and I said our goodnights in the dark, I tried being extra sweet to him, whispering little compliments, rubbing the back of his neck until he relaxed.

'I love you so, Hetty,' he said, winding a lock of my hair round his finger. 'Do you really love me back?'

'Of course I do,' I said. 'There now. I'm so glad you're not angry any more.'

'You're an artful little witch, Hetty.' He reached for the Mizpah ring, turning it round and round on my finger. 'You're mine, aren't you? You'd never run off with a drunken oaf like Samson, would you?'

'Do you think I'm a fool?' I said, and I mock-clouted him about the head. 'Come on – one more kiss and then I have to go indoors.'

I didn't go to bed straight away. Long after Miss Gibson had gone upstairs I sat sewing by candlelight. I cut into a length of new soft white muslin, deciding I would do just one sleeve, but when I had done it I felt I had to complete the job and do the other sleeve too. I was so tired my eyes kept blurring, but I could still see that the new sleeves made the blue velvet look very old and tired, and the hem was beginning to fray.

I went to bed thinking of ways to improve the old costume. When I went to sleep, I dreamed I was wearing the blue velvet gown myself, peering down from the balcony, distracted by love. I gazed into the darkness and saw a figure in the shadows, but I couldn't see who it was.

When I woke, I started working on the Juliet costume again. Miss Gibson didn't have any blue velvet to remake it from scratch. I decided to embellish the worn parts instead.

I stitched silver brocade ribbon around the hem, which

instantly smartened up the dress and made the folds of the skirt hang more crisply. (I only remembered that it would be obscured by the wretched balcony later on, but consoled myself that Miss Royal would like it all the same.) I gave Diamond a length of the ribbon to decorate Adeline and Maybelle's dresses.

Then I started embroidering. I thought of the moon images in the play, and the fact that Romeo and Juliet were called 'star-crossed lovers'. I sewed a shining moon on the front of the dress, and added silver stars at random, knowing they would catch the light when Miss Royal was on stage.

'You're turning that gown into a little masterpiece,' said Miss Gibson.

'Are you sure?' I asked her anxiously. 'What if Miss Royal doesn't like it? Do you think she'll be angry with me for adding embroidery? She might prefer it plain.'

'Then she's a fool,' said Miss Gibson. 'But you can always unstitch it all. Though not before I've taken careful note of your design. It's very similar to the new art that's all the rage in Paris. You've got such an eye, Hetty.'

'Do I have an eye too, Miss Gibson?' Diamond lisped, widening one eye and squinting with the other.

She held up Adeline and Maybelle. Their brocade ribbon was puckered in places, but Miss Gibson praised her lavishly and then made us tea and sponge cake.

Diamond insisted on thimbles of tea and crumbs of cake for her dolls.

''Cos they get as hungwee as we do,' she lisped.

While we were getting ready for the show I held Diamond at arm's length.

'Is your little-girly act all pretend, Diamond?' I asked, looking her straight in the eye. 'All this play with the dolls, and lickle teeny voices, and flouncing about? You don't need to pretend with me. I don't mind in the slightest. I'm just curious.'

'Well . . . I *like* playing,' said Diamond. 'And I like it when people think I'm sweet.'

'I always think you're sweet,' I said. 'But very artful. Now, have you done your stretching exercises? We can't get sloppy. The Little Stars have to be perfect all the time.'

'I'm sick of being a blooming Little Star,' said Diamond, in her old street-girl voice.

She *was* perfect for the performance, though – a lovely little doll herself, landing on my shoulders with perfect precision yet again. When we came off stage I was excited to see Marina Royal standing in the wings.

'Bravo!' she said, embracing us.

'I have your repaired Juliet dress safe, Miss Royal,' I told her happily.

'Well, you really are a Little Star. I'm very grateful. Could you bring it up to my dressing room in the interval after the second act?'

'Certainly,' I said.

I loved it that she didn't mind me visiting her in her dressing room. Lily Lark wouldn't allow any of the other artistes in hers, not even Mrs Ruby herself. Diamond wanted to come too, of course, so I took her with me.

Bertie was left kicking his heels irritably. 'What am I supposed to do, just hang about while you fawn over old Ma Royal?' he demanded.

'Don't you dare talk about Miss Royal in that rude way! I'm not going to "fawn", as you put it. I'm simply returning her costume,' I said. 'I had to do a little repair work for her. She asked me specially.'

'So how much is she paying you?' Bertie asked.

'I wouldn't dream of asking for payment,' I said. 'Not from someone like Marina Royal.'

'Well, more fool you. I never thought you'd be such a mug, Hetty.'

'Oh, mind your own business!' I snapped, and flounced off.

'Poor Bertie,' Diamond remarked as we went upstairs to the dressing rooms.

'I hate it when he interferes and tells me what to do,' I said.

'That's what ladies are supposed to like, isn't it?' asked Diamond.

'Well, I'm no lady – and I hate being bossed about,' I said.

'You boss me sometimes. A lot of times.'

'No, I don't! I look after you!'

'It's all right, I don't mind,' said Diamond. 'You have your little ways.'

'I don't know, one minute you're acting like a baby and the next you sound like a wise little old woman,' I said, grinning at her.

We knocked on Marina Royal's door and she told us to come in. She was in her wrapper again, applying fresh paint to her face, lots of white under her eyes and pink on her cheeks to look like a youthful Juliet. She'd undone her hair, and it tumbled down past her shoulders in great shining skeins, rich red darkening almost to purple.

She looked so marvellous I was awestruck again, scarcely able to say a sensible word.

Diamond had more wits about her. 'Good evening, Miss Royal,' she said, actually bobbing a curtsy.

'Hello, dears. No need for curtsies, poppet. I'm not the old Queen, in spite of my surname!'

'I absolutely love your hair, Miss Royal!' said Diamond.

'And I absolutely love yours, Little Star,' she said. 'So long and yet not a single tangle! You're very diligent with your brushing.'

'Hetty does it for me,' said Diamond. 'If I fidget she threatens to spank me with the hairbrush, but she's only joking.'

'She makes a very good job of you, dear. You look a

regular Alice in Wonderland!' said Miss Royal.

I was beginning to feel a little out of it. I wished my own hair were longer and luxuriant and a more subtle colour than bright orange.

'I've brought you your Juliet gown, just as I promised.' I pulled off the tissue paper with a conjurer's flick and displayed the renovated costume in all its glory.

'Oh my Lord!' Miss Royal gasped, looking shocked.

My chest went tight with fear. 'Don't you like it? I'm so sorry I took the liberty of embroidering it. It was just to cover up the worn patches – but I can unstitch everything quick as a wink if it's not to your taste.'

'It's tremendously to my taste, dear girl. You've turned a dusty old dress fashioned from an ancient curtain into an exquisite gown that is the very *essence* of Juliet. Beautiful new sleeves, set in so neatly – and wonderful embroidery! You're a genius! My, my, I wish you were part of the Parkinson Players. You'd spruce us all up in no time.' She clasped the dress to her bosom and then gestured to me and embraced me too.

I breathed in the heady smell of her lily perfume and greasepaint and felt dizzy with happiness. 'I wish we were too!' I said fervently.

Miss Royal looked thoughtful. She gazed at me and then she gazed at Diamond. 'Hmm,' she said. 'I wonder . . .'

Then the bell rang, warning that the third act would start in five minutes.

'I must get ready! You'd better run along, dears. Now, how much do I owe you, Little Star?'

'You don't owe me anything, Miss Royal. It was a pleasure to work for you,' I said, and then I seized Diamond's hand and pulled her away before Miss Royal could argue further.

'That was a bit silly, Hetty,' said Diamond. 'You spent ages on that dress. She would have paid you heaps and heaps of money.'

'I don't want her money,' I said grandly.

'*I* might,' said Diamond. 'I could buy a new friend for Adeline and Maybelle, or maybe a perambulator to take my girls out for a breath of fresh air. *Why* didn't you want her to pay you, Hetty? You took Mrs Ruby's money when she offered it, and Miss Lark's.'

'They're different. I don't like them as much,' I said.

'Why do you like Miss Royal so?' Diamond put her head on one side and adopted her wise old woman expression. 'Is it because she's a little like Madame Adeline?'

'Not at all,' I said. I was too gallant to say that Madame Adeline was sadly old and wrinkled beside the mature beauty of Miss Royal. They both might be redheads, but Miss Royal's hair was real and abundant whereas Madame Adeline's was only a wig. They were both artistes, but Marina Royal was still a leading actress of great renown, while Madame Adeline was now retired, and had only ever been a circus star.

345

I felt disloyal to Madame Adeline just thinking such thoughts inside my head. She still hadn't written back to us. I'd consulted a map to find the exact location of Mr Marvel's cottage in the country. It might be possible for us to get there and back in a day, though I wasn't sure I trusted trains any more. Perhaps we could try one Sunday, when there was no performance?

'Would you like to visit Madame Adeline?' I asked.

'Oh yes please! And Mr Marvel and all the monkeys, especially Mavis,' said Diamond.

I seized grumpy Stan's broom, propped against the wall in the corridor.

'Jump on then! This is a witch's broomstick and it can fly through the air. It will whizz us to Madame Adeline in less than a minute,' I said, riding it energetically.

'You're a little witch all right!' It was Samson, walking along the corridor, tying a fresh neckerchief at his throat. 'You're a minx when it comes to disappearing acts. Come here, you naughty girl! I haven't seen you for days.'

My heart started thudding. 'Hello there, Mr Samson,' I said, making my voice as childish as possible. 'I thought you'd be at the bar just now, telling your stories and amusing folk.'

'I'd sooner amuse myself,' said Samson. He consulted his enormous gold watch. 'Damn, time presses onwards! You run round the corner, little Goldilocks, while I have a quick word with your sister. Go on! Hop it!'

Diamond stood fast, clinging to me. 'I don't want to!' she said.

'Do as you're told. I'm the boss here,' said Samson, flushing.

'No you're not. Mrs Ruby's the boss.'

'Don't you argue with me, you little tinker!' Samson seized hold of her.

Perhaps he was only going to give her a little shake, but I wasn't having it. 'Leave her alone!' I screamed, grabbing Diamond. Then we ran for it.

Samson chased after us, but stumbled when we got to the stairs. We flew down, almost jumping, and then bumped into half the third-acters strolling towards the wings. We dodged past, and found Bertie.

'What's the matter? Why are you two running?' he demanded.

'We're just having a little race, aren't we, Diamond? Come on, let's race to the first lamppost outside. You race too, Bertie!' I said, as if we were just playing a silly game.

So the three of us raced all the way back to Miss Gibson's and then had to lean against the shop window in a line, wheezing like bellows.

'Oh my,' gasped Bertie, clutching the stitch in his side. 'And I thought I was fit with all that tap dancing!'

'I ran faster than you two, I did!' Diamond said triumphantly. (Bertie and I had behaved like diplomatic parents, slowing down towards the end to let her forge ahead.)

I turned round to press my hot forehead against the cold glass. I saw that Miss Gibson had a new display in her windows: one dress similar to the gown I'd sewn for Mrs Ruby, and a large green shawl embroidered with lilies like the ones I'd invented for Miss Lark.

'She's copied you!' said Diamond, looking too.

'I don't mind,' I said. 'She's been very kind to us. Where would we be without her?'

'Is this our real home now?'

'I suppose it is,' I said.

'No it's not,' said Bertie. 'These are your digs. Digs are only temporary. Mine are too. But *one* day I wouldn't mind betting we have our own little house.'

'You and Hetty – and me too?' said Diamond.

'Bertie, don't. She'll believe you,' I said quickly.

'*I* believe it,' said Bertie. 'Don't you, Hetty?'

'Well, yes. But not *yet*. We're still practically children.'

'I've been fending for myself since I was taken out of the workhouse by Mr Jarvis the butcher when I was ten years old. Young Diamond was half that age when she started earning pennies. And you were barely fourteen when you became a little maid. I reckon we're counted as adults now. Why *can't* it be now? We'll marry, Hetty, to make it all proper. Twinkle here can be our bridesmaid.'

'Oh yes, oh yes! Will you make me a bridesmaid's

dress, Hetty? What colour will it be? Will it have lots of frills?' said Diamond, clapping her hands.

'Stop it, both of you! Bertie, you're being very irresponsible, winding her up like that.'

'Well, you're the one that's forever winding *me* up, blowing hot and cold. One minute it's *Oh yes, Bertie, I love you, of course we'll be together*, and then it's *No wait, I'm not sure, we're just children, I don't think I want to after all*,' said Bertie.

'I didn't say either of those things! Stop exaggerating. And don't let's have all this out in front of Diamond!' I said.

She was staring at us uncertainly, her pretty little face ghostly in the gaslight. 'Are you two playing or are you really cross?' she asked.

'We're playing,' I told her.

'We're really cross,' said Bertie, and he turned on his heel and marched off into the darkness.

'Oh dear,' said Diamond. 'Is he cross with me too?'

'Of course not. No one could ever be cross with you.'

'Mister was, back at the circus. And you were once, before we ran away,' said Diamond.

'Oh, don't remember that, please! I promise I'll never, ever be cross with you again. Now come on, let's get you to bed. And we'd better give your lovely hair a hundred strokes with the hairbrush, seeing as Miss Royal admires it so much!'

20

MARINA ROYAL APPEARED IN the wings to
watch our Little Stars act again the next night –
with Mr Gerald Parkinson. He was peering at us with
narrowed eyes, puffing thoughtfully on his cigar.

When we pedalled off stage, they both made silent
clapping gestures.

'Well done, dears,' said Mr Parkinson.

'What do you think?' Miss Royal asked him.

'I think you have a point,' he said.

We stared at them, not having any idea what they were talking about.

'We'd like a little discussion with you.' Miss Royal glanced round and saw Ivy Green trying to look nonchalant, but clearly listening intently. 'In private,' she added.

'Can you come to Miss Royal's dressing room at the end of the show?' Mr Parkinson asked. 'Perhaps you will be our guests for a light supper?'

I didn't answer for a second, worrying about Samson, but decided to risk yet another unpleasant encounter if it meant supper with Miss Royal and Mr Parkinson.

She saw my hesitation and misunderstood. 'Gerald, darling, they're little girls. They should be home in their beds!'

'They were at the club once with the Rubys, were they not?' said Mr Parkinson.

'Yes, and that's another matter to take into consideration. We want to negotiate discreetly first of all. Tell you what, darlings – come and take afternoon tea with us tomorrow afternoon, at the Queen's Hotel. Will that suit?'

'It will suit splendidly!' I said.

'Then run along now, dears.'

We didn't just run, we skipped! We didn't wait for Bertie, though Diamond wanted to.

'No, don't let's. He's still in a bit of a sulk,' I said. 'Oh, Diamond, imagine! Tea with Marina Royal!'

'What do you think we'll have to eat?' asked Diamond. 'Will it be the pretty pink-and-yellow cake? Oh, I do hope so!'

'I don't care what we eat, just so we can be with Miss Royal. She's so wonderful. What do you think they want to discuss with us, Diamond?'

She shrugged. 'I don't know. They want to talk to us just because they like us,' she said.

'No, I think it's more than that.' My head was whirling. 'Do you think – oh, do you think they might be inviting us to act in their show? They were gazing at us so intently, nodding and smiling. Why else would they be taking such a keen interest in our performance? Perhaps they want to include us in the comical murder play? Maybe I could act as a maid?'

'But you didn't like being a maid, Hetty,' said Diamond.

'I hated being a real one, but acting one would be entirely different.'

'I don't think I'd like to act. I wouldn't be able to remember any new lines.'

'Well, perhaps you could act the little daughter of the house. You could just sit on a rug and look sweet, but not say a word.'

'Could I play with Adeline and Maybelle?'

'Yes! Well, maybe not Maybelle, as she's a little shabby

now, but certainly Adeline,' I said. 'And then, when they do their *Romeo and Juliet* scene, maybe we could be fairies dancing in the moonlight. Shakespeare has lots of fairies in *A Midsummer Night's Dream* so I'm sure he wouldn't mind. You'd make a lovely fairy, Diamond.'

'That's what Mister called me. I don't want to be a fairy,' said Diamond stubbornly.

'Well, you don't have to act at all if you really don't want to. But I rather fancy it myself,' I said.

Fancy it! I longed with all my heart to be a tiny part of the Parkinson Players and share the stage with Marina Royal.

The next day I was restless with excitement, barely able to sit still and sew. I couldn't wait to go to the Queen's Hotel for our afternoon tea. But what *time* was afternoon tea? I was furious with myself for not enquiring. When I was a maid, I served afternoon tea to Mr Buchanan at four o'clock, but when I visited Mama at Bignor, her crotchety old mistress demanded it at three on the dot.

'Miss Gibson, what time is afternoon tea?' I asked.

'Well, it can be any time, dear,' she said unhelpfully. It was difficult to understand her because she was busy turning a hem and had a handful of pins in her mouth.

'What time do hotels start serving it, do you know?'

'I would think around half past two,' said Miss Gibson, inserting another few pins.

Diamond was staring at her in fascination. 'Don't those pins prick you terribly, Miss Gibson?' she asked.

'Of course not, dearie. The rounded heads are in my mouth, see?'

'Don't you try to copy Miss Gibson, Diamond,' I said quickly. 'You'll sneeze or swallow and do yourself endless mischief. So, hotels serve afternoon tea early, at half past two?'

'Yes, but they carry on serving it throughout the afternoon until about five o'clock.'

'Oh goodness. So how on earth do I work out when we're expected?'

'Is dear Bertie asking you out for afternoon tea at a hotel today?' Miss Gibson sounded wistful, maybe hurt she wasn't invited too.

'No, no. Miss Marina Royal and Mr Gerald Parkinson have invited us,' I said grandly.

Miss Gibson winced as if all the pins in her mouth had turned tail and attacked her. She spat them out to speak properly. 'Isn't she that old actress you keep talking about – the one that's joined the Cavalcade? And Gerald Parkinson is her fancy man?'

'No! I mean, yes, Miss Royal is a wonderful, extremely famous actress, but Mr Parkinson isn't her fancy man! He's her manager and he acts too. He's surprisingly good, but still not a patch on Marina Royal. She's utterly magnificent,' I said.

'But she's still an actress. I know you have to associate with them all at the Cavalcade, but I really don't think it's proper taking tea with such types,' said Miss Gibson primly.

'Miss Gibson, if you don't mind my saying so, you're a terrible hypocrite! You're happy enough to make a profit making gowns for all the Cavalcade ladies,' I said.

'I didn't make any profit at all out of that blue gown you were working on. I didn't see a penny for that fine muslin you used for the sleeves, not to mention the skeins of embroidery silk.'

'Oh, that's not fair! You know I'm going to pay you as soon as I get my wages!'

'Now now, don't use that tone to me! I can't really blame you, Hetty, because I know you've had an unfortunate background. You haven't had a mother around to teach you the ways of the world. It's perfectly acceptable to run a respected business and converse pleasantly with Mrs Ruby when she orders gowns from my establishment, but I'd never dream of taking tea with her at a hotel.'

'Then you're very silly,' I said. 'And totally illogical. You had no qualms when you thought we were having tea with Bertie, and *he* works at the Cavalcade.'

'But he's your young man, and a very sweet boy too. Totally devoted, in fact. You beware of taking him for granted! He could easily turn, you know. I'm sure *he* isn't too keen on you running around with painted actresses who give themselves airs.'

'I don't care whether Bertie approves or not. Or you, for that matter! I keep my own counsel,' I said, and I flounced out of the room.

I decided that Diamond and I would have to lurk discreetly opposite the Queen's Hotel, waiting until we saw Miss Royal and Mr Parkinson go inside. It seemed a sensible plan in theory, but it was a chilly afternoon, and Diamond and I hadn't wanted to spoil the effect of our best frocks by covering them with old shawls. We hopped up and down on the pavement, shivering.

'Can't we go inside and wait?' Diamond begged.

'No, I think it's more polite if we join them when they're already at a table. I don't want to look too forward,' I said, wishing I knew more about general etiquette.

'But I'm getting awfully cold. And I very much need to visit the WC,' said Diamond.

After another ten minutes this became a matter of urgency. I needed to go myself, so I agreed that we should go into the hotel. It wasn't as gilded and grand as the Cavalcade and didn't boast a single chandelier, but it seemed formidable even so. A man in livery was standing in the vestibule, staring at us disdainfully.

'I'm afraid unaccompanied children are not allowed in here,' he said.

'I'm not a child,' I said indignantly. 'And we won't be

unaccompanied anyway. We are joining Miss Marina Royal and Mr Gerald Parkinson for afternoon tea.'

'Then please proceed to the Pink Room, where afternoon tea is served,' he said, sniffing.

'But first we require a visit to the ladies' room,' I whispered, blushing.

I felt as if everyone was staring as he directed us down a corridor – but my spirits lifted when we were inside the ladies' room. The facilities were very grand and glamorous. Diamond was so fascinated by the swoosh of water when she pulled the chain that she ran into each and every cubicle to repeat the action. I spent ages washing my hands in the hot water, using a particularly delectable honeysuckle soap. I dabbed a little behind my ears to act as perfume.

There were snowy white towels and free little brushes to tidy our hair.

'Is this money for us too?' Diamond asked, fingering a little mound of pennies in a saucer.

'No, I think that must be for the lady attendant,' I said.

'Oh, how I should like to be a lady attendant in a fancy WC,' said Diamond. 'You could play waterfalls with the water closets all day long and get lots of pennies every day!'

'We're not going to be WC attendants. We're artistes. We like to perform,' I reminded her.

Diamond wrinkled her nose. 'Some of us like it. And some of us don't!'

'Some of us are just plain awkward,' I said, splashing her with water from the tap.'

Diamond shrieked and splashed me back.

'No – don't! Stop it! We're wearing our best dresses,' I said.

We did stop, but even so we seemed to have become very wet. I dabbed at us with the towel, but we were still damp when we emerged from the ladies' room. We peeped into the Pink Room, and luckily, there were Miss Royal and Mr Parkinson, sitting in rose velvet armchairs before a low table set with fancy white and gold china.

'Hello, dears. My goodness, have you recently taken a bath?' asked Miss Royal, looking amused.

'Hetty splashed me!' said Diamond. 'So I splashed her back!'

'You really are just children!' said Miss Royal. 'Well, sit down at once and we'll call for some tea. And absolutely no splashing, nor spilling either!'

I felt my face glowing hot. How could I have acted so foolishly in the ladies' room? I hated being treated like a naughty little girl. Diamond looked a little nonplussed too. We sat very subdued while Miss Royal ordered four teas. She had a way of summoning a waiter out of a blank wall and dispatching him about his business with a wave of her white hand. I wondered if I would ever acquire that authoritative air. I remembered Bertie trying to act grandly in the club, but not quite getting it right. It was such a struggle to master the right manners in fancy society!

Diamond sat fidgeting, running her finger round and round the gold rim of her china plate. She was looking at it hopefully. 'Will there be cake?' she mouthed at me.

'Yes, there will!' Miss Royal told her. 'Lots of cake.'

'Everything's better with cake,' Diamond and I chanted together.

It had been one of Madame Adeline's special sayings.

There were sandwiches first, dainty little cucumber ones, very pretty, but not really tasting of anything. Then there were scones, and they were much better because we were given tiny pots of cream and strawberry jam to go with them. Diamond popped her pot of jam in her pocket when she thought no one was looking. I knew she was taking it home as a present for Adeline and Maybelle.

Then the plate of cakes arrived, and they were truly splendid. No pink-and-yellow cake, sadly, but there were little fruit tarts with whorls of cream, tiny coffee and chocolate choux buns, small slices of lemon cake, and the Pink Room speciality, rose cream meringues.

'Oh, how shall I ever choose!' Diamond wailed.

'You may have one of each,' said Miss Royal.

I hoped she meant I could too. Miss Royal herself ate with gusto, tucking into the cakes, licking cream from her fingers and devouring her meringue with great relish. Mr Parkinson ate hardly anything, just a plate of thin bread and butter.

Miss Royal saw me looking at him with concern. 'Poor Gerald has trouble with his tummy,' she said, patting him fondly.

'Ulcers!' he said. 'Because of all my business worries!'

'And talking of business,' said Miss Royal, 'we have a little proposition for you.' She dabbed her lips with the napkin and sat up straight. 'Your performance is very stylish and the two of you act it out very cleverly. Who taught you?'

'No one,' I said proudly.

'Well, Hetty taught me,' said Diamond. 'I have to act like a dummy dolly.'

'And you do it magnificently,' said Miss Royal. 'Well, we were wondering if you'd care to join up with us Players in the second act? We like to change our comic sketch every month so the Cavalcade regulars won't get bored of us. We've started rehearsing our new little comedy already.'

'Oh my Lord, yes please!' I declared. 'We would absolutely love to, wouldn't we, Diamond? It would be a great honour. We will play any parts. Oh, Miss Royal, thank you so much for giving us such an amazing opportunity,' I burbled.

But something was wrong. Miss Royal was staring at her empty plate, looking stricken.

Mr Parkinson leaned over and patted my hand. 'I'm afraid she wasn't thinking of you, dear girl. It's your little sister we've got our eye on,' he said.

'Oh!' I blushed again, deeply and painfully. 'Well, of course. Yes, Diamond. That will be lovely, won't it, Diamond?'

'Why don't you want Hetty to do acting too? She's much better at it than me,' she said.

'I dare say. I'm sure we'll be able to find her a little part too. But you see we're going to act a comedy sketch of *Alice in Wonderland*. So far Stella, our ingénue, has played Alice, but she's a tall girl and clearly a young woman. We thought it would be funnier with a real child in the part, and you seem born to play Alice, Diamond, with all that lovely long hair.'

'But Hetty has long hair too. Couldn't she be Alice?' asked Diamond.

'She has lovely hair but it's red, like mine. Alice is always fair,' said Miss Royal. 'Haven't you seen the pictures in the story book?'

'I'll read it to her,' I said. I hadn't read it either. I had such a lot of catching up to do.

'Does Alice say much?' asked Diamond.

'Oh yes, she has the biggest part,' said Miss Royal, as if that would please her.

Diamond slumped in her chair. 'I'm not very good at remembering.'

'I'll coach her,' I said.

'That's a good kind girl,' said Miss Royal. 'And of course we'll pay you.'

'Just a little token,' Mr Parkinson added quickly.

He went outside to smoke a cigar. Diamond said she wanted to visit the ladies' room again.

I stood up to go with her, but Miss Royal stopped me. 'You run along, Diamond. I just need a little word with your sister,' she said.

When Diamond had gone, Miss Royal leaned close to me, looking into my eyes. 'I'm so sorry, dear. It must seem so tactless, offering your little sister such a chance and not you. I hadn't quite realized how it would affect you.'

'That's quite all right,' I said stiffly, terrified I might actually burst into tears.

'It's no reflection on you or your acting. It's just that Diamond looks so perfect for Alice. And I meant what I said. We'll find a special part for you too,' she promised.

'It's very kind of you, Miss Royal,' I mumbled.

'Is your heart really set on acting?'

'Yes it is!' I said fervently. 'When I watch you playing Juliet, I just believe in you. It's as if it's truly real. It gives me such a thrill. I can't take my eyes off you.'

'I wish you could have seen me long ago, when I was the right age to play the part,' said Miss Royal. 'About your age, Emerald. Though I believe Diamond called you Hetty. Is that your real name?'

I hung my head. 'Hetty Feather. It's a horrible name.'

'What about Ada Perks? That's *my* real name. Far worse!' said Miss Royal. 'I changed it when I got my first part as Mamillius in *The Winter's Tale*. I wasn't much more than a baby, but I had enough savvy to choose well. Like you. What were our mothers thinking of!'

'Well, actually, *my* mother didn't choose Hetty at all. She wanted me to be called Sapphire, because I've got blue eyes. I should have been Sapphire Battersea,' I said, unable to bear even a little criticism of Mama.

'And does she call you Hetty or Emerald or Sapphire now?'

I swallowed. My eyes were burning as well as my face. 'She's not here any more,' I said, and tears suddenly spilled down my cheeks without warning.

Miss Royal was so kind. She pulled her chair closer and put her arm round me. 'There now. I'm so sorry, dear. I seem to have a knack of saying and doing the wrong thing with you. So who looks after you now, if your mother is no longer with us. Father?'

'Oh no. He lives in the north. He's a fisherman,' I said. 'I don't need looking after. I look after myself.'

But actually I ached for someone to look after me. I loved leaning on Miss Royal's warm shoulder, her arm round me, holding me close. I had a ridiculous urge to climb onto her lap like a baby and be truly comforted. I thought of those long nine years growing up in the

Foundling Hospital, where I'd been pushed and pulled and frequently smacked, but never once held close or kissed.

Then Diamond came running back and I quickly wiped my wet face with my napkin and smiled at her reassuringly. I might still long for my mama, but I had to pull myself together and act like Diamond's mother instead.

Mr Parkinson came back reeking of his Havana cigar, and started discussing our payment. As his company had its own private deal with Mrs Ruby, he would be paying us out of his own pocket. When he said a 'token', he meant exactly that. He offered Diamond half a crown a week, which seemed to me monstrously mean, seeing as Alice had to be the leading part in *Alice in Wonderland*.

'And we will pay Emerald too, of course,' said Miss Royal.

I was offered even less, a shilling – a child's pocket money.

I was tempted to argue, but I sensed that Mr Parkinson wasn't the sort of man to bargain with. I was pretty sure it was Miss Royal's idea to try Diamond out as Alice. He clearly wasn't the sort of man who liked children. When Diamond started prattling on about Adeline and Maybelle, he started yawning and consulting his watch.

'Come along, my dear,' he said, cupping Miss Royal's elbow. 'You need to rest before tonight's show.'

She raised her eyebrows at me. 'Come to the Cavalcade tomorrow at ten in the morning and we will start rehearsals,' she said. 'I know you'll both be splendid.'

'I don't think I'll be at all splendid,' Diamond said to me on the way home. 'I won't have to learn too many lines, will I, Hetty?'

'I'll help you, don't worry,' I said, though I was worried myself, knowing that Diamond would struggle.

'Is Alice a nice little girl?'

'I'm sure she is. We must read the story.'

The toyshop where we'd bought Adeline had several shelves of children's story books. I spotted the little red volume of *Alice's Adventures in Wonderland* straight away. I had several shillings in my pocket just in case we'd been asked to pay for our own afternoon tea, so I bought the book.

I read it to Diamond for an hour or so when we got home. She liked the tumbling down the rabbit hole part. She became intrigued when Alice found the bottle marked DRINK ME, laughing in delight when the author declared it had a 'mixed flavour of cherry-tart, custard, pine-apple, roast turkey, toffee, and hot buttered toast'.

'Will I really have a drink that tastes so delicious when I play Alice?' she asked.

I said yes to encourage her, though I very much doubted it.

She chuckled when Alice grew tiny as a consequence

of the same drink. 'I can do that, look!' she said, crouching in a little ball and looking very sweet.

She liked the idea of a cake with EAT ME spelled out in currants too, though was more disconcerted at the thought of growing very, very tall with a giraffe neck. 'How will they make me do that? Will they stretch me? Will it hurt, like Mister cricking me?' she asked anxiously.

'No, of course not,' I said, though I couldn't work out how they would manage it either.

The story was extraordinary and very funny, but it seemed impossible to stage. How would they manage a Pool of Tears? And what about all the strange creatures? I knew animals could perform. I'd seen Elijah the Elephant put through his paces every day at the circus, and Mr Marvel's monkeys had a brilliant act, but how could there be a performing mouse, or indeed a dodo, which was surely extinct? Then there was a caterpillar, and two frog footmen, a baby that turned into a pig, and a cat with a grin that kept disappearing!

I couldn't work out which part Miss Royal would play. There were no beautiful women in the story whatsoever, just a very bad-tempered Duchess and an even more terrifying Queen of Hearts who kept yelling 'Off with her head!'

Diamond dozed off and I skipped through the rest of the story, puzzling. I couldn't quite follow the plot, especially when they were suddenly at a beach with a

Gryphon and a Mock Turtle and they all danced a bizarre Lobster-Quadrille. How could there be a seaside down a rabbit hole? And why were there suddenly so many playing-card characters?

I searched for another child part that I could play, but there wasn't one. And I was starting to worry dreadfully about Diamond being Alice. She would be on stage all the time, and she had the longest lines of anyone. I wasn't at all sure she would cope – though at least she looked the part.

I got her up early the next morning and showed her the key pictures of Alice in the story book, and she was quite good at striking poses, copying them. She looked calm and composed for the most part, not at all overwhelmed by her bizarre adventures.

'There you are! You'll be perfect, darling,' I said, dressing her in her best blue dress and white pinafore. I knew that most actors wore their oldest clothes for rehearsals, but I wanted Diamond to look the part.

Miss Gibson was annoyed when we said we were off to the theatre for rehearsal. 'But you're supposed to help me sew, Hetty! That's the way you earn your keep,' she said petulantly. 'You spend all evening at the wretched Cavalcade. You don't need to go there during the day too!'

'But we do, Miss Gibson, because we're going to be little actresses now, not just music-hall artistes. Diamond is going to be the star of the Parkinson Players. Alice in *Alice in Wonderland*! We have to rehearse,' I said.

'And I have to make a living, and here I am needing to attend to new customers in the shop all day long because we're so unaccountably busy, and if I'm stuck there, I can't get on with all the costumes, can I?' she moaned.

'I think you're unaccountably busy because of the new designs in the window, Miss Gibson,' I said meaningfully. 'And I will parcel up an unfinished gown each day and take it to the Cavalcade. I will only have a small part and so I can sit in the stalls and sew while Diamond performs. There! You've nothing to complain about now, have you?' I put my arm round her and rubbed my cheek against her fat one.

'Get away with you!' she said, batting me away. 'You think you can charm anyone, Hetty Feather, but it won't work. I haven't forgotten how impertinent you were to me.' But even so she packed us up a little bag of jam tarts to sustain us.

It was a thrill to saunter past grumpy Stan so early and see his surprise.

'What are you two doing here? It's rehearsals only for them actor folk!' he said fiercely.

'We *are* the actor folk,' I said grandly. 'Miss Diamond is going to be the star of their new production.'

But poor Diamond didn't shine. The players were all gathered on stage in various shabby but artistic outfits – worn velvets, tattered silks and trailing paisley scarves.

The very fat person who was actually a man wore tight crimson cord trousers and a grubby dressing gown in daffodil yellow. He was playing another lady again, the fierce Duchess with the pig baby, shaking imaginary pots of pepper and causing havoc, making the rest of the cast laugh.

'Ah, the Little Stars!' said Miss Royal. She was wearing a faded floral tea gown and silver slippers, with several jade bangles clinking on either arm. 'My heavens, Diamond, you look the part in that outfit! Pop up here on stage, dearie. Find her a copy of the script, someone. You'll have to read your lines until you've got it all in your noddle.'

Diamond looked round at me, aghast. I'd tried to teach her to read properly, but she had barely progressed beyond *The cat sat on the mat*.

'Diamond has a little trouble with her eyesight,' I said quickly, not wanting to embarrass her. 'Generally I read the line to her and then she remembers it.'

'Very well,' said Miss Royal. 'Just for today. If it works for you.'

But it didn't work. They went back to the beginning of the scene, with Stella playing the Cook, and the funny fat man playing the Duchess. He told us his name was Harry Hungerford. It sounded familiar. I remembered reading about him in one of Bertie's stage journals. He was a very famous pantomime dame. He didn't have a real baby – or, indeed, a real pig on his lap. He just had a pink cloth with pink sausage arms and legs and an alarming screaming head. He made it cry and squeal very realistically. Diamond stared, fascinated, and Miss Royal clapped her hands.

'There! Look at that expression. Exactly right! Well done, child. You see, Gerald. She's born to be Alice,' she declared.

But when Diamond had to say her lines, she failed miserably. I held the script and whispered the words to her with the right expression and intonation. After several stumbling attempts Diamond did manage to repeat a few lines, but in her usual monotone.

'No, dear. Not in that little doll voice. You're not a ventriloquist's dummy now. You're a real little girl, in a most peculiar situation, but you're very sensible, the only sane person on stage. You say: *There's certainly too much pepper in that soup!* in a lively manner, proclaiming it to the audience, and then you pretend to sneeze.'

Diamond repeated the line syllable by syllable and attempted a very false sneeze.

Mr Parkinson raised his eyebrows and sighed. 'Perhaps this isn't such a good idea after all, Marina,' he said.

Diamond looked miserable. By the time she'd repeated the line five more times tears were pouring down her cheeks.

'Do it *this* way, Diamond,' I said, going over the line

again. 'Look, I'll sit in the stalls, and you can turn your head and say it to me.'

Diamond tried. She turned her head and looked exactly right. She just sounded terrible.

'I'm sure she'll pick it up quickly once she gets used to acting,' I said.

'But we haven't got time, dear. She needs to be perfect by Monday week,' said Mr Parkinson.

'I'll rehearse with her. Don't worry – we'll make it work, I promise.' I tried all day long, slipping Diamond a jam tart as a reward every time she remembered two consecutive lines.

'Jam tarts – how perfect!' said Miss Royal.

'Please, do try one,' I said.

'Mmm, absolutely delicious. Which baker did you go to? We'll order some for the Knave of Hearts scene.'

'Miss Gibson makes them. She's our landlady at the gown shop. I'm sure she'd be happy to provide them for everyone.' I looked at Miss Royal imploringly. 'You will give Diamond a proper chance, won't you? You said yourself, she does look a perfect Alice.'

Poor Diamond plodded her way through the pig-baby sequence one more time.

'She seems to be getting worse rather than better,' Mr Parkinson groaned, clutching his head in despair.

'She's simply tired out now. Surely you can see she's trying her best,' I said.

'But her best isn't anywhere near good enough. This isn't a village-hall tableau, dear. We are a professional company,' he told me.

The word tableau gave me a sudden idea.

'Could Alice not simply strike attitudes *like* a tableau?' I suggested excitedly. 'I think that would work splendidly. All the Wonderland people could act around her while she stands watching quizzically. It would show the difference between our world and Wonderland. I think it would be a fantastically original production.'

Miss Royal burst out laughing. 'You're certainly persistent, Emerald, and clearly a born director. What do you think, Gerald? *Could* her idea work?'

'A mute Alice? Don't be foolish,' he said. 'We're wasting our time. Stella, come, you play Alice once more. God help us, you're not right either – a grown woman who's taller than all the rest of the cast.'

Poor Stella hunched her head into her shoulders. She was only normal size, but of course she couldn't help towering over Mr Parkinson.

'Stand before us and act,' he commanded.

Stella stuttered her way through her encounter with the Duchess, totally unnerved. She spoke in an irritating childish lisp and struck dreadful babyish attitudes.

'I think we'd better abandon the whole idea of doing *Alice*. What were you thinking of, Marina?' Mr Parkinson groaned.

'But it's such a clever parody of the book, darling, with all sorts of risqué references that Cavalcade audiences will adore. I think it could work splendidly as a little set piece. Don't look so woebegone, Stella, you did your best. And so did you, Diamond, dear – and you look such a picture in that pretty frock,' said Miss Royal. She sighed. 'And that wonderful hair!'

'I like Hetty's hair more,' Diamond said, as she always did.

Miss Royal turned and looked at me appraisingly. 'I wonder . . .' she began.

'We can't have a carrot-top as Alice,' said Mr Parkinson.

'We could find her a wig. Haven't you worn a yellow wig in the past, Harry? I'll see if I can fish it out of the props box.'

Oh my goodness! This was *my* chance! I pulled Diamond nearer. 'Would you mind terribly if I had a go at playing Alice?' I whispered.

'Not at all. *I* don't want to be her, ever!'

But Mr Parkinson was frowning. 'I know you've taken a fancy to these little girls, Marina, but I can't really be doing with child performers. They don't know what they're doing.'

'You're totally wrong, sir,' I said, rushing to the centre of the stage. 'I'm sure I could be your Alice. Please give me just five minutes of your time and I'll show you!'

'There, Gerald. You have to admire her spirit! Let us

give her five minutes,' said Miss Royal. 'Hand her the script, someone.'

'I don't think I need it,' I said, truthfully enough, because I'd gone over the scene so often with poor Diamond that I already knew it by heart.

Harry and Stella assumed their places and I opened an imaginary door. I immediately reeled back, hand over my nose, giving little explosive sneezes. I made the too-much-pepper remark as an aside to the audience, shaking my head.

Then I peered at the rolled-up rug on the floor, a strange white smile painted on its end. 'Please would you tell me why your cat grins like that?' I asked, circling the rug warily as if it might grow paws and scratch me.

'It's a Cheshire cat,' declared Harry as the Duchess, in a wonderfully throaty female voice. 'And that's why. *Pig!*'

I jumped, though the Duchess was addressing her unfortunate baby. 'I didn't know that cats *could* grin,' I said.

'They all can,' said Harry, 'and most of 'em do.'

'I don't know of any that do,' I said politely.

'You don't know much,' said Harry. 'And that's a fact.'

'Well, *I* know something!' Miss Royal exclaimed. 'You're a born actress, Emerald Star! Oh my Lord, you little wonder. There, Gerald! See! Admit I'm right!'

'You'd better say so, boss, because the little sweetheart

is Alice to a T, carrot-top or not,' said Harry, and he put his arm round me and gave me a hug.

Even poor Stella clapped me limply with her long pale hands.

Mr Parkinson smiled at me. 'Welcome to the Parkinson Players, child,' he said, but he couldn't help adding, 'Let's hope this isn't a fluke! I need you to be word perfect in every scene, and no fluffing.'

'Yes, sir,' I said.

I looked at Diamond. 'You're sure you don't mind?' I mouthed at her.

She shook her head fervently.

'Then I'm *thrilled*!' I declared, and I actually skipped about the stage. I wasn't being deliberately childish. I was just so ecstatic that I *had* to jump about.

21

BY THE END OF the afternoon we'd gone through the whole play twice. I still had to learn all my lines, of course, but I'd got into the swing of the story now and found myself reacting naturally as Alice. And I'd found a little part for Diamond too! When we got to the scene where the Cheshire cat is up a tree, they stuck the painted rug up on a piece of scenery tree. It didn't look convincing.

'How about using a little person dressed up as a cat?

A little person who could leap up a tree just *like* a cat? A little person who would have hardly any lines to say, but could probably mew very convincingly?' I said to Miss Royal.

She laughed. 'I wonder who that little person could be? Very well. I think it's a good idea, Gerald.'

'I don't,' he said. 'It'll mean further fiddling around, and where are we going to find a small cat costume?'

'That's easy. I'll make it,' I said. 'Diamond, show Mr Parkinson how neatly you can climb up the tree and then balance right at the top, grinning from ear to ear.'

'I won't have to say anything, will I?'

'No, just mew like a cat. You can do that! *Mew, mew, mew!*'

Diamond shrugged, bounded up the tree and squatted there, grinning and mewing for all she was worth. The whole company burst out laughing, even Mr Parkinson.

'Yes, I agree it looks effective. Very well, you pair of little minxes. Go home now. We all need to eat and rest before tonight's performance.'

'Thank you so much, sir. And thank *you*, Miss Royal,' I said.

I wanted to kiss her on the cheek the way I had Miss Gibson, but I was still too much in awe of her to try.

Poor Diamond plodded home exhausted, but I was still dancing on air. I showed off tremendously to Miss Gibson, but she seemed irritatingly unimpressed.

'I don't know what you're doing, throwing in your lot with those actors. They sound like fly-by-nights,' she said disapprovingly.

I was sure Bertie would be thrilled for me. I couldn't talk to him in the boys' dressing room because I didn't want to see them all lolling about in their undergarments. I had to wait till we were in the wings together. He was still being a little standoffish so I slipped my arm about his neck.

'Bertie, you'll never, ever guess!' I said.

'I hate it when people say that,' he said, wriggling away from me.

'Oh, Bertie, do listen! It's absolutely amazing. Diamond and I are going to be part of Mr Parkinson's Players while they're here! Miss Royal asked us. They're going to do *Alice in Wonderland*. It's a children's book, but their play version is more sophisticated, with topical jokes, the sort of thing that goes down wonderfully at the Cavalcade, you know.' I spoke as if I'd been a music-hall artiste all my life.

'So what part are you going to play – Alice?' said Bertie sarcastically.

'Yes!' I said triumphantly. 'Well, they wanted Diamond at first because of her long fair hair.' I looked at Diamond, suddenly remembering to be tactful. 'But then they thought it was rather too big a part for such a small girl.'

'Much, much too big,' said Diamond. 'So now I'm a

funny cat and I get to jump up in a tree and I only have to mew and I can do that – listen.' She demonstrated noisily.

'And so they chose me as Alice. I'll have to wear a long fair wig, but they think they've got one already. Oh, Bertie, I'm so thrilled! Why are you looking at me like that? Diamond doesn't mind not being Alice, I promise you.'

'Well, that's good,' he said stiffly.

'What's the matter with you? *You* wouldn't want to play Alice, would you?' I was joking, but I saw Bertie's eyes flicker. Oh Lord, had I been so concerned about not hurting Diamond's feelings that I'd been tactless with Bertie? 'You don't want to act too, do you? I mean, you've always said you wanted to be a music-hall artiste. You sing and you dance. *Do* you want to act too?'

'Of course not,' said Bertie loftily, but he didn't sound sure.

Perhaps he just wanted to be asked. Was he jealous that I'd been chosen? Bertie had made it in music hall before me. He had worked so hard on his performance, but it was still in the first act. He was only a second-acter because he was a foil to Ivy Green. I'd popped up out of nowhere, been promoted to the second act in two shakes of a lamb's tail, and now had the leading part in the play. I was such a fool. Of course he was struggling with his feelings.

'I'm sorry,' I said softly.

'Why are you sorry?'

'Because I've just been showing off and behaving insufferably. I just had to tell you straight out, though, because you matter more than anyone to me apart from Diamond – I hoped you'd be pleased for me,' I said.

'I *am* pleased,' said Bertie, hugging me to him at last. 'So, are you going to grow your hair even longer and talk in a husky manner and wear odd gowns without waists and have beads clanking down to your knees now that you're an actress?'

I giggled, though I thought Miss Royal looked wonderful, and certainly *had* considered fashioning myself a gown in the new art style.

'*I'm* going to wear a little fur suit with a tail,' said Diamond. 'And Hetty says I can wear special red greasepaint on my lips to make my mouth look really smiley. She's shown me how to stretch like a cat, and bat at people with my paw if I don't like them. She says I'll make everyone laugh.'

'And you will. You two will be the stars of the show,' said Bertie. 'My Little Stars.'

I so hoped he was right. I took the rehearsals very seriously indeed, straining to prove that I could be as good an actress as anyone. Well, I knew I could never be as good as Marina Royal. She was wonderfully scary as the Red Queen, striding about the stage bellowing 'Off with her head!' However, I was pretty certain I was already better than Stella. I wondered if she was annoyed with me for taking over her part, but she seemed relieved more than anything.

She seemed very vague and distracted, mumbling her way through her series of minor parts. I gathered from the way she kept looking at Cedric, the young male lead, that she was hopelessly in love, but he seemed barely aware of her existance. She only came into her own as the Mock Turtle towards the end of the piece, playing it in her natural melancholy manner. She had a surprisingly good singing voice, high and pure.

The whole cast had to join in the Lobster-Quadrille dance, which was very nearly my undoing. I had never danced before and discovered I was hopeless at it.

'It's a very simple routine, Emerald. You're so quick at picking things up, you'll learn it in ten minutes,' said Miss Royal.

It soon became obvious that I'd still be stumbling and getting my feet mixed up in ten *hours*. I wondered if I were simply self-conscious in front of the others, but I was equally hopeless when I tried to practise at home. When I failed to remember the dance for what seemed like the fiftieth time, I threw myself on the bed, thumping my pillow in despair.

'Don't get upset, Hetty. Shall I help you learn it?' Diamond offered.

She really *had* learned the dance in ten minutes, moving naturally this way and that, her feet tapping and thumping and pointing obediently.

'Yes please, do help me,' I said humbly.

Our usual roles were now reversed. Diamond instructed me in every way she knew, being endlessly encouraging, while I did my best to copy her.

'How do you *know* to start with your left foot rather than your right, and to turn round clockwise rather than anti-clockwise, when I didn't even think you could tell left from right, and I know for a fact that you can't tell the time properly,' I said.

'I don't know how I know. I just sort of do it.'

She could also turn perfect cartwheels and walk bent backwards like a crab. She hadn't needed to be taught. She could just do it instinctively.

It took me a long, painful time to learn the dance. I found I was even stumbling through it in my sleep. I practised everywhere I could. Thelma saw me trying to perfect the simple step-tap-tap, step-tap-tap in a corner of the crowded dressing room and laughed at me. But then she stood alongside me and showed me how to do it very slowly until I stepped out properly instead of dithering and hopping all over the place.

'That's it, girl, you're getting it!' she said. 'Then you can progress to this – and this – and this!' She danced the most complicated little routine in her high-heeled boots, her strong muscled legs moving so fast I could barely follow what she was doing.

'You're so clever, Thelma,' I said, clapping her.

'I wish I was,' she said. 'It strikes me you're the clever one. You're already everybody's pet. You'll go far. But you'll have to learn to look out for yourself. Is Samson still giving you grief?'

'Oh, I'm managing to keep out of his way,' I said cheerily.

I was also having to keep out of his so-called aunt's way. Mrs Ruby wasn't at all pleased that Diamond and I were taking part in the play.

'You should have asked my permission first! *I'm* the one who employs you. The Players aren't part of my company, they're just here for the season. They've no right to involve you and your little sister. You'll get distracted and mess up your performance – *if* you can be bothered to get here on time,' she said snippily.

'I'm sorry, Mrs Ruby. I've only been late once, and I'll make sure it never happens again. Our performance will be perfect every night, I promise you,' I said sincerely. She simply sniffed at me, refusing to be mollified.

I didn't really care. I'd rather admired her before, but now I only had eyes for Miss Royal. She was being so kind, helping me with all sorts of little suggestions for playing Alice. Mr Parkinson was the director, but he basically told me to stand here or turn there. He didn't help me *become* Alice.

'No need to take it so seriously – it's hardly Shakespeare, just a little piece of childish comic business to amuse the hoi polloi,' he said loftily.

But Miss Royal had a different attitude altogether. She took all acting seriously. We had long discussions about what kind of little girl Alice was. It was hard for me at first because I couldn't imagine a girl like Alice in the Foundling Hospital. She was so calm, so confident, so curious. She coped splendidly in the bizarre world of Wonderland. I wondered how she'd fare dealing with Matron Bottomly. If she'd shaken her head contemptuously and poked her starched apron and told her she was nothing but a playing card, she'd have been whipped.

I was disconcerted by the long blonde wig Miss Royal fished out of the props box. It was a little big for me, but she managed to tie a blue ribbon tightly round it so that it didn't slip too much. I looked so strange with fair hair.

'You really do look like my big sister now!' said Diamond.

The fair hair somehow made my face look softer, and not quite so pale, and my eyes looked more intensely blue. I peered hard in the looking glass in Miss Royal's dressing room. Did I actually look pretty now? I was so used to being plain.

I couldn't wait for Bertie to see me transformed. I

asked Miss Royal if he could possibly sit in on a rehearsal. She looked doubtful, and said that the company always liked to rehearse in private.

'Oh please, please, Miss Royal. Bertie will be very quiet and very discreet. You won't even know he's there,' I said. 'And it's not as if he's some outsider. He's one of the Cavalcade artistes.'

'It sounds as if you're really fond of him. Is he your sweetheart?' she asked, sounding amused.

I felt myself blushing. 'I suppose so.'

'Well, try not to lose your heart to someone you've only known five minutes, dear.'

'I've known him a long time, since I was a servant and he was the local butcher's boy,' I said.

'Oh, that sounds exactly like a music-hall song! Very well, Bertie can come and watch tomorrow, so long as he doesn't make you lose concentration. You have the makings of a superb little actress, Emerald. I don't want you to be distracted.'

'Oh, I won't be, I promise!' I declared. 'I'm so grateful to you, Miss Royal. Thank you so much.'

It was all wasted effort, because when I told Bertie he could come the following day, he shook his head. 'I don't think I really want to, if it's all the same to you,' he said.

'What? Look, this is a special favour! Miss Royal doesn't usually let anyone watch rehearsals,' I said indignantly.

'I don't want any special favours from Miss Royal, thanks very much.'

'Don't you want to watch me? Don't you care? This is the most important thing in my life!'

'I know it is,' said Bertie shortly.

'Well, the most important work thing. Not as important as you,' I told him, trying to win him round.

'Look, I'll see you on stage next Monday. And every day after that. Isn't that enough? Besides, I've got things to do tomorrow.'

'What things?'

'Look, you lead your life and I'll lead mine,' said Bertie.

I thought he was just bluffing. I hoped he would change his mind and come to the rehearsal after all, but he didn't.

'So where's your constant swain?' Miss Royal asked, peering around the darkened auditorium. 'Is he hiding somewhere?'

'No, I'm afraid he had a former engagement,' I said.

'Oh, I see. Well, never mind. Let's get started. Gerald, are we having a complete run-through this morning?'

We went through the whole play twice. Perhaps it was just as well that Bertie didn't show because I wasn't at my best. I fluffed my lines several times and couldn't get the inflection right on several of the jokes, mostly because I didn't really understand them. I wore the fair wig to try to feel as much like Alice as possible, but I hadn't tied the ribbon tight enough and it kept slipping. I held my neck as still as possible to keep it in place – until Mr Parkinson told me that I looked like a wooden coat hanger and would I please loosen up!

By the evening I felt exhausted, too tired even to eat the coddled eggs Miss Gibson gave us.

She took offence. 'I suppose you've got used to eating oysters with all those acting folk,' she said huffily. 'My simple suppers aren't good enough for you now.'

I tried to explain but she didn't want to listen, and just grumbled on about my taking advantage of her.

'And you're leading your poor little sister astray too! She told me she's playing a *cat* in this wretched play! What are you doing, dressing her up as a heathen animal? She says she has to hide all her beautiful hair inside a hood with ears!'

'Cats don't usually have long fair hair, Miss Gibson,' I said sharply, wishing she'd mind her own business.

Even during our Little Stars routine, I was going over *Alice* in my mind. It seemed easy enough because I'd done it so many times – and yet I was just half a second late pedalling back on stage. Diamond was already springing up to land on my shoulders. I speeded forward and *just* reached the right spot on time, but poor Diamond had to clutch on hard to stop herself falling, and then the penny-farthing wobbled and we very nearly both went sprawling. It didn't happen. I controlled it somehow. We carried on, and rode off to our usual applause.

Half the people in the audience weren't even aware that I'd made a mistake – but we knew. And unfortunately Mrs Ruby had been in her box, watching the show. She was downstairs in two minutes, absolutely furious.

'I knew this would happen! What a shambles! It's because you've been concentrating on this wretched play all day, isn't it? How dare you compromise your performance! I'm paying you good money for a quality novelty act. Your loyalty belongs to me, not to a troupe of actors who are here today and gone tomorrow! One more slip like that and you'll be out on your ears, both of you,' she said.

'It wasn't Diamond's fault, Mrs Ruby. I messed up my timing. I promise it won't ever happen again,' I said, so exhausted and worried that I actually burst into tears, right in front of all the other artistes.

'Look at you, bawling like a baby!' hissed Mrs Ruby. 'When will I ever learn? Child performers might be popular, but they're always more trouble than they're worth. Mop that face – all your greasepaint is running. What do you look like?' She swept out angrily, stamping her glacé kid boots.

Bertie pushed his way through and put his arms round me. 'Don't take it to heart, Hetty. Or you, little Twinkle. She threatens everyone like that. She's just in a black mood because Samson's been playing fast and loose with her. Cheer up!'

'Here, let me help,' said Ivy Green, dabbing at my face with her little handkerchief in the most irritating manner. 'Oh dear, look at these dark circles under your eyes! Perhaps you really *are* working yourself too hard. You need to relax during the day, not rehearse with all those old actors. Take a walk in the fresh air. There's a beautiful little park not far away, with the sweetest ducks on the pond – isn't there, Bertie?'

The last three words were like a punch in the stomach. I stared at Bertie. He looked straight back, but his eyes couldn't quite meet mine. I didn't say anything. I didn't want to give Ivy the satisfaction. But the moment she went on stage to start her act, I said quietly, 'A walk with Ivy in the beautiful little park with the sweetest ducks?'

'No!' said Bertie. 'No, you've got it all wrong.'

'So you didn't go to this beautiful little park?'

'Well, I did, eventually, but—'

'With Ivy?'

'Look, I was simply mooching about town, feeling pretty fed up, if you must know, wishing I'd come to your rehearsal after all. And then Ivy came skipping out of Miss Gibson's after buying some ribbons or fancy whatevers and we walked along the pavement for a bit, and then she said she'd like a little sit down, and we just happened to be near this park—'

'Oh, *I* see.'

'No, you *don't*. It was all totally innocent. Two friends

taking a stroll. I didn't stay with her for long, I swear to you, Hetty, I—'

'Bertie! You're on in two ticks!' Peter Perkins hissed.

'Wait here, Hetty! Just let me get the dance over and then I'll explain everything.' He rushed on stage to do his Ivy routine with all the other men.

'Come on, Diamond, let's go home,' I said.

'But Bertie said wait.'

'We don't have to do what Bertie says,' I said firmly. 'Come *on*.'

'Don't be cross with him,' said Diamond, trotting obediently by my side.

'I'm not the slightest bit cross,' I said, though of course I was fuming. Bertie's stage name was so apt. He couldn't seem to help flirting with any girl who came his way. And Ivy seemed particularly keen. It *could* have been a chance encounter, a stroll, a totally innocent interlude – or they could have spent the whole day walking hand in hand.

How could I know? Why did it matter so much? I told myself I couldn't care less, though inside I cared terribly. But I couldn't fuss about Bertie too much now. I had to concentrate on being Alice.

We were rehearsing full time because there were so many ragged patches, so many little bits of business that weren't slick enough, and the wretched Lobster-Quadrille was still far from perfect. We even rehearsed all day Sunday, in full costume.

'I'd much sooner be having a picnic with Bertie,' Diamond moaned to me. 'It's so hot and itchy in my cat costume. And I rather think I need to go to the WC. How can I go when I'm stuck in all this fur?'

I had to take her off stage mid-scene, and Mr Parkinson glared at us. Even Miss Royal seemed irritated.

The morning rehearsal went very badly. People missed their cues or forgot their lines, and Mr Parkinson kept shouting, which made everything worse.

Diamond got so anxious she forgot to mew, and Mr Parkinson bellowed at her. 'Dear God, you can't say a single line properly so we let you simply mew like a cat, and yet you *still* mess it up! We should have used the rug for the Cheshire Cat. It's a better actor than you!' he exploded.

Diamond burst into tears.

'Don't shout at her like that! She's doing her best. You forget, she's only a child!' I said furiously.

'Exactly my point! I never wanted children in my play in the first place. I told you it would never work,' he said, frowning at Miss Royal.

'For goodness' sake, the child simply forgot to mew and you go throwing a tantrum! And you're conveniently forgetting that Emerald here has been word perfect right from the start and is acting her little socks off. So stop throwing tantrums, Gerald. You've been in the business long enough to know that a bad dress rehearsal means a marvellous performance,' she said.

'In my experience a bad dress rehearsal means an even *worse* performance.'

'Come along, dearies, don't peck each other,' said Harry, smiling benevolently, though he looked terrifying in full Duchess regalia. 'It's not as if tomorrow is opening night at the Shaftesbury or Her Majesty's. We're doing a risqué parody in a seedy music hall in the provinces. Nothing to get het up about, surely?'

'I have my reputation to think of,' said Miss Royal grandly. She couldn't help sounding pompous, but I really felt for her when the rest of the cast burst out laughing. She was clever enough to laugh too, and suddenly everyone was friends again, thank goodness.

Even so, I was disconcerted by Harry's words. The Cavalcade, in all its gold and glittering splendour, seemed so impossibly grand and glamorous, yet the Players clearly looked down on their surroundings, half ashamed to be here. I wondered what the large theatres in London were like. I pictured them in my head: as large as Buckingham Palace, with solid gold fittings and vast chandeliers, the audience in full evening dress every night.

But the Cavalcade was still very important to me, and my part in *Alice* so special. I spent the night feverishly dreaming I was on stage, and everything went horribly wrong. I was stuck in a Blunderland, where my wig fell off, and I opened my mouth and no words came out, and my legs fell off and rolled off the stage during the Lobster-Quadrille.

On Monday morning Bertie came round to Miss Gibson's.

'Come on, girls. I'm taking you out to distract you,' he said.

'Where are we going? The beautiful little park with the sweetest ducks?'

'Stop that! No, I thought we'd go back to Ledbury Hill. You'll help fix a picnic, won't you, dear Miss Gibson?' he said.

'I might be able to,' she said, dimpling.

'We can't go, Bertie! I mean, it's sweet of you to suggest it, but we have to rehearse,' I said.

'No you don't! Old Parkinson said he wanted you all to have a good rest today so you're fresh for the evening performance, I heard him,' said Bertie.

'Yes, but Diamond and I need to rehearse together all the same. And we can't go as far as Ledbury Hill anyway. What if we were late back? Mrs Ruby will sack me on the spot if I'm so much as a second late on stage. No, Bertie. It's out of the question.'

Bertie looked at me. Diamond looked at me. Miss Gibson looked at me.

'Don't!' I said. 'I'm sorry. I'd like to go, truly, but I just couldn't relax and enjoy myself.'

They were still looking. Diamond seemed especially stricken. I struggled with myself. It was so hard. I'd got so used to thinking about myself and my own needs. It was the only way to survive at the Foundling Hospital. No one else looked out for you, so you were lost if you didn't look out for yourself. Out in the world at the age of fourteen, you had to keep struggling, especially if you didn't want to stay a sad little servant for ever.

The only person I'd cared for more than myself had been Mama. She'd meant the whole world to me – no, the entire universe. I'd loved her more than the moon, the sun, every twinkling silver star in the sky. I'd have dusted a thousand houses daily for her, trekked a thousand miles barefoot to seek her out. And where had it got me? I'd found her but I couldn't keep her. She'd died, and I'd felt my heart shrinking, withering into a hard little shell like a walnut.

I loved my father, I loved Jem, I loved Bertie, but not with the same intensity. I'd liked little Diamond from the moment I found her lying under a wagon, sobbing bitterly, but I never thought I'd grow to love her. She sometimes irritated me, bored me, exasperated me – but I'd grown to care about her more than anyone.

'All right, we *will* go for a picnic,' I said.

'To Ledbury Hill?'

'Yes, yes, where else. It's lovely there.'

'Yes, isn't it!' said Diamond, hugging me.

Miss Gibson scurried to the kitchen to start packing a picnic.

Bertie took my hand. 'We don't have to go if it's really going to worry you,' he said.

'I was just being silly. It will do me good to think about something else for a change. And Diamond will love it.'

'And will you?'

'Yes, of course,' I said.

I did have a good day. It wasn't hot and sunny, it was a grey day – positively chilly at the top of the hill, but I made everyone stand in a ring, and Diamond and I showed Bertie and Miss Gibson how to do the Lobster-Quadrille to warm us up. Bertie picked up the steps almost immediately. I expected Miss Gibson to flounder, but she was surprisingly spry and nimble. She couldn't quite manage every intricate step, but she did a remarkable approximation. I knew it by heart but danced in a jerky fashion, as if I were Little Pip. Diamond was the true star, moving with such ease, her blue dolly shoes tapping away.

'Will you, won't you, will you, won't you join the dance!' we all sang, and then we stepped faster and faster until we all collapsed in a heap, laughing uproariously, as warm as toast.

Our picnic wasn't as splendid as the original one because we'd had no time to prepare anything.

'I miss your apple pie, Hetty,' said Bertie.

He didn't cook us steaks this time, but he'd brought thick slices of honey roasted ham, and Miss Gibson had found tomatoes and lettuce and pickled beetroot in her larder. We ate our ham salad with wedges of bread and butter, then devoured a whole fruit cake between us, washed down with pink lemonade.

'Oh my goodness, I'm full to bursting now,' I said, flopping back on the grass.

'So am I,' said Miss Gibson, trying to ease her corset a little.

'I'm the Cheshire cat now and I want feeding!' said Diamond, squatting down and assuming her cat position. '*Mew mew*, I want some food! Nice fishy! And a tasty little mouse for my pudding!'

It was so strange – she could act beautifully when she was simply playing with people she liked.

'Is that what you say in this play of yours?' asked Miss Gibson. 'Is it for children then?'

'Yes,' said Diamond.

'Not exactly,' I said quickly, because there were all sorts of grown-up jokes and asides that I knew would shock Miss Gibson.

'What do you think of the girls being in this play, Bertie?' she asked.

'I think it's splendid,' he replied stoutly. 'I shall be watching breathless in the wings, with my fingers crossed the whole time that it all goes splendidly.'

'Really?' I said. Then, 'Watching with Ivy?'

'She might be there too, I have no idea, but I won't

be aware of her. I'll only have eyes for you two,' said Bertie.

I smiled at him, I smiled at them all. Then I turned onto my front, my head in my arms, and whispered into the darkness, 'It will be all right, won't it, Mama? I want to act so badly. Will I really be any good as Alice?'

You will be wonderful, my love.

It was Mama's voice, speaking in my heart. I knew she always told me the truth. But why did she sound so worried?

22

'I'M SCARED, HETTY,' DIAMOND whispered as we waited in the wings that night.

'Me too,' I said, taking her hand.

Our clasp was damp and slippy. I could feel her trembling.

'But we'll be fine,' I said. 'I don't know why we're so scared now. We've just got to do our old ventriloquist act, yatter-yatter, dance-dance, cycle-somersault through the air, both of us wave, off! Easy!'

But it wasn't easy when we were both so het up. I was horribly aware that Mrs Ruby would be watching. It would be fatal if we made one fluff, one slip. Perhaps she would ban us from being in *Alice* immediately and we'd never get a chance to do even one performance.

'So here they are, the child wonders, our Little Stars!' Samson declared.

We were on! And somehow we worked our way through it. We managed our little piece of patter, and the audience laughed even more than usual. They gasped when I cycled on stage and Diamond sprang through the air. We came off stage in a hurry, desperate to go and change into our *Alice* costumes, but the applause went on, and Samson called us back.

'Where are you, Little Stars? Come and take another curtain call!'

We had to run back and curtsy and smile. I tried not to look in Samson's direction, but I couldn't help giving him a quick glance. He was grinning at me, moistening his lips.

'Quick, Diamond,' I said, and tugged her off stage.

We hurtled back to the dressing room. I stepped into my blue Alice dress and pinafore and tied the blonde wig tight with the hair ribbon, then buttoned Diamond into her cat costume and smeared a red smile across her face.

'I'm even scareder now, Hetty,' she said.

'Don't be scared. You're a cat. You're a lovely smiley

cat who climbs trees and says *mew mew mew*. You're going to have fun being the cat, and everyone will think you're sweet,' I told her.

I rather wished I was playing a little Wonderland creature now, with hardly any lines. I thought of the dense pages of script I had to plough through, line after line after line. I couldn't even remember the very first one! My mind was suddenly empty – no words at all. My throat went dry. I couldn't speak. I caught sight of myself in the speckled mirror and a ghost girl peered back, panic in her eyes.

'You're going to have fun too, Hetty,' said Diamond. 'You'll be a lovely Alice.'

I gave her a hug, and suddenly the words flashed inside my head again, though my voice came out in a croak.

Some of the showgirls were still getting dressed. They wished us luck, and Thelma ran off in her top and bloomers to fetch me a glass of water.

'Here, take a sip or two. You too, Diamond. Whet your whistle!'

We sipped obediently.

'Gawd, Hetty, you're still so white!' She reached into her bag and brought out a little silver flask. 'Take a swig of this. Not too much or you'll choke.'

The liquid burned my throat and made me shudder, but it brought a little colour to my cheeks.

'Better?' asked Thelma.

I swallowed. 'Better!'

'Off you go then. Knock 'em dead, girls!'

'Good luck, kids!'

'You really are the Little Stars!'

They were being so sweet that I wanted to hug them all. As we dashed along the corridor, we passed Benjamin Apple with Little Pip in his suitcase. Mr Apple nodded at us curtly, but Little Pip called out, 'Good luck, girls!' in a muffled voice.

The Parkinson Players were gathered in the wings, ready for our entrance. They all looked surprisingly tense. Even Harry Henderson's expressive face was set rigidly, like a mask. Stella was chewing her lips, spreading red greasepaint all over her long front teeth. Even Miss Royal seemed anxious: she was nibbling at the back of her hand and frowning.

'Oh, what is it? Are you all scared that I'll make a mess of things?' I whispered.

'Don't be silly, darling,' she said. 'You'll be splendid. This is just stage fright. We all suffer from it, especially on the first night of a show. But it will pass, don't worry.'

'Are you sure? I feel so terrible! I think I might be sick,' I said.

'There's a bucket over there if you need it. We always have one handy.' She smiled wryly. 'Oh, the glamour of the stage!'

We waited while Ivy Green finished her vapid little song and dance and then pranced off stage, with Bertie and all the other men in attendance. Bertie broke away from them and put his arms round Diamond and me. He was hot and sweaty from his energetic dance, but comforting all the same.

'Good luck, Hetty. Good luck, Twinkle. You'll be wonderful.' He felt for my hand. 'Where's your ring gone?'

'Alice can't wear a ring. But look, it's on a cord round my neck,' I said, showing him.

He smiled at me. 'That's my girl.'

The stage hands were rushing around getting the set ready. They couldn't construct a real rabbit hole for me to tumble down, of course. I had to climb to the top of a ladder and then act it out slowly, swaying from side to side, pausing every now and then to say a few words. I felt sicker than ever at the top of the ladder, terrified I might lose my grip and fall.

On the other side of the curtain Samson was announcing our new comic play – 'A saucy new version of everyone's favourite kiddy story, *Alice's Adventures in Wonderland*. Remember, Wonderland's that magic place where every bottle is labelled DRINK ME. We'd like that, wouldn't we, ladies and gents? So give a big hand to the Parkinson Players, starring Miss Marina Royal and Mr Gerald Parkinson himself – plus, just for this production, the Cavalcade's very own Little Stars!'

Then the orchestra struck up the strange swirly music Mr Parkinson had found for the introduction, the curtain went up with a swish – and there I was, in front of the huge audience.

I opened my mouth and the words came out, and suddenly I wasn't Hetty any more, or Sapphire, or Emerald. I was Alice, and I'd seen a white rabbit on a river bank and followed him, and now I was tumbling down, down, down . . . and I ended up in Wonderland. Everything became curiouser and curiouser, and I swam in a pool of my own tears, and ran a caucus-race with the whole company and was given my own thimble as a prize by the Dodo (Mr Parkinson with a walking stick and a magnificent papier-mâché beak).

I had a puzzling conversation with a caterpillar (Marina Royal herself, smoking a hookah, sitting cross-legged in a green silk costume), and had a peppery encounter with a Duchess and her pig baby. Then at last I met the Cheshire cat, grinning at me up a tree, and just for a moment I stopped being Alice and was simply myself, praying that Diamond wouldn't fall or mew in the wrong places, because I had to interpret her cat-talk to the audience.

She mewed beautifully, and then I joined the Mad Hatter and the March Hare and the Dormouse for a tea party. I played croquet with a stuffed flamingo in the Queen of Heart's garden (Miss Royal padded out to look like Queen Victoria), and then we all joined the Mock Turtle and the Gryphon and sang and danced, before the final trial scene. This made reference to some recent scandalous affair, and the audience laughed and clapped. I didn't get the jokes, but it didn't matter. I was Alice and I had to take everything seriously.

Then the Queen shouted, 'Off with her head!' and I lost my temper and declared that they were nothing but a pack of cards. They all sank to the ground dramatically – while I told the audience that if they wanted to see them come alive once more, they should return to the Cavalcade the next evening, where they could join me in Wonderland all over again.

Then the cast struggled to their feet and we held hands and bowed. And bowed and bowed and bowed as the audience clapped and cheered. Miss Royal took me by one hand and Mr Parkinson by the other, and the three of us bowed again. Then I was pushed forward to stand at the very front of the stage, dazzled by the footlights, while the audience rose to its feet and clapped me.

I stood there in a daze, hot and sticky under my wig, shivering right down to my stripy socks, unable to believe it. They were all clapping *me*, Hetty Feather, the foundling child! I wasn't a support act any more, I wasn't a ringmaster introducing all the other acts, I wasn't a silent living mermaid in a seedy tableau. I was an actress, the star of the play!

'My little star,' Madame Adeline had once said. Now I was!

There was great jubilation backstage during the second interval. Miss Royal herself hugged me and congratulated me, and then Bertie picked me up and swung me round and round, kissing me in front of everyone. He swung Diamond round too, and declared she was the sweetest little pussycat ever.

Mrs Ruby joined us and congratulated me. 'You've stolen the show, you little minx!' she said. 'Well done! We'll have to devise another little showcase act for you when the Players move on. You're going to be a big draw now.'

Samson came too, a glass of red wine in his hand, and probably the contents of another bottle in his stomach. 'Congratulations, Little Star,' he said, lurching towards me.

He couldn't do anything untoward in front of Mrs Ruby and half the Cavalcade cast. He tried giving my damp cheek a kiss, but I ducked away, pretending to be shy.

I was glad to see that Bertie was too busy giving Diamond a piggyback to notice. Then the bell went to announce the beginning of the third act, and our impromptu party was over.

Bertie walked Diamond and me back to Miss Gibson's. She still thoroughly disapproved of our acting, but even

405

so she had prepared a little party for us. She'd made a special iced sponge cake and opened a bottle of her home-made gooseberry wine. She gave Bertie a full glass, me a half measure, and Diamond a spoonful.

I scarcely slept that night. I relived the whole play again and again, sometimes lapsing into a dream where the whole Cavalcade turned into Wonderland and every-one sang, *'Will she, won't she, will she, won't she,* will *she be a star!'*

Then, at dawn, I woke properly and sat up in bed, hugging my knees. I decided it had been the second best night of my life (finding Mama would always come first). And it wasn't over. I would play Alice again and again and again, until the Players left to start their autumn season up West. I had weeks and weeks of glory still to go.

I didn't realize how quickly those weeks would pass. I started to get desperately tired. Alice was a long and demanding part, and it was sometimes a struggle without the first-night adrenalin to keep me going. During the day I had to sew, and then perform our own Little Stars act perfectly before the play itself. I was strict with Diamond and made her take a midday nap, but I tried to keep going myself. It didn't always work: I would fall fast asleep in the middle of sewing a seam until I stabbed myself awake with my needle. I dozed off after picnics with Bertie, once when we were on our own and he was sweet-talking me.

'Hey, wake up, sleepyhead! Am I that boring?' he said, tickling me with a blade of grass.

'I'm sorry, Bertie. I'm just so tired,' I said, rubbing my eyes.

'I think you need those wretched iron jelloids you see on all the posters,' he told me.

'Look, *you* try doing three jobs each day – sewing for old Ma Gibson, performing on a penny-farthing, and then having the lead part in a play. It's blooming exhausting,' I protested.

'All right, all right, I know I'm not a star like you, everyone's pet and darling,' said Bertie.

But I wasn't going to be a petted darling for ever. It would be over all too soon. The Players were already talking about their new season at the Duke of York's. Miss Royal told me they were there for a full six months, doing Charles Dickens adaptations – meaty two-and-a-half-hour evenings, *David Copperfield* first, then an extended musical version of *A Christmas Carol* in December, and then *Great Expectations* in the new year.

I listened to her in an agony of longing. I wished I was a permanent member of the Parkinson Players! I'd have given anything to act with them for ever – and in *David Copperfield* too! I had my father's copy, and I'd read it at least five times. Perhaps I could play the young Davy, with my hair hidden under a cap. I'd often passed myself off as a foundling boy, when I wanted to see how Gideon was managing.

Yes, I could be young Davy, and perhaps Diamond could be Little Em'ly. She would have hardly any lines – she'd just have to act shy and smile at me, and she could do that standing on her head.

'What is it, Emerald? You look as if you're going to burst,' said Miss Royal fondly.

'I was just thinking how much I'll miss you. How I wish, wish, wish Diamond and I could be part of Mr Parkinson's Players.'

She put her arm round me. 'I'd love it if it were possible. You really have such potential. It's a hard life, of course, especially for a child, but I survived happily enough. It's actually much harder now, when I'm getting old and stout,' she said sadly.

'You look wonderful. When you act Juliet, you honestly look fourteen,' I said sincerely.

'Bless you, child! I wish it were possible for you to join us. But you're on a contract to Mrs Ruby. She made that very plain when we gave you the part of Alice. You and Diamond are legally tied to perform in the Cavalcade for the next three years. Mr Parkinson can't employ you if you've signed a contract to work for someone else. He wouldn't dream of it. So I'm afraid you and Diamond have to stay here.'

'But I don't want to! I want to act with you!'

'Well, perhaps you'll be able to one day, when your current contract is finished. Though heaven knows whether we'll still be treading the boards by then. Let us hope so for both our sakes! Now chin up, dearie. We've another whole week to go. Enjoy being Alice while you can.'

I did enjoy being Alice, but it was a bitter-sweet experience now.

'I shall so miss performing with the Players. Won't you, Diamond?' I said.

'Well, I like being a pussycat in my furry suit. But I wouldn't want to do any other acting. I can't say the words right,' she said.

'I'm sure you could if I had time to teach you. If only we didn't have to stay at the Cavalcade for three whole years. I so want to be one of Mr Parkinson's Players,' I said, sighing.

'But we couldn't really go, could we?'

'No, because of this wretched contract.'

'But we couldn't go *anyway*, not without Bertie!' she said.

It was a shock to realize that I hadn't even thought about Bertie. I felt terribly guilty, and was extra sweet to him in consequence. He sensed I was unhappy, though, and kept asking me what was wrong.

'I'm just going to miss the Players so,' I said, truthfully enough.

'But you'll still have your Little Stars act. And make your pretty dresses for everyone. And have Diamond – and me.'

I must have frowned. Bertie sighed impatiently. 'Honestly, Hetty, you're never satisfied. You always want *more*.'

I remembered Jem saying something very similar when I was little and begged him to take me back to the circus when I'd only just been.

I smiled wryly. 'I can't help it, Bertie,' I said. 'It's just the way I'm made.'

The last time I played Alice was enormously poignant. I wanted to savour that special hour, but it sped past in a flash, and there I was, hand in hand with Miss Royal and Mr Parkinson, taking my final bow. When I stood there on my own, the audience cheering, I felt the tears rolling down my cheeks. As soon as I was off stage I started sobbing.

'Don't cry, sweetheart,' said Miss Royal. 'We're going to Maudie's for a little celebration. Will you join us?'

'Oh, I'd love to!' I said, sniffling.

'I'm not sure about Diamond, though. She looks far too young for nightclubs.'

I looked round for Bertie, who had been standing in the wings, clapping us. 'Do you think you could do me a great big favour, Bertie?' I begged.

'Of course,' he said, smiling.

'Could you walk Diamond home for me? I'm sure Miss Gibson will give her a warm drink and put her to bed.'

'So what are you doing?' he asked. He wasn't smiling now.

'Miss Royal's asked me to come to a little party at Maudie's, to celebrate the end of the show.'

'You're going to the nightclub on your own?'

'No, of course not. I said, I'm going with Miss Royal and Mr Parkinson and the other players.'

'And you want me to act as nursemaid while you go off gallivanting?'

'Oh, Bertie. Never mind. I'll take her home myself, and then I'll go back,' I said wearily.

'No, I'll take her. You'll walk with me, won't you, Twinkle?' he said, offering her his arm.

'Of course I will, Bertie!' said Diamond. 'I like walking with you best of all.'

'There! Someone still cares for me.'

'Don't act this way, please. This is such a big night for me,' I said.

'I know. And I hoped we'd celebrate your success as Alice together,' he told me.

'You're just saying that to make me feel bad! I don't think you had any plans at all,' I said. 'Diamond, be a good girl.'

I marched off to Miss Royal's dressing room and waited there while she played her Juliet scene. She came back looking white with exhaustion, but smiled when she saw me.

I watched while she removed her greasepaint with cold cream, and then washed her face and brushed her wonderful long hair, tying it up in several shining coils. She went behind her Japanese screen and changed into one of her new art dresses, a deep sea green with a shimmering silver thread.

'I love your dress! I meant to try to make you one. I've made dresses for Mrs Ruby and Lily Lark, but I've been so busy the last few weeks. I'll make you one even so, and send it to you in London,' I said.

'That's very kind of you, Emerald. I'd love that. But I already have my Juliet dress. You've completely transformed it.'

'I think *you've* completely transformed me,' I said. 'I always thought I wanted to be a writer, but now, more than anything, I want to be an actress! Do you really think I have talent, or are you just being kind to me?'

'I really think it,' she said. 'Oh, Emerald, you remind me so much of myself when I was young! I feel like your mother.'

'You could be like a second mother to me, now that I've lost my own dear mama,' I said shyly.

My little star! Aren't I your second mother? Madame Adeline seemed to be peering out of Miss Royal's looking glass, her face stricken.

I felt my stomach twist with guilt, but I couldn't unsay the words.

'You're such a sweet intense little creature.' Miss Royal eyed me up and down. 'You look about seven in your Alice costume. I think you'd better take off your pinafore and your stripy socks if you're coming to Maudie's. I'll lend you some stockings. What size shoe do you take? I think you need little heels instead of those pumps. And perhaps we'll put your hair up too.'

She fiddled and fussed with me, deftly transforming me into a young lady. I loved her black stockings with clocks and her pearl-grey heeled shoes with satin ribbons. They were much too big for me, but I rolled the stocking tops over and over above my knees and stuffed handkerchiefs into the toes of both shoes.

Then we met up with the other players and set off for Maudie's. Mr Parkinson gave his arm to Miss Royal. I walked a little behind, until Harry Henderson bowed to me and offered his own arm. Stella walked with Cecil, the young romantic lead. She was clearly hoping he'd take her arm, but he was talking to Alfie, the comic turn. At the rear came Mr and Mrs Greatorex, a middle-aged married couple who had played the Mad Hatter and March Hare to perfection, working a puppet Dormouse between them. I felt as fond of them all now as if they were proper family.

When we got to Maudie's, Mr Parkinson ordered

champagne and oysters for everyone. I didn't touch my oysters, but I couldn't resist the sparkling champagne. I drank it with such enthusiasm the bubbles went right up my nose. They all drank a toast to me – 'Our little Alice!' – and my heart thumped with joy. I downed my glass and then drank another. And perhaps one more. I seemed to have lost count. The bubbles were tickling my insides. I laughed and chatted and bounced about the table, talking to everyone as if they were my dearest friends in all the world.

Then Mr Parkinson looked up and waved at some new arrivals, beckoning them to our table. Oh Lord, it was Mrs Ruby and Samson! Mrs Ruby frowned when she saw me, but Samson grinned. I should have been wary, but now I was this new bubbly sparkling girl, dancing about in her borrowed pearl-grey heels. I waved at them.

'My, my, you've grown up all of a sudden, Little Star!' said Samson.

'She's still a child,' said Mrs Ruby sharply. 'I think it's time you went home, Hetty.'

'She's our little Emerald for tonight,' said Miss Royal. 'But she certainly *is* a Little Star.'

'Yes, look at me sparkling!' I said, and I twirled round and round. The room twirled too, and I had to clutch the back of a chair to stop myself falling over.

'Whoops! I think you're a little the worse for wear, poppet,' said Harry, steadying me. 'Let me help you outside. We'll call a cab to take you home.' He got to his feet unsteadily. 'Oh my, old Uncle Harry's a little bit pickled too!'

'I'm absolutely fine,' I said. 'I'm not going home yet. The night is young!' But I was starting to feel rather ill even so.

'You've had several glasses of champagne on an empty stomach. Here, have an oyster,' suggested Harry.

I heaved as soon as the salty slime touched my tongue. I ran across the room, twisting my ankle in my borrowed heels, and only just reached the ladies' powder room in time. I was sick into the water closet, and felt so ill and dizzy afterwards I knelt on the cold stone floor, clutching my head. This room was spinning too, and it took a great effort to stand up so that I could wash my face in the basin. I rinsed out my mouth, vowing never to touch champagne or a single oyster ever again.

I felt so ashamed I decided to creep away without saying a proper goodbye. I opened the door of the ladies' room – and bumped right into Samson, who was lounging outside the gentlemen's. He had an empty champagne flute in his hand and was leaning against the door, his legs crossed, showing off his elegant patent boots.

'Well, hello there, Little Star.' His voice was slurred. He'd probably been drinking all evening, long before he started on champagne.

'Hello, Samson,' I whispered hoarsely.

415

I tried to edge past him, but he took hold of my shoulder. 'Hey, hey, where are you off to?'

'I have to go home. I – I'm not very well,' I said.

'I can see that. You've been having a little tipple, haven't you, you naughty girl. Come on, you can be honest with old Samson. I'm the last one to be fierce with you.' He patted me on the back, shaking his head and making silly tutting noises.

'Please, Samson, I really do feel terrible,' I said, and I felt the tears spilling down my cheeks.

'What's this! Tears! Oh dear, dear, dear! Don't cry, Little Star. You'll be as right as rain soon enough. Here, let old Samson kiss it better.' He pulled me closer, his breath hot in my face.

'No, please – please let me go,' I said, squirming away from him.

But he was much too big and strong for me. He shoved me against the wall and then started kissing my face with his horrible blubbery lips. He tasted of champagne and red wine and those awful slimy oysters, and I shuddered.

'Leave go of me! Stop it!' I said, struggling.

My hastily stitched Alice dress tore at the seams, the bodice gaping at the front. 'My dress!' I cried.

'What the hell's going on?' Mrs Ruby was standing there, hands on hips, staring at us, looking appalled.

Samson pushed me away from him. 'Now then,

Ruby-Red, don't jump to conclusions. Nothing's happened. Just some passing tomfoolery. Let's go and join the others. Leave the little minx to recover. She's had one too many.' He lumbered towards Mrs Ruby, putting his arm round her. 'Don't frown like that, sweetheart. You don't want to get even more lines on that old forehead, do you?'

I thought she'd slap him. She was breathing hard, her fists clenched. But she let him brush past her without saying a word. She turned to me instead. 'What are you playing at?' she hissed.

'What? Are you mad?' I said furiously. '*I* wasn't doing anything. Samson caught hold of me and started slobbering over me.'

'How dare you use that tone with me! And don't start accusing Samson. I've got the measure of you, you shameless little hussy. Look at you, reeking of drink at your age! You can scarcely control yourself, can you? I've seen you making eyes at my boy. And now, when you can see the man's in his cups and barely knows what he's doing, you thrust yourself at him shamelessly!'

I shook my head, hardly able to believe what she was saying.

'Don't try to deny it! I saw you with my own eyes!' Mrs Ruby spat at me.

'Then you must be blind in both those eyes, because if you looked properly you'd see your so-called nephew was attacking me! I wouldn't touch him if he were the last

417

man alive. I can't stand him – I don't know why *you* put up with him, Mrs Ruby,' I said. The champagne was still pulsing in my blood. My mouth opened and more words came out. Words I should never have said. *'There's no fool like an old fool!'*

She flushed a deep ugly red, a vein throbbing in her forehead. She clutched her throat. 'Get out of my sight,' she gasped. 'You're dismissed. If you dare set foot in the Cavalcade again, I'll have you thrown out. Go!'

I stared at her, trembling. 'But it wasn't my fault. You *know* that! You must know what Samson's like. He can't leave any of the girls alone,' I protested.

'Hold your tongue. Now get out of here.'

'You can't dismiss me, you know you can't. I have a contract to perform at the Cavalcade for three more years.'

'It's only binding for you. I can get rid of you whenever I choose. And that's what I'm doing. You and your sister are dismissed.'

'Well, good! I don't *want* to work for you. We're Little Stars, remember? We're a big draw, you've said so yourself. We'll work at another music hall, maybe one of the London gaffs. You wait, we'll still be stars,' I shouted defiantly.

'Don't talk to me like that, you little fool. There's no music-hall management will touch you, not when I've put out the word. We stick together. Any performer considered trouble is black-listed. Trust me, you'll never work again. Now get out of here before I give you the good slapping you deserve.'

She gave me such a push I nearly fell over. I ran back into the main room, crying my eyes out. I felt disorientated and couldn't see where Miss Royal was sitting. I staggered about, blundering into a chair, dodging round a waiter who tried to steer me towards the door.

Then Harry was catching hold of me, his great bloodhound face still kindly. 'Come on, dear. Come with me. We'll get you a cab,' he said.

'I must see Miss Royal first!' I sobbed.

I spotted her at the side of the room – but Mrs Ruby had joined her and was talking rapidly.

'You can't bother Marina in this state, sweetheart,' said Harry.

'Yes I can! *Miss Royal!*'

She looked over at me, her hand to her mouth, shocked. Oh God, did she believe Mrs Ruby? I had to explain! I tried to push my way towards her and saw myself reflected in one of the ornate looking glasses lining the walls. I saw my dishevelled hair, my tear-stained face, my running nose, my gaping mouth, my swaying body in its stained dress. I looked like a drunk crazy girl from the gutters! I started shaking.

Mr Parkinson moved swiftly towards us. 'Get the girl out of here, Harry,' he said.

'Come along now.' Harry steered me out of the room, down the corridor and out of the door.

The fresh air made me feel fainter than ever. I had to hang onto Harry while he hailed a cab, pre-paid it, and helped me inside. I was crying all the while.

'There now, dearie, don't take on so. You'll be better soon,' he said, trying to comfort me.

But I cried all the way home.

23

I **COULDN'T BELIEVE IT** had happened. I hit my fuddled head with my fists, trying to make sense of everything. I still felt very sick, and the rocking of the cab made it worse. I kept hoping that it was all a terrible nightmare.

When I was first taken to the Foundling Hospital, I'd been plagued by bad dreams where monsters snatched me from my home and started devouring me, limb by limb. When I woke up, I found I was biting my own thumb while a fierce matron in rag curlers slapped me awake because my screams were disturbing the whole hospital. I was left shivering beneath my worn blanket, the other girls whispering insults. I longed to climb into Jem's warm bed and cuddle up close, but I was locked away from him for nine whole years.

I wanted him now. I wanted to feel his strong arms around me, his deep country voice whispering in my ear, telling me that I didn't have to cry any more, he would look after me. Why hadn't I stayed in the village with him? Why hadn't I married him myself when I had the chance? Why hadn't I run away with him?

I'd been so headstrong, so foolish, so sure I was doing the right thing. I'd been so proud of myself for devising the Little Stars act, making Diamond and me the highlight of the show, and then getting the chance to play Alice and become a true star. I was an actress, famous in the town. Folk recognized me in the street, even without the blonde wig. They clustered round me eagerly, begging me for my signature. The ladies gave me chocolates, the men gave me nosegays as if I were a real professional actress like Marina Royal.

Now it was all over – though it hadn't really been my fault, had it? I hadn't deliberately encouraged that hateful Samson. I'd waved, I'd smiled, I'd danced around him, but that didn't mean I wanted him to kiss and paw at me. Why hadn't I gone home the moment he came into the nightclub? Why had I drunk so much champagne when I knew it made me ill? Why had I made such a spectacle of myself, so that Miss Royal stared at me in disgust? I no longer had a contract with the Cavalcade, but the Players would never invite me to join them now.

'Here you are, missy. Home, sweet home. My, you're in a state. I bet your ma will have something to say to you!' said the cab driver as I staggered out onto the pavement.

I thought of Mama and burned with shame. It was bad enough facing Miss Gibson. It was so late she'd given up on me and gone to bed. I had to hammer on the door, still crying. She opened it at last, wearing a nightcap, a shawl round her shoulders, a candle in her hand.

'Hetty! I've been so worried—' she started. But then she looked at me properly and took a step backwards. 'You're drunk!' she gasped. 'And – and your dress is all torn at the front!'

'Oh, Miss Gibson, I'm so sorry. Please believe me, it wasn't my fault. I haven't done anything,' I sobbed.

'What do you mean? You're so drunk you can barely stand! If it wasn't for that innocent little angel upstairs, I wouldn't let you over my doorstep, not in this state. Get up to bed. We'll talk properly in the morning. You do realize, I can't let you live here any more. I knew this would happen, cavorting with all those actor folk.' *She* was looking at me in disgust too.

I ran upstairs as best I could, trying to stifle my sobs.

Diamond was leaning up in bed on one elbow. 'Hetty?' she whispered, sounding frightened.

'Sorry, darling. I didn't mean to wake you.'

'You're crying! What's the matter? And you smell funny. A bit like Samson.'

'Don't!' I burst out crying afresh, casting myself down on the bed.

'There now. Don't cry. Are you sad because you won't be Alice any more?' she whispered anxiously, smoothing my tousled hair.

'I won't be anything any more!' I wailed. 'I've spoiled everything, for you as well as for me. I've lost us our lodgings as well as our position at the Cavalcade. We're ruined, Diamond, and it's all my fault.'

'Tell me what you've done,' she said, holding me close. 'I promise I won't mind, no matter what it is. You're my Hetty and I love you, and everything will be all right, just so long as we can be together.'

So I sobbed out the whole sorry tale, half expecting her to pull away from me in disgust too. But she held me close and did her best to comfort me.

'Samson's a big horrid pig. Poor you, Hetty. I would hate to have him kiss me. Mrs Ruby's horrid too. We don't *want* to work at the Cavalcade any more. We don't want to stay at Miss Gibson's either, though she does give us lots of treats. Still, you've sewn her lots of lovely dresses, so I think we're even.'

'But what shall we do, Diamond? Mrs Ruby's going to make sure we don't work anywhere else. Miss Gibson doesn't want us here any more. Where shall we go?'

'We could go to Bertie's! That would be lovely,' she said.

Bertie! I thought about him, my mind whirling. I put my head in my hands, trying to steady it.

Think, think, think, I muttered to myself.

'We can't tell Bertie about Samson,' I said.

'But he'll believe you, Hetty, I know he will.'

'Yes, he knows what Samson is like. So what do you think he'll do?'

'He'll be very cross,' said Diamond.

'Of course he will. He'll try to fight Samson, won't he? And who do you think will win?'

'Samson,' she whispered.

'Exactly.'

'Bertie *might* win. I'm sure he's very good at fighting.'

'Samson could beat anyone. Remember, they said he used to be a strongman. He'll fight, and Bertie will do his best to fight back – he won't give up, you know what he's like. Bertie will end up horribly hurt.'

'I don't want him to be hurt!'

'Neither do I, Diamond. And then Mrs Ruby might dismiss him, because she always takes Samson's side.'

'But that wouldn't be fair.'

'She isn't fair, you know she isn't. And if Bertie gets dismissed from the Cavalcade, he won't be able to work anywhere else either, she'll make sure of that. It's been his dream to be a music-hall artiste ever since he was small. He loves working here. Remember when we first met him, how he showed off to us? I'll never forgive myself if he loses his job.' I started crying again. What was the matter with me? Why did I always spoil things for the people I loved? I had made Jem unhappy on his wedding day. I couldn't make Bertie wretched too.

I twisted his gold Mizpah ring round and round. No one else could make me laugh like Bertie, no one else could surprise me so, no one else knew me through and through, not even Jem. We were a matching pair, the foundling girl and the workhouse boy, both of us cocky and ambitious and determined. That was why we got on so well – and why we bickered constantly. Perhaps we could never be properly happy together, because we were so alike.

'I can't tell Bertie and wreck his life. We'll run away, Diamond, without telling him why.'

'But he'll be so sad!' she said. 'He'll think we don't care about him any more.'

'I know, but it's the only fair thing to do.'

'I shall miss him so,' Diamond said mournfully.

'So shall I,' I said. 'Oh Lord, my head. It's still spinning.

Never, ever drink alcohol, Diamond. It feels good at first, but then it makes you feel so wretched.'

'I know,' she said. 'My pa drank and drank and we always had to keep out of his way. Well, after Ma died I had to keep out of his way whether he was drunk or sober because he hated me so.'

She said it so matter-of-factly, it nearly broke my heart. It was better to have grown up without a father than to have one who'd sold me for five guineas. When I had eventually found my father, it was a joy to discover that he was a sweet, kindly man, even though I didn't care for his new family.

'Perhaps we can travel up north again, to stay with my father?' I said as we settled down to sleep.

'The fisherman? But you said you didn't like the fish, Hetty,' said Diamond.

It was true that I had hated their staring eyes and gaping mouths, their slimy scales and hot guts – the reek that clung to my hands no matter how hard I scrubbed. I couldn't bear to be a fishergirl again. I could never be part of that harsh salty world – and if *I* couldn't fit in, Diamond would find it even harder, with her startling looks and dainty ways. My fierce stepmother had never liked me. She'd like Diamond even less.

'Perhaps we won't go to stay with my father after all,' I said. 'So where *can* we go?'

I shut my eyes tight and tried to ask Mama.

Diamond answered first. 'We'll go and see Madame Adeline and Mr Marvel,' she said.

'Oh yes! Yes, we will! I don't suppose we can stay there for ever, it's only a small cottage, and we'll have to earn our living, but we could stay a few days. Oh, Diamond, of course, that's where we'll go.'

'And Madame Adeline will call us her little stars and we will tell her all about our act,' said Diamond.

'We will show her! She will be so proud of us. Oh, wait, I've left the penny-farthing at the Cavalcade,' I groaned.

'No, Bertie and I took it. He tried to ride it but he can't balance the way you can, Hetty. He had to wheel it most of the way home. It's in the back yard.'

'Dear Bertie,' I said, clasping my ring tight.

'I'm sure Mr Marvel could ride the penny-farthing, even though he's very elderly. He was always very nimble – he taught me how to tumble without hurting myself. Perhaps we can train his monkeys to ride our penny-farthing too!' said Diamond. 'Little Mavis could scamper up and sit on my head. That would look splendid. We can have a whole new act!'

'For a circus?'

'No, not a circus!' said Diamond firmly. 'I never want to be a circus girl again. But perhaps we could perform in a marketplace? When I used to do my little show folk gave me lots of pennies. Shall we do that?'

'Perhaps,' I said, fighting back tears again.

I'd been a circus ringmaster, a music-hall star, a leading actress – but now it looked as if I would have to content myself with being a lowly street performer. It wasn't just a matter of pride. All my life I had fought to progress upwards, but in the past few hours I seemed to be tumbling down again.

Throughout that long queasy night I thought of Madame Adeline. I conjured her up as she used to be, strong and lithe in her pink spangles, leaping from horse to horse, her red hair gleaming in the harsh circus gaslight. When I slept at last, I dreamed she'd turned into Marina Royal, proclaiming Juliet's speech as she rode round and round, her own red hair unravelling, flying behind her like a cloak. I pedalled hard on the penny-farthing, scarcely able to keep my balance, while clowns threw buckets of water at me and the audience shouted abuse.

When I woke, the room had stopped circling, but my head hammered and I felt so sick I had to rush out to the privy in the back yard.

Miss Gibson was waiting for me in the kitchen, fully dressed, arms folded. 'There! You've been sick, haven't you!' she asked.

I nodded wanly.

'It serves you right. The demon drink!'

'Miss Gibson, you yourself have had the occasional tipple,' I said.

'But I have never been drunk as a lord!'

'I am very sorry. I *was* a little drunk last night, though I only had two glasses of champagne – three at the most. It won't happen again,' I said.

'How could you abandon poor Diamond while you went off gallivanting with that actor troupe?'

'It wasn't quite like that.' I rubbed my forehead, trying to ease the blinding pain. 'But I still behaved very badly. You don't need to lecture me any further. Diamond and I will be leaving very soon.'

She looked a little taken aback. 'There's no need for that.'

'You said we had to go.'

'Yes, but not immediately. In fact, I might just be willing to overlook your behaviour if you're truly sorry,' she said.

'I *am* sorry, but I think we'd better go all the same.' I couldn't bear the thought of staying on at Miss Gibson's now that we were unable to work at the Cavalcade. Miss Gibson might relent, but I knew that Mrs Ruby would never change her mind.

'Well, suit yourself,' she said. 'But don't go telling folk I turned you out on the streets. I wouldn't do that, especially not to a sweet little soul like your sister.'

'I know,' I said. I took a deep breath. 'You've been very kind to us. Thank you for all your help and generosity. Now, I'd better go and wash. Excuse me.'

I ran upstairs, my head pounding at every step. Diamond was already up. She was still in her night-gown, but Adeline and Maybelle were dressed in their coats and bonnets, with all their outfits and little belongings packed neatly into a shoe box.

'I've got my children ready,' she said. 'They're very excited, especially Adeline, because she's going to meet her namesake.'

'We'd better get packed up too,' I said.

It took much longer this time. We seemed to have acquired many more possessions since we started at the Cavalcade. It was a terrible struggle to fit everything into one small suitcase. When I'd succeeded at last, I realized I still had to write a letter, and had to unpack everything again to find my pen and ink and notepad.

'Are you writing to Bertie?' Diamond asked.

'I just want to write a quick note. I still can't explain, but I don't want him to think we just set off without giving him a second thought,' I said.

'May I write him a note too?'

'Yes, of course,' I said, though I knew her printing wasn't really up to a letter.

We sat cross-legged at either end of the bed, trying to compose our letters. It was a struggle for both of us. Diamond's note was very concise:

Deer Burty I wil mis you so Love Diamond

My own letter was also brief:

Dear Bertie,
  Please forgive me. We had to go. I shall always wear my Mizpah ring and whisper its message: The Lord keep us safe when we are absent one from another.
Love from
Your Hetty

I didn't know the address of Bertie's lodgings, and the Cavalcade would be shut on Sunday. When we went downstairs clutching all our belongings, I gave the sealed letters to Miss Gibson.

'Would you be kind enough to give these letters to Bertie when he calls round? And if he doesn't, perhaps you might hand them in to the Cavalcade tomorrow?' I asked politely.

'Why can't you give them to him?'

'We won't be here. We're not working at the Cavalcade any more.'

'What?'

'We're moving on.'

'But where will you go?'

'We're visiting a dear friend for a little while,' I said.

'Have you given Bertie the address?'

I shook my head.

'Poor boy,' said Miss Gibson. She fidgeted with her apron, crumpling the starched material. 'He will be so upset.'

'I know,' I said, and one last tear slid down my cheek.

'Look, you've been a very silly girl, but I'm sure there's no need to rush off like this. I told you, you can stay here, so long as you mend your ways and never come home in that dreadful state again. And although I disapprove of the Cavalcade, by all accounts you two were a big success there. You don't want to walk out of a good position.'

'We have no choice, Miss Gibson. Mrs Ruby doesn't want us there any more,' I said.

'Then work full-time for me, Hetty. I have to admit, you've made a big difference to my business. Your designs are proving very popular. If we work together for a few years, I might even consider making you a partner.' Miss Gibson emphasized the last four words to show she thought this an extremely attractive offer.

'It's very generous of you,' I said. 'But I still think we must move on.'

'Well, at least let me make you breakfast before you go,' she said.

I still felt so nauseous that the very word breakfast made my stomach heave, but I knew we were facing a long train journey on a day when many eating places would be shut.

'That would be very kind,' I said.

433

Miss Gibson made enough breakfast for twenty girls: porridge with honey and cream, then eggs and bacon and mushrooms and fried tomatoes and buttered toast, along with a great brown pot of tea. Diamond and I did our best to eat heartily and so did Miss Gibson, but we couldn't finish it.

'I'll make you up some bacon sandwiches for your journey – and there's a freshly made ginger cake in the larder. You'd better take that too,' she said, dabbing at her eyes with the hem of her apron.

'That's very kind of you, Miss Gibson,' I mumbled. My own eyes were a little watery, and Diamond was openly sniffling.

'I wish I hadn't spoken so hastily last night. I don't want you to go!' she said.

'Oh, Miss Gibson, you had every right to be cross with me, though I swear that I did nothing more than drink one glass of champagne too many. But we have to go, I'm afraid. Thank you for all your kindnesses while we've been staying with you. Please feel free to appropriate all my dress designs, I don't mind a bit.'

'Thank you, dear. That's very good of you. I don't know what I'm going to do without you,' said Miss Gibson. 'It's so hard to find a girl who's truly particular about her stitching nowadays.'

'I know where hundreds of such girls are trained!' I said. 'Don't worry, Miss Gibson. I will find you a substitute girl – and I'm sure she'll be much less trouble than me.'

I retrieved my writing materials and, on a corner of the kitchen table, penned a hasty letter to Miss Sarah Smith. She was the children's author who had taken an interest in me and encouraged me to write my memoirs. She was a governor at the Foundling Hospital and had influence there. I asked her to select a likely foundling – preferably my foster sister Eliza! – and arrange an apprenticeship for her at Miss Gibson's establishment. Eliza was a little young, and I didn't know if she was a truly competent seamstress, but I was sure she'd prefer life at Gibson's Gowns to slaving away as a servant.

Then I packed my suitcase again, and Miss Gibson provided Diamond with a stout bag to carry Adeline, Maybelle and all their possessions. I made sure that Diamond made another trip to the privy, and then I went myself, because I knew that the facilities were meagre at best on long train journeys. I felt a little better with a full meal inside me, but my head still throbbed. It was partly the champagne, partly worry about our future.

What would we do once we'd visited Madame Adeline and Mr Marvel? I didn't want to end up as a street performer. We'd never earn enough, and we couldn't expect Madame Adeline to provide for us. While I was still on the privy, I thought I heard the doorbell go at the front of the shop.

My tummy tightened. Was it Bertie? What was I going

to do if it was? I wanted to tell him everything – and yet I knew I mustn't. I sat there trying to decide what to do. Perhaps I'd been mistaken. It was still very early for a visit. Bertie usually slept till past ten on a Sunday.

I dithered in the privy for another minute or so and then forced myself to go indoors.

Diamond was in the back room, her eyes wide. 'We have a visitor!' she said, grabbing my hand. 'Come, quick!'

24

SHE PULLED ME INTO the kitchen. Marina Royal was perched on a wooden chair, resplendent in a deep navy velvet travelling costume, with two long strings of turquoise beads swinging to her waist. She wore a matching navy hat with a jay's feather set at a jaunty angle. Miss Gibson was standing staring at her, looking uncomfortably like a servant in her black dress and white apron. She held her chin very high, to convey to Miss

Royal that she was a respectable dressmaker who looked down on painted actresses.

'Oh, Miss Royal!' I gasped, blushing.

'Good morning, Emerald. How are you feeling?' she asked.

'Not very well,' I said honestly.

'I'm not at all surprised.'

'I'm so sorry I got in such a state last night. I feel so ashamed.' I hung my head.

'Oh well. I dare say everyone gets a little squiffy sometimes,' said Miss Royal.

Miss Gibson sniffed loudly, making it plain that *she* had never been squiffy in her life. She poured Miss Royal a cup of tea, because she wanted to appear hospitable, but she served it at arm's length, as if she might become contaminated if she came any nearer.

'Thank you so much,' said Miss Royal, sipping. 'Well, girls, I see you've packed your bags. That's fortuitous, because I came here to tell you to do just that.'

We stared at her.

'What do you mean, Miss Royal?' Diamond asked.

'I mean, little Diamond, that Mr Parkinson and I are inviting you both to become members of the Players, our small but select band of actors.'

I heard her perfectly, but I wanted her to repeat the words again and yet again. I couldn't believe it. I shook my head, utterly bewildered.

'Don't you want to join us, Emerald?' she asked, eyebrows raised.

'Oh, Miss Royal, I want to more than anything in the world! But – but you seemed so shocked by my behaviour last night,' I stammered.

'I was shocked at both the Rubys, dear. Appalled at Samson, though I know that such behaviour is typical. Far more astonished that Mrs Ruby could be so foolishly vindictive. She prides herself on being a businesswoman too! She could see how well you went down with the audience. Well, more fool her. She has declared your contract null and void, so you are both free to come to us, my dears.'

'You're sure you want me, Miss Royal? I'm not very good at acting,' said Diamond. 'Are there lots of pussycats in all your plays?'

'Not really, dear. But I'm sure we'll find a little part for you in most things,' said Miss Royal.

'Perhaps she could be Little Em'ly in *David Copperfield*?' I said tentatively.

Miss Royal laughed. 'There, you've been thinking things out in your head already, Emerald.'

'Emerald!' said Miss Gibson, sniffing. 'What are you doing, taking these two little girls and turning them into actors? It's different playing dollies at the Cavalcade and riding their old cycle. That's natural enough, though I can't say that I approve of kiddies in a music hall. But

439

getting themselves up in paint and acting other people, that's different – and in London too! It's child labour, whichever way you look at it. Hetty's hardly old enough to earn her own living, let alone little Diamond.'

'I think Emerald's been doing her fair share of labour here,' said Miss Royal mildly.

'Sewing's different! It's respectable work, suitable for any young woman,' said Miss Gibson.

'I'm afraid we have to agree to differ in our opinions.' Miss Royal stood up. 'We haven't got time for further disputes. The girls and I have a train to catch. Come along, my dears. Say goodbye to Miss Gibson.'

We both hugged and kissed her. Miss Gibson drew away from me and turned her cheek from my kiss, but she clasped Diamond as if she would never let her go. 'If you don't like life with these theatricals, you can always come and live with me, Diamond,' she said.

'Thank you very much, dear Miss Gibson,' Diamond said. She hesitated. 'I don't want you to be lonely. I know you're not very fond of Maybelle because she's so plain, but perhaps you'd like Adeline to keep you company when we're gone? She's very pretty indeed, and you could make her lots of new dresses and display her in the shop window.'

'Oh, Diamond, I can't take your dolly!' said Miss Gibson. 'But I like your idea of dressing a doll for the window. Perhaps I shall do just that!'

'Thank you very much for looking after us so well, Miss Gibson,' I said. 'And you won't forget to give the letters to Bertie, will you?'

'Oh, Bertie!' said Diamond, her face falling.

'We must go right away, or we'll miss the train!' Miss Royal said quickly.

So we left Gibson's Gowns and set off for the station. Diamond carried her dolls and their equipment, and I carried the suitcase. I dithered about taking the penny-farthing.

'You won't really need it now, will you?' said Miss Royal.

I knew she was right, but I was reluctant to let it go.

'It helped us escape from Tanglefield's Travelling Circus, it's served as a vehicle, and earned us a living as a novelty act,' I said, stroking it as if it were a pony, not a penny-farthing.

'You're starting a new life now,' said Miss Royal. 'Actors don't do novelty acts.'

So I left it in Miss Gibson's yard and we hurried towards the station. Mr Parkinson and all the other players were on the platform. A hot, damp porter was struggling with an enormous pile of trunks and cases.

'We'd practically given up on you!' said Mr Parkinson. 'Did it take you a while to make up your minds?'

'No, sir, we decided in an instant,' I said. 'Thank you

so much for giving us this opportunity. I promise you won't regret it.'

'I hope not,' he said.

I swallowed. It was very embarrassing having to ask, but I needed to know something. 'Please excuse my asking, but what sort of wage will you be paying us?'

'It's ten shillings, is it not?' said Mr Parkinson.

'Yes, it was while we were at the Cavalcade, because we were also being paid by Mrs Ruby. But though it will be a privilege to work with your company, I'm afraid Diamond and I won't be able to manage on such a small sum. Please, sir, could we possibly have a little more?'

Miss Royal laughed. 'There, Gerald, we'll have to put on a production of *Oliver Twist* in our Dickens season. Young Emerald would play Oliver very nicely!'

'Ten shillings each,' said Mr Parkinson.

'That's very kind, sir, and a fair enough salary for Diamond as she's a little child, and likely to have small parts. But I'm of working age, and perhaps you'll be kind enough to cast me in bigger parts. I think I might be worth at least a sovereign, especially if I maintain the costumes for the company. So that makes thirty shillings a week for the two of us.' I held out my hand. 'Is that a bargain?'

Mr Parkinson frowned, not at all impressed, but Miss Royal and Harry and the other players were all laughing.

'She's got you fair and square, Gerald,' said Miss Royal. 'I think you're going to have to say yes.'

'Very well, very well,' Mr Parkinson muttered, and he shook my hand, though he was still frowning. I was a little worried that I'd been too assertive. I didn't want him to regret taking us on the very day we joined his company, but on the other hand I had to show him that I wasn't a fool. Thirty shillings for two Players (albeit small ones) was still a very modest salary. I wasn't going to let him exploit us just because we were young. And if he gave us a written contract, I would examine it very carefully indeed before signing.

The train steamed into the station and there was a flurry of activity as the gentlemen Players ordered the porter about and the ladies climbed into the third-class carriage. I had assumed that Miss Royal and Mr Parkinson at least would travel in first-class splendour, but it became clear that even the Principal Players had little money to spare. They didn't go to eat in the dining carriage. They spread checked napkins on their laps and ate pork pies and drank ginger beer straight out of the bottle like the rest of us. Luckily there were enough provisions for Diamond and me, and we shared out our bacon sandwiches. The ginger cake was particularly popular once it was cut into chunks with Harry's penknife.

Diamond ate her share, and fed Adeline and Maybelle

crumbs in a way that made Mr and Mrs Greatorex coo at her, but she started staring out of the window anxiously, especially when we drew in to each station.

'What's the matter, Diamond?' I asked.

'I'm looking out for Little Foxfield. Isn't that where Madame Adeline lives now?'

'Yes, but that's on another railway line entirely. We're going to London. Didn't you understand? We've joined Miss Royal and Mr Parkinson. We're going to be Players now, in a London theatre.'

'I know. I'm not stupid,' said Diamond, a little indignant. 'But I thought we were still going to see Madame Adeline *first*. You said we could go and see her, and I want to so much. And I want to see Mr Marvel and all the monkeys, especially Mavis.'

'Yes, I know, and we *will* go and see them, I promise. But not today.'

Diamond looked desperately disappointed. 'You *said* we could go and see her,' she wailed.

'And we will. Once we've got settled in London,' I tried to reassure her.

'Well, where are we going to live in London?' Diamond asked sulkily.

This was a problem I hadn't addressed. I had assumed that all the Players would live in one big house in a very jolly, companionable way, but this wasn't the case.

'Mr Parkinson and I have our own apartment in

Bloomsbury,' said Miss Royal. 'But it's very modest, with only one bedroom. I suppose one of you could sleep on cushions in the bath as a temporary arrangement, but it would be extremely cramped and uncomfortable.'

I rather liked this idea, but Diamond drooped.

'We really need to stay together,' I said.

'Perhaps you could stay in Stella's ladies' hostel?' Miss Royal suggested.

'They don't take children,' Stella pointed out.

Cecil and Alfie shared a small house with four other young men – it was very crowded and unsuitable accommodation for two girls – and Mr and Mrs Greatorex lived in a converted mews cottage with their grown-up sons and a very elderly parent, so they had no room for us either.

'We'll find you cheap lodgings, girls, don't worry,' said Miss Royal. 'Perhaps Gerald will pay you your wages a week or two in advance so you have the rent money.'

Mr Parkinson ignored this suggestion.

I tried to work out exactly how much money I had in my purse. I wasn't sure how much the rent would be. Miss Gibson had let us stay for nothing because I helped her with the sewing. I had paid rent in Bignor, but maybe seaside rents were cheaper than the capital? Either way, I probably only had enough for a night or two – certainly not a full week.

'Don't look so worried, little 'un,' said Harry, patting

my hand. 'You can come and stay with me until you can afford your own digs. I have a very large living room with comfortable sofas. My amiable landlady has happily accepted the occasional nephew staying with me. I'm sure she won't object to a couple of pretty little nieces.'

'Thank you very much, Mr Henderson,' I said, a little doubtfully. After my experience with Samson I was wary of older men.

'Bless you, Harry, that's very generous of you.' Miss Royal put her head close to mine. 'Have no qualms, you've nothing to fear from Harry. It will all be very respectable,' she whispered.

She was right. When we arrived in London, everyone went their separate ways, which was a little disconcerting. On Monday we were to meet at some rehearsal rooms in a street in Covent Garden, and spend a week practising there before opening at the theatre in Shaftesbury Avenue.

'I live just up the road, in Soho, so it's all very convenient,' said Harry. 'It's not too far from the station. I dare say you two little girls could walk it in a flash, but if I ask my poor legs to carry my stout old body, they'll start to buckle before we know where we are, and there's my trunk to deal with too. So we'll take a hansom and arrive in style.'

I had uncomfortable memories of my trip in a hansom the previous night.

Harry saw me hanging my head and laughed. 'Oh dear, I'll warrant your head's still thumping even now,' he said.

'It is, rather,' I admitted.

'We'll all have a nice cup of tea when we get home. It will make all the difference, you'll see.'

Harry's street was narrow, with grim grey buildings on either side of the road. There was litter in the gutters and strange people lurking on street corners. Diamond put her arms round her two dolls protectively, probably remembering her own childhood.

'I wish we were back at Miss Gibson's,' she whispered to me.

I rather wished it too.

Harry's house was at the end, part of a plain Georgian terrace, the bricks black with grime, the steps cracked, the front door peeling. He knocked at the door with a cheery *rat-a-tat-tat*. We heard light footsteps inside, accompanied by a tap-tap-tapping.

'My landlady, dear Miss Grundy, is coming,' said Harry. 'She uses a cane.'

'A cane?' said Diamond nervously, remembering Beppo's stick.

'To get about, my dear. She's blind, but she never complains. Such a cheery soul.'

Then the door opened and we saw Miss Grundy for ourselves. Diamond had been expecting someone very stern and fierce, swishing her cane. I had pictured a very elderly person in cap and mittens. But Miss Grundy was only a few years older than me. She was the whitest young woman I'd ever seen, apart from her black spectacles. She had limp white hair tied up in a bun, and the palest face, which looked drained of blood. She wore a white dress and a white apron and white stockings and white kid boots, and she was smiling broadly, showing off her small white teeth.

'Mr Harry? I can smell your delightful cologne!' she said.

'Indeed, it is I, dear Miss Grundy.' Mr Harry reached for her ghostly white hand and gave it a kiss. 'I've turned up again like a bad penny.'

'Dear Mr Harry. Welcome home!' she said. Then she turned her head as if she could see Diamond and me. 'And I believe you've brought a friend or two with you, Mr Harry? Welcome to you too, my dears.'

I said a polite 'How-do-you-do,' but Diamond was staring open-mouthed, too astonished for politeness.

'Are you a ghost girl?' she asked. 'You're so white!'

'Diamond!' I hissed, shaking her arm. 'Please forgive my little sister.'

Miss Grundy roared with laughter. 'Don't be silly, dear, I don't mind at all. I admit I'm a bit of a puzzle,' she said. 'I'm real enough, but I have a strange condition. I have no skin pigment, so I'm white as snow. I'm an albino, like a rabbit. And my poor eyes are very weak because of my condition, so I can't make you out at all. I know you're girls from the pitch of your voices. The little one's Diamond?'

'And I'm Hetty Feather, Miss Grundy, though my stage name is Emerald Star. Diamond and I are new members of the Parkinson Players,' I said proudly.

'I'm hoping they might stay with me in my spacious chambers until they have acquired enough cash for decent digs,' said Harry.

'Well, I dare say I can find them their very own room,' said Miss Grundy. 'Come in, come in. This house was left to me by a great-uncle – another albino, bless him, so he wanted to provide for me. I find it difficult to work with my bad eyes, so I take in lodgers. I only accept recommended guests – with my affliction, I have to be cautious, but any friend of Mr Harry's is definitely a friend of mine. Do come in and I'll make us some tea. How rude of me to keep you all standing on the doorstep!'

She led us along the dark hallway and into her living room. It reminded me of Mr Buchanan's, with its huge leather armchairs; its tables covered in ornaments; its glass domes of stuffed birds and cases of blue butterflies; and its landscape paintings set symmetrically along the flock wallpaper. By the fireside Miss Grundy had created her own special corner, choosing items for their feel rather than their looks. There was a velvet chair with tassels, several silk cushions, a small tapestry stool, a little table with a collection of smooth round eggs made out of semi-precious stones, a marble angel with outspread wings, a glazed china bowl of beads and buttons, and a real kitten sleeping in its basket on the floor.

'A kitten!' said Diamond. 'Oh my!' She sat Adeline and Maybelle with their backs against the stool and then knelt beside the kitten, gently stroking its soft grey back.

'Are you getting acquainted with my little Lily?' asked Miss Grundy. 'They tell me she is grey, with a very white face like mine. I hope you like cats, Diamond. Lily would love you to play ball with her when she wakes up.'

'Oh, Miss Grundy, you can count on me!' said Diamond. And when Miss Grundy produced checked pink-and-yellow cake to eat with our tea, she let out a sigh of sheer happiness.

After we'd had our refreshments Miss Grundy felt her way upstairs, tapping with her cane, and showed us to the room at the top of the house that she thought would suit us. It was small, perhaps once a servant's room, but the bed seemed comfortable and the linen fresh. It was a little dusty around the edges and a few cobwebs hung from the ceiling – Miss Grundy clearly couldn't properly supervise its cleaning – but in half an hour we'd made the room spick and span.

'Is this our home now? Oh, please can we stay here for

ever, Hetty? Adeline and Maybelle and I like it ever so!' said Diamond.

She had clearly forgotten Miss Gibson's – though neither of us had forgotten Madame Adeline. We were already in London, which was much nearer to Mr Marvel's cottage in Sussex. I promised Diamond we would make a trip there as soon as possible. Meanwhile we were busy from early in the morning until midway through the evening, rehearsing.

The Players had performed a version of *David Copperfield* before, but our scenes were a new innovation: Cecil had been unable to convince as a small child, so the important opening chapters about the young Davy had merely been referred to in several lines of exposition. But now I was the child Davy, just as I'd hoped. I had several wondrous scenes with my young mother, with the hateful Mr Murdstone, with Miss Royal as Betsy Trotwood, and with Harry got up as a splendid nurse Peggotty. Then there was the best scene of all, the Peggotty boathouse on the sands, with Diamond playing Little Em'ly.

Diamond still didn't care for acting, and found her few lines hard to learn – but every night, tucked up together in bed, I recited them to her again and again until she knew them by heart. I knew that Little Em'ly had a blue bead necklace, so I bought some glass beads from the market near the rehearsal rooms and threaded a necklace for her.

'There you are. It matches your beautiful blue eyes,' I said.

'You have beautiful blue eyes too, Hetty. We're really like sisters!' said Diamond.

'Sister and brother. I'm young Davy now, remember?'

'Poor Hetty, having to be a boy and hide your long hair!'

Diamond simply wanted to look pretty on stage – but I wanted to shine. Inside my head I was Davy all the time. I didn't have that many lines myself, and twenty minutes into the play I disappeared entirely, to be replaced by Cecil as the grown-up David. Privately I thought he made a pig's ear of the part, but I couldn't help that.

Miss Royal was wonderful, of course, though she was confined to character parts and the rather uninteresting Agnes, but somehow she made her silent yearning so powerful and poignant I couldn't look at anyone else in the room. I was happy to watch the play over and over again, but Diamond couldn't help getting fidgety.

I sat her in the corner of the rehearsal rooms, and at first she played quietly enough with Adeline and Maybelle, but she couldn't help muttering to her dolls, making them talk back to her in Little Pip voices. The Players put up with this for a while, but Cyril started to complain that it was distracting. I'm sure he was simply making excuses for forgetting his lines, but Mr Parkinson took him seriously.

'You two girls must stay utterly silent if you sit in on rehearsals,' he said, pointing at us sternly.

'They're being very good, Gerald,' said Miss Royal. 'And it's a very long time for the little one to stay quiet. Perhaps we should let her run around a little every now and then?'

'We're actors, not babysitters.' Mr Parkinson always pronounced the word actors in a particularly plummy voice, 'aaac-tooors'. Diamond and I often copied him to make each other giggle.

'It seems silly to have them sitting here hour after hour when we're not rehearsing their scenes,' said Harry. 'What are you planning for tomorrow, Gerald?'

'We need to do the Dora scenes. The pet-shop owner is bringing some likely dogs to see which one is best playing Gyp,' he replied.

'Oh, Gerald, you old meanie. *I* wanted to be Gyp,' said Harry. He crouched down, surprisingly nimble for such a large man, and started running round on all fours, giving high-pitched barks. He nestled up to Stella, growled at Cecil, and then impudently cocked his leg on him, which made everyone laugh, even Mr Parkinson.

'Tell you what, why don't we let the girls have a day off, seeing as they're not required,' said Miss Royal.

'Yes, very well,' said Mr Parkinson, joining in the fun in spite of himself. He held out an imaginary titbit to make Harry sit up and beg.

'There you are, girls! You can have a little wander around London and enjoy yourselves,' said Miss Royal. 'Perhaps you might like to go to the Zoological Gardens?'

I remember my last trip, the day after the Queen's Jubilee. I thought of taking Diamond for a ride on Jumbo the elephant – though this wouldn't really be much of a novelty to a circus child.

No, I had a much better idea.

25

I WOKE VERY EARLY. Diamond and Adeline and Maybelle were all leaning on me and I could barely move. I planned our journey in my head, turning my Mizpah ring round and round. I thought longingly of Bertie and hoped he didn't think badly of me. I remembered all our squabbles and sulks. They all seemed so silly now. Why hadn't we just enjoyed our time together? I was missing him so much already.

I woke Diamond at six and we tiptoed about as quietly as possible. When we slipped softly down the stairs, we heard Harry snoring in his room, great guttural snorts that gave us both the giggles. We had to hold our hands over our mouths, stifling our splutters. We crept down to Miss Grundy's kitchen for a cup of tea before our journey. She came pattering in herself, her long white hair hanging loose past her shoulders, wearing a white cotton nightgown. Her feet were bare, thin and delicately boned, very white against the dark linoleum.

'You're bright and early today, girls,' she said cheerily. 'Would you like some bread and honey?'

She felt around carefully, taking the bread out of the crock and then cutting it carefully, handling the knife with caution. She kept the butter on one shelf in the pantry, the honey on another, everything neatly in its place so that she could be sure to find it.

She let Diamond lick the honey spoon.

'Please may I share it with Adeline and Maybelle? They are my two dollies,' said Diamond.

Miss Grundy felt each doll with her long paper-white fingers. Maybelle's blunt features and baldness must have been a shock after Adeline's smooth china and flowing locks, but Miss Grundy tactfully didn't remark on this. She even made two fairy-sized sandwiches for the dolls.

'Thank you so much! My girls are very happy now.

But I'd better take your travelling cloaks off, dears, I don't want you to get them all sticky with honey,' said Diamond.

'Are they going travelling today, then? Aren't they rehearsing with you two?' Miss Grundy asked.

'We're not needed at rehearsals today, so we're going to visit a friend,' I said.

'A very, very dear friend,' added Diamond. 'She's like a mother to us, because we've lost our own mothers.'

'Well, I'm sure she'll be thrilled to see you,' said Miss Grundy. 'It's so lovely to have some feminine company. I've nearly always had gentlemen lodgers. Ladies don't always care to live in Soho.'

'We care to live here,' I said. 'Thank you for making us so welcome.'

I hoped Madame Adeline would make us welcome too. I was longing to see her, but I couldn't help fretting.

'Perhaps we should have telegrammed last night, to say we were coming,' I said, when we were on the train. 'It will be such a shame if Madame Adeline and Mr Marvel have gone out for the day – we will have come all this way for nothing.'

'But they can't really go too far. Mr Marvel would never leave all the monkeys for long,' said Diamond. 'Oh, I can't wait to see little Mavis! Do you think she'll remember me?'

'Of course she will,' I said.

'Adeline and Maybelle are so excited.' Diamond made her dolls jig up and down. 'Adeline can't wait to meet her namesake! And Maybelle remembers Madame Addie most fondly, don't you, dear?' Maybelle nodded her cloth head so vigorously she nearly unravelled her stitches.

I was becoming very excited myself. I relived the first moment I'd seen Madame Adeline, when I was a small girl in the village. I'd been dazzled by this fairy-tale woman riding her fine horse, her bright red hair shining, the sequins on her pink costume sparkling in the sunlight. Jem had taken me to the circus and I'd run into the ring to perform with Madame Adeline. She had laughed at my boldness and called me her little star.

Little Star, Little Star, Little Star, I repeated to the rhythm of the train's wheels. I kept a careful eye on all the station names, and at last I spotted Little Foxfield. Madame Adeline's address was very brief: Honeysuckle Cottage, Little Foxfield, Sussex. I imagined a story-book cottage with a thatched roof and mullioned windows, a colourful flower garden in front and honeysuckle in a fragrant tangle around the front door.

Little Foxfield station was deserted, though we were still waiting hopefully for a station master or porter long after the train had chugged out of sight.

'Well, we might as well look for Honeysuckle Cottage ourselves, Diamond. I'm sure it won't be far,' I said.

We wandered down the lane. We passed a few cottages,

but none were named Honeysuckle. I stopped a small child and then a boy ambling along whistling to the birds, but neither seemed to have even heard of Honeysuckle Cottage. After a while the houses petered out and we were left trudging up a steep path, trees and hedges on either side of us. We stopped on the brow of the hill and peered down. More trees, more hedges, many fields – but no sign of any cottage.

'Oh dear, are we lost?' Diamond asked.

'No, of course not. We must simply have gone the wrong way at the station. We'll go back,' I said.

'We will find Madame Adeline, won't we?' Diamond demanded.

'Of course we will.' I tried to sound confident, though I was starting to wonder if there might be another Little Foxfield in a different part of the country altogether.

We trudged back again, our toes rubbing uncomfortably against the end of our shoes because of the steep incline. The station was still deserted, so we set out the other way. There were more tumbledown cottages, but still none named Honeysuckle. Then we saw a small store with a blue-and-white awning.

'Perhaps the shopkeeper will know where it is,' I said.

She was sitting behind her counter, sharing a pot of tea with a man in a navy uniform with brass buttons. Perhaps he was the station master?

'Yes?' said the woman rather curtly. 'What do you want to buy?'

'I don't really want to buy anything, ma'am,' I started politely.

'Then don't come bothering me in my store,' she said, raising her eyebrows at the man in uniform.

'I was just wondering, would you happen to know the whereabouts of Honeysuckle Cottage?' I asked.

'Oh, the whereabouts!' she said, mocking my accent. 'No, I don't.'

'Me neither,' said the man, shaking his head.

'Madame Adeline lives there. A lady with red hair,' I said.

'There's no one with red hair in our village,' said the man.

'And there's Mr Marvel – he's an elderly gentleman, and he has a family of monkeys,' added Diamond.

'Oh, *him*,' said the woman. 'Old Monkey Man? Him that came to live in the old cottage in the woods with some old biddy?'

I couldn't bear to hear her talking about our dear friends so disparagingly.

'Please, just direct us to the cottage,' I said. 'Which path should we take?'

'It's in Larch Woods, over on the left,' said the man, gesturing. 'Can't rightly say which path to take. It's just a matter of following your nose.'

'Thank you for all your help,' I said sarcastically. I grabbed Diamond and pulled her out of the shop.

'What a horrid pair!' I said. 'Come on, let's find this cottage in the woods. We will indeed follow our noses!'

I tried to sound light-hearted, but I worried as we set off into the woods.

I was used to woods from my early childhood, when I played happy squirrel-house games with Jem, but this wood seemed too dark, too quiet, too inhibiting. The branches reached out, the twigs like grasping fingers, and the roots crept stealthily beside the path, intent on tripping us. Diamond held my hand so tightly I couldn't move my fingers. She had her dolls clasped in her other arm, and all the while she tried to murmur comfortingly to them, though she was nearly in tears.

I began to doubt the existence of this cottage. The man and woman in the shop were probably laughing at us now, slapping each other on the back and spilling their tea. Could Madame Adeline and Mr Marvel really live in the middle of this hateful wood? They were an elderly couple now. How could they negotiate their way to the village shop in rain, in snow?

Madame Adeline had sounded so positive in her letters. She had said that the cottage was out in the country, she had told us how she had to clean it and paint it and make curtains and rag rugs, but she had somehow made it sound cosy and comfortable. She had never once mentioned that it was in the middle of a dark wood.

Diamond kept looking about her, glancing fearfully this way and that. Every now and then she stopped, her head on one side, listening. 'What's that?' she asked sharply.

'It's just the leaves rustling in the breeze,' I said.

'Are you sure?'

'Yes! Why, do you think someone's following us?'

'Not exactly. But this wood is just like the one in the picture book,' she said.

'Which picture book?'

'The fairy-tale one. The Red Riding Hood story.'

'Diamond, I promise you, there can't possibly be any wolves in this wood,' I said firmly.

'There could be.'

'There aren't any wolves left in England, not nowadays.'

'How do you *know*? There might be just a few creeping about.'

'Oh, do stop it!' I said impatiently, because I was worried she might be right, even though I knew it was a crazy idea.

We were still bickering when the wood thinned a little – and suddenly we found ourselves in a sunlit clearing. And there was a cottage! It was very old and tumbledown, the brickwork crumbling and cracked. It had a thatched roof of sorts, with many bare patches. But the front door had been given a coat of bright green paint and someone had trained a slender spiral of honeysuckle up a lattice beside it.

'Oh, Diamond, it's Honeysuckle Cottage, it must be!' I cried.

We both rushed forward and started tapping on the green door. The knocker was polished, though it didn't look as if any visitors ever came to the cottage to use it.

'Madame Adeline! Madame Addie, are you in?' Diamond called.

The door opened and an ancient old lady peered out at us, blinking in the light.

We hung back uncertainly, wondering if we had the wrong cottage after all. This lady was surely much older than Madame Adeline. She had sparse grey hair, worn so thin her scalp showed. Her face was very pale, with brown smudges under her eyes. The fingers clutching her robe were shaking. It was the green floral wrapper I recognized, not Madame Adeline herself.

'Madame Addie!' I said.

'My girls!' she gasped, and held out her arms.

The three of us hugged as if we would never let go. But then a little light creature suddenly leaped onto Diamond's shoulder, thin arms clutching her long hair.

'Mavis!' she cried delightedly. 'Oh, darling Mavis! Don't pull my hair now, naughty girl! Oh, you remember me, don't you! But where are all the others? Are they in a cage? And where's dear Mr Marvel, Madame Addie?'

I felt her shaking. 'Gone,' she murmured.

'*Gone?*' I repeated. 'He *left* you?'

'No, no, he – he became ill. And so did the monkeys. Oh, girls, it's been so terrible.'

'Mr Marvel,' said Diamond, her lip quivering. 'Oh please, Mr Marvel can't be *dead*. I love Mr Marvel!'

'Diamond!' I said softly. 'Hush now. Madame Adeline loved him too.'

'But not enough,' she said, starting to weep.

I led her inside the cottage, Diamond following, her arms full of dolls and monkey. The living room was neat and tidy, with little decorative touches: lace curtains tied up with blue ribbon, coloured lithographs of horses on the wall, wild flowers in a jam jar on the scrubbed wooden table. There were two worn armchairs on either side of the fireplace. I sat Madame Adeline in one and Diamond in the other and then went to set the kettle on the hob.

I found two blue-and-white striped mugs and a set of gold-rimmed rose patterned china. This was Madame Adeline's pride and joy, and for decoration only. I made tea and poured it into the two mugs and a rinsed-out jam jar.

'Is there cake?' Diamond asked hopefully.

Madame Adeline shook her head. I peered into her larder. There was hardly any food at all, just an end of bread and a tiny morsel of cheese that would scarcely feed a mouse. I looked at Madame Adeline closely. She'd always been slender, but now she was stick-thin, all long wrists and bony ankles, and the delicate bones in her face seemed to poke through her skin.

I wished we'd thought to bring some food with us. I could have bought a big fruit cake, a bunch of grapes, a bottle of tonic wine . . . How could I have been so thoughtless?

I gave Madame Adeline her tea, and then sat at her feet, leaning my head against her knee.

'Dear Hetty,' she murmured, wiping her eyes with the back of her hand. 'And dear Diamond. My two girls. I never thought I'd see you again.'

'Why didn't you tell us in your letter? Couldn't you bear to?' I asked.

She shook her head. 'It was so sad. I didn't want to upset you, especially Diamond.'

'But we'd have come at once!'

'Yes, I know, but you've made your own lives now. At the Cavalcade! I'm so proud of you both,' she said.

'Well, actually we're not there any more. We're going to be actors in the West End, so hopefully you'll be even prouder.'

I told her all about it, and she nodded and shook her head in all the right places, and did her best to smile. Diamond laid her dolls down flat for a rest and concentrated on playing with Mavis.

'Poor little girl, she's an orphan now,' she said. 'So I

shall make even more fuss of her. How did all the other monkeys die, Madame Addie? Did they all die at once?'

'Yes. Yes, they did,' said Madame Adeline uncertainly.

'And Mr Marvel too?'

She covered her face with her hands.

'Diamond, I don't think Madame Adeline wants to talk about it just now – it's too upsetting. Why don't you take Mavis for a little walk outside? Have you got a lead for her, Madame Adeline?'

We fixed it to her collar, and then Diamond took her out into the garden. We heard them chattering together in a very touching way.

Madame Adeline uncovered her face. 'The monkeys didn't get ill. They were attacked by a fox. Mavis was the only one who escaped, because she's so nimble,' she whispered.

'Oh goodness, how dreadful.'

'Marvel kept them in their big travelling cage in the shed at the back of the cottage. It was partly to please me. He'd have liked them in the house, but I didn't like the smell. The monkeys didn't mind – they were used to their cage, they probably preferred it. At least, that's what I told myself. Marvel doted on his monkeys, you know that. He gave them such tender loving care. But he was getting older, much older. I've no idea how old he was, he wouldn't tell me, but he was sometimes forgetful – he couldn't help it. And one night, after feeding them their supper, he didn't remember to latch the cage properly. I should have checked. But I didn't, and in the night the fox came.'

'How terrible!'

'Don't tell Diamond. It would upset her so. She loved those monkeys. Thank goodness Mavis escaped. We found her right at the top of the tallest tree. It took hours to talk her down, and she was traumatized for days. So was Marvel. He couldn't bear it. He blamed himself. He just took to his bed. I tried to comfort him, but I could do nothing. He wouldn't eat, wouldn't drink, wouldn't get up. He didn't want to live any more. He died at the end of the week.'

'Oh, Madame Adeline,' I said, putting my arms round her and rocking her. I kissed her poor scalp.

'If only I'd loved him more, Hetty. He was a good man, a kind man, a sweet soul. We got along well together, but I wouldn't really call it love, just friendship. He might have lived on if I'd been more tender with him,' she wept.

'He was very, very old. I think he'd have died no matter what. You know what those monkeys meant to him.'

'I'm old too, Hetty. Look at me! I can't bear to peer in a looking glass now – I'm such a fright. I think my time is coming soon too,' she whispered.

'No it's not! You just need building up. You've got so very thin. Madame Adeline, please don't mind my asking, but have you any money now? I don't think you've been eating properly,' I said, hoping she wouldn't take offence.

'I have money. Marvel had saved a great deal, bless him. But to tell the truth, I haven't felt up to making my way through the woods and then facing the villagers. They've never really accepted us. They look down on circus folk. The woman in the stores is very unpleasant.'

'Then it's simple! You must move away.'

'I haven't the energy to sort everything out and put the cottage up for sale. I don't know where to go, anyway. I've travelled all my life. I've no roots any more, no relations that I know of.'

'Yes you have!' I declared passionately. 'You have us, Diamond and me! We'll be your family. We'll pack up now, take the keys and visit a solicitor. There must be one in the nearest town. Then you must come back to London with us. We will live together, you and me and Diamond – and little Mavis too.'

'Oh, Hetty, don't! Stop being so sweet to me, you'll make me cry. You can't burden yourself with a sad sick old woman.'

'You are sad and sick, but I'm going to make you well and happy again, you wait and see,' I said. 'You won't be a burden. You will keep house for us when you're stronger, and look after Diamond when I'm on the stage. You will be our mother and we will be your loving daughters, I promise you.'

I coaxed her out of her old wrapper and into her best dress. I found the pink gauze shawl she used to wear over her spangled costume, and arranged it round her thin shoulders. Then I dug deeper into her wardrobe and found her red wig. I combed it out carefully and then gently put it on her head, sweeping the long strands into a loose bun and securing it with hairpins. I found an old stick of carmine and outlined her lips, and then rubbed just a smidgeon on her white cheeks.

'There!' I said. 'You look in that mirror now!'

She looked and wept a little, but managed to smile too. She sat back in the chair while I roamed the rooms, trying to think what to take with us. I couldn't bear the thought of leaving Madame Adeline here. I was still terrified she might take to her bed like poor Mr Marvel.

I didn't know how we could possibly carry everything between us – but we didn't need to.

'I don't want anything,' she murmured. 'Just a change of clothes. I lost my home when I left my wagon at Tanglefield's.'

'And we had to leave it there when Diamond and I ran away,' I said. 'But perhaps one day we'll be able to get you a new wagon, Madame Adeline.'

'I think my travelling days are over, Hetty,' she said.

'Then if I get to be a really rich and famous actress, we will have a big house with an even bigger garden, and you can keep your wagon there. We could even have a paddock, and you can find a foal with a patch on his face like Pirate,' I said.

'Dear Hetty. You've always been so good at making up stories,' she said. 'Do you still keep a journal?'

'I gave it up a while ago. There didn't really seem any point any more. But perhaps I will write down everything that's happened to me this past year. Goodness, so *much* has happened!'

'And then, if you're really rich and famous, perhaps someone will want to publish the story of your life?' said Madame Adeline.

'I used to hope that would happen,' I said. 'I was such a silly child!'

'I think you're the sort of girl who can make anything happen,' she said. 'You always manage to find me!'

'We're going to stay together for ever now,' I told her.

Diamond could hardly believe it when she came skipping back to the cottage, Mavis riding on her shoulder and tenderly gripping her ear. 'Madame Addie's coming to live with us? How wonderful!' she said, clapping her hands.

Madame Adeline wandered through the cottage one last time, laying her hands on everything as if saying goodbye. Her hands lingered on her rose-patterned china. 'I bought it piece by piece, and displayed it all week in my wagon, before packing it up carefully to travel to the next place. Not a single piece broke – there's not even a chip or a crack,' she murmured.

'Then we'll take it with us,' I said. 'You'd better pack it yourself. I don't think I have the knack.'

It took a while for every piece to be carefully wrapped in old material and stacked neatly, cup in cup, saucer on saucer, plate on plate, in an old basket, but it seemed vital work. When we were outside the cottage at last, Madame Adeline carefully tore off several strands of honeysuckle and tucked them in the basket too.

We had to undertake a long and complicated journey, back through the woods to the station, onto the train, off again at the next town to find a solicitor and give him the keys of the house and various instructions, and then on the train again to London. By this stage both Diamond and Mavis were fast asleep, Mavis tucked between Adeline and Maybelle like a furry third doll.

It was pouring with rain when we reached the station, and we were loaded with bundles. Madame Adeline insisted on paying for a cab. I felt extremely anxious as we climbed out in front of Miss Grundy's house. She had already been kind enough to let Diamond and me stay with her, and we hadn't even paid her any rent yet. Perhaps it was too much to seek shelter for Madame Adeline too. She could have one of the attic beds while Diamond and I shared the other, and she had money to pay her way – but even so it seemed an imposition. And then there was Mavis. Most landladies would surely draw the line at circus livestock.

I was hesitant about ringing the bell, though we were all getting very wet. I hoped Harry might answer the door, but I heard Miss Grundy's light feet and the tap of her cane.

'Hello, my dears!' she said cheerily as she opened the door. 'My, I'm glad you're back from your trip. It's been raining so hard. Little Lily came back soaked when I let her out in the back yard for two minutes. Come in and get dry, girls. You must look like two little orphans in the storm.'

'Well, we're actually three orphans, Miss Grundy,' I said hesitantly.

'No, *four*!' said Diamond as Mavis scampered out of her arms and up onto her shoulder. The little monkey chattered anxiously.

Miss Grundy squealed, startled by the sudden noise. 'It's a little creature! What kind is it?'

'I'm terribly sorry, but it's a little monkey. I promise it's very sweet and well-trained,' I said. 'I do hope you don't mind.'

'A little monkey! Oh, I'm sure I love monkeys!' Miss Grundy declared. 'I wonder if it would like Lily's basket? She often spends the night curled up with me.'

'That's so kind of you! And could our dear friend possibly share our room overnight, as it's much too late for her to find other lodgings? She will of course pay you,' I said.

'Of course! Do come in. Shall we all have a cup of hot chocolate? Dear Harry's out with some of his chums, but

I dare say he'll be home soon. I take it you're another friend of his, Miss . . . ?'

'It's Madame,' said Diamond. 'And she's not Harry's friend – not yet anyway – she's *our* friend, Hetty's and mine.'

'She's like a mother to us,' I said, smiling at Madame Adeline reassuringly.

She was looking desperately pale and I could see she was trembling, but she held out her hand and managed to say in her thrilling stage voice, 'How do you do? I am Madame Adeline. I knew these dear girls when we all worked at Tanglefield's Travelling Circus. I used to have an equestrian act.'

I took off her soaked shawl and attended to Diamond, while Miss Grundy tapped her way up and down the stairs to get towels from the linen cupboard.

'An equestrian act?' she repeated politely.

'She used to have six rosin-backed horses – she was the star of the show,' I said proudly.

'There was talk of my joining a circus when I was a little girl, because of my unusual appearance,' said Miss Grundy, pouring milk into a pan, careful not to spill a drop. She put it on the stove and spooned chocolate powder into four mugs. 'I didn't have any special skills. How I wish *I* could have had an equestrian act. Six horses, you said?' She looked out into the hall hopefully, as if all six might come trotting through the door.

473

'All gone,' said Madame Adeline. 'I have no act now. You get thrown out of the circus when you get old. I'm simply a sad old woman with no followers, no friends, apart from these two girls.'

'They suggested I join a troupe of clowns,' Miss Grundy told us.

'Oh no, you wouldn't want to work with clowns!' said Diamond.

'You're absolutely right. I didn't care for the idea of being laughed at. From the age of fifteen I tried my hand at various occupations, but I wasn't a success because of my eyesight. When I was employed as a nurserymaid, little boys ran away from me. When I worked in a shop, bigger boys stole from me. When I worked in a factory, grown men played tricks on me.' Miss Grundy smiled bravely. 'But I'm a very lucky girl: my great-uncle took a shine to me. He left me this house! Now I'm a landlady, queen of my own little palace, forever making new and interesting friends.'

We sat down at the kitchen table and drank our hot chocolate. Miss Grundy poured warm milk into two saucers for Lily and Mavis. They weren't at all sure about each other. Lily hissed and Mavis screeched, but as long as Lily stayed on the floor and Mavis perched on Diamond's shoulder, they didn't come to blows.

Miss Grundy opened a cake tin. We'd eaten all the pink-and-yellow cake but she found half a loaf of madeira.

'It's a little dry,' she said, touching it delicately. 'I'll spread it with raspberry jam to liven it up.'

It was a delicious combination. The colour crept back into Madame Adeline's cheeks as she chatted to Miss Grundy, telling her all about her circus experiences. By the time our supper was finished they seemed like old friends.

Then Harry swept in, a little the worse for wear, but very mellow and jolly. He gallantly kissed Madame Adeline's hand and complimented her on her red hair.

'I'm surrounded by Titian beauties,' he said. 'There's you, dear Madame, and young Emerald here, and old Marina at work. Thank goodness you're a snow-white maiden, Miss Grundy, to add a little variety to my life.' He bowed low to each of us and then staggered off to his bed.

We went to our beds too. Madame Adeline worried about Diamond and me having to share, but we assured her we preferred it.

'It's much more cosy,' said Diamond. 'In fact, you might feel lonely by yourself, Madame Adeline, so perhaps you'd like to borrow my doll for the night? She's called Adeline. Isn't she pretty? I named her after you.'

Madame Adeline declined her namesake's company. She fell asleep almost immediately, clearly exhausted. She looked so vulnerable with her wig on the bedpost. I was so concerned about her that I crept out of bed several times to peer at her in the moonlight. I felt all the old agony I'd suffered when I visited Mama at the hospital. I'd lost her much too soon. I couldn't bear it if I lost Madame Adeline too.

But she woke early in the morning, dressed quickly, applied a little colour to her face and adjusted her wig. By the time Diamond and I came downstairs Madame Adeline had helped Miss Grundy prepare breakfast and swept and dusted into the bargain.

'I've never had a paying guest be such a help before,' said Miss Grundy happily, frying a great pan of bacon for us all.

We ate a hearty breakfast. Harry enjoyed two platefuls, in spite of his celebrations the night before. He took a great shine to little Mavis and fed her choice titbits. Then we had to rush to the rehearsal rooms, while Madame Adeline and Miss Grundy sat down with a fresh cup of tea and planned their day.

'I wish I could stay with them,' said Diamond wistfully. 'I quite like being Little Em'ly, but I'd much, much sooner stay Little Diamond and play back at Miss Grundy's.'

'I know, but it will be fun to have a proper run-through of the whole play,' I said.

It turned out to be anything but fun. People kept forgetting their lines, or bumping into each other, or suddenly corpsing, cracking up with nervous laughter. As the day wore on, Mr Parkinson grew more and more irritable, reducing Stella to tears and even being a little savage with Miss Royal.

She stuck her head proudly in the air and behaved impeccably, repeating a line again and again until he was satisfied, but during the brief lunch break we heard them having a furious row out in the corridor.

'I don't like them being so cross,' Diamond whispered.

'Don't worry, chickie, they don't really mean it,' said Harry. 'They always get a bit tense at this stage. And I dare say the dress rehearsal will be even worse, a positive nightmare. Though a bad dress rehearsal means a good first night, every actor knows that. On Monday night it will go splendidly, and then everyone will be all smiles, you mark my words.'

26

THE DRESS REHEARSAL IN the theatre went surprisingly well, though there were various hitches with the lighting, and the stage hands frequently failed to find the right prop. But the actors were nearly all word perfect. Diamond *did* forget her lines once, and had trouble saying 'Mas'r Davy', but she looked so sweet skipping about the stage it didn't really matter.

I stopped being Hetty altogether. I was little Davy

Copperfield and I'd fallen in love with Peggotty's enchanting little niece. Peggotty was no longer Harry, the funny friend I saw slopping about in his yellow silk dressing gown every morning, a little the worse for wear after the evening's carousing. He was my dear nurse, who mattered as much to me as my mama.

At the end of the performance Mr Parkinson gave us copious notes, but all the actors still seemed anxious. They all thought like Harry: if a bad dress rehearsal meant a brilliant first night, a *good* one must surely mean the exact opposite.

'But isn't that just a silly old superstition?' I said.

I was trying to be comforting, but they all turned on me.

'What do you know, you ignorant little girl?'

'You've only been in the company two minutes and yet you think you know it all!'

'You're right out of order!'

Even Miss Royal shook her head at me. 'When you've been in this business as long as I have, Emerald, you'll learn when it's better to hold your tongue,' she said sharply.

I was so shocked I felt tears prickling my eyes.

'Oh, for goodness' sake, don't be a cry-baby,' she snapped, and turned her back on me.

'How do you hold your tongue, Hetty?' Diamond asked me in a muffled voice on the way home. She was trying to grasp her slippery pink tongue and talk at the same time, so she wasn't having much success.

'It's just a figure of speech,' I said, in a little voice. 'I hate it that I upset them all.'

'Cheer up, chickie,' said Harry. He was smoking a large cigar, and we had to take care to avoid its fumes and ash. 'An actor can't help being superstitious. It's the nature of the beast. It might seem silly to you – indeed, it *is* silly – but it's unwise to point this out so vehemently! Especially if it *does* all go wrong on Monday night. They'll say you jinxed it.'

'That wouldn't be fair!' said Diamond loyally.

'They'll want to pick on Hetty anyway, because she's so good at acting,' said Harry, puffing away.

'I'm good?' I said. 'Do you really think so?'

'I know so. And you do too. That's why the others are all on edge, especially Marina.'

'I thought she *liked* me.'

'She does, a great deal. But she's also an ageing actress, long past her prime. It's very hard for her to see someone new and fresh and talented. She never had any cause to be jealous of poor sappy Stella, but you're the genuine article, Hetty Feather, and you're getting everyone wound up,' said Harry. He inhaled deeply to make his point and then had a coughing fit. It became so violent, he had to bend over while Diamond and I patted him on the back.

'I don't think that cigar agrees with you, Harry,' I said. 'I didn't even know you liked to smoke.'

'I can't smoke in the house. Miss Grundy doesn't care for the smell,' wheezed Harry. 'I only smoke in the street. One of *my* little superstitions is to enjoy a fine Havana cigar after a good first night. And as it looks as if the performance is doomed, I thought I should enjoy it now instead.'

'Seriously?' I said, stricken.

'No, no, dear, I'm just pulling your leg.'

'You're not to pull Hetty's leg, you'll hurt her!' said Diamond.

'Shall we pull yours instead, little Diamond?' said Harry, handing me his cigar. He seized hold of her, swinging her round one-handed and tugging at her stripy socks with the other, while she squealed and struggled.

I peered at his cigar and tried one little puff. Then I was the one bent over, coughing and gasping, tears streaming down my face. I already knew that I never wanted to drink alcohol again. Now I added tobacco to my list of forbidden substances, fine Havana cigars in particular.

I had never thought I was superstitious myself, but now I began to fear that the opening night would be truly dreadful – and that somehow it might be my fault. I lay awake on Sunday night, manically chanting my way through my part, but the words faded from my head, just

481

as they had done before when I played Alice. This was worse. Whole paragraphs disappeared entirely. I couldn't even remember my opening lines. I saw myself on stage, sweating under the spotlight, my mouth opening and closing soundlessly like a goldfish until the audience started booing.

I sat up in bed, clutching my chest. My heart was thudding so hard I feared it would burst through my skin. Diamond was fast asleep, thank goodness, as was Mavis in Lily's cat basket, but Madame Adeline stirred.

'What is it, Hetty?' she whispered.

I crept over to her, shaking. 'I can't do it!' I whispered. 'I can't remember my words! I shall go on stage and die! I've jinxed myself, and now I can't act at all.'

'Of course you can act, child! I watched you day and night at Tanglefield's, playing the role of ringmaster to perfection. You're simply suffering first-night nerves,' she said, putting her arm round me. 'You will do splendidly, I promise you. I believe in you, Hetty. Now you must believe in yourself.'

'Will you come and watch me, Madame Adeline?' I begged. 'Mr Parkinson says we can invite special family and friends for the opening night.'

'Of course I will,' she said, clasping my hand and squeezing it. 'Are you inviting anyone else? Perhaps Miss Grundy?'

Harry had already invited Miss Grundy as *his* special

guest. There were so many people I'd like to invite. Some were neither family *nor* friends. I'd have loved to invite Matron Pigface and Matron Bottomly from the Foundling Hospital, just to see their expressions when the red-haired child of Satan came bounding onto the stage. I didn't think Miss Sarah Smith would approve of my new profession either, but she would appreciate the literary content of the play. My older foster sisters would tut and act superior, though they might secretly be envious. Gideon would love to see me in a play, but he wouldn't leave Mother – and she would be shocked. She'd been appalled when I joined Madame Adeline in the circus ring as a tiny child.

What about Jem? Oh, how I'd love Jem to see me, and Janet too, but they'd have to stay in London overnight after the performance, and where would they go? I couldn't ask Miss Grundy to accommodate yet more friends. Father was even further away, though how wonderful it would be if he could see me playing the young David Copperfield when he had given me the precious book. And Mama . . . I ached for Mama. I so hoped she would be proud of me.

I'm always proud of you, Hetty, she said when I crept back to my own bed. *You're my own dear child. I can't wait to see you act on stage.*

I was still desperately anxious, but I was comforted by Madame Adeline's presence in the next bed, Diamond's warm little body nestled against my own, and Mama safe in my heart.

There was one more person I longed to invite. I longed and longed and longed to invite him. I lay awake thinking about him, turning the ring on my finger. I didn't fall asleep till the room was starting to turn silvery-grey and the first birds were singing outside the attic window.

When I woke up, the room was bright with sunlight, in spite of the drawn curtains, and the bedroom was empty. Running downstairs, I was astonished to find it was nearly midday. Madame Adeline and Miss Grundy were baking cakes together, Diamond was teaching Mavis a new trick, and Harry was sprawled in his dressing gown, reading a newspaper on the sofa, with Miss Grundy's kitten comfortably draped across his large stomach.

'Good morning, Miss Rip Van Winkle,' said Harry. 'Or should I say, good afternoon?'

'Take no notice of Harry, dear. What would you like for breakfast?' asked Miss Grundy.

'I'm so sorry I slept in. I feel dreadfully lazy,' I said.

'Yes, you absolutely wouldn't wake up, even when I gave you a little shake,' said Diamond.

'I think Hetty was awake half the night.' Madame Adeline smiled at me. 'You needed to sleep on, dear. Do you feel rested now?'

'I think so,' I said.

I didn't really know what I felt. My head was still whirling, and every time I thought of the evening's performance I felt sick. I could only manage a couple of bites of toast for breakfast, and a mere mouthful of egg-and-bacon pie for luncheon an hour or so later.

I was glad to see Madame Adeline eating heartily. Diamond ate enthusiastically too, and Miss Grundy cleared her own plate, though she always ate slowly, taking care not to spill anything. Harry usually wolfed his meals down and hoped for seconds, but today he was only toying with his food.

'It looks as if you and I have first-night collywobbles,' he said to me. 'I think we should go for a long walk to clear our heads and stretch our tense muscles. Let's all go!'

Harry's idea of a long walk was an amble to St James's Park, where he flopped down on a bench by the lake and fed the birds crumbs, but it was enjoyably diverting all the same. Passers-by sometimes stopped and stared because we were a motley crew. There was huge Harry and chalk-white Miss Grundy, fragile Madame Adeline with her defiant bright red hair, and pretty little Diamond laden with two dolls and a monkey on a lead. And there was me, Hetty Feather, brought up a mile or so away, and yet only let out to see London once in those nine long years.

Folk had stared then, that day of freedom on Queen

Victoria's Golden Jubilee. They'd shaken their heads at my old-fashioned brown frock, my white cap and tippet and sleeves, my thick darned stockings and worn boots. I was obviously a foundling child, an object of pity and contempt.

I wondered if anyone would guess that I was a foundling now. We walked back to Miss Grundy's via Shaftesbury Avenue. We paused outside the theatre, looking up at the posters. There was a beautiful full-length portrait of Miss Royal in her prime. Her name topped the bill. Harry was photographed too, a head-and-shoulders portrait, with *Hilarious Harry Henderson, world-famous character actor* written underneath. He muttered the wording to himself approvingly.

Diamond and I didn't get a photograph, but our names were there, albeit at the bottom of the poster.

And introducing our Little Stars Emerald and Diamond, child actors extraordinaire!

'Look, Diamond! Do you see our names?' I said excitedly.

'What does that funny long word say at the end?' she asked.

'*Extraordinaire.* It's a foreign way of saying we're extraordinary,' I said.

'And so you are,' said Madame Adeline.

'Extraordinaire! Extraordinaire!' Diamond sang, twirling round and round.

'Extraordinaire! Extraordinaire!' Harry sang in a deep fruity voice, copying Diamond's little-girl dance.

'Extraordinaire! Extraordinaire!' Madame Adeline sang, and she hitched her skirts to her knees, and twirled too, her thin legs suddenly showing their strength.

'Extraordinaire! Extraordinaire! Oh my goodness, we are all extraordinaire!' I sang, and I danced right round them in a circle.

I tried to murmur *extraordinaire* to myself hours later, shivering in the wings, waiting to go on stage. Marina Royal was acting the first scene with Stella, who was playing my mother. Miss Royal played Aunt Betsy Trotwood to perfection, so neat and particular and impatient, fiddling with her bonnet strings and twitching her crinoline. Stella was clearly very nervous and stammered her lines a little, but it didn't matter because my mother was supposed to be afraid of this alarming relative. At least she was word perfect. My own lines darted in and out of my head, frequently disappearing. How could I hope to be *extraordinaire* if I stood on stage like a dummy, unable to say a single word?

I've never known you at a loss for something to say, Hetty!

It was Mama, there inside me, gently teasing me.

'Oh, Mama, I'm so scared,' I told her. 'I know I've performed hundreds of times before. I've shouted in the circus, I've been a Little Star, I've played Alice – but this is different. This is a proper theatre in the West End and it's real acting and I don't think I can do it.'

Yes you can! I'm so proud of you. Good luck, darling girl!

'Good luck, my dear!' Miss Royal whispered, coming off stage in her crinoline. She gave me a hug. I felt her trembling, and realized that even she got nervous on a first night.

Then Harry appeared in the wings in long skirts and apron, a splendid Nurse Peggotty. 'Come along then, Master Davy,' he whispered, in character already.

We went on stage hand in hand. I don't know whose was clammiest, his or mine.

For a moment the lights were so dazzling after the dark wings that I hung back, startled, horribly aware of row after row of faces, like apples stored for the winter, but I let Harry lead me to the armchair in the centre of the stage. He sat down, showing his long lace drawers, which made the audience chuckle. I perched beside him and asked, 'Were you ever married, Peggotty? You are a very handsome woman, aren't you?'

The audience laughed out loud now, and Harry played up to them, but I stayed solemn, because I was little Davy and I was fretting about people marrying. I read from my book about crocodiles, and then Stella came in with Mr Parkinson, playing my soon-to-be stepfather, Mr Murdstone. Mr Parkinson seemed to grow in stature, towering over me in a sinister fashion, and I flinched away.

Then Peggotty and I were dispatched to the seaside and entered the magical house on the beach made out of an old black barge. Diamond came skipping on stage in a simple frock, her blue beads about her neck. I heard the audience give a sigh of appreciation because she looked so pretty. I thought her pretty too – after all, I was little Davy, falling in love with her at first sight.

We went for a walk on the beach hand in hand, chattering together. Diamond stumbled a little over her speech about the finery she'd like to deck her Uncle Dan in, but I helped her out, suggesting nankeen trousers and a red velvet waistcoat, and it sounded utterly natural.

Then I had to return home, and now Mr Murdstone lived there with my mother, and was so cruel and unkind to me. I had to recite my lessons to him but I was so frightened I couldn't remember the words. Oh, I knew that feeling well! Then he became terrifyingly angry and seized hold of me, ready to beat me. I thought of all the unfair punishments the matrons at the hospital had inflicted on me, and bit his hand in a fury.

The audience cried out in support, and booed when Murdstone punished me. I was sent away to school and met Mr Micawber (Harry again, now in a yellow waistcoat and checked trousers). I sought refuge with Aunt Betsy Trotwood – a wondrous scene with Miss Royal! Then I met the Wickfields and the horrible Uriah Heep, and then – oh dear goodness, then I came off stage and Cedric took over, playing the grown-up David. Young Davy didn't exist any more.

'Did I do it right, Hetty?' Diamond asked anxiously.

'You were a wonderful little Em'ly,' I said. 'Did you enjoy yourself?'

'Sort of,' said Diamond. 'I still don't really like acting but I love wearing my blue beads.'

I gave her a hug.

'Listen, Diamond, I promise you don't ever have to act again, not if you don't want to. I'll do all the acting for both of us – and I'll buy you a new bead necklace each time I get a new part.'

We were meant to go back to the dressing room and wait till the very end of the play, when we were to join the rest of the players and take a bow. Diamond did slip back to check on Adeline and Maybelle, who were tucked up in an old shawl, having a nap. I'd persuaded her to leave Mavis safely at home, tied up so she couldn't do too much damage in the house, while Lily darted about, teasing her.

I stayed in the wings, caught up in the drama. I knew they were only ordinary folk under their greasepaint and wigs, I knew it was just a play, I knew we were in a theatre with hundreds of folk watching – but it also seemed *real*. I watched Cedric as if he were my own self grown up. I laughed, I cried, I hissed at Uriah Heep – and at the end I cheered. As soon as the curtain went down the other players beckoned, and Diamond and I ran on stage too.

We all took bows and the audience went on cheering. I peered into the stalls and all those apple faces became real people. I saw dear Madame Adeline clapping and clapping, tears running down her cheeks – and Miss Grundy standing in her white frock and whistling, especially when told Harry was taking an extra bow.

'You two girls bow too!' Harry insisted.

Diamond and I stood hand in hand. She did her little curtsy and I made a stiff little bow, because I was still in character as Davy. Then Cedric and I stood together and bowed to each other as well as the audience, before giving way to Miss Royal and Mr Parkinson. Of course, they were the stars – but I was experienced enough with audiences to know that Diamond and I were a real success. I was actually called back for another encore. When I took off my cap and let my long red hair fall past my shoulders, there was a gasp, because few people had realized I was actually a girl. There was another burst of clapping and this time I curtsied.

Miss Royal came and put her arm round my shoulders. 'You'll remember this moment for ever, little Emerald,' she said, and I knew she was right.

There was a celebration backstage, with champagne

flowing, but this time I wasn't tempted, though Harry rubbed his hands and was obviously preparing for a long and happy night. Diamond and I drank a glass of lime cordial with Madame Adeline and Miss Grundy. I suggested going home first, determined to show everyone that I was being sensible this time.

When we went out through the stage door, we found quite a crowd gathered there, wanting to congratulate the actors and ask for autographs. They were mostly waiting for Miss Royal, but to my delight they clamoured for our autographs too.

Diamond struggled to print her name, but I signed *Emerald Star* with a flourish. At first I chatted to each person as I wrote, but more and more people crowded round. I was aware that Madame Adeline was starting to look very tired, though Miss Grundy was bouncing about excitedly. I signed more quickly, scarcely looking up.

'I don't want an Emerald Star signature – Hetty Feather will do me,' said a voice.

I looked up and gasped. I saw a small square figure in the darkness. 'Bertie! My own dear Bertie!' I cried, and I threw my arms round him and hugged him close.

Diamond came leaping over and clung to him like a little Mavis, squeaking with excitement.

Madame Adeline and Miss Grundy stood back tactfully, a little bewildered.

'I can't believe you're actually here, Bertie!' I said. 'How did you know it was our first night?'

'Well, *you* certainly didn't tell me,' he said, shaking his head at me. 'Whatever possessed you to disappear like that?'

'Didn't Miss Gibson give you my note?'

'Yes, she did, but it was so cryptic it was worse than useless! I had the devil of a job tracking you down until I came up to London and saw that poster outside the theatre. *Why* didn't you tell me you were going?'

'I couldn't tell you why, Bertie, because I was so worried you might do something reckless,' I said. 'I still can't tell you.'

'You don't need to! That big Harry was drinking with some of the lads till dawn the next day – he was full of it. I nearly went berserk when I heard! I had to teach that Samson a lesson. I wasn't going to have him mauling my girl and getting her sacked!' he declared.

'Oh, Bertie, *did* you hit Samson? Did you teach him a lesson? Oh, you're a hero!' Diamond exclaimed.

Bertie shrugged. 'I guess I hit him once or twice, taking him by surprise. But then he started hitting me. And kicking too. Still got the marks to prove it, so mind your cute little feet on my kidneys, Twinkle.'

'He beat you up?' I asked.

'Of course he did,' said Bertie. 'Look!' He set Diamond down and stood under the gas lamp, grinning ruefully.

'Oh, Bertie, you've lost your front teeth!' I gasped.

'And I've lost my job and all. Mrs Ruby got rid of me right away.'

'That's what I was scared of! What are you going to do?'

'I'm looking round the London halls, seeing if someone will take me on. I'm working on a new act. I've had enough of Flirty Bertie. I'm the Gappy Chappie now.' He exaggerated his grin and sang:

'I'm the Gappy Chappie,
And I guess I'm small and square,
Yes, I'm the Gappy Chappie,
With the maddest hair.
I'm the Gappy Chappie,
I know I shouldn't stand a chance,
But I'm the Gappy Chappie,
And you should see me dance!'

Then he started a new tap-dance, while singing:

'Watch my two-step,
My me-and-you step,
With a little twirl,
Yep, I'll get any girl!'

He ended with a flourish. I clapped, Diamond clapped,

Madame Adeline and Miss Grundy clapped, the auto-graph hunters clapped – even complete strangers clapped.

'That's wonderful! But, Bertie, how will you get work if you're blacklisted? If Mrs Ruby puts the word out, none of the halls will take you,' I said anxiously.

'That's nonsense. You're a fool to fall for that spiel, Hetty. She hasn't got that sort of power. She's Queen of the Cavalcade, but it's just a little provincial gaff compared to these ones in the Big Smoke. I should have tried my luck here before. You wait and see – I'll be a star too one day,' said Bertie, with some of his old swagger.

'I know you will!' I said.

'But I won't be a patch on you, girl.' He took my hand and lowered his voice. 'You're still wearing my ring then?'

'Of course I am. I've never taken it off.'

'Does that mean you're still mine?'

'Yes, it does!' I said.

'Then you're a little cracker,' said Bertie, and he kissed me there and then, in front of everyone.

Diamond clapped her hands. Madame Adeline and Miss Grundy laughed, while the crowd around us whistled and cheered.

'How long have you been in London, Bertie? Have you found digs for yourself?' I asked anxiously.

'I've discovered a lovely airy room, completely rent free,' said Bertie.

'What do you mean?'

'I've been dossing down on a park bench for the last three nights,' he told me, laughing.

'We can't have that, young man. Any friend of Hetty and Diamond is a friend of mine,' said Miss Grundy. 'Such special friends too!' She squeezed Madame Adeline's arm. 'We'll find a spare sofa for him, won't we, Adeline.'

'Oh yes, yes, yes!' said Diamond. 'This is the best day of my life! We're all going to be together like a proper family. We *will* stay together, won't we, Hetty? Do you promise?'

I took a deep breath.

'I promise,' I said. 'I'm absolutely certain.'

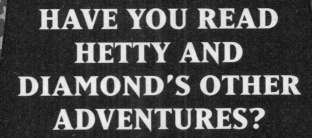

HAVE YOU READ
HETTY AND
DIAMOND'S OTHER
ADVENTURES?

HETTY FEATHER'S
FIRST AMAZING STORY

*Victorian orphan Hetty is left as a baby at the
Foundling Hospital – will she ever find a true home?*

ALSO FROM THE WORLD
OF HETTY FEATHER

Hetty's time at the Foundling Hospital is at an end –
will life by the sea bring the happiness she seeks?

ALSO FROM THE WORLD
OF HETTY FEATHER

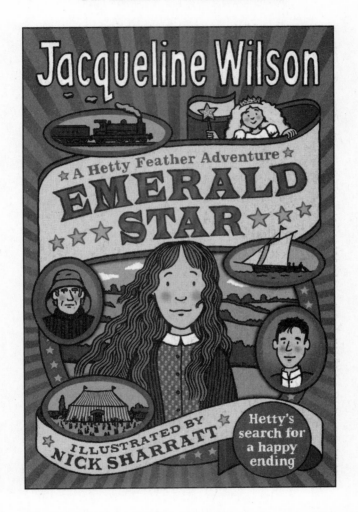

*Following a tragedy, Hetty sets off to find
her father – might her true home be with him?*

ALSO FROM THE WORLD
OF HETTY FEATHER

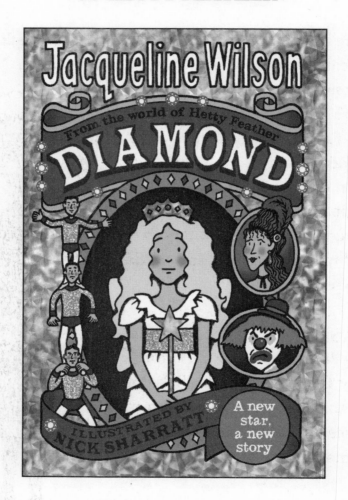

*The crowds adore little Diamond, but life at the circus
is too much to bear. Could her beloved Emerald
hold the key to a brighter future?*

VISIT JACQUELINE'S
FANTASTIC WEBSITE!

There's a whole Jacqueline Wilson town to explore! You can generate your own special username, customise your online bedroom, test your knowledge of Jacqueline's books with fun quizzes and puzzles, and upload book reviews. There's lots of fun stuff to discover, including competitions, book trailers, and Jacqueline's scrapbook. And if you love writing, visit the special storytelling area!

Plus, you can hear the latest news from Jacqueline in her monthly diary, find out whether she's doing events near you, read her fan-mail replies, and chat to other fans on the message boards!

www.jacquelinewilson.co.uk